ALWAYS FALLING *Behind*

BETH GELMAN

This book is a work of fiction. Names, characters, places, and incidents are the product of the author's imagination or are used fictitiously. Any resemblance to actual events, locales, or persons, living or dead, is coincidental.

For information, address Beth Gelman directly at BethGelman.com or at BethGelman Writes@gmail.com.

ISBN: 979-8-9899467-7-8 (KDP Paperback)

ISBN: 979-8-9920340-1-1 (Ingram PB)

ISBN: 979-8-9920340-0-4 (Ingram HC)

Summary:

Never hitch a ride with a stranger...unless he's hot.

I'm Abigail Farnsworth-Burton. ADHD'er extraordinaire. Aspiring artist of mediums I'm not practiced in and chef of meals I've never eaten. And now, heiress. Basically, it means I now own more assets than I can wrap my head — and my limited organizational capacity — around.

So, of course, my car breaks down 400 miles shy of my new mansion. And, of course, the only guy offering a ride looks intimidating as hell...until he opens his mouth. I didn't care that he tripped over his words every time he spoke to me. I figured if he were a real killer, he'd be smoother in his script. Bad guys are never this hot...right?

And Elias McGinnis is anything but scripted — unlike the voice in my head that seems intent on my eventual downfall.

My one saving grace is my new friend, Amy The Great. She always knows exactly how to get things done. Too bad she's a chicken.

But old money attracts new enemies, and focusing on anything is impossible with my sexy live-in mechanic. If I only had a plan – and some actual cash. Oh, and a car.

Always Falling Behind *is a fun and steamy rom-com that shows people with neuro-divergent brains living their best lives.*

Always Falling Behind is the first book in *The Dazed and Confused* series by Beth Gelman. This is the conclusion to *The Perfect Lessons.*

[1. Romance 2. Contemporary romance 3. Romantic comedy 4. Mental Health romance 5. Satire 6. Healing love story]

Copy Editor: Dione Benson

Formatting Editor: Cindy Ziegelman Enterprises LLC

Cover Design: 100Covers.com

First Edition

Contents

Dedication   1

Chapter 1   2
A Quest

Chapter 2   9
Meeting Elias

Chapter 3   19
Elias and Abigail Start Their Journey

Chapter 4   27
Hitting the Road

Chapter 5   36
The Inner Workings of Elias

Chapter 6   44
The Final Hour

Chapter 7   54
Double Deeds

Chapter 8   61
Give Me My Keys

Chapter 9   67
Kitchen Chaos and Garden Grossness

Chapter 10   84
Meeces to Pieces

Chapter 11   94
All Hope is Lost

Chapter 12   106
Goodbye for Now

Chapter 13   113
Hello ATG. Goodbye, Elias

Chapter 14   120
Under Scrutiny

Chapter 15   132
First Day Realities and Goodbye, Aunt Eleanor

Chapter 16   145
Planting Seeds

Chapter 17   155
Staking My Claim

Chapter 18   164
Getting Into the Weeds

Chapter 19   178
Taking the Plunge

Chapter 20   190
A Day in Hell

Chapter 21   198

Reunited with Seneca

Chapter 22   206

The Girls Are Back At It

Chapter 23   213

Besties in the Village

Chapter 24   227

First Dates and A Vision for Seneca

Chapter 25   237

To Know Me is to Love Me

Chapter 26   247

A Three-Way Pact

Chapter 27   262

Found Money and Philanthropy

Chapter 28   274

Purging and Pretenses

Chapter 29   287

Out With the Old

Chapter 30   296

Shared Spaces

Chapter 31   309

A Not So Subtle Night

EPILOGUE   323

The Grand Illusion

About the Author   335

    Follow me at:
    Visit my website and Join my Newsletter:

Acknowledgements   338

Mental Health Organizations   341
The Road to Better Living

1. A Peek at The Perfect Voice   344
    The first book in the Perfect Series

Dedication

To Evan and Sam,
Someone once told me I couldn't achieve greatness.
That was their biggest loss!

Never underestimate your abilities,
and your capacity to achieve them.

There is greatness within you.
Your job is to cultivate it and bring it out for the world to see.

Believe you can, and you will!

Love, Mom

Chapter 1
A Quest

A BIGAIL

My dilapidated, once-red Toyota Corolla shuddered under the weight of all the belongings I had stuffed into its every available space. Audible sounds creaked from the suspension while I threw myself on the trunk lid, securing it shut for a journey I couldn't have imagined I'd be taking. First, a call from a lawyer who claims I am the sole living person in a family line dating from 1832, then having to notify my less than stellar boss, bosses actually, that I have to leave immediately to claim an inheritance from someone like me could never be responsible enough to accept. My name may be Abigail Farnsworth-Burton, but my AFB initials spell out my actual life, "Always Falling Behind."

I looked at my apartment building, one last time vacillating from what was great about this opportunity to obstacles known and unknown. I opened the driver's door and, when my tush hit the torn, black leather seat, I slammed the door, desperately trying to keep my shit together. In truth, my mood matched the weather perfectly—gloomy. The impossible task ahead of me was well beyond my capacity. With no one in the world to guide me, I put my car in drive and headed out of the run-down apartment building parking lot and prayed to God that taking this risk would be better than the pathetic life I was currently living.

The address the lawyer provided was several states away from where I'd been living. Once a Detroiter, I moved to Chicago with a friend, Seneca, to help her dad start a grocery store. My skills, or lack thereof, didn't give me many opportunities for other occupations, so I figured, "Why not," and made a move. It wasn't that I didn't have potential; I did. My high school art teacher, Mrs. Rose, said I was a gifted artist in many mediums, but what she didn't tell me was that my inability to focus on one thing at a time would be a lifetime nemesis. At the persistent urgings of my teacher, my aunt finally agreed to get me some counseling. After countless surveys and emotional tests, Dr. Hastings proclaimed I had ADHD. Yes, the dreaded Attention Deficit/Hyperactivity Disorder millions of people like me struggle with daily.

"That doctor is a crackpot and has no idea what he's talking about. Besides, who does he think will be paying for all those medications he insisted you needed?" My aunt blustered the whole ride home from that appointment. Did I need medication? Wasn't I doing okay in school? Sure, I was scatterbrained at times, but I was a teenager! We all were that way.

As I entered the I-90 Expressway toward Mystic, Connecticut, my engine rattled in retaliation for the high speeds it was usually not forced to take. Dolton, Illinois, was not known for its extended infrastructure; therefore, "Little Red" didn't have to exert herself often. Fourteen glorious hours of silence were in front of me, and all I had were my thoughts and a cassette player my Aunt Eleanor gave me for the trip, along with her collection of 1980s music she insisted were classics. *Whatever.* My car had wheels with mildly balding tires, torn leather seats, sporadically working windshield wipers, and a snarky engine that spoke when irritated. Beyond that, I traveled on a wing and a prayer.

Tapping out the worn tunes on my steering wheel helped burn off my trepidation about my future. The lawyer was sweet and kind in his words, "You remind me of my granddaughter, full of spunk, creativity, and potential." What the hell was "potential" anyway? Was it a finish line? A magical place where money fell from trees, pool boys brought me margaritas, and I had no cares in the world? That stuff may happen for some people, though surely not for me. That wasn't going to happen, especially given my troubled beginnings.

The whoosh of semis barreling down the road had my hands white-knuckling through Chicagoland traffic. I didn't think I could endure fourteen hours of this, except I had little choice. I'd been driving since I was sixteen, only not on jam-packed roads like these. It was time to turn off into a rest area.

I planned to take two days to get to my destination. It was a great plan. Seven hours each day. No stops, fast food, and lots of hyperfocus. One hour into my trip had me rethinking my excellent plan. I forgot about bathroom breaks. That would add at least two more hours to my two-day trip. Sleeping, that was another thing. Twenty-minute naps every few hours would have to be enough for me to get to Connecticut. It would have to be because I didn't have money for a hotel, let alone the gas my gas-guzzling car required. Yes, this would be my new plan—finally, a solid path to my non-specific future. I should probably call my aunt and let her know I was okay. That would be the responsible thing to do as soon as I got back in my car. Except I didn't.

An hour later, I awoke to my phone blaring Journey's "Don't Stop Believin'." *Shit!* When did a few minutes of shuteye turn into a full-on nap? I dug into my pocket and pulled out my phone, loaded with cracks from when I threw it across the room last year when I lost yet another job. It was my aunt. *Shit!*

"Hey, Aunt Eleanor, I was just getting ready to call you." Yeah, right. An hour ago.

"Hey, yourself. You forgot to call me so I could send you all your medical records. I'm moving in a couple of weeks, and you should have these for your next doctor appointments. Where can I send them?"

My mom's sister, Aunt Eleanor, raised me from age four. She did all the mom things my mother would have done, except my mom died of cancer, leaving me an orphan. Where's my dad? Ha! More like a sperm donor without a forwarding address. I never knew the guy, and I'm not looking now. I had the basics my aunt could afford to provide, along with some sage advice about stuff I can't remember, but I'll know them when I need them. I was sure of it—sort of. That was my plan, and I was sticking to it.

"I wish I could tell you I have an address, except I don't. I'm moving to Connecticut, and the place I'm moving to may or may not be working out for me. Can you give me a few days? I'm sorry I didn't call last week when you left a message. I totally forgot, and then this move came out of nowhere, and now I'm trying to keep it together to get this inheritance figured out." I pleaded for more time. I always did. I knew it annoyed her, but I couldn't help it. Maybe that ADHD thing was real.

"Inheritance? What in the world are you talking about?" she barked at me as if I was an idiot. I may be many things, but I'm *not* an idiot.

"Listen, Aunt Eleanor, I have to get back on the road and can't talk while driving. I'll fill you in on everything later. Bye!"

I promptly pushed the end button, threw my phone on the passenger seat, and shoved my fingers through my loose hair. It was time for a pep talk. I did them daily—several times a day, if necessary—this time to shore myself up for the next leg of my journey.

"You got this, girl. Breathe deeply. Settle your mind. You only have one thing to do: get to Connecticut in one piece," I uttered to assure myself. I huffed air out of my lungs to pump myself up, then threw my gearshift into reverse, squealing the tires as I completed a two-point maneuver back onto the expressway. There was one thing I was very good at, and that was talking myself into anything I wanted. However, thinking through the details of how to get the job done, not so much. As I mentioned before, that was how I gave myself the call name, Always Falling Behind.

I'm the queen of two steps forward, one step back. I chuckled, "If my ancestors who left me this giant inheritance could see the person who would one day claim their legacy, they would have rewritten their trust." Anthony Brickner assured me this trust was ironclad—with one minor adjustment: to claim the one hundred and sixty acres, mansion, and pool, I didn't have to be engaged or married as previous inheritors once had. New legislation made that antiquated statute obsolete; now, all I had to do was claim the deed within thirty days of the bequeath. I spent a whole night searching the internet for what all these words meant, most were four-dollar words requiring a college degree. I may have graduated high school, and I may not be an idiot, but I didn't have either a college or law degree at twenty-four, and I wouldn't ever have one, to be sure.

Two more hours of nerve-racking trucks and high-speed drag racers, and I was done for the day. My stomach grumbled, my bladder was near to bursting, and the needle on my gas tank pointed at zero. I guess it's Cleveland or Bust. Knowing I would most likely never be in this city again, I pulled into a gas mart three miles down from my exit. Whenever I could focus properly, I could be pretty efficient, this being a perfect example: bathroom, food, and fuel. I was feeling proud of myself after suffering through a disgusting unisex bathroom and stomaching a leathery hot dog spinning on a slow roller from behind a glass partition. Not wanting to make another pit stop in an hour, I purchased a small bottle of water, some Skittles, and a bag of corn chips along the way. Healthy eating certainly wasn't a top priority; for the record, it never was nor had been. I'm a survivalist, I have no ego, and I don't measure myself against any other person, mostly. I grabbed the white plastic bag and walked with my head held high back to my car, pondering where I would stop for the night. Surely, I could keep going for a few more hours?

As I unlocked my car, a young man a little older than I asked if I wanted to give him a ride.

"A ride? I don't think so." I may be poor, but I was taught not to give strangers a ride.

"I could pay for your gas. Come on, driving alone must suck." He prodded, giving me a wink.

He did look sexy in his tight, black T-shirt and ripped faded jeans. His hair flopped over his left eye and pierced through its strands to my chest.

"I'm good, thanks," I replied, quickly getting into my car and locking the door.

As I pulled away, he stood with his hands on his hips, staring at me like he lost his prey for the night. Good! The distinct feeling of dodging a bullet passed through my mind, feeling my mother's presence like I always did when I had a serious decision to make. I didn't know how I knew she was with me, but I did. That protection had never steered me wrong, and her protection was definitely concrete tonight. Thank God!

Chapter 2
Meeting Elias

ABIGAIL

I jerked awake, disoriented, and felt like I slept in my car. News flash: I did. My eyes were lightly crusted over, and my messy hair nested around my puffy face. My rearview mirror wasn't kind to me this morning, and no amount of finger-combing would fix this look. The sun began its ascent as I reached behind me to dig out my purse when I noticed a young kid staring at me through my windshield. I collected a clean shirt, deodorant, purse, and phone charger and exited the vehicle carefully to use the hotel bathroom. My luck, I'd trip over my feet and create another embarrassing moment for all to enjoy.

As I stepped onto the curb, I looked at the boy and said, "Stay in school, kid, or this could be your life." His mother grabbed him by the collar and gave me a pained look like I was some creeper. Truth be told, I creeped myself out most mornings. I needed a new life, a new look, and a guardian angel to turn my ship around.

A polite society would have been disgusted by the sink shower I completed before anyone could walk in on me. Thank goodness the braid I locked into place suggested I was a sweet girl; however, the bright red lipstick I applied said otherwise. My dark raven hair and fair skin implied one of two things: with makeup—a vampire; without makeup—a starving orphan. I went with option "C" today and added some demure eye color, no liner or mascara, and some tinted moisturizer, minimizing my opaque skin to appear "alive."

In case anyone cared to reach me, I turned my phone back on, continued to charge it for a few more minutes, and opened the email from Mr. Brickner, the attorney, confirming the address to my new abode. I reset my navigation and calculated I was approximately six hours from my final destination. Sadly, there weren't any messages, texts, or shared memes. Even junk mail missed my box. With any luck, I'll arrive mid-afternoon and be able to sleep in my new bed shortly after that. Wish me luck.

As I traveled through the highways and byways of our great nation, I saluted each bridge emblazoned with a general's name and slowed down to enjoy the hills and plains springing to life. Small purple and yellow flowers pushed their way to the sun, reminding me that we get a chance to start a new cycle of life every year. This spring was going to be my best cycle of life yet. I wished I had someone to share it with.

Two hours into my inspirational morning, my engine light went on. The last time that happened, my gas cap wasn't on right, so I pulled off on the side of the road to double-check I put it on correctly when I filled it up this morning. Careful of traffic coming up behind me, I slid out of the car and inspected the cap, noting that everything was in order. I calculated the chances of how far I could push my limits and get to Mystic without the engine exploding; then I hatched a new plan. First, I'll drive fifty-five miles per hour not to tax the engine too much. I'll top off my windshield wiper solution. I vowed not to use the heater or air conditioning. Perfect. I can do this!

I looked carefully, pulled back into traffic at the slower pace my plan called for, and added my hazard lights to my plan, just in case. A moan cried out from under my seat like a ghost, ready to re-enter this plane. Then, a crunching sound erupted under the hood. *Jesus Christ! What the hell was happening?* An exit appeared, and I didn't think twice about taking it. I threw the gear shift into Neutral and coasted up the exit ramp. More groans and a popping sound emanated under the hood, then smoke! *Oh shit, smoke!* Swiveling my head, I looked for a gas station. I prayed for my mother's intervention and aimed Little Red into the driveway of "Elias's Fixer Upper." *What the hell kind of name was that?*

Smoke plumed from under the hood as I pushed in the clutch, threw the gear shift into Neutral, and cut the engine. Like a cheetah on the prowl, I leaped out of the car and ran into the building for help.

"Help! Help! My car is going to explode!"

ELIAS

A wild creature barged into my garage screaming at the top of her lungs, and my first instinct was to yell at her to calm down. After eyeing her appearance and the desperation on her hysterical face, I thought better of chastising her and looked where she pointed. She was correct; her car looked like Vesuvius, ready to blow. I grabbed the fire extinguisher off the wall and marched over to her vehicle as she ran behind me, wailing about Little Red. Who the fuck was Little Red?

I hosed the smoke, pulled my work gloves from my jumpsuit, and unlatched the hood. The sickening smell of oil cooking on the engine led me to believe this girl got lucky. Three more minutes running, and it would have caught fire. Hosing the whole compartment down gave me a minute to look off in my periphery to this young woman folded over at the waist and bawling into her hands. Once I was sure the car was no longer alive, I put down the extinguisher and walked back over to explain what options she had regarding the disposal of her vehicle.

"Uh, miss?" I tempered my big voice so as not to frighten her. "Are you going to be alright?"

She sniffed several times, then removed her hands from her face, and my jaw dropped. I didn't notice it when she first ran into my shop, but she was a dream. Well, not a dream, like a blonde bombshell. No, she was actually *in* a dream I had last week. I dreamt of a fair, long-haired girl with dark hair and a small frame. She was in distress, and I was supposed to save her. That can't be right. I've never had a premonition in my life. Why now? I couldn't see her face exactly in my dream, yet everything else about her was the same.

I pulled myself together and reminded myself that she needed to know her options, so I began rather mechanically delivering the news.

"I'm sorry to inform you that your ride is dead." *Very eloquent. Nice job, dummy.* "Sorry. What I meant to say was that you need a casket for that heap." *Stop! Just stop.* "Okay, what I'm trying to say is . . ."

Her eyebrows narrowed, "I get it! My car is long gone, and not a fucking thing can make it work again. Thank you for your assistance, but now I have to think." She stormed away to sit under one of the maple trees lining my parking lot. Her hands returned to her face, and she started hitting her head. Nope! That's not happening on my watch. I looked over at my other technician, who came out of the garage while this girl went ape-shit, I jutted my chin toward the girl; and quickly walked back over to see what I could do for her.

"Hey, listen," I knelt before her, trying to get her attention. "Please stop hitting yourself. It's not your fault."

She wouldn't stop, and I began to get angry. Why would she do that to herself?

"Stop!" I grabbed both her wrists and pulled them down to her knees. She was surprisingly strong for such a small person. "This isn't your fault. Your car is old. Given how packed your car is, I'm not sure where you're coming from, but you made it here safely. That's all that matters."

Big, hazel, watery eyes stared at me blankly. Her lashes were dewy, and the smudges of darkness under her eyes led me to believe she either hadn't slept much or had a difficult past. It was her lips, though, that captivated me—the delicate "o" between her pillowy, Cupid's bow upper lip and the entire bottom one. They were stained red and so expressive even when they weren't moving. She was fascinating.

"It's not all that matters to me. It's the *only* thing that matters to me. I can't be stranded. I have to be somewhere tomorrow, and, if I don't make it there, I don't know what to do." I let her wrists go and pulled a clean handkerchief out of my pocket. It was such an old-school thing to do, but I was an old-school kind of guy. Hankies weren't just for runny noses. She dried her eyes and whimpered.

"Thank you. Although I have no idea what this is."

"Hasn't anyone taught you about hankies? It's a standard gentleman's accessory. It's like a tissue you wash." Her quizzical expression made me laugh, and then she hummed a pretty sound. "There, that's better."

She dabbed her eyes and wiped her nose, then looked at me and extended my fluid-filled cloth. "Did you want this back? It's gross now."

I chuckled. "Keep it. You never know when you'll need it again." I smiled at her and stood up. "Let me help you up." I extended my hands, and she took both, laying her tiny palms in my giant, calloused ones. We both looked at them, perplexed. Tingles went down my spine when we touched. Her timid smile made me hard, and that was my cue to let her hands go and walk back to the garage.

I could hear her shuffling behind me, trying to keep up. I was a big man and no match for this little flower. This, whatever it was, wasn't going to go anywhere. I needed to return to work, forget my stupid dream, and let this woman get on with her life.

"Hey, uh, mister!" She called after me. "What do I do now?" Her expression was pathetic and needy.

Under my breath, I spoke to myself and finished with a sigh. "I can help you dispose of your car, but that's all I can do. I'm sorry, ma'am." *I'm an ass.*

"I understand. Is there a bus station nearby? I saw one pass a few minutes ago," she panted, swinging her arms toward the road.

I stopped, turned toward her, and consented, "It's a mile down the road. Where are you headed?" *It couldn't hurt to know.*

"Mystic, Connecticut. I have to get there by tomorrow. Can a bus take me there?"

"Sure. That bus you just saw? You missed it."

"Okay. I'll get the next one. Could you drop me off at the station? I need to take my things."

"Well, the problem isn't getting another bus. The problem is that was *the* bus going that way until Saturday." I pressed my lips together, seeing the irony of her situation.

This tiny person let out a litany of expletives that any marine would be proud of. "Why does this shit always happen to me?" The waterworks continued to the point of her almost vomiting.

"Hey, hey. If you give me a minute, I might have another option for you. Hang on." I held up my pointer finger, nodded my head encouragingly, and sprinted into the building.

"Paul!" I hollered at my tech under a hoist. "Can you cover tomorrow for me? Sorry for the short notice, but this lady needs some help, and we were going to shut down for a long weekend anyway. What do you say?"

He placed a hose under the Chevy 250 engine, cranked open a valve, and emptied the oil into a splash pan. "Helping a lady out in distress, huh?" He winked twice at me.

"Fuck off. Can you help me or not?" I stood with my chest out and my hands on my hips, trying to be as intimidating as I could.

"I've got you, boss. Go save your damsel in distress," he smirked and slid back under the pickup.

I shook my head to clear my ridiculous thoughts of "saving" this girl. I had a dream, not an epiphany. Maybe she was a girl in a dream and not my dream girl. I could feel my muscles tighten at my shoulders and neck, and I hadn't even committed to asking her if she wanted my help. I could help her pack her crap up in boxes and UPS them to wherever she was going and dump her into a taxi. Provided our town had one—and they don't. Her option, singular, was for me to drive her. Let's hope she doesn't cry again when I offer my hair-brained idea.

With hands in my pockets and a flush of heat coming on, I walked up to what's her name and stopped in front of her. She had returned to the tree, with her shapely legs tucked under her chin, and waited for her to look up.

"So, I had an idea that would solve your problem. Do you want to hear it?" I toed the earth and hung my head down, enjoying how her hair cupped around her jaw when she lifted it. She was young, confused, and wary.

She picked at the ripped denim at her knee and looked back down after acknowledging me. "What?"

I squatted down to get her attention and spoke quietly. "I had planned to close my shop for a long weekend anyway, and I didn't have any specific plans other than watching the hockey division playoffs and drinking beer. I could drive you where you need to go."

The cock of her neck coupled with my being pushed to my ass with two rather strong palms should have been my red flag. She popped up and backed away from me like I was a snake ready to attack.

"What the fuck did you just say? Should a young girl get into a stranger's vehicle and let him take her anywhere? What's *wrong* with you?"

She didn't wait for an answer and stalked again across the parking lot. She looked all around for what appeared like another human being to bear witness to my proposition. I wasn't getting on her crazy train. Though now that I'm rehashing what I said, I did sound like a creeper.

I ran ahead and blocked her way, pressing my hands together and begging her to listen.

"Hey, come on. I'm sure that sounded bizarre, even to my ears. The reality is that you don't have any other options. I promise I'm not a pedophile or a serial killer. I'll even have our police chief come down and vouch for me. I only wanted to help."

She stared at me, shifting her eyes from my mouth to my eyes, to my arms, then my chest. Now *I* was starting to feel violated. What was she doing? Sizing me up? I could crush her with one hand. Shit, I could shot-put her to the next county with one hand tied behind my back. It had to be my beard that scared her. It wasn't long and scraggly, nor nice and tight like those city boys wear it. It looked manly, sexy. At least, that was what a few women said about me when they thought I wasn't listening.

As she finished her inventory of my features, she dropped her hands to her sides and confessed, "I'd be breaking every lesson I've been taught about not speaking to or going with strangers, but, if I do say yes, I want that police chief's approval."

I chuckled and extended my hand, saying, "I'm Elias. Elias McGinnis. Proprietor of this here establishment." I bowed slightly at the waist and gave her one of my signature smiles. She laughed back shyly, extending her tiny hand to mine. "Abigail Farnsworth-Burton. Always Falling Behind." I sensed her predicament and gave her a wry smile.

"Not today, sweetheart. Destiny may have brought you to my door, but your situation is temporary. Mark my words." As we shook hands, that zing of electricity shot up my arm again. The look Abigail gave me took that jolt and sent it straight to my dick. She had to trust me. I wouldn't let her down.

Chapter 3

Elias and Abigail Start Their Journey

ELIAS

The blue lights of the police chief left my parking lot to go onto its next assailant, not before the chief giving Abigail his testimonial of my good character.

"Wait here, and I'll get my pickup. Then we can get you loaded up. We'll be on the road as the sun comes up tomorrow." I smacked my hands together and pulled open my desk drawer to grab my keys.

Abigail leaned forward with both hands on my desk, giving me what looked like her stink-eye. Most of her hair had fallen from whatever hairdo she started her day with today. Those red-tinted lips now looked blush pink, and I wanted to lick them. Pull it together, man. You're saving her, not planning an assault on her. No wonder she felt a creeper vibe.

I must have made a sound because she cocked her head again to the side. This time, though, I saw the red flag and stepped back immediately. "What did I say?"

After a deep breath, she stood straight and pushed her hair behind her ears with those delicate fingers. *Stop!*

"That might be your plan, but it isn't mine. I must be in Mystic by Friday morning, not Friday night."

"Mystic? As in Connecticut? That's almost four hours away." She gave me a no-shit-Sherlock look.

She shoved her hands onto her hips and shifted her weight aggressively. "Where did you think I needed to go? To the Walmart the next town over? I have a deadline, buster, with or without you." Pressed lips and large puffs of air pumped out of her body like a dragon. *Note to self—Beware of the Dragon Lady.*

ABIGAIL

WTF? Who was this guy? First, he douses the impending flames of Little Red, and then he lights a damn fire inside me moments later. Next, he offers me kindness with a cloth tissue. Who uses shit like that anymore? Ah, yes, he told me. Gentlemen. I wouldn't have known what one of those was because, remember, no dad. Not even a goddamned distant cousin. I did have an uncle, though. Let's call him a relative, not family. I remembered Uncle Ted as a cool guy when I was younger. When I turned twelve, he bolted, and I'd never seen him since. When questioned years later, Aunt Eleanor said he had some business. For five years? *Sounded more like a prison sentence.*

The final insult this Elias-guy made was that *his* offer had a radius attached to it. After I thoroughly assessed his caramel-colored eyes and long lashes, his too-small-for-his-face ears, that silky-soft beard, tree-trunk arms, thick thighs, and his rock-hard chest, I determined that, if he killed me, the view would be spectacular.

"Elias. Thank you for the offer to drive me. I'm sorry you offered without knowing the specifics of this trip, though it was naive on your part not to ask before offering. Here is what you need to know. I have an inheritance to claim, and, for reasons I don't want to get into, it has to be claimed by this Friday. Today is Thursday—afternoon. We have to leave now. Not tomorrow morning. The Office of Deeds closes at four o'clock on Friday, and I have to claim what's mine before then. So, what's it gonna be?"

I eyeballed him, challenging him to back out of his offer. I may be tiny, but I can be a force when pushed.

He rolled his eyes and then located his keys in the drawer, dangling them in front of my face.

He scrubbed his face aggressively. "I'm in. But we're leaving tomorrow. I have a car to finish this evening, and it can't wait. Go ahead and start grabbing stuff out of your car. I'll find some boxes or tubs to throw them in so they don't slide around the pickup bed. After that, you can either wait for me to finish working, and then we'll eat, or take a half-mile walk down the road and eat at the diner yourself."

Five minutes later, Elias returned with three boxes and two giant tubs for me to start packing my stuff—alone. Without so much as "good luck," he went back to work, and I spent the next twenty minutes figuring out how to Tetris my stuff into the truck bed so it wouldn't fly away driving down the highway. When I arrived at Mel's Diner, the sun was beginning to set. The walk down was calming, and my nervous system began to relax. I felt like Little Red

Riding Hood walking over a sparkling stream via a covered bridge. The spots of red and yellow wildflowers that sprung up along the side of the road promised better times to come.

An older woman in a pink uniform and white apron cracked her gum while asking me for my drink order. "Lemonade, please." I smiled back. She didn't deserve my foul attitude. I was down to my last seventy-five dollars and didn't want to waste it on food. Who knew how much money it would cost to claim the deed and how long it would be until I saw a dime from the inheritance?

My drink and french fries arrived. "That's all?" the waitress asked. "Yeah, for now." I had no intention of getting anything else. I still had some Fritos I got from my front seat that I could rely on later. A large, ominous shadow appeared behind me. "Get her a burger, too, Bev. I'll have my usual." It didn't take a genius to know who overruled my decision, though I was hungrier than I let on.

Elias sat down and winked at me. He sure knew how to disarm a girl. "Just because I'm letting you drive me to Mystic doesn't mean you're the boss of me." I tried not to laugh and instead pouted. A big-barreled laugh sang through the air and felt like a stereo subwoofer humming through my chest. It felt good. Ticklish.

"Trust me, sweetheart. I don't want to be your boss. You're boss enough. I was being selfish when I ordered you a burger. I can't imagine spending hours with you hangry." He laughed a little softer, but still, that ticklish feeling permeated my chest.

I gave him a demure look and delivered a smartass snipe: "I'm sure you're no prize either." I drank deeply from my lemonade.

He had the decency to nod and looked out the window, avoiding my gaze. He was unavoidable. A goliath of a man blocked my vision of the rest of the restaurant. I may not be worldly, but this guy must pull tree trunks out of the ground with his bare hands with such powerful-looking arms. It was a struggle to keep my hands at my sides, envisioning what his full beard felt like. Wavy and somewhat kinky in texture, not that I could see him up close, but it didn't lessen my desire to keep looking at him.

Our food arrived, and the waitress forgot to leave the ketchup. Luckily for me, Elias extended his eagle-length arm over to the following table, making his bicep pop to attention. Whoa! What kind of routine does this dude do to make muscles like that? I was just about to ask him when my mind kicked into gear, alerting me that I would say something inappropriate, and I shoved a french fry into my mouth. Occasionally, my impulsivity could be controlled when I only had one thing to focus on, and I could concentrate on those arms all day.

"Abigail?" Elias stared at me in concern.

I shook my head like a bobblehead, "Uh, yeah?"

"Where did you go? It looked like you spaced out for a minute. Are you okay?" His forehead, etched with fine lines, shared his concern. Reading nonverbal cues had always been difficult, though it became easier as I got older.

I drank some water, looking at him over the rim of my glass and assessing his concern.

"Sorry, I, uh, sometimes do that. I'm sorry if it made you feel uncomfortable. A lot has happened these past few weeks. The stress must be catching up to me." Not wanting to talk more about it, I took a bite of the burger, and my eyes rolled back in pleasure at the taste. It was so good. My last regular meal was almost a week ago, and this one bite produced a visceral response I couldn't have held back.

"Wow! This burger is amazing!" That sounded more like drunken, slurred speech. "So good!" Juice dripped down my chin, forcing me to set the burger down and wipe my lips.

He stared at me with a look that could only be described as perplexed. I don't know why, but I picked up my burger and dove in for another tasty bite.

"You have a . . . drop." He pointed at his cheek. Not understanding, I pointed to my cheek and cocked my head to the side.

"Yeah—not there, but . . ." He pointed to my other cheek, and I wiped again. Still not happy with my attempts, he licked his thumb and reached across the table, brushing his wet digit across my cheek to remove whatever was there. Torn between disgust and lust, I sat there in awe at the gentleness of this massive man and the kindness he offered in helping me get whatever it was off my face. Most people I've encountered would have shown annoyance or thrown a napkin at me, yelling to clean it off.

"There. Some juice splattered on your cheek." He grimaced, sitting back, perhaps realizing what he did invaded my personal space. Or maybe he was stunned too that he touched me without permission? Either way, he was freaking adorable. Shyness in such a big person was sexy. I liked it.

"Thank you." I dabbed at my cheek once and looked back at my food.

We ate silently as the dinner crowd picked up, and the room became noisier. My knee started bouncing with the inferred tension between us. I needed to hurry up and leave before I combusted. It wasn't just him that added to my tension; it was the idea that I would be stuck in a vehicle with him for over four hours tomorrow. I wanted to touch his beard and see firsthand how his face felt in my hands. I wasn't a shy person without things to say. What could I say that would be interesting enough for a guy like him?

"Abigail? You're doing it again." He held his sandwich inches from his face when he spoke; a smile crept up at the corners.

"You're sitting too close." What did I say? "I mean, you don't know me well enough to . . . well, anything." I jumped up, unable to sit another moment. "I'm going to the bathroom," I stormed off in the wrong direction of the restrooms, forcing me to about-face and walk past his smug face again. *Argh!*

This was all too much for me. I opened a stall, threw down the seat cover, stepped up onto the seat, and crouched, making myself as small as I felt. Did I think I could pick up and move across the country without a million things going wrong? Who did I think I was to deserve a ginormous inheritance, let alone from a family I never knew existed? Now, I have a complete stranger extracting a feeling I also never knew existed within me. I needed a therapist. I needed medication. I needed a friend, a mother, a father. I had none of it, and I was terrified. The tears began seeping from my eyes, creating a puddle on the cover, and I covered them ashamedly. I was spiraling downward, and, even though I knew it was a bad thing for me to do, I couldn't help it. Minutes went by, and the stall whipped open—*crappy lock.*

"I knew you weren't okay; you were gone too long." He barely got through the door and stepped inside the stall with me. Like before, he gently pulled my wrists back so he could see me face-to-face. "It's going to be alright. I've got you."

My whole body shuddered to hear his words. *I've got you*, he said. I felt what he was saying for the first time in my life. He had me. I wasn't entirely sure what that entailed, but a wash of calm passed through me, swallowed my tears, and shot back so I could pull myself together. I reached for some toilet paper, but he pushed my hands aside and pulled a long wad off the roll for me. That simple act was what I hoped he meant by, "I've got you. To think, this was the second time in two hours, this man did what had never happened in my whole life—showed me compassion.

"Thank you, Elias." I wiped my eyes and blew my nose, feeling more together. He stepped back and offered his hand for me to step down, albeit wobbly for crouching like that for so long. He backed up and out, letting me pass around him to the sinks, where I splashed some water on my blotchy face. "I'm a wreck, Elias. Are you sure you still want to drive me to Mystic? I can't guarantee this won't happen, or something worse, again."

His jaw ticked under that blanket of wavy, kinky hair, and he palmed his beard thoughtfully. "I'm still in. You are an enigma, Abigail, and I like a good mystery. So, if you don't mind me trying to unravel you, let's keep to our plan. Wait! That didn't sound right. I don't want to physically unrav . . ." His cheeks blushed, and his eyes looked horrified.

I chuckled and put my hands on my hips, "I knew where you were going with that. No worries. I'm still hungry. Let's finish eating and go." I didn't wait for an answer, marching past him and out of the bathroom.

Chapter 4
Hitting the Road

ABIGAIL

My things were secured in the pickup bed. Elias packed a small cooler with water, healthy snacks, and a giant pickle. Last night was something to behold. He drove us to his home two miles from his shop and showed me around like a drill sergeant indoctrinating his new cadets.

"Here is the bathroom. You'll sleep here. Breakfast at seven. We're out the door by seven-thirty. Any questions?"

Yeah. I had a few. He marched himself into his bedroom and shut the door. No "need anything?" or "help yourself to whatever you want." Nope, none of the above. I've made it my life's work to blend into any surroundings, and this won't be any different. I had already grabbed my backpack filled with what I needed for the night. I stayed in my clothes, brushed my teeth and hair, and rebraided it for the night. The dark blue leather recliner sat across from a sixty-inch television mounted above a rustic wood mantel. That would be my resting spot for the night. I would stay alert, mostly, and not give him the option to join me on his couch. It did look comfy, though. A wide cushion covered in an equally wide blue plaid with giant tufted pillows lined up along the back would be enough room for me to sprawl out on. The rest of the room was between Early American and Bachelor Hand-Me-Down decor. It fit Elias. Big, soft, rugged, and thoughtful.

I grabbed a hand-knitted afghan and threw it over my small frame as I pushed back into the recliner, grateful for a safe place to sleep tonight. At least, I hoped it would be safe. It's much safer than sleeping in my car, for sure. I played on my phone and scanned my emails, hoping to find a message from Seneca or my aunt. Both needed my attention once I got settled. The only exciting information was from that attorney informing me of my inheritance.

I hope you have arrived safely in Mystic, Abigail. This is a reminder that you have until five tomorrow night to claim your property. Should you have any difficulties or need anything explained, please call my direct number below, and I'll get it straightened out immediately. I should have mentioned earlier that twenty thousand dollars is in your trust to help you get on your feet. Please spend it wisely.

Best wishes. Henry Brickner, Esq.

"Holy shit!" I screamed, smacking a hand over my mouth—finally, a port in an ocean of shit. I suppose Elias, too, was a port. I laughed out loud, more like a hyena. I was in shock, wrapping my head around this new information. I closed out of my email and started to get up to do a happy dance.

"What's wrong?"

I jumped out of the chair like it was on fire.

"Jesus Christ, Elias! You can't sneak up behind me like that. You scared me to death!" I struggled to control my breathing while he laughed through his big chest.

"You didn't hear my door opening or the floorboards creaking as I walked across the room? Or the light being turned on? You do get engrossed in your thoughts and tune everything out, don't you?" He said it in the most lighthearted way I almost missed his sarcasm. I was warming up to his soft-spoken speech, and it was unsettling. My aunt started speaking to me sweetly when I went to live with her at four. By eight, her tone held annoyance, and, by twelve, it became accusing, like I was trying to be an asshole. High school was a disaster, and, quite frankly, I was happy to move out two weeks after graduation just to be rid of the anxiety she caused in me.

I paced the floor, pondering how much of my condition and situation I should share with him. It had to be something substantial, or he'd think I was a Looney tune.

"I suppose I should mention that I have ADHD, and that has something to do with my responses." I slid back onto the chair, curling my legs underneath me. He walked around to the couch I coveted and squatted deeply until he was low enough to rest his ass.

After leaning back, with his arms crossed—yet relaxed—he reached up and stroked his beard again. "Yeah, that would explain a few things. My cousin has ADD. He takes medication. Better living through chemistry, I say. He would have been miserable and friendless for the rest of his life if it weren't for his meds."

I burst into tears, hanging my head in shame. Streams of water left my eyes, and all I could think of was how pathetic I was. "I-I'm miserable and friendless!" I screamed. My logical self needed to sleep—like the dead kind of sleep. I couldn't think clearly, and everything Elias said seemed like a minefield of emotions going off like fireworks, except his face stayed unaffected.

"I'm sorry. I shouldn't have yelled. I need some sleep." I reached under myself, pulled the blanket around me, and closed my eyes. I decided that keeping my new fortune to myself would be smarter. I didn't know this man and didn't want to be taken advantage of if he knew. Maybe if I kept my eyes closed, he would turn off the lights and disappear. Instead, I felt him lean over me, kiss my forehead, and whisper encouragement.

"You've been under a lot of stress. Everything will work out; just be patient."

His footsteps made a significant noise as he crossed the room and turned off the lights. The sound carried down a short hallway toward the kitchen, where I heard the pipes lightly bang and water fall into a glass. Moments later, through my slitted eyes, I saw him carrying two glasses of water. He set one on a coaster for me while taking the other back to his room.

Who was this guy? Something about him felt so familiar. His mannerisms were comforting and gentle, like those of a grandfather or dear uncle. The way he moved and shood affection made my heart flutter. Was it affection, though? You would think he knew me, too, the way he kissed my head, held my wrists, and looked at me. He looked at me, not through me. So strange. I must have passed out because I was on the couch covered in a thick fleece blanket when I woke up. He didn't . . . he couldn't have . . . I shook my head, waking up to the sun peeking through the curtain and over some trees. I was too consumed with the smell of coffee. The mystery of how I got on the couch was forgotten.

ELIAS

This girl slept like the dead. An hour after she tripped out about not having friends and being miserable, I walked out to check on her before crashing for the night myself. I carefully scooped her into my arms and settled her onto the sofa that would allow her to be more comfortable all night. I fetched a pillow from the hall closet and a heavier blanket to help her sleep deeper. From my cousin Dell's mom, I learned about the benefits of heavy bedding on light sleepers. It changed Dell's sleep immediately for the better. Luckily, I didn't hear a peep out of her until two minutes ago.

She entered the kitchen, rubbing her eyes and mumbling. I took a chance and grabbed a mug off the counter, filled it with coffee, and handed it to her.

"Creamer is in the fridge, and sugar is on the table," I offered. "I wasn't sure what kind of breakfast eater you were, but I'm happy to fix you some eggs or pancakes." She stopped rubbing and gave me big hazel eyes that looked like a deer in headlights.

"Did you say pancakes?" Her hopeful grin was precious.

"Yep." I walked to the pantry to grab the mix. "Want anything in them?" I waggled my brows, tempting her to share her favorite toppings.

She took two steps forward, holding her mug and bringing it to her full lips. "Chocolate chips? Cinnamon? Syrup?"

I grinned, enjoying her shoulder shrug and tip of her chin toward the cupboard I had my hand in.

"I've got you. Get yourself cleaned up, and I'll have these ready in ten minutes. We have to leave soon, and I have a few chores to do before we go."

Without a word, she spun on her heel and glided out of the kitchen, hands still wrapped around that mug. I wanted to be that mug. The rim, the cup, the handle. All of it, so long as her hands and mouth were on it. How long had it been since I was with a woman? No date came to mind, so too long was the answer. Abigail was a girl. Not more than eighteen, by my calculations. I'm over twice her age, and I had lustful thoughts about her. For my mental health, I'm going to blame these feelings on that weird dream and too many months of not being with a woman. I had enough issues to invite unappreciated affection from an unsuspecting person. Though she didn't seem annoyed about the kiss on her head last night or wiping some hamburger juice off her supple cheek. *See! There I go again. Stop!*

Forty minutes later, we were on the road, ready for what I hoped would be a great adventure. I hadn't closed the shop for over three days since I bought it five years ago. My life as a mechanical engineer was too stressful. I had always wanted to work on cars and not much else. When the opportunity came up, I jumped on it and never looked back. My parents weren't too happy. Leaving a six-figure career didn't bother me as much as it did them. Did they think I would be back with my hand outstretched for a loan? Or worse, be sleeping on their sofa for an indeterminate time? I saved over half of what I made from the previous ten years to change my career, and I was known to be a bit of a savant regarding the stock market. At least, that's what my broker called me. That's how I could afford to buy this service station and start fixing cars without a mortgage. *Not too bad for a country guy.*

"Elias!" I slammed on the brakes. "What? Are you alright," I panted. I carefully pulled the pickup over to the side of the expressway and looked deeply into her eyes.

"Am I alright? Are you okay? Your eyes were glazed over, and I thought you were having an embolism." She had both hands on my forearm, patting it all over for what appeared to be a pulse.

"Are you trying to find my pulse?" She nodded vigorously. I tried not to laugh outright, but this girl was hilarious in her attempts to "help" me. "Sweetheart." I cupped one of her hands and squeezed two fingers together, placing them on the underside of my wrist. "Here. This is where you find a pulse."

The look in her eyes made me sad as if she didn't know what to do. I touched the space just below her ear and exhaled audibly. "And here."

Her lids drooped, and her breathing hitched. *Christ. I had affected her. She affected me. This needs to stop.* I pulled my head back abruptly.

"These are called pulse points. You count how many times your heart pulses in sixty seconds to know how fast it beats." I shifted my head away and looked over my left shoulder to see if the traffic was clear for re-entry.

Abigail spent the next few minutes putting her fingers at each pulse point to ensure I wasn't fooling her. "You're right. You can measure the beats. How do you know so much about this stuff?"

Good question. "I don't know. I remembered it from a high school health class or a doctor's show. It's basic stuff."

She laughed. "I guess I missed that whole class. I don't have a TV, so—oops! —I missed that, too."

I was getting annoyed with her self-deprecating comments. It didn't help her, and it didn't feel good to hear her saying those things about herself.

"I tell you what. Let's play a game." She nodded, thinking this was a terrific idea.

"What kind of game?" Her lips pressed together, concerned.

"It goes like this: every time you say something negative about yourself, you put a quarter in this cup." I held up an old water cup from a fast-food place I hadn't thrown away.

"Why?" She said hesitantly.

I shook my head as I spelled this out for her. "I'm tired of you putting yourself down. I'm sure you have amazing talents and exciting experiences that would be more interesting to me or anyone else instead of tearing yourself down."

"So, you're saying that I'm annoying, and you don't want to be around me anymore." She harumphed and threw herself back in her seat, crossing her arms around her pert breasts. *Not fair.* I tried again.

"No. That isn't what I'm saying. Let me try again. If I called myself weak, you would think I was being ridiculous, right?" She nodded her head. "That's different than I'm feeling weak today. Do you see the difference?" Her pink lips pushed forward as she drilled her stare through my windshield.

"Abigail. Are you mad at me? I only want you to see that your words matter and say a lot about how you think about yourself." She huffed again. "I think a lot about you and like what I see." Her smile bloomed.

"So, you think about me a lot, do you?" Her arms uncrossed, and she pivoted in her seat, raising her left knee near the center column.

I felt my face flush. Why couldn't I say things without embarrassing myself? "I meant to say that you are different, and I like that about you." Oh my God. Words! I need to find better words. I sound like I'm in love with her. *Geez.*

"So, I'm different, huh? Like weird different? Embarrassing different?" Her eyebrows ruffled, and she glared at me like the imbecile I was.

Wait. Did she giggle? She didn't. She did!

"You're pulling my leg, aren't you? You're naughty." I said the word, and my dick vibrated at the possibility of that statement.

"Me? I've never done a naughty thing in my life!" She burst out laughing, and so did I. This was fun. She was fun. What kind of fun could we have in the next three hours left of our trip?

Chapter 5
The Inner Workings of Elias

A**BIGAIL**

Toll roads are boring. Elias was anything but. He rattled off random facts about the area he currently lived in and mechanical concepts that have evolved. I listened intently, not for the information, though it was interesting and telling about him. No, I listened because I liked how his mouth moved with his beard. I liked the crinkles at the corners of his eyes and the rise of his ears when he smiled. His laugh, well, you know that already.

"How many tattoos do you have?" *Wow! That was random.*

He looked at me oddly since he was presently informing me how the telegraph system evolved similarly through the high-tension lines bordering the tollway.

"Uh, seven, I guess. Some connect to others, but I've only gone to one artist, and only that many times. Do you have any tattoos?"

"Seven. That's a lot." I pointed to the one that peaked from his long-sleeved shirt to his hand. "How far up does that one go?"

Again, he shot me a look. What did I say? Inquiring minds wanted to know.

"You ask a lot of questions." He smirked and pointed to his shoulder. "Satisfied?"

I bit my lip, "Very."

I was disturbed to see my hidden ingénue emerging. I shifted forward again and willed my mouth shut. He swallowed hard, and that tick in his jaw reappeared again.

"Sorry. Impulsivity is a problem for me. Stop me if I make you uncomfortable." Why couldn't I think first and speak second? My aunt chastised me for doing that often, which was another reason for giving me a hard time. What do you know? She was right.

He pursed his lips, thinking while cows, fences, and windmills whooshed by our windows. Sometimes, time flew by on our drive, and others were slow and awkward. Here we were again, being awkward.

"Why don't you tell me where we're going and what you plan to do when you get there?" I saw what he was doing. Mr. Brickner did the same thing when I got amped up.

"I don't know all the details, only that a lawyer called to inform me that a family inheritance was left to me, and I had thirty days to claim it in Mystic, Connecticut. He said there were one hundred and sixty acres, a mansion, and a pool. Why did he think telling me about the pool would clinch the deal? I don't know. I don't even swim."

Elias tapped the steering wheel with his thumbs to the beat of the country music playing low on the radio. "You don't swim?"

I twisted in my seat, throwing my arms forward in annoyance. "That's what you took from my story? Seriously?

Elias, you missed the whole point of this trip!" He sounded like me.

He chuckled. "Continue." His smirks were patronizing, and I wasn't a child to be mocked. I snarled my upper lip at him and continued.

Sitting up straight, I placed my hands in my lap and primly repeated what Mr. Brickner described to me.

"The inheritance (cough, cough) was created in a heritage trust handed down through my family's female line, dating back to 1832. I have no idea how this was possible because on the days I did pay attention in history class, only first-born men usually received the lion's share of an inheritance. The attorney said it wasn't important at this time to know, but I should hurry up and claim what's mine." I drank from the water bottle I stashed on my door, recalling the conversation from a month ago.

"I'm curious," he inquired, "Why did you wait so long before starting this trip? You said you had to claim this by tomorrow but had a whole month." His forehead scrunched up, and his lips pressed together—another sexy look to file away.

"Did I mention I had ADHD? P-R-O-C-R-A-S-T-I-N-A-T-I-O-N." I spelled out each letter like a nail in a coffin. "Time is elusive to me until a hard deadline becomes evident, and even then, I perseverate on failing and then fall behind again. It's a cycle I can't seem to break. A therapist years ago recommended medication to help, but my aunt vetoed it, saying, 'It isn't affordable, and I will do just fine without them.'"

"Wow! Your aunt didn't give this the attention it deserved." He hummed to himself.

"Nice pun. Again, Elias, you missed the point. I did procrastinate, but once I finally got around to notifying both my bosses, at least I thought I told both my bosses and then my landlord, it was almost three weeks later. That's why tomorrow is my drop-dead date. Understand?" I sounded patronizing, but I was annoyed.

ELIAS

We drove in companionable silence for the next hour, playing a game called *Truth or Lie*. Abigail chewed on the inside of her cheek, pondering my answers. She twisted her fingers around one another, making tiny sighs that made me too aware of her proximity. The toll road was busy this time of day, and the cops were everywhere. I knew Abigail had a deadline, yet paying fines for speeding wasn't part of my plan.

"Lie!" she blurted out. There is no way fortune cookies aren't Chinese!" If she had nuts, she'd have busted one by now.

"It's the truth. On my honor, I hope to die. It was the Japanese. Look it up."

I loved being right about Abigail's unabashed reactions. She ripped out her phone and searched for "the real truth." She cracked me up.

"Unbelievable. My whole world has shifted. Don't tell me anything else. I might explode or fall into a coma. I'm not sure which." She yawned, massaged her scalp with her fingers, and curled herself tighter; sleep was the winner.

She looked adorable and vulnerable, with her head resting on her arm on the center console. Whisps of silky black hair fell from her braid, and I fought the urge to rub those strands between my fingers while she peacefully slept. My luck, she'd wake up freaked out and feeling violated. *Oh God, Elias, who wouldn't?* I did notice a slight dusting of freckles that adorned her nose, cheeks, and corners of her eyes. She looked ethereal. How could such an angelic sleeping beauty one moment transform into Vesuvius the next? She told me about her condition. I wasn't naive to her plight. I had my own bag of tricks that I dealt with, namely, not being a clear communicator under pressure, which was a big reason I got out of mechanical engineering. The higher the stakes, the higher the pressure, which equaled more erratic communication on my part. When building bridges or buildings, precise instructions and execution are critical to the excellent health of its future occupants or travelers. People's lives were in my hands, and although I was talented, my ability to share my vision, issues, and the rest was, well, incomplete. After ten years of battling myself and my bosses, I chose "Door #2" and left the corporate world for a quieter life, limiting how many people I worked with in one day.

Nature called, and I pulled into the next rest stop, parking next to an elderly couple struggling to get out of their car. I couldn't open my door, so I passed the minutes giving all my attention to Sleeping Beauty drooling on my leather. I succumbed to my better senses and stroked the top of her head under the pretense of trying to wake her up. Her head settled into my palm when she shifted her weight, and another jolt of electricity ran through my body. The fact that she wasn't trying to entice me didn't go without notice. My imagination had built a whole life of its own around her, and it didn't matter that I had no idea who she was, whether we were compatible, or if I could live with her drooling like a baby on all my stuff. *It was worth trying.*

"Abigail," I whispered. Do you need to use the bathroom?" I stroked her cheek with my knuckles. Her skin was so soft that I did it again. "Abigail, wake up." Nothing. Only a snort. I was afraid if I used more force, she'd throat-punch me in her panic to wake up—or, worse, scratch my eyes out. I tried once more and pulled back on the defensive. "Abby! Wake up!"

She snapped to attention, screaming, "What? What's happening?" She whipped her head to the left, but when she whipped back to the right, she yiped. "Ah. Ouch. Oh my God, I can't move my neck." She whimpered, and I felt her pain.

My hands smacked onto my head, and I wondered what to do next.

"What can I do to help? You must have slept on it funny. Here . . ." I looked out the driver's side window, and, finally, it was clear to open. I jumped out and ran to the other side, jerking her door open. I stepped up onto the running board, hoping to support her head.

"Can you turn toward the driver's side? I'm going to release your neck, okay?"

"As long as you can make this pain stop, do it." She daintily shifted to her left thigh while dropping her right off the side of the seat. I pulled the jean jacket she wore over her shoulders and down her arms. The idea of undressing her was erotic, giving me questionable confidence in relieving her pain. I sealed my mouth so as not to make any untoward noises. Next, I stroked my left hand down her arm while gently putting pressure on her neck to lengthen the tendons and muscles that were in spasm.

"Lift your shoulder if you can, then drop it again gently. I'm going to apply light pressure to lengthen the area. There, that's good again. Exhale each time." I continued the process until I could feel the tension recede. Unfortunately, as her breath evened out, mine became labored.

"How are you doing?" I asked, hoping we could be done. I needed some relief, and my time was running short.

"Better. Would you mind rubbing my shoulders for a few minutes? Maybe up my neck?" She asked innocently enough, though she moaned when I began squeezing her shoulders. I pressed my fingers lightly into her scalene muscles, eliciting a slap on my forearm.

"Ouch! There! That's killing me."

"I can feel it. You have to breathe and let me get it to loosen up. Put your head on my chest here and let me try to work you from this angle." That sounded provocative, but she leaned back without being pressured. "Better?"

"Yes."

"Okay. Close your eyes and concentrate on breathing. I should have this worked out in a few minutes." If only the smell of her hair wasn't floating into my nostrils. A soft peach perfume unsettled my nerves, and I carefully dug my fingers along each tendon's ridge until they relented. A few minutes of attention on each of the three adjoining muscles brought an audible, "Yes!" from Abigail, and I almost blew my wad. Christ! She had no idea what she did to me. Being the responsible adult, she *wasn't* going to know either.

"Excellent. You did well. Let's hit the head and get back on the road. We have a house to claim." I took her hand and helped her up. Alarmingly, she looked strange and perplexed. Did I say something wrong again?

"What?"

"*We* have a house to claim? You mean my house, right?" Her hands were on her hips, my help long forgotten. "Yes, of course.

Your house, madame." I bowed slightly at her high-handed statement.

"Just checking." She bit her lip, reminding me she was a teaser, and I fell for it again.

I took her hand, "Let's go, princess."

Chapter 6
The Final Hour

A BIGAIL

Elias was so serious. Getting him to lighten up took a lot of work, but I was determined. Over the next hour, I would hammer him with a barrage of questions to get to the nut that sat in the middle of his rock-hard abs. After I was done with him, he'd be an open book, and then I could get him to do anything I wanted. It's not that I'm evil, though I have an agenda. Not having much parental supervision growing up allowed me to learn life in a completely different way—from the streets.

Don't underestimate the value of watching people in the wild. Parents who reprimanded their children in public to businessmen melting into little boys when they lost big deals. I saw it all. I took mental notes and used those lessons to establish patterns in people that any clinical psychologist would applaud. I didn't need a lot of backstory to come to my conclusions. However, some information could swing my opinions dramatically. People are generally the same unless they've been traumatized or raised by wolves. We all, mostly, want the same things. Maslow had it right, except at the top of the triangle. Actualization is subjective and not an altogether solution to a finish line in my opinion. The one thing I was blessed with was the ability to read people despite my handicap. My teachers were always impressed at how quickly I could spin my approach to working with teammates after spending only a few minutes with them. It's my sixth sense. After three high school psychology courses and years of YouTube education, I believed I had the equivalent of an undergraduate degree in psychology. Either way, Elias would crack open like a walnut at Christmas.

"So . . . tell me about where you grew up, Elias." I looked at my chipped nail polish nonchalantly, promising myself I'd remove it the first chance I had.

He gave me a quick look, then focused on the road again. "Me? Uh. You know, a usual background. Strict parents, church, football, rugby, homework. Usual." His mouth twitched. Did he want to add something? Why was he so tongue-tied?

"Huh. Elias, my childhood didn't include any of those things except homework. Yours sounds predictable."

"Yeah, predictable and boring," he mumbled annoyingly.

I meant to say it as a compliment. Nothing was predictable in my life. I wish it had been. Maybe I wouldn't be such a spaz all the time.

"I didn't mean that as a judgment. It's reassuring to know what to expect and not be always on high alert. Tell me something else. Did you have a girlfriend in high school? A dog? A cat? Bunk beds?" I asked as sweetly as I could. I even twisted in my seat to show engagement. *See that? Psychology.*

"Aren't you full of probing questions this afternoon? I didn't realize emptying your bladder made you so talkative." He smirked and then laughed full-out.

"Ha ha ha. You didn't answer any of my questions. Do I have to repeat them, or are you smart enough to remember?" I snarked back.

"Yes. Dog. No bunk beds. I was an only child." His brow knit slightly, admitting that to me.

"Me, too." I shared.

"A girlfriend? A dog or an only child?" he asked.

How could eyebrows morphing from scrunched to raised be so sexy? His smile was full and beautiful and stretched to his eyes. Although I couldn't see most of his mouth through his beard, I could see the fullness of his lips while he laughed. I liked that, too.

"I'm an only child. My mother died when I was four. Why didn't your parents have more kids?" *Shut up, Abigail. That's rude.* I blew through an explanation of my mother's passing, not giving him an opportunity to comment on it I only knew two things about her passing: sudden and painful.

"My parents weren't the most demonstrative couple. They didn't share much with me on purpose. They would say, 'What happens in a marriage stays within the marriage.' I suppose they had their reasons, but I learned later on that my mother suffered through several miscarriages and gave up on trying again." He rubbed under his eye as if he had an itch.

I looked like a fool. When would I learn not to speak every word in my nosey head?

"I'm sorry, Elias. I didn't mean to pry. I'm sorry for their pain and loss. You deserved to have a sister or brother." I fingered through the loose tendrils of hair that had fallen from my braid.

"It's all right. I had friends and, like I said, a dog, so that was cool. How about you? Friends? Pet?"

I'm happy he changed the subject. In my earnest attempt to get to know him, I alienated him. Geez, I was a real ballbuster.

"I have an aunt who raised me. I wasn't the easiest kid and made her life difficult at times. I stayed at my friend Seneca's house in high school, mostly since my aunt worked the afternoon shift. It was a good arrangement and kept me from being a juvenile delinquent. Any pet I would have had would die a painful death since I wasn't around to feed or love it. I was invisible."

I muttered the last three words, feeling sorry for myself. I'd vacillated from "poor me" to "I'm free to do what I want my whole life."

"Abigail. Listen. Neither one of us had a perfect childhood. Make no mistake about that. What I wouldn't have given to do what I wanted, how and when I wanted." He let out a chesty chuckle. "My parents would have had an aneurysm if I chose to hang out with friends after school instead of being on a team or doing homework." He shook his head slowly and rolled his eyes upward.

"Aren't we a pair then? Two opposites of the spectrum, and yet we haven't killed each other—yet." I slapped my knee and laughed.

He looked at me funny, "A pair? As in together? You and me? I'm just driving you somewhere, not hitching up with you." He sniped at me.

My jaw dropped in shock. I didn't suggest that at all. He was so literal I wanted to punch him in the arm. It's good that I didn't because I might have hurt my hand.

"Don't be an ass!" I shouted, and he began to laugh.

"Are you mocking me?" I kept shouting and getting angrier by the second.

"Are you mocking me?" He shouted back, trying not to laugh again. Unsuccessfully, I might add.

Realization kicked in. I was the one being duped this time.

"Ha. Ha. Fine. You got me. Well done." I smirked and turned forward in my seat. "Nice to know you're a quick learner. I'd hate to have to spell everything out for you."

"You can spell anything you want for me." His white teeth shone brightly.

"How about S-H-U-T U-P?" I crossed my arms and stared out the window, chewing my bottom lip. This guy was getting under my skin.

"Don't be a spoil-sport. We're almost to our destination, and you're going to need my help to drag all your crap into your new mansion." He reached over and gave me a light punch in my arm. If I weren't being cheeky, I would have yelped in pain, but no, I wouldn't give him that. No way. No how.

"About that, Elias. When we arrive, I have to go to the courthouse's Office of Deeds. Then, I have to go to the realtor's office for the keys. I want to buy you lunch for helping me out, and I will pay you back for the gas as soon as I get a job or inherit a bunch of money." I smiled sweetly, framing the back of my fingers under my cheekbone.

That barrel-chested laugh roared once more, and I felt a connection to him I had never felt with anyone else in my life. How ironic it was that he came into my life when he did. *Thanks, Mom.*

ELIAS

Abigail was a contradiction. She's smart and funny one minute and naive and severe the next. She vacillated like a pendulum on a grandfather clock. Keeping up with her was exhausting, but I'm loving the challenge. When she mentioned us being a pair, I had to keep from slamming on the brakes. Instead, my brain knocked against my skull at the idea that such a pairing would be outrageous. And tempting. And hot as fuck. For the past twenty-four hours, I've been chastising my libido for even thinking about her in any other way but as an acquaintance. Sometime today she mentioned being 24, and I was hugely relieved, I wasn't having illicit thought about a minor. *Shit!* I was over a decade, and then some, older than her, and I felt like a pervert indulging in that kind of thought. It was her lips that distracted me the most. They were so expressive with that tiny Cupid's bow in the middle of her upper lip. When she wasn't speaking, her lips rested in a tiny *o*, and I wanted to put my finger over the top of it and imagine that mouth sucking on other things. I'm a sick asshole. She probably hasn't even been with a man, especially not one of my size and girth. My frame wasn't the only overdeveloped part of my physique. Doing car repair work did most of the heavy lifting that kept my body in shape, though bailing hay twice a week for a friend wasn't child's play. When I quit my engineering job, I also quit the gym. I felt claustrophobic, stuck behind four concrete walls and a bunch of prima donna assholes looking at themselves in the mirrors. Get over yourselves and get outside in the free fresh air.

"Elias, did you hear me?"

I shook my head clear. Had she been calling my name for long? "Uh, no. What did you say?"

"Your navigation thing said to exit right in one mile." She looked at me like I was, I don't know, weird.

"Oh shit. Yeah." I put on my blinker, looked in my side mirror, and swerved right in enough time to exit. "Sorry," I muttered. *Geez, man, stop distracting yourself.*

"Are you sure you're okay? We still have to drive ten miles to claim my deed. Do you want me to take over?" She was talking fast and sounded concerned. Was I driving that badly?

I dragged my hand over my face and pulled myself together. "Let's stop for lunch, and then we can drive the rest of the way."

"No."

No? "Why not? I'm starving, and you said it yourself: I could use a break from driving." I stared her down, attempting to intimidate her into giving in.

"Pull over, now." She pointed to a gas station and unbuckled her seatbelt before I even pulled in. "I'm not taking chances that the Office of Deeds closes early or the person who does whatever needs to be done drops dead. We are going to make the claim now, then we can eat. Got it!"

She actually shouted at me while unlocking the door and exiting the vehicle. Seconds later, she whipped open my door and continued her rampage, "Get out! You're taking a break." She grabbed my hand off the wheel and tugged with all her might to get me to move, and, as much as I wanted to oblige her, I stayed seated.

"Why aren't you moving?" she whined, bracing her foot on the running board and pulling harder. "Why are you so big anyway? You're like a freak of nature. A human tree or something." Her continued attempts of moving me turned into anger and then to tears. *Damn it.*

I jumped out of the cab and sat down on the running board. "Abigail. Why are you getting so upset? We have plenty of time to get to that office. Maybe we should call and ensure they will be open in an hour. How about that?" I know I sounded patronizing, or even parental, for that matter. She needed reassurance I couldn't give her. I stood up, reached into the center console for her phone, and handed it to her. "Here. Make the call. You'll feel more in control, knowing for sure."

She sniffed and wiped away her tears with the back of her hand. "I can't screw this up, Elias. I just can't. If I don't do things immediately after I think about them, I forget to do them. It's not intentional or self-sabotaging; it's only that my brain doesn't process things the same way others do."

My instinct was to pull her into my arms and give her strength, except she needed to muster her strength to get through this on her own. If there is one thing I have learned about Miss Abigail Farnsworth-Burton, she's a survivor and very clever. She survived daily on her own; she'd been doing that for years. What could I do that she wasn't already doing for herself?

I tipped her chin up, letting myself get lost in her hazel-green eyes. "You've got his, Abby. Believe in yourself." Her expression morphed into shock.

"You're right. I can do this. I have to do this myself." She chanted each statement like a coach speaking to their team. "Elias . . . thank you."

I pulled my hand back, stuffed it into my pants, and watched her make the calls. She asked many questions while pacing back and forth next to my truck. Like the pervert I am, I watched her tight, pear-shaped ass swish by me over and over again. I wanted to squeeze both cheeks—hard. Her small breasts stretched her T-shirt, making the words, "Try Me," more like an appetizer than a challenge. When she yanked the end of her braid, forcing it to unravel in wavy, dark brown tresses, I had to stand up to give my dick more room. Fuck, was she gorgeous. I waved at her, pointing to the building, letting her know I was stepping away. I waited to see her nod before I ran to the bathroom to relieve myself. This guy needed immediate relief, and getting the job done didn't take much more than a few pulls. This trip better end soon or I'm unsure how safe this woman would be around me.

I returned to see Abby sitting on the running board, rebraiding her hair. *So sad for me.*

"So, how did it go? You were on the phone for a while." I stood over her, waiting for her reply.

"Pretty good, I think. Susan Somebody is at lunch and won't be back until one-thirty, so I guess we should eat now. They needed Mr. Brickner's phone number to ask some outstanding questions, and, until he responds, we can't finish the transaction. I called the realtor and asked that he meet us at the courthouse at three to drive us out to the house and show me around, but he said I had to go to his office. I hope I thought of everything." I let her ruminate a few more minutes while I looked around for a place to eat.

"Sounds like you did all the right things." I knew that she hadn't, though. It wasn't my place to get involved; I certainly wouldn't make her feel bad. "Get in the cab and we'll start driving in the right direction. We'll stop along the way to eat, okay?"

She expelled a long sigh, "Fine." Her shoulders sagged as she walked around the vehicle and hopped back into her seat. "I guess I can wait two hours."

"You'll make it." I attested, and drove down a picturesque, tree-covered road.

I didn't know her past well enough to discern if she understood that claiming the property was the easy part. I'm confident she hadn't thought about turning on the utilities, changing the locks, cleaning a furnace, and everything else a potentially dilapidated mansion might need. I couldn't handle this for her. I had my own business with my own responsibilities. Abigail would get some fast lessons in home ownership whether she wanted to or not and the only thing I could do after I dropped her off was wish her luck.

Chapter 7
Double Deeds

ABIGAIL

My hands had begun to sweat, and my armpits weren't much different. I felt like every pore on my body chose this moment to ooze out any extra liquid it possessed. As we pulled into the courthouse parking lot, I could feel my lunch churning eerily. I wasn't sure which, my mouth or my ass, would erupt, but as soon as Elias threw the gearshift into Park, I ran for the building in a panic. My body had never behaved this way before, and it scared me to death. Chills ran down my spine, and goosebumps blanketed my arms. Nausea created panic, leading to hyperventilating, and then—nothing.

"Do you know her?" I heard a woman ask.

"Yes. She must have fainted. She wasn't looking too good after lunch. I've got her. Thank you."

He did have me—wrapped in his arms like I was a baby. Sweet Lord, this felt good. I was feeling much better after passing out, but my breathing was still coming in short bursts.

"There you are. Are you okay? Did you hit your head? Does anything hurt?"

"No." Though the butterflies that zinged around my belly were the opposite of what I had experienced a few minutes ago.

He looked at me as if I were under a microscope. Assessing. Concerned. "I'm fine. I didn't hit my head, though my hip is sore. I must have landed on it when I fell. What happened?"

"I'm not sure, though I have my suspicions. I saw you fainting as I ran to the building after you bolted."

His thumb rubbed my jawline, making me lightheaded again.

"You scared the shit out of me."

"Yeah, sorry about that. I felt nauseous and ran for the bathroom, then I felt out of breath and wanted to crawl out of my skin. I didn't know what was happening, and then, BAM, everything went dark. I'm so thirsty." I said as I smacked my lips together.

He grinned. "You had a panic attack, and your body shut down to reset."

"What the hell are you talking about? Why would I have a panic attack? I've never had one before. Why now?" I pushed off his ridiculously large pecs, storing that bit to process later, and sat up shaking my head.

"Why now? Seriously, Abby? Do I need to spell this out for you? Your whole life is about to change, and you're asking why now? Geez-Louise, woman. Take a beat and figure this out."

His exasperation was palpable. I suppose a smart girl like me could figure this out if I could slow my breathing down. Listening to his words swirl around my brain, I began to piece together everything that happened to me this past month. Add in the past twenty years, and, logically, this all made sense. I hummed to myself.

"I see your point." I rubbed my eyes and slowly stood up. Elias caught my elbow when I swayed slightly away, keeping me from a possible face plant. "Could you get me some water, please? I'm going to sit down for a few minutes and get my bearings straight."

That lovely, annoying man rushed to do my bidding while I prepared myself for my meeting. I had a lot riding on this move, and my past did nothing to assure me I was making the right decision or that I could run and maintain such a massive piece of property. What would my ancestors have to say about this? Come to think of it, I felt like Mulan from the Disney movie. I needed my ancestors to guide me and a sidekick to keep me from losing my ever-loving shit. Maybe Elias would want the job. *A girl could dream, right?*

Elias strode through the lobby carrying a cup of water like a teacup on a saucer. "Here. Drink this slowly."

Why do people always say that? Does it make a difference how fast it goes down? I'm not stricken with a swallowing disorder. I just panicked, and rightfully so. He watched me swallow and then asked if I was ready to get this meeting over with.

I stood up carefully, rubbed my eyes, and exhaled deeply. "Let's do this." I clapped my hands and walked halfway down a hallway before I realized I didn't know where the hell I was going. Then, I walked back to the directory board to find my way. I swear I was a three-dimensional cartoon at times.

Attempt number two was successful, as Elias opened the glass door for me to pass through. "Control your breathing and listen to the details of what they are telling you. I'll take notes on my phone if you want." I nodded in appreciation. I was positive I wouldn't remember half of what was shared with me, but I was thrilled I had Elias around to help me.

Two women sat at desks across the room from the counter I was in front of.

"Hello. I'm Abigail Burton. I'm here to see Susan. Is she available?" I smiled warily, hoping Susan-Somebody would appear and say, "Sign here," and I'd be on my way—no such luck.

The blonde in a tight pencil skirt and flouncy blouse sashayed up to the counter, eyeing Elias. She flipped her blonde locks over one shoulder and boldly stared him up and down. To his credit, he blanched and pulled me to his side for what appeared to be protection.

"Hi there. I'm Susan." *Excellent.*

I pushed the envelope Mr. Brickner supplied, which contained the inheritance, the completed Connecticut claim paperwork, and a notarized letter from his office stating the authenticity of this claim.

I smiled sweetly at her shellacked face, "This should be everything you need. I believe you spoke with Mr. Brickner this morning. Is everything satisfactory?" I stood there waiting for a full two minutes with a painted-on smile and dug the heel of my tennis shoe into the arch of my other foot. I'd seen molasses move faster than this Barbie-Want-To-Be. She had one eye on the document and one eye on Elias, and I was done.

"Elias, dear, would you mind waiting here while Susan does her job." Okay, maybe not so smooth, but I wanted my papers stamped now. He looked down at me and smirked at my endearment.

"No problem, sugar." He whispered into my ear using a husky voice that could melt panties. *Ugh.* Pretending we were a couple could get me into a lot of trouble. *Big trouble.*

Susan returned to her desk, stamped each paper, notarized them with her seal, and signed and dated each document. After glaring at me briefly, she approached the counter again and handed me my paperwork.

"Congratulations, Miss Burton. That is quite a large estate to inherit. I hope you'll have help restoring it to its former beauty. I'd head to the library and do some digging around for historical documents to show you how much work you're looking at. Good luck." She gave me a wink like she had a secret, or maybe it was a disorder affecting her eye. Either way, I hadn't planned to see her again ever—goodbye and good riddance.

"Thank God that's over." I breathed my first full breath in an hour. "Do you believe that bitch? She was too busy ogling you to do her job and pay attention to the customer—me!" I stomped out of the courthouse toward Elias's truck without a glance to see if he was following me.

"Why aren't you saying anything?" I yelled over my shoulder. I stopped short when he didn't respond. I turned and found him standing ten feet behind me with a goofy grin and his hands on his smallish hips. "What?!" I snapped at him.

He took a few steps closer, "Miss Abigail Burton, are you jealous?" He was mocking me again. And like a dumbass, I took the bait.

"What? Me? That's ridiculous." Without waiting for a response, I ran to the truck's passenger side and waited for it to unlock. I didn't have to wait long as a long, muscled arm reached over my shoulder and pulled on the handle. I could smell his aftershave, or whatever it was that smelled like fresh laundry and mint. This man had unarmed me with a clean shirt. I'm pathetic.

The heat from his breath passed over the shell of my ear, exacting the response I knew he wanted.

"No, I'm not jealous," I said stubbornly.

He pressed his chest into my body, boxing me in tighter.

"You are. Face it, Abby. You like me, maybe even want me, don't you?"

I could hear the smile in his voice. I'm not practiced in the art of seduction, but damn it, he flipped all my switches, and I was helpless to him. I wanted something from him. What exactly wasn't yet clear.

I swallowed hard, focusing on speaking without stuttering. "Elias. You're like no one I've ever met. I don't know exactly what that means, but you intrigue me, and, therefore, I do like you." *Ta-da! I'm safe for now.*

He turned me about quickly, put his massive hands on my hips, lifted me like a bag of groceries, and held me in mid-air.

"I like you, too," he said deadpan. The crinkles at the corners of his eyes and those pearly white teeth spoke volumes to his words. He pulled me to his chest, put a soft, chaste kiss on my cheek, and then placed me carefully onto the seat with a wink. He swung my legs inside. *Oh, God, no.* He shut my door and strutted around to his side of the vehicle. Peacocks didn't preen like he did, and my insides turned to goo. I'll have to add adorable to his growing positive qualities. The soft pillows of his lips lingered on my cheek for the few silent miles we traveled to the realtor's office. My next hurdle would be more challenging—I was sure of it.

Mr. Brickner promised to have the realtor turn all the utilities on before I arrived. The trust included a small operating fee that would cover the initial start-up. I knew I had money to get the place up and running again, although I couldn't possibly know what it would cost to fix anything I hoped my learning curve would be quick and painless.

Chapter 8
Give Me My Keys

ELIAS

The moment I met the realtor, I knew Abigail would freak out. Not a panic attack but a full-on meltdown. This ancient man with the patience of a flea in his suede-patched houndstooth jacket that smelled of mothballs wasn't listening to a word Abigail was saying.

"I was promised these keys would be available after 2 p.m., and it's 3 p.m. Mr. Brickner verified that the property was mine, and I've shown you the paperwork. So what's the problem?" Her eyes twitched, and her hands bunched at her sides, ready to explode. I thought it best to stand off, giving her time and space to work things out independently. I was her crutch, not her fixer.

"Miss, uh, what's your name again?" His dismissive tone wasn't lost on her.

"I've told you three times, Abigail Farnsworth-Burton. Why are you giving me such a hard time?" she said. I'd give this guy another minute before pinning him to the wall.

"Yes, Farnsworth. I knew your family back when. They were nothing like you. Wait here, and let me dig through the back for those keys."

She whipped around, mouthing silently, "Nothing like me? What the fuck? What's *your* name, buddy?" Her hazel eyes glowed under the dim light. Her chest heaved in frustration, and she looked hot as fuck. Usually, I was tongue-tied. However, this little minx unraveled my tongue when her honor was at stake. My words flowed out of my mouth before I realized what I was saying to this old geezer.

"Hey! Buddy, what's your problem? And what kind of crack is that to make to one of Mystic's newest citizens? Has she done anything to you personally?" I was offended by this dude's attitude. Poor Abby was made to feel less than, and that didn't sit right with me. He gave me some side-eye and walked through the door behind the counter. *Jerk.*

While we waited for Grandpa to get her keys, I walked up to her, put my hands on her slim shoulders, and looked her straight in the eye. "This jerk doesn't know you or what you're made of. Be polite but stand your ground. You deserve this opportunity, and this guy has no right to take potshots at you. Got it?"

I squeezed her shoulders again and nodded. I turned her around to face the counter again and rubbed her shoulders until the man returned.

He shuffled up to the counter, carrying a skeleton key hanging from a brass ring along with two more modern keys. "It's been two years since I've seen these keys. Here. Sign this document, and I'll find someone to drive you over to the house and show you the place." He threw the keys on the counter and shoved a bulging yellow envelope at her. The way he brusquely handled her paperwork made him as hospitable as a corrections officer.

"Clarence!" He bellowed across the room. Another older man shuffled over to us. At least he forced a smile on his face.

"Coming, Henry. Hello, kids." His voice crackled like sandpaper.

"Take these people to the old Farnsworth property and show them around. Don't take too long, though. We have a gin rummy game starting in an hour. Don't be late," the old fart warned.

Clarence made a three-point turn and aimed himself at the front door. "Come on now. I don't want to miss Edna's rhubarb pie."

I looked at Abby and took her hand. Clarence told me to follow him to the house, but I was sure I could use my truck navigation and arrive, fix the front gate, and make dinner before he arrived. I'm not against the older generation. I like them a lot. I just wanted to move this day along and put my feet up.

The short path lined by trees opened to a majestic, whitewashed mansion with four massive columns in the center main section of the home and four half columns on either side of the middle. My jaw dropped, and I almost forgot to put my truck in Park.

"Geezus, Abby. You really are an heiress. How many square feet did that document say this was?" I looked at her in awe. She swayed in her seat, and I pushed her shoulder upright. "Abby! Are you all right?"

Quietly, she opened the door and walked directly to the center of the driveway, making a panoramic study of the view in front of her.

"It's so beautiful I want to cry." She moved toward the left side of the house and continued her walk down the straightaway, her head pivoting from side to side.

There was another door on an angled porch on the side of the house. What must have been a mauve wreath hanging on the door now looked like a muskrat chewing on its tail. *Disgusting.* She kept moving forward to what previously could have been lush, beautiful gardens, but, again, everything was dead, matted, and musty.

Abby turned back to face me. "Why do you call me Abby? I'm Abigail." *Wait! What? Where did that come from?*

My eyes went wide, and my hands floated in front of me, hands up. "Uh, I don't know. When did we go from a beautiful house to me calling you Abby?"

Her face went stern, and her hands pushed into her hair. "Sometimes my thoughts get jammed and emerge at weird times. Never mind that. I'd like you to call me Abigail like everyone else does."

I made a "whatever" face and walked back to the front of the house. Clarence finally made it in his 1982 Dodge K car, and I wanted to get the grand tour over so I could get back on the road and home by midnight. He handed A-B-I-G-A-I-L's keys to her so she could have the honors, and, when she did, no lie, two bats and a flock of flies flew over our heads. God help us for what we're going to find next.

"Holy shit! That better be the only critters alive in there," she exclaimed.

Still affronted by her earlier remark, I zipped my lips and took stock of all that needed attention. Why? Who knew? I wasn't staying, and I wasn't fixing anything, so why did I get the nagging feeling I was?

Clarence stepped onto the checkered, linoleum foyer and didn't move. He pointed to everything instead.

"This is the dining room and, beyond that, the kitchen. To the right is the salon, and a grand living room is on the other side of the room. The giant mirror is original to the house. This piano was a gift from a seafaring family I can't recall exactly. Sometime at the turn of the 20th century." He took two steps to his left at the bottom of the curved stairway to the upper level.

"Notice the pastoral mural hand-painted back in the eighteen hundreds. I can't remember who did it. Upstairs are five bedrooms and a study. The side door has a separate entrance to this floor from the driveway, and the last bedroom down the hall has a hidden stairway down to the kitchen. It must have been servants' quarters at the time it was built. Any questions?" Clarence made to walk out the front door when Abigail huffed.

"Mr. Clarence. Is the electricity turned on? The water? Gas? Or will I live in the dark and bathe in a nearby stream?" I liked her sass. I liked that she remembered to ask those necessary questions before he left. Whatever disability she claimed to have, she was managing this transition quite well. Unless, of course, you count the meltdowns and panic attacks. Seriously, though, anyone being thrown into her circumstances would have felt the same way.

I smiled, showing encouragement and how proud I was of her. "Great questions. Where's the fuse box, too? The furnace and water heater, as well." *Sorry. I had questions, too.*

Clarence made another three-point turn back to point again. "Mechanicals are in the basement. The light switch is at the bottom of the stairs through the kitchen. Electricity is on, but water and gas won't function until tomorrow. Mr. Attison didn't get notice of your arrival until yesterday."

He gave a small wave and carefully shifted one leg over the threshold onto the porch and then the other. You had to give him props for his dexterity, given his age. I hoped I still could move at all at his age.

I followed him outside and brought Abigail's things into the foyer and front room. She'd have to figure out where she would like to sleep and every other decision alone. I grabbed the last of her things from my truck, and the only thing left was her soft scent in the cab. I was preparing to give her my goodbyes when I heard a scream from the kitchen.

"Abigail! What's going on?"

Chapter 9

Kitchen Chaos and Garden Grossness

ELIAS

I ran through the dining area and down the short hall to the kitchen, where I found Abigail standing on the counter, her hands in her hair and shock written all over her face.

"Hey! Hey! What's going on? You sounded like the boogeyman was ready to carve you up."

She snarled at me, pointing to a whip-like tail attached to a furry body in an open can on the floor. *Nasty.* I'm not a fan of vermin, and I wouldn't doubt this place was riddled with them. Why did I get the feeling I wasn't leaving tonight?

"Elias! Get that thing out of here. I'm freaking out!" Her screams turned to whines and she yiped every time that thing moved.

"Obviously," I muttered. "Don't worry, milady. Your prince in not-so-shining armor will protect thee." I grabbed the first thing I found on the counter and raised it above my head like a knight defending his lady, poised to attack that little bugger.

"What the hell, Elias? You can't kill that thing with a whisk. Grab the can and throw it out the door!" Even through her hysteria, she made sense. Ensuring my hand wouldn't be mauled, I slipped on an oven mitt that hung off the stove handle and approached the can stealthily. I snagged it up in one shot, held it out like it was on fire, and then ran across the kitchen to chuck it out the side door. The thought of Abigail assisting me was ridiculous since she continued to hop from foot to foot on the counter, squealing like a stuck pig.

I leaned against the door, forcing myself to calm down. When I walked around the corner, Abigail sat on the counter, her face buried in her hands. My mind raced with so many visions of what I could do to her on that counter that my pants became uncomfortable. My ego got the best of me as I walked over and pressed myself between her legs to hug her. Seated on the counter, she was two feet shorter than I, but she managed to grab my shirt, pulling us into an embrace. I pulled her thighs tightly into my hips and kept her there, knowing she could feel my growing bulge. I breathed in her soft scent laced through her hair that had come loose during her despair. I spread my hands wide, hoping to feel more of her sexy body. She was so small that my hands touched each other as I held her tightly. I wanted to kiss her, long and deep. I'd been fantasizing about how she'd taste. Sweet? Salty? Both?

"Elias, please don't leave me here alone. I don't know what I'd do if you hadn't saved me. This house is so old there has to be more of them. I'll never sleep knowing those things are running around." She gripped me tighter, nuzzling her face against my chest. *Damn!* She's right. I couldn't leave her until traps were set and this place was scrubbed down. Her courage up until now was remarkable. She faced her fears like she knew what she was doing, but we both knew it was all a facade. She trembled under my hands, and—my fellow auto tech, Paul, was right—I am a sucker for a damsel in distress. This wasn't the first time I was dragged into someone else's drama through tears. Ironically, I wanted to stick around this time and see how this all played out.

My hands slid from her hips up to her shoulders and gently rubbed circles on her back, savoring her sweet smell and delicate curves. "I'll stay tonight and make sure you're safe." We stared at each other for a long moment. Her pert nose and tiny freckles distracted me to no end. The *o* that parted between her lips beckoned to me, and I couldn't wait any longer to taste them.

I slowly bent down, memorizing every detail of how the corners tilted upward, and her eyes fluttered closed when I leaned over her mouth. I felt paralyzed breathing her in. I knew I was taking advantage of her vulnerability, except I couldn't move away. I closed the gap between us and gently kissed her plump lips. Her small moan was permission enough to penetrate her mouth longer and deeper. I pressed my tongue deeper into her mouth, making her moan again. She pushed her hands into my beard, found my jaw, and pulled me tighter still. Time stopped, and the world fell away. Magical was the only way to describe what just happened. My head flashed of a previous time; no, it transported me back to a time in history when I kissed these lips before. It was incredible. I knew these lips. They felt like home.

"Elias," she purred into my beard. "I feel like I've known you forever." She looked into my eyes again, and I saw it, too. That strange attraction I had to her before. Could we have known each other from another time? I know people who believed in past lives, though I never believed it myself. Now I wondered.

I lifted her down to the floor, releasing the hold she had on me. I rubbed my forehead, confused about that flash from the past, what she had said, and that kiss! Abigail had a hold on me I couldn't explain. I liked it, but it confused me.

"Elias. Say something. You don't look so good." Her concern was adorable. If only I could describe my thoughts and feelings clearly, she would think I was as batty as the ones that flew out her front door.

"You taste good," I said as I licked my lips. *Brilliant!* Of all the things you're thinking about, your primitive caveman brain goes with taste. *Idiot!*

She smiled slowly, not letting my stupid statement infiltrate her mood. "You taste good, too. Chocolate and peanuts," she giggled.

I chuckled. "I'm kind of a sucker for a candy bar after lunch. Come on. Let's walk around the house and see if we can find some cleaning supplies—and I can take you to the hardware store—and clean up this place." I took her hand and led her back around the corner to a set of stairs leading to the basement—the haze of our kiss lingering in the air without discussion.

I kissed her, and she kissed me back. Wishing for more was greedy. Nonetheless, I wanted more. Her eyes were soft and slightly hooded, and if I were someone other than myself, I'd have taken her right there on the fucking counter. She called me a caveman earlier, and she wasn't too far off. I needed to get away from her now, or I would be the rat bastard in this scenario.

I shifted gears and stepped back.

"Let's find the basement door and see what we can find to clean up this place."

Besides some mustiness, the basement floor had poured concrete. Someone must have updated this house since several spider-webbed cracks tracked across the floor, not to be outdone by the real webs tucked all over the place.

"Didn't that old dude at the realtor's office say this used to be a bed and breakfast?" Abigail led me to the corner where several brooms, mops, and buckets were stacked against a wall.

"I think so. Actually, two previous owners used the house for B&Bs. The guy said the house has been empty for almost three years, and the last Farnsworth who occupied the house was over twenty years ago. I suppose each owner had it for fifteen years."

I loved her math. We gathered what we could, and I patted her back, pushing her toward the stairs like a lost child. I caught the light switch with my elbow and kept going. "Not quite, princess. Let's do some research tonight and see what we can find." Her brows knit at my new pet name for her. *Not changing it.*

She reached the top of the stairs before I could clear the landing when I heard a crash.

"Aahh!" She screeched.

"You have to stay! You can't leave me alone!" She launched herself at me as all my things fell to the floor. Sometimes she acted so childlike, and others, well . . .

I burst out laughing and held her tightly. "I said I would, Abigail. Did you forget so soon?"

ABIGAIL

The way his chest rumbled when he laughed made me ticklish. The vibrations were so loud I was forced to laugh.

"I didn't forget. I was hoping you'd meant it and not placate me like others have done," I frowned. So many times, people said things like that to get me to go away, but it hurt. I tried to pull away and pick up the stuff I dropped, but he wouldn't let me go.

He took me by the arms and looked at me like he would shake me to death.

"Listen to me, Abigail. I will say this once, so pay attention. I am a man of my word. I only speak the truth. I would never say anything deliberately to hurt you. Do you understand me?" His stare held me in place and I knew I could trust his word.

"Yes." I whimpered. Is this what it was like to have a father? Being scolded into submission? He was serious, and I stepped forward. "I believe you."

He dropped his hands and stepped back, not wavering in his stare. "There are many things you don't know about me, Abigail. Being dishonest or dishonorable is not part of my constitution. Now, let's look through these cupboards for more supplies."

He walked away without looking back. I think I just learned the bottom line with Elias. His word was his bond, and I could bank on it. When in all my life has anyone been that honest with me? My aunt, I thought, was honest with me, except she didn't tell me anything about this inheritance. Did she know and was hiding it from me? I knew she barely just tolerated my existence, so I couldn't trust her to tell me the truth. She wouldn't follow up with medication for my condition, and she never, and I mean never, did anything more than was minimally required to get me through school. Just the basics. Argh! *Now I have a headache.*

I rubbed my temples as I walked back to the entryway by the winding staircase. The carpet was gross and had to go. The wood railing was ornate and would look amazing after it was cleaned and polished. *Note to self: watch videos on how to clean antique wood.* There wasn't a mudroom like a modern-day home, leaving me to comb through each bedroom suite for cleaning supplies. I noted every laughable update that covered up the beautiful wallpaper and fancy materials on the furniture. Who does that? *Another note to self: learn what all these materials are and how to maintain them.*

As I browsed a bookshelf in the last bedroom, I noticed a leather-bound journal with papers stuffed inside it sitting above the rest of the books on the shelf. It caught my attention because it had a brass hook with a bangle hanging off the binding. I gently pulled it off the shelf, and a picture fell to the floor. My jaw dropped open as I studied the image. It was me with one of those loose bun hairdos that the olden people used to wear. We had the same eyes, nose, and space between my lips Was this my great-great-grandmother?

"ELIAS!" I screamed again hysterically.

A thunderous sound emanated throughout the house. I kept staring at this picture, trying to reconcile how similar we looked.

"Abigail!" He gasped. "I swear, if you're not dead or dying, I'm going to kill you myself." He looked surprised that I hadn't fallen through the floorboards.

"Look. At. This!" I shrieked. I shoved the picture at his face, and his reaction was priceless.

"You . . . She . . ." He looked back and forth between the picture and myself at least three times. "Unbelievable. No one could ever dispute you were her heir." He returned the picture, shaking his head and pulling at his beard. "What's that?" he said, pointing to my other hand.

"You won't believe this, but it's a journal. Hopefully, it's hers," I said, pointing to the picture he held between his thumb and forefinger—a dainty pose for such a large man. "Come here," I motioned for him to join me on the couch behind me. "Let's look at this together."

Elias sat beside me, towering over my shoulder to see what I was seeing. "*The Personal Diary of Agatha Farnsworth.*" I read aloud, tracing the gold script on the leather cover. Our collective "Oh My God" was not only funny but revealing. He understood that finding this journal was a link to the past.

"Abigail, you found the Holy Grail to your house. Open it."

We settled back against the crushed cushions to travel back through time together. Page after page of details revealing my family's history. Every item Agatha ordered, from fabric to wallpaper, was noted.

I read an entry from April, 1845:

Ten yards of chintz for parlor pillows. Twenty yards of brocade for master bedroom curtains.

Eight yards of matching dupioni silk for the duvet cover. My guests need to experience our good fortune, and after what we'd been through starting out, I'm never sleeping on anything resembling burlap again!

I looked over my shoulder, "Whoa. Sounds like there is more to that story. These materials must have cost a fortune even by today's standards." I rubbed my cheek, imagining her making this list, considering her comfort and that of her guests. She sounded like a very thoughtful woman.

I read about her gardens, their business, and what was happening in their social life back then. All were written down so carefully that I could picture their lives as it unfolded in 1845. How fascinating was it that I stumbled upon it at this precise moment? It's mind-blowing.

I shut the book, thanking the Heavens for finding it. My life had taken a turn I couldn't have imagined, and an honest, caring man helped me reach my goal. At that precise moment, I promised my ancestors that I, Abigail Farnsworth-Burton, would not mess this up. I would be successful no matter what.

I jumped up and grabbed Elias's hand. "Come on. We have work to do."

Like two whirling dervishes, we drove to the Mystic Village and retrieved everything we needed to clean this place from the attic to the basement. I had no idea how long Elias could help me, so I took advantage of his "hunting" skills and purchased twenty mouse traps, a jar of peanut butter, and an all-purpose toolkit to handle simple jobs. Let's face it: I'm not a handy person but I am willing to learn. I needed a plan to get this place functional again—fast!

"Hey, princess. I'm hungry." Elias announced as we hauled our loot to his truck. We went past a pizza place earlier. "I'm stopping to get a pie. What do you want on yours?"

I buckled myself in and yawned. "Hawaiian pizza." I drilled my fists into my eyes, realizing it was almost eight o'clock. I was emotionally exhausted and physically whipped. It was time to stop for the day. Even the mouse situation didn't supersede my need to sleep.

"Gross. I'm getting you your own pie. Fruit and pizza is not a thing." He grimaced and put the truck in reverse, leaving the hardware store.

"You don't know what you're missing," I said, rolling my eyes at him. He harrumphed in response.

We sat in companionable silence as he drove to the pizzeria. He ran into the place, ordered, and suggested we hit the convenience store across the street for drinks and snacks to get us through the night.

By the time we returned to the house, the sun had set, making the house look spooky. We forgot to turn on the lights or even lock the door. *And I thought I was the forgetful one.*

While Elias investigated the boiler, I wiped down the kitchen tables and chairs with the disinfecting spray we purchased. It was April, and, although the days were warmer, the night still chilled my toes.

"Wahoo!" He must have been satisfied since I heard a whining sound downstairs and a gust of air bursting through the radiator next to the table. Dust spewed onto the very things I had just cleaned. *Hmm.* Thank God something in this house worked. The kitchen faucet spewed some brown goo, turned to a yellow pee color, and stopped altogether.

Elias danced into the kitchen and swung me around giddily. "Not too bad, if I say so myself. That mechanical engineering degree finally paid off." He grabbed a bottle of water from the counter and glugged it down. "Let's eat!"

We discussed why he left engineering and what his aspirations were for the future. More importantly, how long would he hang around here before returning to Pennsylvania? I needed to work on my plan, but Elias had made himself indispensable. Sadly, I would have to say goodbye soon and figure out how to handle this home alone. My inheritance offered enough money for repairs, though that wouldn't last long if I didn't prioritize these repairs. The question on the table was what to do first—repairs or updates.

I finished my first slice of pizza and saw Elias staring at me again. "What? Do I have sauce on my face?" I reached for a napkin when he put his hand on mine.

"No. I was admiring you."

"Admiring me?"

"Well, more than just admiring you. Um, that picture you showed me of your great-great-grandmother, she has the same mouth. That same little *o*. I have this strong compulsion to kiss it or touch it with my finger." He pulled his hand off mine abruptly. "Sorry. That thought was supposed to stay in my head. Now I've made things awkward."

This big, burly man blushed right down to his chest and heated me along with him. I remembered that smoldering kiss from earlier. I wanted to feel more of that. I stood up slowly, walked around the table, and stopped behind his chair. My hands slid to his shoulders, massaging the stress away he felt from speaking his truth. They were hard like boulders that stiffened each time I kneaded the muscles, and I could hear his breath quicken at my touch.

"Please don't feel embarrassed," I whispered behind his ear. I hadn't realized how much stress these past twenty-four hours had also been for him. I tipped his head to the side and pushed my forearm up and down his neck to help him relax even more. Switching to the other side, his soft grunts increased when I found the right spots. Mostly, I enjoyed his flesh's warmth and how easy our connection was.

"I like making you relax. It's ironic how soft your skin is when you're so hard everywhere else."

"You don't know the half of it. Nor should you." He muttered the last part.

"Well, then tell me more." Though I have my charms, I'm not smart enough to be a game player. I have, however, been disparaged for my impulsive nature. I was too aggressive to attract men, per my aunt. I've also been called a "loose cannon" on more than one occasion, but that didn't put me off trying to uncover this thing between Elias and me.

My thoughts were interrupted as Elias pulled my arm over his shoulder like a wrestling move, ducking himself down as I fell into his lap. His hand locked onto my ass to steady me while the other cupped my neck and pulled my face within a breath of his lips.

"No more words," he whispered and planted a panty-melting kiss on my waiting lips. A surge of adrenaline ran through my body, igniting every cell to bursting. I tasted the spice of his pizza as his tongue glided over mine. I loved pepperoni. We grappled in each other's arms, moaning our pleasure, giving into the moment. The way he sucked on each of my lips was so erotic I didn't know whether to laugh or cry. My hands pressed into his pecs and ran down the six-pack he had hidden beneath his henley. I wanted to peel that material off him immediately if only we didn't have to break our kiss.

His big hands worked up my spine and downward again, finally finding my small breasts. There were so many sounds to file away and review them later, each unlocking the mystery of his body. He spun me around to straddle his legs and kissed me straight on. I loved his soft beard, tickling and teasing me as he deepened the kiss. His light brown eyes opened between kisses, and that strange connection I had felt earlier returned. I knew his soul. I had to. How do two completely different people connect so quickly if they didn't?

"How did you learn to kiss like that? It's so sexy." I said.

"Then be quiet, and let me do it some more," he said. *You don't have to ask me twice.*

Moments turned to minutes and then a complete lapse of time. We clawed at each other until we were both exhausted. Guilt washed his face for a brief moment.

"Damn, girl. You wrung me out. I don't think I've ever kissed anyone like that before." He wiped his brow, dropping a single kiss to mine.

"I think I blacked out somewhere in there. You short-circuited my brain," I panted. "Give me a minute to come back online."

I'm still baffled at how our connection could be so intense. My guess was that we had thirteen or fourteen years between us and entirely different backgrounds. We were both on different trajectories, yet fate threw us together. Was Elias my destiny? I can't explain how comfortable I felt when he was with me. When he touched me, I wanted to melt against him. And, God forbid, he kissed me. I'm overwhelmed with feelings I've never had before. Feelings of hope, safety, constancy, and something else I can't articulate. I couldn't wrap my head around him, walking out my front door and never seeing him again. Fate couldn't be that cruel, could it?

My desire would have to wait, even though the unmistakable bulge in his pants was tempting. I needed his help and wouldn't be a "loose cannon" this time. I needed a plan before I went to bed. Before I freaked out, I had to know what I could expect from Elias. I don't want to be alone anymore. I don't like the freedom I boasted about earlier *that* much. I wanted him.

"Hey, princess," he cooed in my ear. "Where'd you go?" He stroked my hair and kissed my ear.

Hmm. Words. I needed words.

"Elias."

"Yeah, baby."

I needed to get off his lap. I couldn't think straight with his hands in my hair. I slid off his thick thighs, pushed my hair back behind my ear, and clasped my hands in front of me. Like a freight train speeding through the night, my thoughts also zoomed through my brain. Unfortunately, I didn't know which one was more important.

"Elias, you are addicting and very distracting. My brain doesn't know what to do about you. On the other hand, my body is quite happy to stay in your arms indefinitely. I have to figure out a plan tonight. I need to know what tomorrow will bring, or I won't be able to sleep. Which reminds me, where do you want to sleep tonight—and don't say my bed because I'm not ready for that." *I mean I am, just not now.*

He chuckled. "Your brain really doesn't stop, does it?"

He stood up, hovering over me as he cupped my jaw and kissed my forehead sweetly, followed by a tight hug. "Let's build your plan."

The pizzas were combined into one box that barely fit into the refrigerator, and we threw our garbage into the can at the island's edge.

Elias suggested we make three lists. Over the next hour, we collated my needs, wants, and requirements, ranging from water and electrical inspections to new towels. I leaned on him for his expertise in engineering to know what mechanical things were necessary for my safety. We broke those lists down and fitted them into a neat timeline of where to begin cleaning, repairing—and future projects.

I sat across from Elias, plotting, planning, and having the best time until I yawned.

"Ugh, it's almost midnight, and we haven't figured out where we're going to sleep. Shit!" I grabbed a bucket of cleaning supplies and dashed up the back stairs. All thoughts of Elias were forgotten.

I'm unsure which bedroom I landed in, but thank goodness it had a reasonably tidy bathroom. Sold! I'm sleeping here. I opened the linen closet and was pleased to find several sheets and pillows still resting on the shelves. They would have to do for tonight because I wasn't washing them. Relieved that I didn't have to sleep directly on an old mattress, I made the bed and returned to the bathroom for a cursory scrub down with a water bottle. Please, God, get me through the night.

Thirty minutes later, feeling more confident, I ran back down the stairs to get another bottle of water, pillow, and blankets when I saw Elias sitting on the front sofa, staring at a figurine.

"What are you looking at?" I sat down next to him, my arms still clutching my things.

"She looks like you," he said quietly, continuing to stare.

Long rivulets of curls fell off the shoulders of a porcelain girl. Pink, full lips sat prettily on an oval face. Her dress was fitted in the bodice with a low collar adorned with lace. The skirt billowed layer by layer to her feet and was tied around her waist by a thick, satin-like ribbon that hung over the tucked layers behind her. The most fascinating part was how she was looking over her shoulder. Sweetly and demure, with brown eyes turned upward.

"She's captivating, like you. Honestly, if I didn't know better, it looks like you posed for this piece." His eyes locked onto mine.

"I don't know what to say. It's unbelievable how much it looked like me. Someone must have commissioned it back then. Let's call her Agatha." I wanted to lighten the mood. So many things in this house were triggers to the past, and my connection to it grew stronger and stronger every moment. "Let's find you a place to sleep, okay?"

I watched him stand and head to the front door, ensuring it was locked this time, then over to secure the side door. I continued watching how he double-checked his movements, turning off lights as he went. Nodding his head confidently, he followed me up the front stairs past the pastoral mural intricately painted between the floors.

"Pick a room. Any room at all." I quipped like a carnival midway barker.

Without hesitation, he said, "Yours." I gulped. *Don't look at him. Don't give in. Be strong!*

"I don't know, Elias. That doesn't sound like a good idea. I just met you." I shuffled my feet down the matted carpet toward my room.

He stopped me in my tracks, pulling me back to his chest. "I promise to behave."

The rumble in his chest launched a fleet of butterflies in my belly, and moisture began pooling between my legs. I wanted to trust his words more than my desire to attack him during the night. The real question was, could I be trusted not to cross the line between us?

I bit my lower lip and melted into his hold. "This is a bad idea," I muttered, shuffling back down the hall. "Follow me." His chest rumbled, and he pushed me forward. This was going to be a long night.

Chapter 10
Meeces to Pieces

ABIGAIL

I knew this was a bad idea from the beginning.

Elias agreed to sleep above the covers with a blanket while I slept between the sheets. This arrangement would have been fine had he kept his shirt on. Beyond his magnificent, bulging shoulders and pecs, he had that intricate tattoo that baffled me. I felt like a deprived child turning off the lights while wanting to trace every line of his artwork. Elias fell into a deep slumber immediately, snoring lightly at my back. As for me, shutting down my hamster-wheel-of-a-brain took considerably more time. I'd developed a ritual that ensured I'd fall asleep within ten minutes; unfortunately, the added variable of Elias made it impossible.

I flipped and flopped for the first hour. The second hour was packed with identifying noises that crept from the basement to the skittering of God-knows-what in the walls and attic. Committed to a successful day tomorrow, I wrote down my concerns and forced myself to only think about breathing deeply and puppies. *Who didn't feel happy thinking about puppies?*

Crowing of a chicken jarred me awake a few hours later, and I planned to find that sucker and cook him for dinner. Four hours of sleep wasn't going to cut it today. I needed at least six to be functional. Determined to get those last few hours, I pulled my pillow over my head and started my ritual again. Yes. I could feel the shroud of sleep hovering closely when a tree fell on my body, pinning me to the bed. *Please, kill me now.*

"Settle, princess." The gruff voice said, heaving me up against his hot body. My body froze, and several thoughts buzzed through my cloudy brain, none giving me a reasonable answer. Instead, I focused on Elias's breathing, trying to match mine to his. His hold on me sent tingles down to my toes, and I felt like purring when he tucked me under his chin. My brain drifted in and out of consciousness while my body seemed to float above me. I smelled the smooth skin behind his elbow and marveled how, even after a day of travel and sleep, he still smelled of fresh laundry. Exploring him more, I pressed my lips to his bicep, trying not to wake him but sneak a taste of his essence. To my surprise, he pulled my hips closer, giving me a clearer picture of what I had awakened.

"I said to settle down, not rile me up." He rubbed his face alongside mine, igniting my core. "I'm moments away from making you truly exhausted. Just keep sampling me. I dare you." His throaty threat put every cell in my body into overdrive.

Poking the bear was never a good idea. I've gotten into plenty of trouble over the years doing just that. However, this scenario had plenty of opportunity for mutual benefits if I was willing to pay the price.

"You should stop smelling so good. It's your fault I can't go back to sleep." I breathed in his beard, noting the shampoo I had used at his house.

That did it. He flipped me over to my back without warning and pulled on my bottom lip. "You've been warned." He growled.

He pulled back the blanket and unwrapped the sheets around me. I noticed his shirt was back on from when we first got into bed, but now, one hand reached behind his head to pull off his shirt while the other sat low on my chest. His eyes never left mine, and I knew at that moment unspeakable things were about to turn my life inside out.

"I'm taking your shirt off. You'd better say 'stop,' or I'm going to ravage you until you pass out." I heard words, but my eyes were glued to the most perfect chest a woman could ask for. Elias didn't possess one of those muscle man bodies. He had deliciously sculpted meaty muscles that a woman could sink her hands into.

I must have waited too long because he shoved my shirt over my head and pinned my hands to the mattress. He pressed his flesh to mine, and I saw stars. His chest was covered in an exquisite display of soft, straight hair that reached from nipple to nipple, traveling downward in a straight line to his jeans. My heart nearly leaped out of my chest, absorbing every divot this man had earned. I only wished I had my hands to trace the paths he showcased for me.

Air escaped my throat in short bursts as I struggled to stay conscious. His kiss was scorching, and the noises he made only ratcheted up my desire.

I turned my head to the side, fighting for air. "Elias. Please. I can't breathe. I need to touch you.

He yanked his hands back only to cup my small breasts, kneading them delicately. When he plucked each nipple, jolts of electricity ran directly to my apex. I clawed at his back, grasping for traction, when something scurried over my head.

"Fuck!" He hollered as he pulled me up to his chest.

I held him tightly, trying to understand his reaction. "What was that?"

"God damned mice! That's what." He scrambled off the bed, pulling me with him. "Come on. I don't care what time it is. It's time to set those traps."

He'd get no pushback from me, only from my aching pussy. She was mad, and sad . . . and wanton. *Bad kitty!*

"There!" I sighed, falling back into a wing-backed chair. "This house is rigged like the Ninja Warrior Challenge for mice. No mercy!" I raised a fist, pledging to overthrow the mice population of Mystic.

Elias walked toward me, drinking from a water bottle, "The warrior princess had spoken. Woe be unto vermin everywhere!" He punched the air alongside me. We were two weirdos united in our quest. He's a lot of fun. Now, if we could return to where we left off, we'd both have more fun.

He read my mind as he looked down at my face. "Later."

I stuck out my lower lip, pouting like a petulant child. I'll own it. I was robbed of pleasure, and I wanted redemption.

Resolute, he replied sternly, "Don't give me any lip, even if it's those lips. We have phone calls to make to a carpenter who will seal this damn house from animals, the cable company, and a water tester guy to make sure there isn't any lead in your water supply. After that, its cleaning, cleaning, and more cleaning. Come on, cupcake."

He reached for my hand, expecting me to grab hold, but I wasn't budging.

"Cupcake?" I sneered. "I'm a princess, like you said," and stood alone. Without looking back, I strutted across the living room, the dining room, and into the kitchen to dump several water bottles into a pot to boil.

Moments later, Elias caught up with me, adding dish soap to the water after it cooled down. I was executing our plan from last night without his directions. This was my house, and I was the master. No one believed I could follow through with anything, but not this time. I would prevail. Besides, how hard was it to clean a house?

I heard him clearing his voice, obviously to get my attention. "I'm going to go out on a limb here, and guess you haven't cleaned any antique surfaces before, right?" He looked down his nose at me. *Okay, he always looked down his nose at me because he was a foot taller than me and then some. So frustrating!*

I blew a strand of hair off my face while holding that damn bucket. "No. You know, it's not rocket science, right?"

He walked across the kitchen and gently tried to take the bucket from my hands, except I wasn't letting go so easily.

He shook his head. "No, princess. It's not rocket science, just science. There is a ton of mold around this house, and wood, especially old wood, is a prime mold-collecting material. Here, put these on, and let me get you a bucket of distilled vinegar."

My face scrunched up at the possibility of my house being riddled with mold spores, which freaked me out. I did have a touch of asthma, and that kind of environment could be a problem.

"Huh, the things you learn. What else are you holding back, Mr. Offerman?" Two years ago, while watching his sitcom, I watched an interview with that celebrity. It surprised me how many celebrities had marketable talents beyond acting.

He smirked. "Well, look at you being in the know. Engineers are required to research various materials, including aged wood. I'm not just a pretty face, 'ya know." He slapped his knee at that one.

"Ha. Ha. Pretty? Meh. A prima donna for sure." I giggled, lowering my goggles to my eyes and pulling up the latex gloves he had thrown at me.

He set the empty vinegar bottle on the counter and reached into his pocket for his phone. I didn't hear it ring, but, before I knew it, he had spun around and snapped a picture of me looking like a wasp movie reject.

"This is a keeper!" He retaliated, fisting the air in triumph. Fine. He may have won that round, but this would be a long day, and there were plenty of opportunities to snap incriminating pictures of him as well. *I'm thinking of a butt-crack photo to keep him in line.*

Our plan of attack today was to complete the kitchen and then make our calls. Later, we'd wipe down my bedroom and all the bathrooms while we wash some laundry. At least we could sleep safely and soundly and eat comfortably. The best news so far was the water guy could come before noon, and the cable would be turned on tomorrow.

I'd never been a good cleaner. My aunt—whoa, I'd better call my aunt—would stand at my bedroom door, arms crossed, tapping her toe on the hardwood, waiting to find fault in everything. From making my bed to hanging my clothes correctly, nothing I did was to her satisfaction. I suppose that is why she gave up after three years of trying to "train" me and closed my bedroom door. Fine with me. The only task I accomplished to her satisfaction was cooking, though not so much for cleaning up. I can cook a mean lasagna and a colorful salad. My beef stew is the bomb, and my breakfast casserole is delish. Whenever I did something, I'd get in trouble for, I'd cook a meal to get her off my back. Then, to be sure she saw how repentant I was, I vacuumed the house. Nothing says, "I'm sorry," like a freshly vacuumed floor.

I missed cooking. Maybe Elias will take me to the grocery store later so I can cook him a delicious meal in gratitude for his help. I could offer food and my body in exchange for electrical help. That was my tender. *I needed a job.* He would leave me tomorrow, having made sure I wouldn't explode or drink lead from the pipes. I had to accept that he went well beyond the call of duty getting me here and staying until I was settled. Those lips and arms and, well, everything about him, I suppose, would have to be fantasy fodder for the time being.

I shook my head clear of him and continued to scour the hardwood floors in the foyer with vinegar solution until my bucket was filled with black sludge. I hauled myself upright, feeling my lower back complaining. Hard labor was not for the dazed and distracted. My kind of people worked hard at slaying dragons in video games or breaking a sweat making pizzas. I took a moment to imagine housemaids cleaning every nook and cranny back when my great-great-grandmother was the mistress of the house. She had to have help. I needed to read more of her diary soon to know how she ran this giant home. Keeping the kitchen, bedroom, and bathroom clean was almost too much for me now.

My daydreaming ended abruptly when I heard knocking at the front door. I pushed my loose hair behind my ears, straightening myself as I approached. This was my *first visitor!*

"Hell-o?" I said as I looked left to right. There wasn't anyone there, and yet I distinctly heard a knock. "Hello!" I called out again, stepping onto the porch.

"Whoa. What's this?" A chicken sat on my porch—a real one. Bright marigold-colored feathers, a bright neck, and a crown that looked more like a comb puffed up all around it. I'm not up on my chicken anatomy, but this bugger looked healthy to me. The bigger question was why it was on my porch.

"Hey, little dudette, what brings you here?" *Don't judge me talking to a chicken.* "Were you the one knocking on my door?"

It just sat there, looking me over as if I were the scary one. I bent down warily, ready to jump back if needed. I'd never touched a chicken before, so I felt compelled to reach out and take a chance. Oddly, it let me—once. The second time came with a peck.

"Hey, be nice, or I'll cook you for dinner!" Learning my lesson, I backed up into the doorway and shooed it away. What the hell? Everyone else in the world gets a stray cat or dog. I get a chicken.

I returned to the kitchen, collecting my bucket and rags for water. Elias was standing on a step stool wiping down the fixtures and ceiling. I took my time drinking my beverage, zoning in on his high, tight ass in his soft, worn denim. His back stretched his rock band T-shirt tightly as he balanced his hand above his head.

The tattoo sleeve that I hadn't time to study was breathtaking. Gears, pistons, and clocks adorned his bulging left arm, appearing as though it moved when he bent his elbow. I almost choked when he whistled through his teeth.

"Like what you see?" he growled—*busted again.* I needed to be more clever about how I ogled him.

"Looking for a compliment?" I said flirtatiously.

"Only if deserved, ma'am." *Who's the flirt now?*

"You're gorgeous." *Shit! I needed a better game.*

"So are you." He winked back.

"Now that your head is full of yourself, I'd like to make you a thank you dinner this evening. You've done more than any stranger should for a damsel in distress. Would you take me to the grocery store later?" I toed the vinyl floor, embarrassed I had to keep asking for favors.

He reset the bulbs on the fixtures he was fixing and stepped off the ladder. My heart bubbled thinking about what he'd do next. To my delight, he walked over and kissed me on the top of my head.

"Whatever you need," he whispered behind my right ear. I may be impulsive, but being brazen hasn't been part of my DNA until now.

I licked my lips, deciding how to respond. His biceps called me, and I traced the grooves to his elbows. Every molecule in my body wanted to attack him right there and then. I felt paralyzed with what to say or do, so I looked at the crinkles at the corners of his brown eyes and took the coward's way out.

"That's a long list, and you have a life to return to." I studied the clock on his shoulder, wondering what had led him to this design.

I slid between him and the counter and prepared a new wash bucket. I had an upstairs to get to, and standing around making googly eyes didn't get the job done. I finished my task and turned to see him staring down at me. My core clenched, and my resilience to make a break for it started to fade.

"See you upstairs." *Damn it! That's not what I meant.*

"Uh, I mean to clean. Not the other thing. I, just . . . never mind. Later." I pointed upward and rolled my eyes, feeling like the biggest idiot to walk the earth. I mumbled self-deprecating words up the back stairs. I'll have to drop at least a dollar into that stupid cup Elias put on the counter for saying bad things about myself. I moved through the room until I passed an antique dresser with a marble counter and tarnished mirror. I set my bucket down and looked at my face, remembering how similar I was to my grandmother. I pulled my hair from the fallen braid hanging down my back and scooped it up like Agatha in her picture. I wound the topknot like she had and bunched it into my hair band. I gasped at how quickly I went from the present to the past. It warmed my heart that by wearing my hair this way, I found such a complete and satisfying connection that I left it that way while I wiped my bedroom down from ceiling to floor.

Feeling accomplished two hours later, I rested in the empty hot tub. An idea a previous tenant thought would be appropriate for a period home. It was an eyesore. Regardless, I jumped in and began emptying my thoughts and worries. That's where Elias found me. Half asleep and nearly dead of exhaustion.

Chapter 11
All Hope is Lost

ELIAS

I found her lying with her feet raised onto one of the whirlpool seats, one arm draped over her face and the other on her thigh. I stiffened at the image she created, including the new hairstyle. I stroked my beard, deciding whether to let her know the water guy had arrived or kiss her awake and fuck her in the tub where she lay. I rearranged myself in my tightening pants, focusing on being a responsible adult and not a horny bastard. She had to wake up either way, so why not have some fun with it?

I kneeled at the platform around the tub and placed my hands on her shapely thighs, massaging downward toward her feet. I'd never taken the time to massage someone this way, and shame on me for missing out on how erotic it could be. Her breathing stirred alongside my own. Her hums of pleasure were a tough aphrodisiac to ignore, but I stayed true to my decision to behave.

She sighed deeply, squirming under the pressure of my hands. "That feels so good. Don't stop." *Don't stop. That seemed to be my constant struggle.*

I gave her arches a quick squeeze and grabbed both her ankles, pulling her down flat into the tub.

"What the hell!"

"Time to get up, princess. The Waterman cometh." I chuckled at her expression and offered my hand to help her up.

"I don't wanna get up," She whined like a child yanked from slumber. Besides her petite frame, nothing else about her resembled a child. Her breasts dipped out from her bra as she crawled out of the tub. Her pear-shaped ass was high and tight, and I fought the urge to grab both cheeks.

"Sorry, sweetheart. Work calls. He wanted us to open all the faucets so he could empty the lines. Get yourself together, and I'll take care of the bathroom while you open the hot tub faucets."

I maneuvered around the excess furniture to complete the request, and, by the time I returned, she had left the room. Relieved to have diverted another precarious situation, I ran down the back stairs to the kitchen. Something odd struck me as I descended the stairs that I'd not recognized in myself. I never returned to the relationship game after being hurt so badly in my last relationship. I'm starting to see why I'm so freaking horny around this woman. I lived like a fucking monk. Never going out and never getting laid. And, most definitely, I'm not connecting to someone who woke up everything about me. Leaving her was getting harder and harder.

Tomorrow. I need to leave tomorrow. I needed a clean break and lots of distance to put what's happened in the past forty-eight hours into perspective. Abigail was right. I had a life of my own. One that didn't include her. One that offered me consistency, reliability, and surety. These few days were more fantasy than real life. It was fun, but reality called, and I'm not sure how I felt about that.

April nights have always been inspiring to me. The sun rises earlier, providing those peaceful moments, coffee in hand, watching the world wake up to endless possibilities. As the sun set later, yellows, oranges, purples, and pinks begged for my attention, reminding me of what I had accomplished. Running into Abigail wasn't just an opportunity to help some needy girl. It was life-changing. Watching her fight for her place in the world had been inspiring, and it sparked a dream inside me that had remained latent for a moment. I needed to return to welding, a hobby while studying mechanical engineering. While the process of welding was required, the actual art of welding wasn't. Unfortunately, I couldn't afford that luxury at the time and put it on the backburner indefinitely. Abigail was a force, and, after spending time with her, the possibility of welding again triggered a fire within me. Being creative again made my hair stand on end, and I couldn't stop this feeling if I tried.

The water guy wasn't here more than an hour, and we had a bucket-load of errands to run so Abigail could manage on her own, starting with food. Her tiny hand rubbed my shoulder, getting my attention.

"What's going on in that head of yours?" she said.

I scrubbed my face, setting my dreams aside for now. "Just thinking about how you'll get around when I'm gone. Have you thought about what you'll do?"

My hands landed on my hips while I watched her face morph into panic, concern, and resolve. "I'll go tomorrow and see what I can find. I can use some money in the trust for a down payment on a reliable car. I don't need anything fancy. I'm not going anywhere but here for the foreseeable future."

And before I knew what I was doing, I opened my big month. "Let's look at some options tonight, and I'll drive you to look at them tomorrow." *Prince Charming to the rescue—again!*

She clapped her hands like a child. "You will? Really? Elias, you're my hero!" She jumped up and down and danced her way to my truck. I turned the ignition and flung my arm over the backrest as we backed out of the drive.

"What kind of man would I be leaving you stranded at a multi-million-dollar estate without a ride?" I clicked my cheek and gave her a corny smile. We drove down the country road heading toward the village square in companionable silence until my stomach rumbled. "What are you making me for dinner, princess?"

Her red lips pursed as she thought. She grabbed her phone and started typing. "Tell me what you like, and I'll make a list."

I spewed off a dozen things I liked, and she typed furiously, getting it all down. The tip of her tongue touched her top lip as she worked. She was focused and serious about her task until she dropped her phone on the console, declaring "done" and closing her eyes. We reached our destination and collected two buggies worth of staples and fresh food to last two weeks. Hopefully, that would be enough time for her to get a car and a job.

As we checked out, she made another declaration.

"I'm going to continue in the tradition of those who came before me." Whatever the hell that meant.

"Come again?" I dropped a watermelon onto the conveyor belt and smiled at the clerk.

"My house," she said, lifting four cereal boxes onto the belt and looking at me like I was stupid. "It's going to stay a B&B. After I make you dinner tonight, you'll see how good a cook I am." Her newfound confidence was adorable.

I patted her shoulder. "No doubt you can achieve whatever you put your heart into."

Abigail stopped emptying the basket; her face melted into a pout. Tears fell from her green eyes, forcibly stealing the air from my lungs.

"Abby. What did I say? I take it back. I'm sorry." I grabbed her shoulders, pulling her past the basket and into my chest.

She sniffled and wiped her eyes. "You're the second person who has said that to me in weeks. No one has said that to me my whole life. Do you think I can pull this off?"

I looked from her to the cashier and the three people standing behind us waiting to check out. Now was not the time to say the wrong thing. She didn't need a grand entrance into her new community with theatrics in a grocery store. I pulled her close and whispered in her ear.

"Absolutely. Don't let anyone tell you otherwise," and kissed the top of her head. "Now, let's finish up and let these people get on with their evening."

I turned her around and finished with the last few items. The groceries were packed, paid for, and returned to our buggy. We exited the line without glares of annoyance or big sighs of relief. Only one woman smiled at me, assuming I handled my woman and the situation well. And the gifts kept coming.

ABIGAIL

I snagged a free, local newspaper off the stand when we left the grocery store. While I prepared chicken piccata, Elias read off several car ads that sounded reasonable. Ironically, it wasn't what he said that caught my attention but the lilt in his voice as he read them. That man loved cars.

"Do you think we have enough sunlight to walk out to the barn? I am dying to know what's in there."

I dropped spaghetti into a boiling pot of water and placed the dredged pan-seared chicken into a glass pan we found earlier. That needed twenty minutes to cook, and I began setting the table with one of the many sets of china found in the multitude of cabinets lined up in the main dining room.

"Seriously! What do cactus mugs and historic homes have in common? Nothing!" I spoke out loud, commenting on all the other crap the previous residents draped around the room. Dollar store valentine garland coiled around a gorgeous wood-framed mirror, rubber chickens lying on a ceramic woven basket filled with plastic eggs, and endless tchotchkes disparaging this gorgeous, grand home. I'm going to dispose of this crap as soon as humanly possible, starting with this crappy garland.

I drained my pasta in the porcelain farm sink and selected one of the many unmatched serving bowls to mix in butter, olive oil, and garlic. I should be elated that the previous residents left everything behind when they moved. It would save me a fortune not to buy it all myself, though several things are well past their usability, like this filter.

"Would you like some wine with dinner?" I called across the room. He didn't answer, and I turned, confused, putting the pasta on the counter. I went to look for him when my timer went off, aborting my mission. Setting the chicken on the stove to settle, I called into several other rooms without a reply. The light flashing around by the barn had me concerned that Elias may have been abducted. In a thriller movie, this would have been a sign to barricade myself in the house, but Elias was out there, and I had to find him.

Cupping my hands around my mouth, I screamed his name and a bell sounded in the distance by the barn. *The Shining* be damned, I'm going toward the light. I followed the overgrown path and saw inside the open door.

"Elias! Are you in there? Please tell me you're alive!" He popped up from behind a car like a jack-in-the-box.

"You aren't going to believe what's in here. It's fucking fantastic! If I weren't a potty-trained grown man, I would have pissed myself." I burst into laughter and walked farther inside. I dug deep and prepared to act as excited as he was because I didn't have the heart to disappoint him.

"Holy shit, Elias. It's a car and —a riding mower!" *Okay, I was excited about the car but had to force myself to be excited about the mower.*

"Lady Luck is on our side. If I can get this thing going, you won't need to spend money on a car. As exciting as that is, it's not what I'm excited about." He pulled at his beard, his eyes wide with possibilities.

I looked around the room, viewing all the standard garden tools, including a wheelbarrow. There wasn't anything in particular that would make me whoop and holler. "You're going to have to help me, Elias. What's got you so excited?"

He marched back and forth several times, his feet stomping the ground. "It's concrete. The floor is concrete!" His priceless expression was entertaining, but I still wasn't getting it. He rushed toward me and grabbed my shoulders. "Do you know what you can do with a concrete floor?" His eyebrows hit his hairline, and his eyes shone with delight. "Ugh, you can do *anything* on it! Weld, for instance, fix cars, sculpt, build – anything!" He marched around the large expanse, perusing all the nooks and crannies like a man on a mission.

Hmm. He's right, I suppose. If we're dreaming, I pictured a pottery wheel under the loft area, or, with more light, I could paint. Dreaming of the future was a luxury I couldn't afford in the past, which made planning my future seem awkward and selfish.

"I see it, Elias. I do. You're so clever. Besides fixing cars, do you do those things you mentioned?" Did he have hidden talents like me? I liked seeing these other sides of him. Besides, why was he so excited about those things in my barn? Unless . . .

"Would you use this space for something other than fixing my car? I could get you some cheap rent if you ask nicely." I snarfed, laughing at myself.

His feet instantly froze.

"Would I like to use this space?" He rubbed his forehead, and he looked like he might hyperventilate. "I-I don't know. I'd have to think about it. I live so far away, and . . ."

He walked out of the barn abruptly, leaving me baffled and alone. I shut off the lights, shoving the heavy barn door closed, and wondered why he was so upset. I followed the path back to the house and began plating our now cold dinner. A few minutes in the microwave will remedy that until Elias emerged.

"How about some wine? I know I'd like a glass." I muttered the last part, annoyed.

"Sure." He mumbled back, uncorking a bottle and placing it on the table. He silently poured us water and sat down with a thud. I watched him warily as I placed our warmed dinners on the table. Something wasn't right about his mood.

"Elias, are you alright? You looked spooked out there." I knew I was pushing him, but he went from such a significant high to a crushing low that it seemed rather bipolar.

He cut his chicken and pushed it through the lemon sauce before he put his fork down with a clink.

"Here's the deal. Let's rent you a car for a week or two. I'll come back next weekend with my tools and get that Buick running. If it holds, then you can return the rental. If not, I'll take you to find a suitable replacement. How does that sound?" He nodded like he had the whole thing worked out, never mind the erratic behavior, which he avoided altogether.

I rubbed my eyes, dragging my hands down my face, having no other ideas. "Sure, that would be great. Thanks, Elias."

He pressed his lips together with a mock smile and began eating dinner.

"Wow. This is good. Did you follow a recipe?" He gobbled more chicken into his mouth, leaving the juice on his beard. *Something for later, I suppose.*

I chuckled. "Maybe years ago, but, no, I've tweaked every recipe I've ever followed. Unfortunately, my budget hasn't allowed for elaborate meals like this one. I'd be happy with just the pasta on most nights." He frowned at that.

He wiped his face and beard with a napkin as his face morphed to menacing.

"Don't take this wrong, Abigail, but you need fattening up. Not a lot, just some." He dove back into his food, hoping to shut his mouth.

"You think I'm a stick? Most guys would love a chick that looked like a stick. Who the hell are you, man?"

I'm sorry that my life conditions have interfered with your opinion of how my body should look. That's what I wanted to say. Unfortunately, I agreed with him. I wanted more curves. I didn't have the budget to create them. Maybe now that I have some cash, I can change that.

"I'm sorry. I should have kept my mouth shut. I only want you to be healthy." He reached over the table and took my hand. "You can't do anything without your health, Abigail, both physical and emotional health. Please promise me you'll take care of yourself when I go tomorrow."

Well, shit. What was I supposed to say to a guy who says sweet things to me, even if he says them awkwardly? I felt physically healthy, though a nutritionist might think otherwise. It was my mental health that swung like a pendulum, especially when I didn't do well. Not all of us can afford a therapist, you know.

His face shone with genuine concern. I came around the table as he watched me intently. He turned to me, and I placed a hand on his face. "I'll do my best if you'll do the same." My thumb brushed his jaw through his thick beard, and his silky hair reminded me of Seneca's dog. Come to think of it, the way he was panting in front of me also resembled her dog when he was petted. "Are you my new best friend?" *Jeez! Stop thinking out loud!*

He pulled me into his lap, licking his pillowy lips. "If there's an opening, I could *see* myself as your best friend. Am I allowed to kiss my best friend," he said in a deep, throaty voice. *Gulp.*

I looked up through my lashes to the gleam in his eyes, knowing I was opening up a can of worms, even considering his kiss. "Please."

He dove into my mouth, searing my lips with his lust. He was a fantastic kisser. His hand ran down my sides, pulling me closer until he picked me up so I could straddle his thick thighs. My hands threaded through his soft locks, and I pulled his head closer, trying to get closer. He consumed me. He moaned, then I groaned, and—together—we became a symphony of pleasure that resonated deeply between us.

I pushed on his chest, desperate to breathe. "Elias, I can't breathe. You're a lot of man to handle."

He liked that. He kneaded my ass with his big, strong hands. He released today's stresses yet built new carnal stressors in my soul. I wanted this man so badly. It's been over two years since I was with a boy, and rest assured, he was no boy.

He smirked as he licked my neck into my clavicle. "You haven't even seen the best parts." He continued his onslaught of wet kisses down between my breasts and back up again. I turned my head more, giving him more access as he nuzzled behind my ear, and, damn it, if he didn't find an erogenous zone I didn't know existed.

Minutes later, he pulled back, out of breath and heaving. "If you want to save this food, you have three minutes to put it away and get upstairs, or I'm going to fuck you 'til Tuesday on this table."

Chapter 12

Goodbye for Now

ELIAS

True to my word, I chased Abigail up the main staircase, smacking her ass as she scurried up the steps as fast as she could. I loved that ass. She had no idea how the flip of her hair or the licking of her lips sent my mind reeling with ideas of how to use her assets for my pleasure. My latest pastime was when she shook her hair and then patted down her body from her perky tits to her tiny round ass looking for her pen. I would have offered to do it for her, but I didn't want to destroy the illusion that I was a gentleman. *Ha! If she could only read my mind.*

Abigail reached her bedroom door, planting herself inside the door frame with her hands pressing both sides with her delicate hands. Her eyes were wide, and her chest heaved from being chased, and my pants got even tighter.

"You know that if you enter this room, you're coming back here. You know that, right?" She didn't move, waiting for my answer.

Was I coming back here? There were many reasons to come back, although I have many more reasons to stay in Pennsylvania, for one, my business. Did she understand that we—I—couldn't possibly drive back and forth every weekend? I had obligations, clients, and a mortgage, for starters. My friend needed my help on his farm. I wouldn't say I liked change. I didn't know this girl. Would I drop everything so that we could be together?

What if I could move a few things around so we could get to know one another better? Then maybe—maybe . . .

It was then that I decided to try. I hadn't tried to be in a relationship for far too long. My raging erections are proof that I needed physical touch and, even more, emotional stimulation. Abigail was worth it. I'd try, and, hopefully, things would work out better this time.

I looked deeply into her eyes as I approached the doorframe. "I'm coming back, Abigail."

The trepidation painted on her face, waiting for my answer, melted away. She sighed, resting her head on my chest and wrapping her arms around my waist. I held her tightly, feeling her firm tits press against my ribs and her warm breath through my T-shirt. "We'll figure something out," I whispered into her ear. I began tickling her sides, not letting her go when she shrieked.

"But for now, I'm going to leave you breathless in more than one way." I scooped her in my arms, carried her to the king-sized bed, and threw her onto the duvet. She shrieked again, a naughty smile extending to her beautiful hazel eyes. "Any last words before I change your life for the better?" I ripped off my shirt, making a point to flex my muscles.

"Fuck, Elias. You better make this good. I'm desperate for a real man," she said, choking out her words. What she implied was very telling. Was she saying she hadn't been with anyone who had pleasured her? Or that she hadn't had sex before?

I rubbed my forehead. "Please tell me you've had sex before?"

She laughed at my concern. "Yes, Elias. I've had sex before. Just bad sex." She played with the embroidery on the duvet, presumably shy about her past experiences being less than fulfilling.

I crawled up the bed high enough to hook my arms under her thighs and yank her to the side of the bed. My satisfaction with the "whoop" sound she released was encouraging. "Well, in that case, let me assure you that those times are over."

I twisted off the button to her jeans and, without bothering with the zipper, pulled them urgently off her lithe body. Her hollowed stomach and the pink flush from her chest to her face excited me more than I could ever remember. I released myself from my low-slung jeans and boxer briefs in two pulls.

"Geezus Christ, Elias! I don't know if I can take all that." She pushed herself higher on the bed, creating too much space for my liking.

I pulled on myself, showing her just how big I could get. "Relax, princess. I'll fit. I'll make sure of it."

I let her stay pressed up to her pillows. My time would be best spent enjoying her little pussy once I got these little white panties off her. I pressed my face to her mound, inhaling her scent. Every sound she made convinced me she wanted this. She wanted me. I sucked her through her cotton hipsters, pressing my tongue as deep as the fabric would allow.

"Christ, you smell good," I croaked like a water-deprived prisoner. I traced my finger along the creases between her thighs as I sucked her again, pulling back the fabric even more. I wanted her soaking. Willing and ready to take me. I knew I was a big man. I knew equally well what was needed to make taking me a pleasant experience. Some women couldn't relax enough, making the whole situation awkward. That wouldn't happen this time. I promised myself that, if the time came, I would make this first coupling a memory of blissful enjoyment.

"Eli. You're killing me. You're making me delirious with what you're doing down there. Don't stop." She wasted no time pushing both hands into my hair, trapping my head between her wanton thighs. I wouldn't disappoint her. *Not a chance.*

Slowly, I hooked my fingers in the fabric and slid her panties down her toned, creamy legs. Goose bumps broke out all over her body, and I smiled at her excitement. "I like looking at you like this. You're so beautiful, Abigail." I dragged one finger down her middle from her neck to her belly button, pausing once to see her eyes roll back into her head when I traveled the short distance down to her pussy. "I'm going to make you scream my name, sweetheart."

I wasn't bragging. I knew how to excite a woman and use my skills to make Abigail delirious with want. I dropped flat to my belly to gently pull apart her labia lips, exploring her bud pulsing before my eyes. My mouth watered like a starved man, flattening my tongue and slowly licking her from one end to the other, revealing her sweetness. Her arms flailed above her head, smacking the pillows as she screamed my name. I smiled wickedly, knowing I had only begun her torture. When my head was free, I completed a second pass and finished with a light, torturous swirl around her cherry. She hissed and sucked in a hard breath of air, letting me know she was enjoying the attention I lavished on her pussy. I wanted her wild and desperate, and she didn't disappoint.

When I lifted my head enough to see her glazed eyes trying to watch me through the slits, I spoke quietly, reminding her to stay relaxed. I reached forward and slid my third finger into her mouth. "Suck," I demanded. And she stared at me in awe. *Fuck!* She sucked my finger to the back of her throat, making herself gag in return.

"Fuck, Abby. You are one surprise after another." I let her suck a few seconds more before pulling them out and driving them into her hot, wet pussy.

"OH. MY. GOD! I'm going to come. Shit, Elias. Don't stop!" Her back arched, and her hips bucked against my mouth unabashed. She may not have been able to verbalize what she wanted, but her body conveyed *precisely* what it needed.

Watching this young woman explode was transformative. She twisted and flailed and, when her summit was reached, she melted into the mattress a whole other person. Soft. Compliant. Relaxed. In the few days I'd known Abigail, I'd never seen quiet and relaxed, even when we slept last night. I could feel the gears in her head moving. Stillness released crinkles at the corners of her eyes and the tension in her jaw. Even her lips relaxed more, opening to an *oo*. I crawled up her lithe body, kissing my way to those perfect lips, to slip my tongue in her mouth, praising her performance in between breaths.

"You taste spectacular." *Kiss.* "You make me so fucking hard." *Kiss.* "I need to be inside you." *Kiss.*

Her delirium prevented anything more than sighs and hmms. I was pleased with myself, knowing I knew the magic formula to disengage her brain. It was my new superpower. I felt needed and desired in a way I hadn't ever experienced. Even my last girlfriend didn't appreciate me like Abigail, and I dated her for two years. Was I that desperate to be accepted that I'd hold onto someone that long? My eyes were slowly opening, and the sprite before me was the culprit. I wanted more.

"Elias?" I felt a finger sliding across my forehead, tracing my worry lines. "Where did you go?" she whispered.

It seemed I had a habit of vanishing in my head when my thoughts overtook me. "I was thinking of how incredible you are."

"Aww. Aren't you sweet?" She lifted her head to my nose. "I have an ever-growing fondness for you, too. Especially that wicked mouth. So naughty."

I chuckled. "I have other naughty parts if you're ready to receive them." Her pupils blew wide, and my grin turned devilish.

"Do you have protection?"

"I do."

"Thank God! I can barely take care of myself, let alone a spontaneous love child. Wrap it up, man!" I laughed at her delivery. She was a funny one.

Her brain was back online, and her sassy mouth was back to one hundred percent. I didn't waste a moment jumping off the bed and tripping across the room, looking for my wallet. "God dammit, Abigail! Have you seen my wallet?"

"Bathroom," she mumbled, rolling onto her stomach and pushing her long hair off her face.

"Right." I bolted to the bathroom, jamming my shoulder into the doorframe. *Shit!* Sometimes being a giant was a pain in the ass. I found my wallet and almost cried when I slid out the crackly foil packet. *How old was this thing?*

I strolled back to the bedroom, steering clear of walls and doors, reading the expiration date on the foil. "Uh, Abby. I've got some bad news." I held up the packet with the anguish written all over my face.

She rolled onto her side, propping her head on her hand. "Oh no!" she gasped. "Really? This is my life! Two steps forward and one step back. Dammit!" She smacked the covers with her free hand.

Feelings of letting her down blanketed me from head to toe. Again, I felt inadequate and embarrassed. "I'm sorry, baby."

I must have looked pathetic because she threw back the covers and sat on the end of the bed, speaking directly to my cock. "You will not be denied."

Chapter 13
Hello ATG. Goodbye, Elias

A **BIGAIL**

I heard the sounds of a chicken bawking at the side door. I swear I'll cook that chicken if it does this again. I saw Elias had already left the bed when I jerked up from the soundest sleep in my life. If I hadn't needed to go to the bathroom so badly, I would have rolled around in the sheets for another hour. As it was, Elias was leaving today, and I wanted to spend as much time with him as I could.

This bedroom offered filtered sunlight through the west side of the property. Antique, lacey shades adorned the leaded glass windows, and a distant memory of my mother's bedroom flashed through my mind. I wondered what she'd say, looking at the almost grown-up daughter she birthed. Hopefully, I wasn't a complete disappointment. I was trying. I was. Today would be another turning point in this adventure when I took up the yolk of this property on my own. There was still massive amounts of cleaning in every room in the house—mounds of junk to sort through, assessing the value of each piece. Dollar store junk would find its way to the curb. However, many items needed a trained eye, and I think we both can agree that it wasn't me.

My head began to throb from that damn chicken repeating its toxic shriek until I ran down the side stairs and flung open the door, prepared to scream back.

"Stooooppp . . . " The chicken immediately shuffled backward, though it was brave enough not to leave the stoop. I pushed open the screen door and almost stepped onto the largest brown egg I'd ever seen. "Oohh! What do we have here?" I bent down to pluck the oval out of its clever "nest." The chicken continued staring me down, possibly looking for praise.

"Elias!! Come here now!" I called back into the house, realizing my habit of screaming his name would lead to dire consequences. In the meantime, I took pity on the poor feathery girl and gave her the praise she well deserved. "Good girl. That was a great gift you gave me and very clever in your choice of nest." She clucked her reply and wandered back into the garden.

I felt his heat on my back and the anger on my neck. "You better have damn good reason to be screaming my name like that."

I stepped aside as I pushed open the screen again, pointing to the hilariously deposited egg. "It looks like your giant-ass shoes make for a good nest, big guy."

What the fuck? "There'd better not be any slime in my shoe, or that bird is dinner." I threw my head back, laughing until my belly hurt.

"I said the same thing." I gently slapped him in the chest. "Did I just make my first friend in Mystic?" I snarfed.

"Princess, you making friends with a chicken certainly tracks with your personality. What will you call her?"

I picked up the egg and turned it thoughtfully in my hand as I walked past Elias to the kitchen. *Hmm? What does one call a chicken?*

"How about Amy? I had a childhood friend named Amy. She called herself *Amy the Great*. I wasn't sure why, but she was confident—like this chicken."

He rubbed his beard, presumably contemplating my story. "Why the hell not? *Amy the Great* it is."

Our morning became a frenzy of mechanical lessons, warnings of complacency, and stolen kisses. Lunch came and went, and Elias disappeared again. Once I found him in the barn, I retraced my steps to see him with a tape measure, a tiny notebook, and a pencil behind his ear.

"Hey, you. What are you measuring?" I tentatively entered the space, creating a catalog of artifacts hung from the rafters to the webby corners under the hay loft.

He looked startled at my presence, shoving his notebook into his back pocket. I needed to see what he had written and knew that, to extract it from his very appetizing spot, I'd need a plan. I swung my hips to distract him and pressed myself to his chest, wrapping my arms around him tightly.

"Last night was amazing. I was hoping we could—you know—do it again before you leave?" I ran my hands over his ass, slipping the notebook out carefully. "Please," I begged for effect.

He looked at me quizzically. "You don't have to ask me twice or to look at my notebook." *Dammit! Busted.*

I had the decency to look contrite and handed it back to him. He took it in one hand, took my hand in the other, and walked me back down the path to the house when his phone rang.

"Go upstairs. I'll be there in a minute." He commanded. *Yes, sir!*

By the time he returned, I was naked and wrapped in a sheet, awaiting my next order. Except, the look on his face didn't say he was sticking around.

He sat on the bed, stroking my hair, twirling the ends around his thick fingers. "That was my assistant manager. The mayor's kid blew up his new car and needs me to fix it immediately. I'm sorry, princess, but I have to go."

He bent his large body over mine and kissed me deeply, searing the memories of the past three days upon my lips and heart. If I'm being honest, Elias terrified me. Beyond his size, his eyes permeated my soul, and I found the right combination of words and mannerisms to calm my hamster wheel of a brain. I wanted more from him but knew my time with him had ended. Who knew if we'd see each other again? He said he would come back to Mystic—to me. I wasn't so naive that I believed him. He had a life before me and will have a life after me. Once again, it was time to evolve, and this new beginning could be the springboard to a future I could only have dreamed of. If ever there was a time to believe in myself, it was now.

It was a slow recovery from his dizzying kiss. I knew I had to let him go.

I stared into his big brown eyes, threading my fingers through his silky, wavy hair. I will add this tactile memory to all the others

I've collected and run on a loop for the rest of my life. "I'd like to be selfish and duct tape you to this bed. You'd be my handyman, literally and figuratively." I smirked, tracing the shell of his ear and making his chest rumble. "I'll miss you, Elias. You saved me—literally. I won't ever be able to repay you, but I will send you gas money as soon as I get a paycheck. Thank you for everything." He kissed me lingeringly, pulling my bottom lip and whispering promises of returning soon. I desperately wanted to believe he'd be back. I'd pray that he did. Until then, I'd suffer silently.

Reluctantly, I released him from my embrace, turning toward him as he righted himself on the floor. He pulled his shirt off the back of the couch where it landed last night and pulled it on. The view was spectacular, and I wished I had my phone to take a picture. He must have read my mind.

"Up here, princess, look at my face." He flashed a devilish smile. "You really should take a picture. It'll last longer."

I was out of bed in a flash and yanked my phone from my jeans pocket, diving back into bed, ready to snap the perfect personal pleasure pose for tonight.

"Ready!" I exhaled heavily after my dash around the room.

We both laughed like children as he stripped off his shirt again, flexing his biceps in several manly poses, demonstrating how delicious he looked.

"Hang on," he called and spun around. I didn't know what he was doing until he slowly turned back to me with his hands in his hair, and my jaw dropped. His low-slung jeans dropped several inches lower, revealing a deep V and a dark brown happy trail.

"Geezus, Elias. I might still use that duct tape on you yet. You are so fucking hot." His smile pulled to his eyes, and I wanted to cry at my impending loss. I snapped three more pictures and dropped my phone into my lap, mentally exhausted.

"What do you have for me, princess?" He stalked back to the bed and yanked the covers off me. *Fuck.* He bent over me again, sucking and pulling on each of my nipples until they looked like ripe roses. I threw my head back, and, before I knew it, he was taking a spank-bank full of deviant photos. "Fuck, yeah. You're so sexy, Abigail. I'm going to miss this tiny body."

I watched him gather the few things he had around the room and stuff them into his duffle bag. The sadness in his eyes was visible, and I didn't want him to go. I still couldn't believe my luck at having met such a man. I'm not a trusting person, though it was effortless with him. Trusting in his word was all I had; I'd make sure he knew that.

I dragged myself out of bed and pulled on my jeans and a T-shirt, leaving off my undergarments. I didn't have time for those luxuries now; Elias was leaving me.

"I'll walk you out," I whispered, following him down the side stairs to the driveway where he had parked.

He put his bag on the front seat of his truck and turned to face me one last time.

We both started talking and laughed.

"You first," I said.

"Abigail. This place, you, has been one hell of a trip. I couldn't have possibly planned anything like these past few days, and I would do it again to meet you. You've changed me; I don't know if that's good or bad. I'll think about it more, but I'm sure you cracked me open in a way I hadn't expected . . . thank you." Giant arms pulled me tightly against his solid chest, and I listened to his heart thump softly in his chest for several minutes. Who knew when I'd feel this safe again? "Do you remember what I said about renting a car for this week? You have a plan. Stick to it. You have my number if you get stuck." He kissed me softly. "You can do this, Abigail. You will succeed. I believe in you."

For the first time in my life, someone believed in me. Someone encouraged me and my plan. Maybe this time I won't fail. Or better yet, I will have the courage to pick myself up and keep forging ahead with a positive attitude. Elias believed in me, and I wouldn't let him or me down.

I pressed both hands to his chest, copping one last feel, "Thank you again, Elias. You've made a difference in my life, too."

I pushed back and let him board his vehicle as I rubbed my damp eyes. He rolled down the window after he put the truck in gear. "Tell Amy the Great she will need a new nest for her eggs." He winked and rolled backward down the drive, leaving me empty and alone.

Chapter 14
Under Scrutiny

ELIAS

I'm such an idiot.

My parting words were about a chicken and not that I'd be back soon. Or, even better, I'll miss you—no wonder Abigail was crying. I'll call her later and see how she's doing.

The drive back from Mystic was boring, and I spent the whole time rehashing every conversation we had on our way down there. She really was a spaz. Keeping up with her conversation ping-pong took practice. But when she was direct, it was refreshing, if not startling. I don't think Abigail could ever have a hidden agenda. She's transparent most of the time, unlike my last girlfriend. Oria was always pulling punches and making me feel like I was the one who always goofed up. In retrospect, those red flags got me out of that relationship. I was constantly taking the fall for her lack of planning or bad decisions. Abigail always had a plan. They weren't sound plans, but at least attempted plans. Regardless, I wasn't wasting two more years of my life on someone who blamed me for their problems.

Enough. That was then, and this was now. A new beginning with an exciting, gorgeous, unpredictable, and creative person was underway, and I felt alive again. She came out of nowhere like a whirling dervish and, gratefully, into my arms. Abigail flipped a metaphorical switch in both my heart and my head, alerting me to new possibilities. Where usually I'd be attracted to a taller, more robust woman, Abigail was slight, undernourished, and scrappy. But, those eyes! Hazel and luminous, with long dark lashes set evenly on her delicate face. The smudges under her eyes revealed volumes of struggle and concern. You could tell she'd been hurt; her inflections also said so. Sometimes sharp in tone, her indifference seemed commonplace. Suspect even. She expected me to be annoyed with her, and, when I wasn't, her perfectly bowed eyebrows raised in speculation. I didn't know from moment to moment if she trusted me, though her circumstances forced her to try. I set her straight on that point from the get-go, and it seemed as though we had made progress. I may be obtuse or clinical at times, but I was honest and forthright to everyone. Conversely, no one would know that unless they'd spoke to me to reveal my character. I'd made hiding from people a thing of the past. At least, I'd hoped I was.

Now that I was back in my garage, my attention on Mayor Mitchell's kid's car absorbed my time for the rest of the day. I know the kid caused the problem, though it's his dad's fault for not teaching him how to care for the car properly. No ounce of coolant or oil was found in any of the appropriate chambers. Duh! I swear kids are getting dumber each decade. High schools insisted on sex education, so why didn't they insist on Automobile Maintenance 101? Come on!

Usually, I'd hand this off to my number two guy, Paul, but after taking four days off of work, I gave him a few paid days off as a thank you for holding down the fort. A few hours later, I called the mayor and texted his son to come in for a complimentary maintenance training class. Hopefully, I won't have to see this entitled little shit for anything other than an oil change every few months. Keeping the mayor happy had paid off on a few lucrative fleet deals that paid the rent around here and given me a pretty nice nest egg. If I played my cards right, I could open another location soon.

I'd never been a big dreamer. Data and logic have always steered me in the right direction, except, of course, in relationships. They were the farthest thing from logical. I needed a beer and some guy time. My buddy, Reilly, who I helped on his farm, was the perfect person to help me analyze my adventures with Abigail.

"Since when are you into picking up women?" Reilly poked at me.

"Never. She picked me up." I scrubbed my face, still not understanding how quickly I had come to Abigail's rescue.

"She must have, cuz in the ten years I've known you, you've never had to pick up anyone. Women flock to you. It's too bad you're too stupid to see that. You must be damaged."

I laughed hard at that one. I was damaged. I knew my worth, as well as my appeal. I just never made it a point to dwell on them. If put in front of an intelligent, pretty girl, I would be smitten. Those bombshell types scared the shit out of me. They're like predators without boundaries.

"I think I need a new friend. You know me too well. What's with you? Still enjoying the honeymoon phase of your new relationship?" I waggled my eyebrows, having turned the tables.

"So far, so good. Meghan travels often, and I'm unsure how I feel about that. She'll be gone for two to three weeks at a time, and, when she does come back, she's not emotionally present. Her work promised this pace wouldn't last long, though I wouldn't hold my breath since it's been like that for two months." Reilly took a long pull from his beer and hung his head when the glass hit the table. My friend needed a real partner in his life. He worked too hard not to have someone appreciate him and what he was trying to build.

"Sorry, buddy. You deserve better." I fist-bumped him and took a deep drink myself.

"Not that's any of my business, but are you going back to see this girl? You seem rather intrigued by her." Reilly stared me down warily.

I sat back, crossing my arms over my chest, pondering my options.

"Reilly, this girl is incredible. She's strong, yet silly and smart, and definitely missing a few filters. She's so direct that it startles me sometimes. To your question, though, I promised her I would. I think there's something there. Something more than physical." I silently screamed my enthusiasm and slammed the table, making it wobble.

"Whoa there, big fella. I'm happy for you, but she's two hundred forty or so miles away. From what you told me earlier, she isn't moving any time soon. How will it work exactly?"

Little did he know I'd been running probability studies in my mind day and night. My calculations all pivoted on her wanting this as much as I did. I couldn't afford to open another business in another state without investing in her emotionally and her truly committed to me. My life was beginning to look like a season from the Netflix series *Love is Blind. (Yeah, I watched last season. No judgment.)*

"Is it possible to make that decision without more time together? I want her to want me, not just because I can fix a car or trap mice. She needs to get to know the real me. The dork, the freak, the boring . . ."

"Dude. You're anything but boring," he reassured me.

"Oh, contraire. To someone who doesn't understand art or why I help a pathetic friend like you instead of partying like a rock star, I'm boring. Abigail is anything but boring. Honestly, she appreciated my sense of humor, even when it was at her expense. She's cool. You'd like her."

He nodded his head. "I can't wait."

It was getting late, and we made plans to fix some fencing on his farm that weekend. I dragged myself home to create a project flowchart of how this relationship needed to go so that I could invest in Abigail and our future together. I knew there were more variables than I could account for, but I was determined to navigate this part of our relationship as rationally as possible.

Honesty? Check. Abigail didn't have a hidden agenda. She's very transparent.

Looks? Double check. She wasn't an obvious beauty, but she glowed from the inside out, and her hazel eyes beamed sex appeal. Don't get me started on her ass or her long, silky hair.

Stability? This is where things got sketchy. Abigail's family life didn't do much to give her confidence or nurture her talents. Forget the financial piece; she was a wreck.

Possibilities? Everywhere! I'd build a business out of that barn. I could explore my passion for metal sculpting, and she could make pottery, paint, or anything else her heart desired. Her home had been a bed and breakfast for years. Was there nothing keeping her from repeating that tradition while she explored her passions?

On the surface, we were worlds apart. I was college-educated. She was life-educated. I was raised with structure and little emotional support. She was like her new "friend," Amy—cage-free and openly squawked her emotions for all to hear. However, under deeper analysis, we were both broken in similar ways. We didn't get the love and nurturing we desperately needed when we were young. This precipice was our hurdle to get over—that, and two hundred forty miles.

My relocation project management project looked like a spider web that all led to the same conclusion: our relationship could be a massive train wreck or the adventure of a lifetime. The real question was whether we believed in each other enough to try. I broke out in a cold sweat just thinking about it.

ABIGAIL

I had to shut down my emotional brain after first having a bawling session. Relieving myself of all my pent-up feelings these past few days was not only cleansing but necessary. I had to get this house in order, and my plan wouldn't execute itself on its own. I needed to take action.

Today was a purging day. The mounds of dollar store junk went into a black garbage bag immediately and were dragged to the curb. I didn't know when garbage day was, but I didn't care. I may be ADHD, but I was meticulous once I started a project. By lunchtime, I had gone through the living room, dining room (what a joke that looked like), front sitting room, and the foyer. Three trips to the curb topped off a clear sign there was a new owner, and people started to stare.

"Hi!" I said, waving at two women on the other side of the secluded road I lived on.

Slight grimaces marked their faces with fake waves. I recognized that, though I may not know these women, I might need their help at some point and should introduce myself. Being a good neighbor doesn't take much effort, and that's all the motivation I needed to walk the rest of the drive to meet them.

"Hey. I'm Abigail. I just moved in. So much junk to move out." I laughed like we all knew this little gem of knowledge. "What's your name?" I sounded like a first-grader. I should have added, "Will you be my best friend?"

They looked at each other apprehensively—a secret language between them.

"Um, welcome. I'm Maggie, and this is Jennifer. We live a block down the way. Welcome to the neighborhood." The thick blonde offered her hand as a peace offering.

"Yeah, welcome. Where did you move from?" The tall brunette probed.

I bit my lip, deciding how much to tell them about my past. It wasn't their business. If they were like that old jerk at the Office of Deeds, then they didn't need to know anything about me.

I shook each of their hands with a sincere smile. "It's great to meet you both. Once I get myself and this house together, I'd like to have you over for coffee." *Yes. Coffee, not lunch or dinner.* "I'm originally from the Detroit area via Chicago." *Good answer, Abigail. Short and sweet.*

"I don't have my phone, but maybe we could exchange numbers? You could text me with your info when you have a minute?" It was a question, not a commitment, so I hoped they'd follow through. Again, I'm not interested in shallow friendships, only a helping hand on occasion.

They looked at each other again and answered simultaneously, "Sure."

One minute later, I was back in my house shaking after giving them my number. Meeting new people was the most awkward thing in the world. People were checking you out, making comments about your looks, and judging your character before you barely said a word. If that weren't enough, what should I say to them? I knew nothing about them. Was that why people talked about the weather? Whatever. I met enough new people today.

After a peanut butter and jelly sandwich and an apple, I finished my fortification with a rather large iced coffee. Caffeine was the cure to my dopamine insufficiency, says *Psychology Today*. It's my inexpensive medication without a prescription. Since my aunt wouldn't pay for it, I did some research of my own. Caffeine became my drug of choice.

Revved up and ready to go, the next step in my twenty-step plan was to sift through drawers and drawers of housewares, boxing up anything that required an expert eye. Still unsure of everything else, I bagged them up for review later. I couldn't believe how many china cabinets full of glasses, plates, and other knick-knacks were stuffed to the brim. There must be a set of plates from every decade since the turn of the 19th century. I counted thirty-two sets. Of course, not all were complete, and some were downright ugly. Those went into the donation pile immediately. Another dozen sets were simple and usable but not to my taste. Those got boxed up for donation, as well. Three sets had gold banding around the edges and were adorned with intricate designs. Those stayed and would be great for fancy meals. *Listen to me! Fancy meals. When have I ever been to or made a fancy meal? But, maybe…*

As the streaks of light poured through the windows, I faded. I'd been working hard for hours when I looked around and was pleasantly surprised that my anxiety faded, too. The worst of the clutter was gone, and I could start seeing the original beauty this home once had. Tonight, I'd read through Agatha's journal and research all the fabrics she used throughout the house. Like the antique wood, these fabrics were delicate, if not fraying. I made a list of phone calls tomorrow for lawn care, painting, and other restoration projects. I needed a vehicle that worked, and, though Elias said he'd be back next weekend, I couldn't take the chance of not having a car to run errands.

Elias. I wondered what he was doing now. I wasn't so needy that I had to speak with him tonight, but I would answer his call if he did. I went upstairs, showered off today's grime, and braided my hair. I liked how it left a soft wave in my hair after it dried. Call it a cheap perm, but the price was right. FREE! I skipped down the back stairs into the kitchen and warmed up leftovers while adding more details to my growing lists. Elias checked the electrical systems, so I felt safe. However, those disgusting bugs and vermin had to go.

"Pest control!" I said in an *aha* declaration. I didn't expect an answer, but I was known for talking to myself, complete with answers and narration. *I can't possibly be the only person who does this. I just can't.*

After my late dinner, I followed Elias's orders and locked all the doors—twice. I turned on the outside lights and ensured the stairways weren't cluttered with boxes or bags in case I had to escape quickly. How would he know to do that? "Safety first," I could hear him say. Fine. I went upstairs, stopped in the second bedroom on the right, pulled Agatha's journal off the shelf, and proceeded to my bedroom.

I stared at her picture, tracing her eyebrows, lips, and jawbone. It was uncanny how much we looked alike. The hallway walls were cluttered with sepia photos of men with beards and deadpan faces. I didn't know which was my great-great grandfather's yet. I could spend months researching my family alone, though it wouldn't change my attitude about them. Anyone with the presence of mind to plan for their grandchildren far into the future had a good heart. And, for that, I finally felt at peace. Agatha's predestined manifestation made me the benefactor of their generosity and I promised to make them proud.

I don't know when I stopped working on my research, but, when I woke up, there was drool on my pillow, my back ached, my hamstrings felt like guitar strings, and my hair! Oh, my, it was a swarm of locks resembling a wasp's nest attacking my face. My phone buzzed under the covers, and worked feverishly to unwrap my head to find it.

"H-hello." *What happened to my voice?*

"Good morning, princess. Did I wake you?" My throat closed at his deep greeting, and my thighs clenched. There wasn't a better sound in the world than this man's morning voice. *His afternoon and evening voice were pretty damn good, too.*

Hmm. "Yeah. What time is it? I don't remember falling asleep." Finally free of my hairball, I threw back the rest of the covers and tried to stand. "Ow. Ow. Ow." I muttered.

"Are you alright?" His concern was sweet.

"I'm fine. I think I overdid it yesterday, moving boxes of junk out of the house. I need to find my yoga mat and stretch out." I looked at my phone, noticing it was early, like before eight early.

"Why are you up?" I finally found my walking legs and hobbled across the room and down the short hallway to the bathroom. Yikes, was I a mess.

I heard the rumble in his chest through the phone and the smile in his voice. "Some of us have day jobs, princess. I just wanted to be sure you were okay after your first night alone."

I propped up the phone on the counter and turned on the speaker while I washed my face and pulled my hair into a ponytail. "Remarkably, yes. Especially since someone wasn't distracting me all day." I giggled.

He made a snarfing sound. "Are you referring to me? I wasn't distracting. I was helpful. There's a difference."

Preparing my toothbrush with paste, I replied sweetly. "Tell me more." I began brushing in earnest.

"Well, for starters, stopping you from using abrasive liquids on antiques was very helpful and protected your assets."

I smiled. "That's because you like my assets."

He laughed. "That I do. On that note, not to sound needy, but did you miss me?"

My jaw dropped. I thought the same thing last night, and now he verbalized it. I liked having him around. His vibe was calm, assuring, and sincere. I can't remember ever having these sensations in my life. It felt like what home should feel like. *Hmm.*

"Abigail? Are you still there?"

I was. I had to say something. Something clever, yet affirming. "You betcha I did."

That sounded too big in my mouth. Did I scream that? What happened to clever?

"Sorry. What I meant to say was I did—I do—miss you." I swear I could hear his gears turning in his head. "Take your time, Elias." My hand slapped my mouth. *Shut up, woman!*

I heard him clear his throat, "Abigail, I've been missing you since I met you."

Chapter 15

First Day Realities and Goodbye, Aunt Eleanor

ABIGAIL

By the time indicated on the wall clock, we had been talking for more than fifteen minutes, when l I heard someone hollering in the background. We rushed our goodbye and promised to check in later tonight.

Keeping my promise to stretch, I pulled out my yoga mat from the closet and put my body back together. Today, I would take things slower. Do only the necessary things, especially those phone calls. The weather had broken from frosty to moist these past few mornings; however, today, a balmy breeze passed through the leaves of the giant weeping willow in the front yard. I remember seeing a wrought iron table in the backyard and deciding it belonged on the front porch, along with a cement statue of a Labrador. After rummaging through the garage for a device to move everything, a red Radio Flyer wagon peeked at me from behind a gaudy yellow screen.

"Yes! There you are. You've been hiding from me." I knew I'm talking to myself, but I'm good company. "Let's put you to work."

Four trips later, from front to back, I placed these pieces strategically so I could enjoy my coffee and people watch. *The plan was to watch, not engage.* Growing up, I'd never seen a willow tree until meeting Seneca. Her apartment building in Chicago had one out front. We would sit under it, talking about everyone who came into her dad's store saying judgmental things about them. I'm not sure why we felt that was funny at the time. Could I claim to be young and stupid? In retrospect, we weren't hurting anyone, only that we were small and petty. Thank goodness that phase of our lives was over. It was time to catch up with my friends and family. I hoped they remembered I was alive.

I started with my Aunt Eleanor. I hoped she kept my stuff. I dialed and waited while her very annoying ringtone beckoned her to pick up.

"Where have you been? It's been three days, and you haven't called or texted. I was beginning to think you weren't ever going to call."

Her voice was accusing and harsh. Newsflash, Auntie! The phone works both ways. Why didn't you check on me? If you thought something was wrong, why didn't you reach out? *So much for the caring, concerned aunt routine.*

"Hi, Aunt Eleanor. Hello to you, too." Two could play that way. "I've had my hands full with, you know, moving, car troubles, money troubles, and house troubles, just to name a few things. How are you? Is your move going well?" I hoped my patronizing tone came through loud and clear. God forbid my life should be a priority for a while.

She harumphed. "Don't take that tone with me, missy. I've been up to my ears in moving, job changes, and gout. Unlike you, I have real responsibilities, so where can I send your junk?"

See? That right there was why I didn't have any respect for her. Me not having responsibilities? What the fuck? Did she not know why I moved? And, also, why were my things junk and hers so precious? Once I got my stuff from her, I was done with her. After overhearing a private phone conversation with one of her friends, she made it clear she never wanted me; therefore, I didn't feel obligated or dutiful. It's a wonder I turned out as good as I did. *Thanks, Mom, for the great beginning of my life.* I gave her my address and promised to reimburse her if it was too much of a financial hardship. My whole existence with her was summed up in one saccharine minute.

"Aunt Eleanor, thank you for your sacrifices in raising me without warning. I know you had to give up your personal life to keep me alive and well, and while I greatly appreciate that, I hope you won't feel obligated to keep in touch after sending my things. I'll be fine."

Strangled, guttural noises akin to a gag, were my last words with the woman who technically raised me. I felt numbness throughout the day as I tried to remember any positive, outstanding childhood moments. Beyond my first birthday, after my mother's death, nothing came to mind. It felt tragic in some ways, like another death I had to mourn. It made me feel out of control and alone. It explained my behavior at times, which was impulsive and unfiltered. It could be the unbalanced chemistry in my brain or my subconscious acting out. Either way, it was problematic. I hoped I would outgrow one or the other, but that was a stretch.

After a cup of coffee and a sleeve of cheap, packaged chocolate chip cookies, I called Seneca. She'd lift my spirits.

She answered on the first ring as a good friend should.

"Abigail! Girl, I've been waiting for your call. What took you so long?"

Seneca had, and I quote our sixth-grade teacher, "diarrhea of the mouth." She was one run-on sentence after another. It was charming at times, though mostly hilarious, to see her get passionate about everything.

"Ugh! How long do you have? My story is like a saga. But—it does come with a hunky guy." I baited her, and she ate it up.

It took me the better part of a half hour to give her a vivid account of my travels, Elias, and my house. Generous amounts of drama and imagery poured out of my mouth until I got to Elias's departure. My throat closed off, and I went silent.

"Abs. Where did you go? Are you okay?"

I cleared my throat, hoping that was why I couldn't speak, except it wasn't. It was the thought that Elias wouldn't come back and that the future he painted would never happen. I felt gutted.

"Sorry. My thoughts about Elias are complicated. I'd never thought past the end of the week since I was always in survival mode. I don't know how to think about him and where he fits into my life. Frankly, I'm still trying to figure out how I will be able to keep this place, let alone take care of it."

My voice cracked, and the heaviness of everything I had to endure until now sat like a pit in my stomach. The added responsibilities felt like I was having a heart attack. I could barely take a full breath.

"Seneca. I think I'm having a panic attack. I can't breathe." I waved my free hand before my face and began pacing around the room. The walls were closing in on me, and there wasn't an escape route. I bolted from my seat and started walking around the circular driveway, snapping my fingers.

"Hey. Hey. Slow your roll. I can hear you snapping your fingers. You need to stop and breathe. Come on. Breathe with me." She did this thing with me every time I had an attack. It made me more anxious when I began the deep breathing exercises, but I started to settle down after a minute. To this day, I don't know why my brain couldn't think of doing that on my own. First, Seneca, and now, Elias. How did he know to do this exercise? Did he have anxiety, too? I'll have to ask him next time I see him.

"Thanks, babe. I'm better. What would I do without you?" I smiled as I walked down the side drive, taking in the buds preparing to pop open.

"You'd collapse, and when you woke up, you'd breathe normally. Of course, your head would be cracked open, and you'd have a black eye and a broken arm." Her voice cackled through the receiver.

"Very funny. Then you'd have to come here and be my nursemaid until I healed. Are you ready for that kind of commitment?" *Having her here wouldn't be so bad, right?*

She clucked her tongue, "Be careful what you wish for. I wouldn't mind a little vacation in Connecticut. My dad's store isn't doing well, and I think he's considering shutting it down. Would you mind if I stayed with you for a bit? I could help you with stuff, and we could watch movies and eat popcorn like we used to until the middle of the night." Silence drifted between us. I fondly remembered cuddling each other, watching a horror movie, and then diving into the Romance Channel to lighten the mood.

"Sen, you are welcome to come for as long as you want. You are the chosen sister I never had. Give me a shout when you're on the way." My chest fluttered excitedly at the idea of Seneca coming to stay with me. She grounded me, and I needed that desperately. "I love you, girl."

"I love you too, boo. God knows I need you to braid my hair." We laughed and made promises to speak again soon. She was good medicine, and I needed more of it.

The rental car company dropped off an inexpensive sedan at midday. Since I'd be going back his way to do some errands, I appreciated not being charged extra for a chase car. Today's errands included the library, a craft and material store, the grocery store, and one of those giant warehouse stores for a security system Elias demanded I install.

"You can't be out here all alone with all these buildings. You need cameras all over this place. Get one, and I'll install it next time I come down." I wondered when that would be.

Mystic Library was a converted mansion home similar to mine but more rustic. The vaulted ceiling was lined with thin boards slotted in long panels surrounding a wood medallion-like centerpiece in the center. The floors were covered with ancient rugs, and the walls had chubby baby pictures dating back to their origin in 1878. I couldn't wait to get my hands on my family's documents.

A loud "meow" screeched near my feet when I turned to find a librarian.

"Well, hello, kitty. Sorry, I almost tripped on you." Seriously, what's a cat doing in the library? I found the main desk and was sent down the hall to the historical records section. *Hmm. I didn't know that was a thing.*

A sweet-faced little woman lifted her head and smiled at me—finally, an approachable person.

I smiled. "Hello. I'm Abigail Farnsworth-Burton. I could use your help finding my family's historical information."

Her raised eyebrows should have been a red flag regarding my name. First, the lady at the Deed's office, then the old guy at the realtor's office, and now this chic. Was there some big secret about my family that I was the last to know? She pulled open a drawer, pulled out a set of keys, stood, and signaled me to follow her.

"I'm Micah," was all she said as we walked down another hallway, down a flight of stairs, and into the basement. If I didn't know better, I'd swear she was going to kill me down there.

She stopped abruptly, unlocked a door, and pulled a set of white cotton gloves from her pocket.

She pinched a small smile on her face. "Here is where your search will begin. Start on this shelf and continue reading through those volumes." Ten, to be exact. Handing me the gloves, she turned and walked away, only to stop short again. "When you finish those, you'll want to go to the courthouse and ask Ellen to direct you to the property archives to better understand the Farnsworth Estate's operational history.

I fell asleep after the first three volumes. Reading articles was worse than history class with Mr. Ruggers. The silver lining to these first books was that I learned about the area's growth, the logging business on the Mystic River, and my great-great-grandfather's contributions to feeding this up-and-coming city, along with finding sustainable development in the production of trees. *So, this was how the old guy made his money.*

I returned upstairs to return Micah's gloves and a list of articles I needed to be copied.

"Oh, hello, dear. How did it go?" My eyes looked to hers over her reading glasses, appropriately hanging from a beaded necklace.

I rolled my eyes, "Let's just say I'm not ready for a final exam." I chuckled, and she did as well. "I'd like to make some copies of the articles in a few sections. Could you help me with that? I want to build a scrapbook for future visitors at the house."

Micah made a bright *hmm* sound. "Visitors, you say. Will you be keeping the home as a bed and breakfast?"

I knew she was phishing and wasn't wrong, but I wasn't ready to commit to anything now. "Maybe. I haven't decided yet. There's still so much to do there." I winked and smiled. She reciprocated and stood to take my list. "I don't need this right away. I'll be back and finish my research. Would you hold onto them until later this week? Can I pay you for all the copies when I pick them up?"

She pursed her lips. "I suppose so. By the way, I'm embarrassed to ask, but I was hoping I could take a walk through the house sometime. I've always wanted to see the inside. I fancy myself a bit of an antiquarian. Are many original pieces of furniture and artifacts still in the home?" She pressed her hands together in prayer, tapping her fingers like a hopeful child. I couldn't resist giving in to her request.

"So many," I said. Micah gasped. "If you could give me a week, I'm still combing through the house and making piles of items with questionable antiquity. Do you think you could help me figure out what is an antique and what is a knock-off?"

Micah was full-out clapping at this point, and so was I. This woman was the hidden gem I'd been looking for. Ideas swirled around my brain like a tornado. If Micah liked antiques, wouldn't other people? If Micah wanted to tour the place, wouldn't other people also pay to take a look? The book I mentioned to her earlier could be in a gift shop at the end of the tour, and recipe cards could be purchased for authentic meals initially prepared in the house. There was no limit to what I could do with this gift, and Micah was the catalyst to get me fired up.

"I would be delighted to have you over. Would next Thursday work for you?" She turned and ran for her purse, pulling out a tiny paper calendar.

"It's a date!"

It was too late in the day to look through the sewing store, though I managed the warehouse and grocery stores. By the time I got home, the sun was low in the sky, and two eggs were nestled in my crocs on the side porch—dear sweet Amy. I'd have to build her a proper nest. If she kept delivering eggs, I'd put on those few pounds I'd been hoping for. I was tired of having a body like a boy.

I sat down in the front parlor, the proper name as disclosed in the annals of the Farnsworth Estate, to tidy up my to-do list for tomorrow. It appeared that my plan of zipping through all these tasks was naive. Research took time. Lots of time, including appealing to people's sense of kindness to find what I was looking for. It was exhausting. Tomorrow, I decided to do some gardening, build Amy's nest, and watch YouTube videos on recommended cooking channels. This home could produce so many income streams if I could stay focused, getting even one of them going.

My phone buzzed with a familiar number, and I smiled, remembering his kindness.

"Hello, Mr. Brickner, to what do I owe the honor of your call?" I giggled at my formality.

He chuckled back. "You're still alive and doing well, I hope. I needed to hear your voice to determine whether you were distressed or thriving."

"You're the best. Thank you for keeping me on your radar. I'm doing well—most of the time. I won't lie, this is a lot to manage, but I'm giving it my best shot."

"I knew you would. Establishing a household for anyone, Abigail, is a huge undertaking. The fact that you made it this far is commendable. Keep baby-stepping through this, and all will work out."

His sincerity in his pep talk was so uplifting that I believed I could conquer this giant task. My only hesitation was if I could keep my insecurities at bay.

"Thank you so much for your support, Mr. Brickner. You're my guardian angel. I appreciate you calling."

"My pleasure. I'll call again soon. Remember, you can always reach me at this number."

The wind picked up as I stared out the windows. The willows swished elegantly like hulu girls, and I prayed that my mind would work in that fashion one day: fluid, graceful, and unpanicked. Being kind to myself, I took a moment to pat myself on the back. I had survived four days. Not only did I survive, but I thrived moving this monumental project forward. Maybe there was hope for me? Time will tell.

A sudden jerk woke me up, and I gasped. What the hell? Oh. I must have fallen asleep. The house was pitch black with no moon to guide me, so I used the couch to find my way to what I thought was a clear path, but I smashed my shin on a rather pointy table instead. *Crap! That's going to leave a mark.* I pawed the table to find the lamp I remembered was there and twisted the dial. Happily, it worked, and I didn't have to find the first aid kit to fix more bumps and bruises. After turning the foyer lights on, I turned off the end table lamp, chastising the table profusely.

"Bad table!" I yelled, shaking my finger at it. "Don't do that again!" Trust me when I tell you I didn't wait for a reply. *It's a table, for God's sake.*

I admired the original pastoral mural painting along the curved staircase. If my eyes weren't so blurry, I'd appreciate it more. I might take my coffee break tomorrow on the stairs, enjoying the details. It wasn't especially elaborate, but it was simpler compared to other pastorals I'd seen in my humanities class in high school. It was intriguing, though, I could make some notes to include in my brochure when I got around to making one.

My bed called me, and I obliged. Since I arrived, each day has been jam-packed with activity. At the end of each day, the blessing had been falling into Elias's arms, followed by greedy kisses and snuggling—well, mostly. Last night was hard without him, and tonight wouldn't be any easier. When he stroked my arms, stress released instantly, and my brain calmed. I wondered what he was thinking right now.

"Sweet dreams, Elias." I texted, not being able to hold back. Was I being too needy? Second-guessing myself was as natural as breathing to me. Perhaps he liked needy women? Maybe he got off on it? I could get off on him easily.

Moments passed, and the response dots began, stopped, and started again. I knew that hesitation. "Don't say anything stupid." Or worse, lewd.

Then the sweetest message in the whole wide world came, "Only if I'm thinking about you." *Swoon! See, I wasn't kidding.*

"Aren't you the sweetest? As it is, I am thinking about you. I can't decide if trying to start the car or the tractor would be better tomorrow morning?" I loved to bait him.

"NEITHER!" came the following text. "Step away from the vehicles, Abigail. I mean it. I'll get to them this weekend," followed by an angry face emoji.

I jumped up and down and danced around the room. Elias was coming back like he promised. Wahoo!

"Yes, sir. That's a hard no to touching the vehicles. Got it."

"Behave yourself, Abigail."

"Or what???" I knew, but the rush of warmth between my legs egged me on.

"LOL. Oh, princess, you are in trouble." The GIF he sent was a hunky guy waving his finger at the camera.

"#Promise /#Notpromisetobegood." Sent with a GIF from a *Schitt's Creek* episode. I hope he gets the reference. I loved that show.

"'What you did was impulsive, capricious, and melodramatic...'" *Laughing smiley face.* I guess he did watch that show.

"Haha. You get me! Good night, handsome." I was horny as hell after that conversation.

"Good night, princess."

I reached over and plugged in my phone, feeling too turned on to fall asleep. The nap I took earlier didn't make sleep easier. I knew a good way to relax and had no shame using both hands to massage my small breasts. I envisioned his face, as I squeezed my tits tightly, wishing they were his. My right hand slid down my narrow body and slipped inside my moist panties. I pressed small circles around my clit igniting my desire, and, moments later, Elias' name whimpered off my lips as I came. A wash of calm and sleep passed through my body, my mind wandering to new possibilities. I wished there a way to find out if we had a past life together. We must have because there is no other way our attraction could be so strong.

Chapter 16

Planting Seeds

ELIAS

It was Friday morning, and my mechanic, Paul, was under a 1972 faded red Chevy Camaro. The suspension was shot, and the owner was hell-bent on fixing his "baby" for a car show in a few weeks. Paul slid out from under the car, and I handed him a pickle fork to release the suspension ball joints before I headed out for the day.

"It's all yours, big guy. Call me if you run into any trouble. I'm heading to Reilly's farm for the day. I'll be back around dinnertime to check your work," I jibed. Paul didn't need his work checked. He was the best in the suspension business, and I was lucky to have him. However, my experience as an engineer has taught me to have more than one set of eyes on a project, verifying nothing was overlooked. No lives were going to be in peril on my watch.

I reviewed my text conversation with Abigail last night. That girl set me off like a rocket. It's too bad I promised my time to Reilly today, or I'd be in Mystic, sinking into unfinished business by nightfall. My breathing became short, thinking of how close we were to consummating our new friendship. Her silky hair and dazed look when she looked at me made my cock swell. Last night was too much. I had so many images in my mind of that rare beauty that when I grabbed my engorged shaft, I jacked off in less than a minute.

Several minutes passed as I conjured up more images of Abigail. It was time to snap myself out of it. I felt like a teenager riled up by the remote possibility of being with a girl. Sadly, few girls had the patience for a dorky, tongue-tied giant. I was more than muscles.

The short drive to my friend's farm provided ample time to call in a grocery order at the grocery store in Mystic. I'd pick up some supplies and not waste our precious time together. Last night, I ordered extra tools to keep around her house so I wouldn't have to transport my whole garage to fix her car: a few jacks, a ratchet set, oil, some tarps, and other necessities. I'd bring my extra air compressor before I drove down this evening and by the end of the weekend, she'd have a safe, reliable car. My penchant for efficiency would be coming in handy on these trips.

I arrived at my destination and quickly messaged to Abigail that she should expect some packages today and to put them in the barn. She'd probably think they were bombs otherwise. I chuckled at that.

Reilly walked out of his house holding a chipped coffee mug. "What's up, loser?" This was one of the main reasons he was my best friend—humor.

"Loser? You're the one with a broken cup, a broken fence, and a broken nose if you don't knock it off." I brought my hands to my chest, mocking a fistfight.

"Are you threatening me?" He feigned shock, his hand to his chest.

"I'm no more of a threat to you than Abigail's chicken." I gave him the finger in warning.

He turned and walked away, waving a hand in the air. "I don't know what the fuck you're talking about, and don't bother telling me. Let's get to work."

A previous client of mine paid me in part for an old golf cart that I had gifted to Reilly when he bought his farm. It made it much easier to move around the property for jobs like ours today. Beyond being economical, it gave us a reason to build a putting green, *okay, not so green,* at the back end of his property. I can't even begin to tell you the depths of emotion we spilled out there with no one to hear or judge us. We were brothers in so many ways. Leaving this guy would be a hardship for me if things worked out with Abigail. I'd have a lot to process if I began a life with Abigail.

"Elias!" he yelled, smacking me in the bicep. "You're doing that thing again. Do you want to putt first or work first?"

Sometimes, I wish I wasn't so transparent. My mind takes a little vacation, and, poof, my face goes to stone. Reilly didn't care, but he knew that I tuned out everything when I was deep in thought. The only time that had been a problem was when we tried smoking cigars in college. My mind drifted, and my cigar fell onto the couch, and it caught on fire. I was oblivious to the whole thing until the smoke detector went off. That was the first and last time I used flammable items indoors.

I scrubbed my face, refocusing my attention, and muttered, "Work."

We traversed his forty acres for several hours, checking all the fences, measuring and replacing rotted wood, rewiring fences, and even restoring his chicken coop. By mid-day, we made some sandwiches, grabbed a six-pack of beer and putters, and headed to the back forty to relax.

"So, what did you mean about Abigail's chicken? And don't think you're leaving here without telling me about this new love interest of yours. You've been alone too long to know this girl has put a spell on you." He nudged my shoulder and winked at me.

Where to begin? I had already told him I was helping a stranded customer last week and couldn't come over to bale hay. He didn't think anything of it, and I sure as hell didn't know what would transpire from that ride. There was a lot to unpack, so I bullet-pointed the highlights, hoping that would be sufficient.

"The girl I told you about, Abigail, inherited a large property in Connecticut and was freaked out about how she could manage the place. It was getting late by the time she got her deed and the keys. She begged me to stay after seeing a mouse; frankly, I was too tired to drive the four-plus hours back home anyway. I helped her with a few mechanical things and made sure the house was safe to live in, and then . . ."

I paused, remembering the details. "And, then, she hugged me. I hadn't been hugged in years, and it felt good, so I hugged her back, and that led to kissing, and then . . ."

How much detail did I have to relay? "She, uh, and I, uh . . ." I scratched my head, stalling.

"Tell me you didn't fuck her?" Reilly barked, horrified.

"No!" I barked back. "But I wanted to. Almost did. Twice. She wanted to, but . . .

"But what?" He moved in closer.

"Fucking mice infestation," I said, scrunching up my face.

"Seriously? That wouldn't have stopped me."

"Shut the fuck up. That goddamned vermin ran across her pillow while I was getting busy."

"Whoa. Yeah, well, maybe that would have stopped me. Gross." He shivered.

"So, no hot sex for you. Poor Elias. High and dry." He bent over laughing.

"STFU, asshole. It was painful. Abigail is special. I want to see where this relationship leads. I've never met anyone like her. If you're nice, I'll let you meet her soon." I smiled, imagining that meeting.

"You shut the fuck up. You damn well better let me meet her. After your last love disaster, you need a quality control inspector, and I'm your guy." He pointed a thumb at his chest with a shit-eating grin.

"You're hired, but this girl is a no-brainer for me. She's funny and quirky. She is smart and creative, and she doesn't play mind games. The downside is that she is impulsive and possibly unreliable, but the jury is out on that one. I like that she is direct and doesn't hold back on her opinions. I feel comfortable knowing she believes in me and isn't put off by my inability to use the right words in certain situations. I think she likes me for me." My chest expanded, and I felt a rush of warmth all over my body. This feeling was so foreign that I was stunned by its impact.

"Geezus, Elias. You're in love with her, aren't you?" Reilly's expression mirrored my own.

"If this is what love feels like, then maybe I am." The rumble in my throat felt funny. We both sat silent in this moment, digesting what this new paradigm could mean for our friendship. "Let's give it some time, hey?"

"You bet, buddy. I've got you. But, Elias, if she's the one, don't let anything stop you, even me." He extended his fist for me to bump, and we gathered up our mess and headed back to the house. I needed this time to talk through my feelings. Reilly was a great friend, and I trusted his opinions. I was relieved he didn't balk at how quickly my relationship with Abigail moved. Destiny was destiny. It made life more exciting that way.

The roughly four hours of travel time provided an opportunity to check in with my parents. I'll admit that I haven't been as diligent as I should have in keeping in contact, but they could pick up the phone, too. It wasn't a question of love. I did love my parents and did whatever it took to keep them safe. However, the desire to connect deeply has long been put to rest. They didn't have cell phones, "Why would I want people to call me at all hours of the night?" My father would intone, and the answering machine had been dead for a long time. The "ridiculous" idea that I would need to contact them in an emergency was "insignificant." No wonder I had trouble voicing my feelings.

"Hello," my mother timidly answered the phone. Always the submissive, she let my father make all the decisions in her life. I'm surprised he allowed her to answer the phone.

"Hello, Mother. How are you?" Slang wasn't a language in my home. We spoke slowly and clearly so there were no misunderstandings. My friends thought I had a pole up my ass since I couldn't shut that behavior down when I left the house.

"Elias, is that you?" *No, Mother, it's the other son you don't have.* I didn't say I didn't learn sarcasm in college. I'm pretty good at it if I say so myself.

"Yes, it is. I haven't spoken to you or Dad in quite some time and thought I'd check in to see how you are doing?"

She cleared her throat. "Oh, why, yes, we are doing well. Dad sprained his hand changing a light bulb last week, but it's healing nicely," she said, unaffected.

"How did Dad sprain his hand changing a light bulb?" I held my annoyance at bay for her benefit.

"It was the stepstool's fault. It moved while your father was on it, and he broke his fall using his hand." Again, completely unaffected.

"What!" I was affected. "How did it move? Was it on level ground? Did he turn around on it, and his weight shifted it?" My parents were well into their late seventies, having had me in their forties. They shouldn't be on stairs anymore just for this reason. "If you need stuff done around the house, I'm happy to come out occasionally to help or hire a handyman," I admonished her.

"I wouldn't dream of imposing on you that way. Hiring people costs too much, and your father can still handle most things around the house. Our new neighbor helps us with the snow, and Mrs. Fielding comes down the street when I need her. We're fine here."

Why did I feel so impotent with my parents? They had an answer for everything except for common sense. "Aren't you and Dad getting a bit old to be climbing ladders?"

The gasp she expelled was one I knew well. I was in trouble. "If this is why you called, I will hang up. You need to respect your elders and offer support, not condemnation." She sounded like a Sunday morning sermon. *Fine.*

"My apologies, Mother. I was only concerned about your well-being. How is your health?" Scraping together my sweetest-concerned-son's tone, I continued, "I hope well."

"I have no complaints, not that I'd share them if I did." *So stubborn.*

"I hope they are minor if you did have something going on. Is Dad home?" I was done with this conversation, though moving on to one with my father wouldn't be any better.

"Unfortunately, you just missed him. It's Bridge night at the VFW, and he won't be home for hours. I'll tell him you rang."

"Thanks, Mom. Be well." I tried for compassion, but my mouth felt dry as sandpaper.

"Goodbye, Elias." The incredible loneliness after that call left me numb. There were no I miss yous, or thanks for calling. God forbid asking about my welfare or if I needed something. When I turned eighteen, I was handed a white envelope with five hundred dollars and the title to the car they provided. It was inferred not to ask for anything else unless I was destitute or dying. I was neither—just a desperate-for-validation son.

I continued driving in silence, stewing in sadness about how different my life would have been had my parents shown any emotional support. Hoping for a different outcome was the very definition of insanity, so I put a cork in this downward spiral and shoved those feelings down to my toes. I was on my way to an emotional hurricane and couldn't have been more excited.

My grocery order was ready when I arrived, and I added a few bottles of wine as an afterthought. I'd drink bourbon straight from the bottle if I thought Abigail wouldn't bluster. I didn't drink often, but when I did, my keys were taken away, and I was directed to a toilet post haste. I didn't expect anyone to lift me off the floor, so binging on the couch was the only place I knew I'd be safe and not a burden. As an adult, I've put my fall-down-drunk days behind me—at least, I hoped so.

When I pulled into Abigail's driveway, I shut off my headlights and killed the engine, engaging in a stealthy surprise. Then, from my truck, I called her cell and waited for her answer.

"Elias! Are you still coming? I made dinner." I loved the genuine excitement.

"I'm still coming, though I'm going to be later than planned. Go ahead and eat without me. I'll call again when I get close." I could hear her voice deflate through the phone.

"Uh, okay. Drive carefully, okay?" She tried her best to put up a good front.

"See you soon, princess."

I waited ten minutes, hoping she would stay in the kitchen while I walked around to the front door. I pushed the bell and prepared myself for whatever reaction she might have had.

Moments later, she flung open the door and dropped her fork on the floor. "ELIAS!"

The way her face morphed from shock to delight to annoyance was priceless. "You are such an ass! You tricked me!"

That didn't stop her from launching her petite body onto my chest. She climbed up my legs to my hips to rest her head on my shoulder like a toddler needing protection. Tingles ran up and down my spine, receiving her unadulterated joy. All this excitement should happen when people don't see each other for a while.

A tightness grew in my groin that needed addressing soon, and I didn't care if a damn elephant ran across our bed tonight; I was claiming this woman once and for all.

Chapter 17
Staking My Claim

ABIGAIL

Shock sizzled through my body as I looked at my man standing on my porch. Waves of relief and anticipation launched me onto his body, climbing up to embrace every inch of his being. He dropped two bags of groceries to wrap both arms tightly around my back, hushing me softly, "It's okay. I'm here now."

His eyes sparkled as they looked into mine, mischievous and appreciative. I imprinted this expression into my brain to never forget it. It spoke volumes about how he felt about me. He wanted me, and I desperately wanted him. The way his hands massaged my middle back, sliding down to hold me by my ass cheeks, felt erotic and made me blush.

"Could we eat before you devour me with your eyes again?" I'm just saying—a girl has to have energy for sexual endeavors.

"Is that what I was doing?" His devilish smile and powerful hands said it all.

I pressed a soft, barely opened kiss to his full lips. "Uh-huh," and kissed him again, delving deeply into his smooth, pillowy lips. He squeezed my ass cheeks again as he slowly released me to the floor.

"Nothing is going to distract me tonight, Abigail. No mice, no nothing. Do you understand me?" I nodded compliantly. "Good. Let's eat quickly and get settled upstairs. I'm locking this place down now."

Elias was true to his word. After a quick rundown of the week and enjoying a delicious flank steak stew I found on a cooking channel, he gave me a two-minute head start up the stairs. I dashed to my bedroom, brushed my teeth, removed the acid taste from the tomatoes in the stew, and washed off the day's sweat with a washcloth. I wasn't savvy with sexual preferences, but I knew B.O. wasn't a turn-on for most.

He was shirtless as he stalked into the bedroom. Raw and full of swagger, he ran across the room, picked me up, and tossed me on the bed. He was severe, and I quivered with anticipation.

"Should I be afraid, Elias? You still look like you're starving." A nervous laugh erupted from my throat. I pushed farther up the bed, praying I wasn't in over my head.

"I haven't been able to look at or touch you all week. Of course, I'm hungry." And, with that, he plucked the button at the top of his jeans and dropped his pants and boxer briefs to the floor. His cock bobbed and twitched, making my mouth salivate. It was huge, throbbing, and veiny.

"Any final words before we consummate this friendship?" He waggled his eyebrows and clutched his dick. My brain exploded with so many questions; sadly, I could not articulate any of them.

"Be gentle," I said, whispering. His eyes shot up, concerned.

"But you said you'd had sex before," he said, dropping his cock and blanching.

"I have, but, like I said, it was bad sex. You a-are such a big man, and I-I'm so small. And . . ." I hope I won't have a panic attack. Wouldn't that be my luck? He'd think I was a freak and too much trouble, and . . .

His hands extended to my face, presumably assessing if I was worth the trouble. "Breathe, Abigail. You'll be fine. I promise not to hurt you. Talk to me. Let me know what you're feeling. If I'm doing anything that hurts you, then tell me. Please tell me if you'd like me to try a different way of doing anything I try. We're learning each other's likes and dislikes. It's part of the coming-together process."

He leaned in, searing my lips with his. I completely understood that kiss. It translated easily to, "I still want you." My heart soared at his tenacity to listen and encourage without annoyance. Elias never stopped impressing me.

Elias took my left hand and wrapped it around the root of his cock. "Hold me like this, sweetheart. Tighten your grip as much as you like." I did as he instructed. "Yes. Again." His eyes never left my face when he reached for my right hand. His instructions were explicit, and my clit throbbed, knowing I was pleasing him.

My hands stroked his massive, veiny staff. I found it fascinating both aesthetically and functionally. The velvety tip oozed liquid, and I leaned forward instinctively to taste it.

"Damn, Abigail. Yes! Keep doing that. Put the whole thing in your mouth." *The whole thing? Not possible.*

I flicked my tongue along his slit, enjoying the sound he made when I popped off the top. I felt powerful. I managed to fit the crown of his red, pulsing cock into my mouth and moaned at how erotic this was. He gasped in appreciation. I was bringing him closer with every lick, pump, and flick. I flattened my tongue and took a long, wet pull from the underside of his shaft, exploring every sound I could get out of him.

"Fucking Christ, Abigail. You're incredible. I-I'm almost there." He had his hands on my shoulders, stabilizing me so I could use both my hands equally. I increased my efforts, and he panted my name as he exploded on my tongue, neck, and chest. "Aabby! Fuckin'-A. I don't think I've ever come that hard in my life."

His chest heaved for several moments, regaining his composure. I looked him directly in the eyes as I pushed his come down my neck and onto my breasts. I felt so alive, dirty, and powerful. I did this to him. My hands. My mouth. He smiled from ear to ear, watching me play with his fluids on my tits like I was finger painting.

I looked up again as I licked my fingers. "It's sticky."

He burst out laughing.

"Yes, it is. Do you like it?" My fingers were still in my mouth when he asked, so I nodded my agreement. "Should we do that again?"

More nods. The guttural moan slipping from his throat was intoxicating and heady. That was my new favorite sound.

He propped me up on the pillows and kissed me deeply. "You taste like me, and now I'm going to make you scream my name so loud your neighbors down the street will hear you." True to his word, he drove me wild with pleasure concluding with a pinch to my clit and two fingers that reached so far into me I thought I could see his fingers moving inside me.

"I'm almost there. Elias, don't stop." He curved his fingers so that I bucked up and came hard onto his fingers. "Eeeliaass! Yesss!"

Bursts of shiny sparkles lit up behind my eyes, and I thought I died. Being with him this way was an experience that brought tears to my eyes. I sniffled, and my chest convulsed at the enormity of my emotions. It felt like a dozen locks opened inside me, releasing dead, gritty stuff trapped around my soul. I was lighter physically, emotionally, and spiritually. Is it possible Elias felt this way, too?

"Abigail?" he said, touching my jaw and rubbing the tears from my face. "Did I hurt you?" Elias was always so thoughtful.

I rubbed my eyes, grimacing at how stupid I felt. "No. You didn't hurt me, Elias. You exorcized me."

We erupted into contagious laughter. The mood shifted as our connection deepened.

Elias tucked me into his side, rubbing circles on my arm. "I shouldn't be saying this so soon in our relationship, but you feel like home to me. Safe. Nonjudgmental. Appreciative." The air went still. What else would he confess to me?

I used my free arm to rub circles over the divot in the center of his chest. The swell of his pecs increased in the hollow, and I could tell he was struggling with his emotions. I had so many myself that I couldn't articulate well enough to share them. There was one, however, I knew deep down was true.

I rolled over onto his powerful chest and tapped his chin. "I feel the same way, too." His eyes crinkled, and his nostrils flared. The bulge between us grew again, and my eyes widened.

"Let me show you how much you mean to me."

He flipped me to my back and attacked my mouth like it was his last meal. I could barely breathe as he twisted his tongue in and out while he kneaded my breasts ruthlessly. Elias had always been strong, though not unleashed like he was now. The sheer power of his hands was incredible, and he could tear me to pieces with those paws. He pushed me deeper into the pillows, nipping my neck as he went. Every suck was a brand leaving no doubt I was his.

He explored my body like Lewis and Clark explored our new country. He staked his claim on me, and I was his to own. His iron fingers wove their way across my hips and stomach and morphed into feathers when he reached my dripping pussy. I was ready for him, and I made sure he knew it.

"Now, Elias! I want you now." I arched off the bed, bucking up when he inserted one, then two fingers into my depths.

"It's not too late to stop, Abigail. I can wait."

I sat up immediately. "Shut the fuck up! Get your cock in me now before I duct tape you to this bed and ride your cock until it explodes."

I'm not sure who the hell said that, but that bitch was spot on. I never knew I was that sexually deviant before. It bordered on kink, and I rather liked her. Given the way Elias responded, I believe he liked her, too.

"Yes, ma'am." He pushed my knees wide and high. "Keep them there. Take a deep breath and exhale slowly when I tell you. Got it?"

"Yes, sir."

He moaned deeply at my reply and lined up his throbbing cock to my entrance. He nudged the head, watching my face carefully and looking for signs of distress. *None here.*

He inserted two fingers again, pulling out my fluids and rubbing them onto his cock. Low, sinful grunts erupted from his throat, communicating his bliss. He wasn't alone in that feeling as he penetrated my pussy. His mouth went slack, and my eyes fluttered shut as I adjusted to his size.

"Exhale, Abigail. Slowly," he demanded, and I did exactly as he instructed. The immense pressure of his intrusion stretched so completely that I feared I would never walk again. I panted over and over again, trying to relax and enjoy the sensations. He pushed harder into my tight pussy, and after several tortuous pumps, I took him down to his hilt. "Fuck, Abby. You're so tight. I could stay here forever."

His confessions of pleasure caused me to clench around his shaft, eliciting a cry worthy of a warrior going to battle.

"I'm not going to last if you do that again."

From the voice of my new alter-ego came a resounding, "Fuck me harder!"

Elias was compliant, if not thorough. He drilled his hips into mine, grasping my hips so tightly that I whimpered. Sweat covered his brow as he plowed into me. I knew my pussy would never want another man's dick ever again.

He shifted me into a new angle, and my head rocketed to another universe.

"Yes! Yes! There! Yes, there! I'm going to come. Ahh. "Blood-curdling screams ripped from my throat. I clenched again, and he bellowed my name.

"Ab-by! Fuck, I'm coming, too. You're killing me." His hands left my hips and moved to my knees, changing the angle of my pelvis again.

"Dear God!" I screamed even louder than before. He hit a spot I never knew existed. My mind went blank, and I lost the ability to speak. The same stardust I experienced earlier returned with more tears of joy. I was the luckiest girl in the world to have a man who knew what he was doing. Never before had I experienced sex like this. I'd never been with a man like Elias, either.

He released my legs carefully, allowing me to stretch out completely. I brushed the dampness from his brow and tenderly kissed his swollen lips. I was falling for him, and it made me shiver. Imagining more experiences like this was a dream come true. I draped myself over his chest and fused our foreheads to read his mind and feel his feelings. Our hearts thumped together, filling me with hope that we would beat the odds and find a future together. Every moment we spent was valuable and meaningful in the short time we knew each other. I've read about star-crossed lovers or arranged marriages; those couplings were as far out as ours, and many of them worked out. Why couldn't ours? My heart ached all week without him, and look what happened once we were back together. It was lightning on a summer's night—bright, electric, and terrifying. It was everything I'd hoped love would be, especially for me.

"I can hear you thinking. Tell me." He whispered into my hair, threading his fingers through the strands.

Feeling undeserving, I couldn't look him in the eyes. I kept my cheek firmly attached to his lightly hairy chest. "Are we meant to be together? And how will we know?"

I couldn't say it more straightforward than that. I wish I knew about relationships, adulting, and, well, everything. I wasn't naive. I learned relationships took a lot of work, but I didn't have a good example to follow. My mother was dead, my father was nonexistent, and my aunt didn't exactly exude warmth and inclusion. I was free falling and scared shitless.

He rolled me to my back again, straddling my hips. I was literally stripped bare with no defenses, left to feel exposed and vulnerable. Our eyes locked onto one another, and we interlocked our hands. Seeing how tiny my hands were against his was funny, yet somehow they fit. We pushed and pulled our arms forward and back, and he surprised me by jerking backward. I was thrown off guard, and being the sassy woman I am, I yanked his arms toward me.

"Just like this, princess. We'll flow until we don't, and then we will right ourselves when we are off-center. As long as we have trust and humor, we'll find a way. I promise."

Chapter 18
Getting Into the Weeds

ELIAS

"Where did you put the tape measure? I'm heading out to the barn to work today."

I announced my intention like we'd been married for years. I needed to remember this was her house, not mine. "Does that work for you, Abigail?" I said amending tone of voice.

Abigail had been up since dawn watching online shows about *Best Bed & Breakfast Meals That Keep Them Coming Back.* Compliments of Amy, her pet chicken, fresh eggs were deposited into the new-and-improved nest made from an old basket and straw. Amy the Great provided our breakfast and would be a great asset to Abigail's new business, especially if Abigail agreed to another chicken as a companion for Amy, thus producing more eggs. I approved of Amy one hundred percent until she began bawking in the morning. One slip and that bird was dinner. I'm not a fan of being jarred awake. Besides, didn't a rooster own that job?

Abigail slipped off her earbuds and looked over to me. "What?" she deadpanned.

Oblivious to my request, I did a one-eighty turn and tried again. "Tape measure. Barn. Going now. You coming?" For effect, I raised my eyebrows and pressed my lips together, waiting for a response.

"Ooh! Are we going to fix my car? Why do you need a tape measure?" She genuinely had no idea what the tape measure was for. From her perspective, I suppose she had no idea what my plans were for that space. Of course, she was confused. I'd been planning and positioning equipment in my head for the past week. The tricky part was knowing what kind of work area she'd enjoy.

She walked to the last drawer in the center island, reached in, and pulled out the tape measure. "Here you go," she said casually.

I walked past her and grabbed her hand. "Come on, let's get that clunker running," I said.

We worked together, unloading my tools from my truck and carting them down the path to the barn. From the back of the house, you could barely see the corner of the structure, although the weathervane at the top was clear as day. I suppose that would be helpful from the kitchen window to know what the winds looked like.

My plan included a thorough lube, oil, and filter. Then, a coolant flush. I'd top off all the fluids and then crank the ignition. This car would start without more work if I addressed all the basics. That was wishful thinking. I had no idea how long this car had been sitting in the barn. After my initial inspection, my suspicions were correct. She'd need a new fan belt, brakes, rust removed from the brake pad rotors, and, if all went well, this piece of shit would sing like a star. It took a little ingenuity, but I found a parts supplier with everything I needed to make this 2005 Buick Skylark renovation happen as soon as next week. Abigail texted me that a giant box arrived yesterday and was delivered to the barn as requested. I unpacked my tools, unloaded my air compressor from my truck, and got to work on the L.O.F.

In the process of my work, today became Abigail's first course in car maintenance and restoration. I explained how to drain the oil, and she learned that not having the pan placed directly under the drain plug would douse her in oil.

"What the fuck, Elias!" It was like a comedy skit watching her mouth gaping in astonishment and then rolling around on the floor, thinking she was on fire.

Her second lesson was how to replace a battery. After her insistence on changing the oil herself, I put my foot down on her handling the battery on her own. I couldn't take the chance of her killing herself.

"There is an order to disconnect and reconnect a battery," I lectured. "The proper sequence could mean life or death." I pursed my lips and nodded, insinuating I was the master of this process. *(Except I was. I had a degree to prove it.)* "Put your hands over mine and say the order of the removal process."

"Left, then right."

"Good. Now lift the battery out." Okay, she toppled over like a teapot, trying to lift it from its cradle. *My bad.*

"Aahh!" Her legs flipped in the air, and I grabbed her hips just in time for her to stamp a strip of oil across her forehead and cheek. I swallowed hard. Seeing my girl covered in motor oil and grease was a huge fucking turn-on. I'm such a gearhead.

"Sorry about that, princess. I forgot to tell you how heavy that thing is." I reached into my back pocket, pulled out my phone, and snapped a picture of her messy face. Satisfied, I used the rag to clean off the oil, hoping she wouldn't punch me in the nose.

"Are you okay?"

She grabbed me by my flannel shirt and pulled me to her lips. I didn't move until I felt the soft, wet tip of her tongue press between my lips. Her exhale sparked a flame deep in my groin, and I gathered her ass in my hands, carried her around to the trunk of the car, and set her down gently.

"You better not post that picture on social media, or your nuts will hang from my rearview mirror," she threatened. I crossed my heart and used my fingers to make a scout's honor sign, pressing her back to the hood for another kiss.

"This is not part of today's itinerary, Abigail." I choked out between kisses.

"You need to be flexible, Professor. Things pop up. You have to deal with them." She licked my neck to my ear, whispering, "Your student needs special care only you can provide."

I groaned. "Fuck, Abby. If you want special treatment, you've got it. Don't tell your friends that your teacher is a pervert."

"Pervert, Elias?" She pulled back, confused.

I cleared my throat and shook my head—*stupid words. Always getting in the way.* "Let me rephrase, horny as fuck was what I meant to say." Her eyes widened, and her wicked smile was the green light I was waiting for.

I pulled out my wallet with a fresh condom, waggling my brows that I was prepared this time, and yanked my pants down to my ankles. While she pushed her sweats off, I was busily sheathing myself, and, by the time I was finished, her legs were wide open.

I froze, taking in the gorgeous display from her face to her pussy. What I wouldn't do to take a picture of that.

"Take me, Elias." Like a starter's gun firing, I mounted her with one purpose in mind: ecstasy.

I felt like a damn caveman grunting and rutting against her wanton pussy. She tore at my hair and encouraged me not to stop. *Trust me, I had no intention of stopping.*

"You're so fucking big! I love it!" Her pleasure was the only thing on my mind. I basked in her ability to trust me, letting me do with her what I wanted. And, fuck, I wanted to do everything with her.

The stretch my cock made on her pussy lips was sinful. My eyes rolled into my head, relishing the slippery glide of our union. Every sound heightened my desire, and, before I knew it, I was ready to blow.

"Are you there?" I implored her.

"Yes! Yes, now!" she cried.

I pushed her legs to her shoulders and drove my cock even deeper. Our voices echoed off the walls as we came together, panting with pleasure.

"Fuuuck!" My release almost brought me to my knees, it was so perfect. This woman was going to kill me, and I'd die willingly, knowing it was her who did it.

Moments passed, and I rolled off her. Both of us stared at the rafters, giggling together. Me, a grown-ass man. Giggling made me laugh even harder. I couldn't tell you why Abigail was laughing, but acting like a couple of teenagers fucking on a car in a barn in the middle of the day sure had me grinning ear to ear.

I helped Abigail to a seated position, and every time our eyes connected, we laughed again.

She pushed her hair back behind her ears, rolling her lips into her mouth.

"I think I should re-enroll in this class again just to be sure I caught all the nuances of car maintenance. I rather enjoyed the final exam." She extended her neck forward and dropped her face into her hands, chortling. She was adorable.

I arranged myself back into my pants, stepped up to her crumbled form, and pulled her into my chest. I rubbed her back in slow circles, enjoying her humming each time I completed a full turn.

"Yeah, about that. No more lessons for you today, or you'll need to keep that rental."

I rubbed her upper arms and pulled her back to see her mischievous hazel eyes. "Go and find something else to distract yourself with. How about cutting down those overgrown plants in the garden? I'll come out soon and help you figure out what weeds and actual plants are. And don't forget to put your pants on." *I couldn't help myself.* "How about we plant a small tree so you can watch it grow?"

She slid down the trunk and straightened herself out. Her head hung like a petulant child. "I'd rather you plant something else in my garden."

Damn, girl! "Out!" I bellowed. My resolve might have been shrinking when she was around, but my dick was painfully growing in awareness of how naughty this woman could be.

My stomach gurgled angrily. I was so busy working that I didn't realize I hadn't eaten. Walking past the garden, I overheard a conversation I thought I'd never hear.

"You have no idea how lucky you have it, Amy. I honestly have no idea where you came from, and I don't care. You're like Elias, except you lay eggs instead of fixing stuff."

She pulled at some weeds and tossed them into the wheelbarrow—*very clever, princess.* Amy strutted in a circle, displaying her bright yellow plumage.

"You think you're prettier than he is? No offense, girl, but did you see his muscles? How about that mechanical tattoo? It looks like it's real when he moves his elbow. It's so cool. Oh, and those thick, strong thighs? If you saw those babies in action, you'd squirt out a dozen eggs." *Geezus.*

Amy scratched at the dry earth, demonstrating how strong her skinny chicken legs were—at least, that's what I think she was doing. Abigail, bless her soul, kept the conversation going.

"Yes, ATG. Your legs are great, too." She reached to pet that dumb bird, and Amy let her! Did she think she was a dog? Or a cat, for God's sake? The way she rolled her neck against Abigail's hand was exactly how my childhood dog did.

"You better wash your hands when you're done giving your bird a massage." I cracked myself up, and kept walking toward the house.

"Jealous!" Abigail launched at me.

"Bu-gawk!" Amy echoed, and I repeated the annoying sound back.

How the hell did I end up in this chicken coop paradigm?

I quickly made two peanut butter and jelly sandwiches and washed a few apples. After filling my water bottle, I collected my lunch and ate it on my way back to the barn.

"Lunch is on the counter. Don't forget to eat." I don't think she heard me. She ranted about who knows what while Amy continued nodding and flaring her red crown.

I was ready for my first attempt at turning over the engine and prayed that was all it needed. To my dismay, the engine sputtered and died several times before it occurred to me that perhaps I should check the gas tank—empty, of course. Some engineer I am.

I looked around for a gas can, finding one—a little dented but still workable. Now it was a trip to the gas station. Wasting time on this chore made me anxious. Maybe Abigail could go for me. I walked out to where I'd left her and found her sitting alone.

"Did Amy's mom call and ask her to come home?" I cleared my throat, trying not to laugh.

"Ha. Ha. It was her father who called," she deadpanned. "Where are you going?"

She followed me into the house, where I noticed her lunch on the counter. Not on my watch. I felt like an old-world mother forcing food on her guests.

"Go and wash your hands. We're going to the store, and you're eating lunch on the way."

Her eyes shot daggers. "You're not my father. You don't get to tell me what to do." Her hands were firmly placed on her hips as she stuck out her tongue. *Little brat.*

We stared each other down. I wasn't budging, and it looked like she wasn't either.

"You're acting like a child." I pointed a finger at her.

"You're acting like an ass!" She pointed one back.

I grabbed my keys and wallet off the counter and stormed out the side door to my truck. I'd give her a chance to come to her senses; if not, I'd haul her over my shoulder. Didn't she know that she needed to eat? Abigail constantly commented about how she thought she had a boy's body. I, of course, disagreed. However, my opinion didn't matter as much as her assessment of herself—*such a girl thing.*

The passenger door whipped open, and Abigail climbed into the cab. She looked like a stuck pig with an apple in her mouth and a PB&J in her wet hand. She'd get no style points from me, but she complied, and I was happy we could get on our way. It was a short drive to the village center and I let her eat her lunch silently.

She turned abruptly in her seat, and I was perplexed.

"Happy?" she hurled at me.

I paused. "That you've eaten? Yes. That you don't remember to eat? No?" My tone was admonishing on purpose. She needed to take better care of herself. All those years of insufficient food or money weren't an excuse anymore. She could afford those things now and needed to do them regularly.

"Why are you so obsessed with me eating? Does it offend you in some way?" Her accusation was almost on the mark.

I rubbed my forehead, concerned that my next words might send me packing. I pulled into the gas station, turned in my seat, and made it a point to get her attention. She needed to see how earnest I was.

"I did some reading on your condition, ADHD. It's common to forget to eat, take medications, or any number of things. It's more than that, though. You're an adult, Abigail. You have to take responsibility for your good health and well-being. I want that for you and would do anything to help you make that happen. It's just . . ." Here was the hard part. "You have commented about how you look, and I think eating more regularly would remedy that point of view. You're hot, just as you are, but your opinion counts the most. I won't bring it up again. Sorry."

I turned and exited the vehicle. I chanced a look at her when I grabbed the gas can and closed the door. She twisted her fingers in her lap, biting her lips raw. I caught her looking at me through my peripheral vision but didn't acknowledge the glance. At this point, I don't know who I'm more angry with: me or her. Why was I making this my problem? I couldn't care more than she did, right? I let it go. Over and done. Finito.

Topping off my tank and filling the portable gas can, I felt that I needed to repair the damage I had caused. I drove us to the hardware store, hoping Abigail would forgive me.

"Let's pick out some things for your garden. Pots, seeds, gloves, soil." She nodded. I grabbed a cart and headed to the garden section. "Have you thought about what vegetables you'd like to grow? I'm sure those recipes you've been looking at would taste even better with homegrown veggies." I tried to sound encouraging, but she answered without excitement.

"Yeah. I guess. I'll look at the seeds, and you can get whatever else you came here for." *Ouch.*

I was dismissed, and she walked to the round stand with all the seeds on them, twirling them around haphazardly.

I shook my head sadly. I well and truly fucked this day up, I sure knew how to put my foot in my mouth for a guy who hardly says anything to anybody. I found a case of motor oil for both the car and the tractor in case she wanted me around to fix it, a couple of fifty-pound bags of potting soil, gardening gloves for both of us, a bag of kettle corn from the vendor outside, and, when she stepped up to the counter, four packets of seeds.

She still wasn't talking to me, and it was time to clear the air.

"Can I take you for ice cream? I have a hankering for something sweet." I didn't wait for an answer as I held her door open. I dropped the tailgate and haphazardly chucked everything inside, shoving the door back into place with enough force that I may have bruised my shoulder.

"Only if you're buying," she sassed after waiting for me to return. I hoped she was softening up again. I didn't want to spend our time arguing.

The Sugar Shoppe was similar to an old-style ice cream shop, except they sold chicken wings out of the back door. The back wall was filled with giant glass containers filled with candy, and the front counter was lined with various styles of glass sundae cups. The chalkboard menu listed thirty-seven flavors, and two additional boards described concoctions that simultaneously made my mouth salivate while my stomach turned smelling the grease from their kitchen. Who puts savory and sweet in the same store? Yuck!

We made our selections and sat at a table that could be found in a French bistro. We ate silently, though I could sense how loudly Abigail's brain worked. Mine wasn't any different. I had dozens of things I wanted to say and confess, except each could be labeled a minefield. I wanted to trust her to be levelheaded about each one, but that wasn't who she was. Abigail was anything but levelheaded. Her adjectives could best be described as impulsive and sensitive, with a noun thrown in: firecracker! Mine were sensitive, tongue-tied, irreverent. I rather liked the last one, but not everyone gets that.

My stomach tightened, and I put my spoon down. She needed to hear some things, and if I didn't bring these to her attention, then who would?

"Abigail. Give me your hands." I needed to feel our connection and for her to feel the same way. Her eyes shot up, and she slowly put down her ice cream cup and spoon.

I closed my eyes, praying that everything from my mouth was appropriate and kind.

"I don't know where to begin except to say I feel strongly about you. I didn't ask before but would like to do so now. Would you like to date me?" My mind started to fry when her jaw dropped. What was going on in her head?

She squeezed my fingers, and hope rippled through my body.

"No one has ever asked me that before. I'm not stupid, but what does that mean—for us?

I interlaced my fingers through hers, keeping our eye contact strong. "It means that I will come down and visit you every weekend that I can, and we will figure out what our likes and dislikes are together. It means that when you're unhappy with me, or vice versa, we won't run from each other but to each other. It's a commitment, Abigail. An adult, levelheaded decision that consistently puts the other person's priorities at the same level as our own. If we can do that, we might be discussing a more permanent arrangement in the future. Does this answer your question?"

I kissed the back of her right hand, enjoying the steady beating of her increasing pulse.

"So, you'd be my boyfriend, and I'd be your girlfriend . . . a, and we'd only date each other—wouldn't?"

I chuckled. "Yes. Exclusively."

She hummed quietly as her eyes shifted left and right along the pattern on the table. Her leg bounced, and I got nervous. Minutes went by, and nervousness became anxiety. I breathed slowly, preparing to speak when she injected her reply.

"I'm afraid, Elias. I don't think I can handle being rejected again. I like you so much, but I'm afraid you'll get bored with me or think I'm too much work and leave me like everyone else has. I'm broken that way, and it hurts too damn much."

She tried pulling her hands from mine, but I wasn't having it.

"Would it make you feel better knowing I feel the same way? I've been hurt, too, Abigail, especially by my parents, the people who are supposed to stand by my side forever. And—as the woman from my last relationship said—I'm also pretty boring. I feel broken, too, but I don't feel that way with you. You make me feel alive, and you're never boring. Hardly. You challenge me, encourage me, and think I'm some mechanical genius. Of course, I am a genius, but you recognize that in me and aren't insulted when I talk over your head. Okay, that sounded patronizing. Strike that, but you know what I'm saying, right?"

Oh my God, too many words. When have I ever used so many words?

Her leg stopped bouncing, and I felt a verdict coming in.

"Doesn't it wig you out how similar we are? The fact that we found each other in this giant world is astounding. It seems predestined." She put our intertwined hands on her forehead. "I think we should at least try being in a relationship since the universe went to all the trouble." She turned her face to kiss my hand, and a jolt of electricity shot me out of my seat. I let go of her hands in exchange for her body and lifted her into my arms, searing her lips on my own. She agreed to be mine, and we'd work everything else out later. I could feel layers of stale, putrid thinking fall off my body, readying itself for a metamorphosis. I was reborn and overjoyed to start a new adventure with Abigail that went beyond lust and favors. If we did it right, we'd put new roots into this property, making our future a jewel for all to adore.

Chapter 19
Taking the Plunge

ABIGAIL

It's official.

We decided to take the plunge into a relationship. My body vibrated almost to the point of nausea, hoping that I made the right decision. I'm not one of those girls who spent time planning her future with the perfect man. I couldn't afford to do that in any sense of the word. If I had, Elias would be my Superman. His only characteristic that got under my skin was that he was always right about everything, including knowing my body better than I did.

It took Herculean effort not to jump on him all day long. He turned me on like an Energizer Bunny and those batteries are built to last. After the second time I jumped onto his back while he measured out spaces in the barn, he put me in a time-out.

"Put your horny little ass over there, and don't move." I should have been hurt, but I was turned on even more.

Once I understood what the measuring tape was for, I shifted mental gears and began to imagine a future filled with things I was passionate about for the first time in my life. We outlined the floor with blue masking tape and moved junk around to represent where I would put a pottery wheel, paints, and a small kitchenette. Running into the house whenever I was hungry or thirsty was a colossal waste of time.

Elias—being Elias—suggested I invest in insulation and a bathroom so we could work year-round in this space. I would never have even considered that if he hadn't mentioned it. He worked feverishly, making notes and sketching floor plans for us to review later this evening. He made lists of must-haves and wants so I could build out this space at a comfortable rate without putting myself in a financial crisis. That got me thinking.

I sat in my "time-out" chair and sent telepathic messages for him to look at me.

"Why are you over there?" *It only took two minutes.*

"I'm thinking." I wrapped a piece of hay, left over from Amy's nest, around my finger, liking the texture on my hand.

"About what?" he asked, strutting across the barn as if he owned it. *Wait!*

I beamed at his sexy smile. "How would you feel about owning some of this space?"

His head jerked, and his irises blew wide.

I stepped into his space. "Come on. You must have been thinking about using this space for more than fixing my car, right?" I stood, allowing my hands to fall onto his hips.

"You'd do that? Rent me space?" His expression was priceless. My heart fluttered, and I did a little happy dance, shifting side to side.

I nodded several times, not able to control myself. "I do. I mean, I would." *Freudian. Again, psychology videos.*

"How can we have a relationship only on the weekends? What if you opened a repair shop in the barn? Nothing huge, just enough to make your time here worthwhile."

He picked me up, wrapping my legs around his back.

"Let's get one thing straight, princess. Seeing you is always worth the time and energy to travel here. Everything else is gravy." His lips said everything I wanted to hear. "In response to your question, the thought had crossed my mind. You may have noticed that I taped off a large portion of the barn. Tell me you figured that out on your own?"

Did I? I suppose I did, but it didn't sound like that in my brain. It sounded more like blah-blah, I want Elias to stay, blah-blah, he can't leave his business, blah-blah, I want Elias to stay. It wasn't until I opened my mouth that a complete thought emerged.

"Sort of. It's only that I don't want your business to suffer if you're gone too much. You know I can always use your help, and I'm getting used to having you around to talk to. You may have noticed that Amy doesn't communicate so well." I chuckled, playing with the fabric on his flannel shirt.

"I'd like that a lot, princess. We can figure something out that would benefit both of us."

And, from that moment on, we were a team. I'd never been on a team, so I was excited to pick his brain and build another great plan that included this remarkable man.

"Hello?" A man hollered.

"Oh, shit!" I jumped out of his arms, almost falling to my knees, righted myself, and continued running toward the house. "It's cable guy day!"

A white pickup was backing out of the driveway when I waved my arms for him to stop. Seeing me doing a weird dance on the drive was enough for the guy to drive back and get out of his car.

A good-looking guy about my age extended his hand. "Hi. I'm David. I rang your doorbell several times and then yelled for you. I figured you'd forgotten about our appointment."

Out of breath, I panted a cordial reply, "Sorry about that. I forgot that you were coming today. Follow me." I took David on a home tour, pointing out where the existing cable connections were and where I'd like more to be installed. The barn, for example.

I felt David was checking out more than the cable system as we moved from room to room. By the time we got to the barn, his breathing had picked up, and I didn't have a chance to put down his gentle advances. Under the guise of being a good listener, David walked beside me into the barn, a smidge too close for my comfort. Elias took notice and took care of that for me. He can be very intimidating upon first meeting him.

I choked out sweetly, "Elias. Meet David. He's the cable guy. We could install a TV for football games or watch YouTube out here. What do you think?"

He wasted no time sidling up next to me, tucking me under his armpit. "Definitely, sugar."

I snorted. Poor David. He was no match for Elias.

"Why don't you tell David what you want, and I'll start lunch?" I attempted a cool wink, but my eyes cramped. I must have looked like I was having an attack because Elias coughed. I turned quickly and beelined for the house.

Not long after, Elias reappeared with a piece of paper and a frown.

"This guy wants to charge you a thousand dollars in cable boxes and labor. That's ridiculous!"

What did I know? I'd never had to have cable installed. I used my phone for everything and worked too much to need a television, let alone cable.

"I'll have to take your word on that. It does sound like a lot. What if we only install cable boxes in the guest rooms? I want us to have one in the barn, though. It will be our workspace, and we should be happy out there. Right?"

He pulled at his beard. That was his thinking posture. It was cute and telling. "You make a good point. We can upgrade whenever you want. I told him you'd call him tomorrow to schedule the approved work. Order us YouTube TV. We can get everything we want from that."

See? This is why I love this guy. He's skeptical yet reasonable, frugal yet accommodating. We're going to work out. I know we will.

I handed him a grilled cheese sandwich with a jar of pickles. "Thanks for helping me with that decision. I'd be broke without your help."

"David would have been in your pants if I wasn't here. Come to think of it, you'd have gotten free labor for life if he had his way."

We both burst out laughing; he wasn't wrong.

Elias spent the rest of the afternoon on the phone with his service station manager, Paul, working out this new arrangement. I spent the rest of the afternoon searching the web for B&Bs within one hundred miles of my home. I wanted to offer competitive amenities and an experience different from most B&Bs.

I let Elias know I was leaving for a while and went to the closest drug store for note cards, markers, and Elias's favorite candy. My next stop was at the hardware store to get a corkboard to pin up my ideas. My plan was going to be epic! A *master storyboard* for my future. Elias was going to love this. I made one last stop at the grocery store and returned home with my arms full of bags.

When Elias entered the house, I had already started a homemade spaghetti sauce and was washing a head of lettuce. The dining room table was filled with color-coded ideas broken down into categories: house, barn, gardens, and customer experiences.

"Whoa! What do we have here? Look who's been a busy beaver this afternoon." I could have taken his tone as patronizing, except I was too damn proud of what I accomplished in a few short hours. If I was industrious, he should praise me.

I made a beaver face and chomped my mouth. "Tis I," I replied with a bow. "I have so much to show you after dinner."

He kissed me quickly and walked toward the sink to wash up. "Then let's eat. I'm starving."

"Do you want to share your notes first, or should I?" I shifted from foot to foot, energized wanting to share first.

"You should probably go first or go to the bathroom because you look like you're going to pee your pants." He pointed to my feet.

"Awesome!" I blurted out, unable to hold my excitement back another moment. "Check this out. The yellow cards are for house ideas, the pink for the barn, the blue for customer experiences, and the green for the gardens. Clever, right?"

Without waiting for a reply, I continued dancing around the table, laying down all the cards like a professional presentation.

"I've added numbers to each card, so I know which improvement I'd like to do first, and a line to add the total amount for each project. I still have a lot of research to do to find those numbers. If you have time to help with any of these projects, all you have to do is put your initials on the card, and I'll know that you want to be included in either the decision-making or doing the work."

An hour later, I had outlined every project and fallen into one of the dining room chairs, buzzing and exhausted. Moments passed, and Elias stood up silently, putting his initials on only five of the fifty cards in front of us.

He walked behind me, putting his strong hands on my shoulders. "You have outdone yourself, princess. I'm so proud of you."

After several minutes, he walked around the table, and our eyes connected with newfound appreciation.

"You sat there the whole time and said nothing. I didn't know if you were truly interested or bored." I said as his eyebrows shot up.

"Bored?" he laughed. "You are nothing if not entertaining. I was fascinated, Abigail. The woman who keeps putting herself down made a comprehensive, compelling plan to build this home into a destination worthy of the best gardens in the world. A corn maze? A sculpture garden? A community garden? Geez, woman! How did you come up with all these things?"

I had the decency to blush because I had no idea where these ideas came from. They popped into my head, and I wrote them all down. I wanted to thank my mother for the influence that inspired them.

"Thank you, Elias. You have no idea how amazing that makes me feel to be supported this way. Now it's your turn—wait!" I jumped up and ran into the kitchen, pulling out the candy I bought for him and returning to the dining room. "Here, this is for you because you're so sweet." I clasped my hands together, placing his treat on the table before him.

His sheepish face was adorable. "You're the sweet one. Thanks for thinking of me." He pulled my head down to meld his lips to mine. We both moaned as his tongue slipped inside my mouth, searing me with desire. The room became warmer, but he didn't touch me. How did he have so much self-control?

"Wait for it, Abigail." He waited while I returned to my seat, pulling out his notes from earlier.

"I'd like to think all my ideas were original, but you have proved me wrong. Many of the things you suggested for the barn I have on my list. We should consider some partition between my repair work and your creative space, mostly for safety, but for security as well. We don't want your clients to waltz in and help themselves to dangerous equipment. Agreed?"

I nodded my approval.

"You should know that I, too, have a passion for art and would like to get back into metal sculpting. That fits perfectly into your idea of a sculpture garden. This leads me to my next question: Would you like to have a display area for your work so that you can sell your art? I could also sell mine, giving our sculpture garden a revolving inventory to attract repeat customers. What do you think?"

My jaw dropped. "You've thought of everything!"

He rolled his eyes. "Not everything. I want you to love what you're doing here as much as I want you to be able to monetize your talents. Why should you have to work somewhere you hate when you could create beautiful artwork to sell in your backyard?"

I could feel tears welling behind my eyes, overwhelmed by his thoughtfulness. Moreover, he believed in me as an artist even though he hadn't ever seen my work. Shit, I haven't painted or made pottery in years. I could be a total disaster, and yet he believed in me. I was truly grateful for him appearing in my life. More importantly, I'm terrified I'd let him down.

My face flushed, and a tear slipped from my eye. "Hey, sweetheart, don't cry. You've got this. If you don't want to go this route, don't. It won't change how I feel about you." He wrapped his arms around my back and kissed my head.

I sniffed harder and got up. The room started to close in, and I felt claustrophobic. I paced in front of the ginormous antique mirror hanging on the living room wall, noting how ridiculous I looked after each pass. I was neurotic, ungrateful, and unworthy. I didn't deserve his love. I didn't deserve this house. I'm an imposter to my circumstances. Sweat poured down my forehead, and I screamed.

"I. DON'T. DESERVE. THIS. I'M GOING . . .TO LET YOU DOWN! I let everyone down." I mumbled the last part. "I need some air."

The front door slammed as I stormed through. I inhaled deeply the cool evening air, trying to pull myself together. My feet hit the gravel circular drive, and I walked, and walked, around and around. The buzzing inside my head sounded like a swarm of killer bees directed solely to take me down. I was drowning in despair and responsibility. Every time—and I mean every time—I got ahead in life, I fell down backward. I was Abigail Farnsworth-Burton, Always Falling Behind, and I wasn't taking Elias down with me. He had to get out before I ruined his life. He had to save himself from my delusions of grandeur and stupid plans. He was a good man and deserved more than I could give.

I returned to the house to find Elias exactly as I left him. He spun an index card between his finger and the table, breathing deeply based on the heaving of his muscular chest.

"You have to go," I demanded.

"No."

"Yes," I said more emphatically.

"No, I don't," he also said emphatically.

"Elias. I don't know how to tell you this, but you're making a huge mistake making these big plans with me. I'll let you down. It's what I do. Don't paint me as someone I'm not. You have to leave."

I could hear my voice in and outside my head. I sounded hysterical, unstable, and neurotic. He couldn't possibly want someone like me. I'd even noticed that what I was experiencing was a panic attack. That's how aware of my situation I was.

"Please, Elias. I would hate myself if I hurt you. Save yourself and go." I fell to my knees, begging him to think of himself.

He got up, walked to the kitchen, and returned with a water bottle. "Drink."

Without muttering another word, he turned and exited the side door as my panic crept up into my throat. He was going to leave me. He would give up on me like all the others. My self-sabotaging predictions were coming true. I'm such a loser.

The side door slammed shut minutes later, and Elias reentered the room with a beet-red face—a finger pointed harshly in my direction.

"Who the hell are you to tell me that I can't handle my feelings about you? Do you think I'm so weak that I can't handle a few tears and some well-earned panic? You emasculated me. I'm a fucking grown man with the emotional aptitude to know you're a fucking train wreck, but I can't seem to breathe if you're not around. Get over yourself, Abigail. I'm tired of you living in your head, thinking about how your life sucked before you met me. You should ask yourself if you have been happy since meeting me. You should ask yourself how much better you are when we're together, not how you're going to destroy me. Let me decide if you're good enough for me. That's my decision. Not yours."

He spun on his heel and slammed the door again, leaving me alone to process what an ass I am. I didn't think that what I said was selfish. He did make me feel better about myself. I felt whole with him here. Maybe he was right, and I wallowed in my past too much. I cried some more. *I'd made a mess of things again.*

I drank the whole bottle of water and hiccupped. Was I good enough for him? Could I be patient enough for him to decide about me? My chest ached thinking about the void his leaving would create. He's right. I had to try and put my paranoia aside and stay present to figure this all out. The past had to stay in the past for our future to shine.

I picked up his untouched bag of candy and walked outside. He wasn't standing in the driveway, so I headed to the only place that made him feel good: the barn. Silently, I crept in the door and found him squatting on my thinking chair, head in hand. What I did to this man made me sick. How could someone so small tear down such a huge man? It was unfair.

I kneeled on the hard concrete before him, placing the candy at his feet, and sat quietly. Minutes went by without him looking at me, but when he did, my stomach dropped. His eyes were red, and his nose was running. My hands shot to my mouth in shame, and my tears joined his.

"I'm sorry," I whispered.

Time stood still as no words passed between us for what felt like an eternity. I broke him. This was all my fault.

I tried to speak, but my throat wouldn't cooperate. The words cracked out one at a time when my vocal cords connected. "Okay. I'm going to go now. Please stay, Elias. I don't want to lose you."

Leaning back on my heels, I stood and backed away from him. Shame blanketed me, leaving me no other choice but to go. I ran to my room, stripped out of my dirty clothes, and slid under the covers as if they were a cave where I could hide from the world. My brain hurt, and the only person responsible for that was me.

Chapter 20
A Day in Hell

ABIGAIL

Amy knew something was up because she hadn't blasted her morning squawk. Even the birds held their tongues. To complete the mood, it was overcast, and rain threatened from the east. To quote my favorite childhood book, *It was a terrible, horrible, no good, very bad day.*

My bed was empty and cold. Where was my human furnace? The room felt flat and uninteresting without his smell. The worst part was not waking up to his brilliant, devilish smile. I missed that smile. I flung the sheets back, slid into yesterday's clothing, and departed for the kitchen. I smelled coffee, and my heart fluttered, knowing he hadn't abandoned me.

I entered the kitchen sheepishly, afraid of what I might encounter. Elias stood there eating toast and staring at the microwave. He turned slightly when I entered the room and turned back to sip his coffee. My brain was swirling, but my body needed his closeness, and I walked directly to his chest, pressing my face into his shirt. I inhaled deeply, wishing he would wrap me in the safety of his arms. Behind his deep blue henley, I heard his heart thudding and prayed our budding relationship was still happening. His arms never reached for me as I'd hoped, but he did speak to me.

He sipped again, placed his cup on the counter, and stepped back.

"I'll be done with your car today, and then I'll go."

He left so quickly that he didn't give me a chance to respond. I had so many things to tell him. I rushed to the door and then stopped. Did I carefully think through everything he said, or was I being impulsive again? If I wanted a thoughtful, kind, sinfully skilled, sexy man like Elias, I would need a bulletproof plan.

Cosmopolitan magazine said that vulnerability is the most important thing in making a man love you. Shit! I'm the most vulnerable person in the freaking world. So much so that I was pathetic. Thing number two was to let him fix something. Duh! He's done that ten-fold. Hell, he's doing that as I make this stupid list.

I continued reading the article, carefully considering all the suggestions. Number eight needed some fortification, so that was where I'd begin.

I found my notebook in my backpack and started writing down my thoughts using my high school teacher's suggestion of including the WWWWW and How Method. Who? Me. What? My fears? Where? Both his home and mine. When? Now, before I fuck it up anymore, and he leaves forever. Why? Because I liked him a lot. It was the "how" that sent me pacing. I circled a path from the dining room through the parlor and foyer, then back through the dining room, smacking my pen against my head all the while. Walking helped me think, and the tapping was my ADHD. On the third turn, I saw the figurine he was holding last week, the one that looked exactly like me in a formal period dress.

Her face was contrite and demure, like a girl of her age back then. *That* was what I needed to show Elias. I was sorry for making him feel less than the man he definitely was, but, mostly, I felt so poorly of myself that I would give up on us before we even got going. My high school counselor called it fatalism—everything was predestined to fail. I knew better. I needed to woman up and make my destiny a reality.

I didn't need a therapist to tell me I needed to remove the rose-colored glasses from my past and cast a new, more vivid tone on my future. The real question was not whether I should but if I could shed the past for a brighter future. It was time to search the web for some free therapy. It didn't take long to find; I only needed to convert it to myself and my situation.

Two hours later, I had a letter for Elias. I folded and taped it shut, applied my only lip gloss, and kissed the paper several times before setting it, along with the figurine, on the center island. It was time to put my plan in motion, and I prayed Elias would accept my tokens of apology. I made his favorite PB&J sandwich, BBQ chips, and a heaping helping of pickles on a double-lined paper plate. I tucked a fresh water bottle under my armpit, grabbed my gift, and walked out the side door. *Please forgive me* was my mantra said on every step to the barn. I was so focused I almost tripped over Amy, who nodded her bright red crown several times as I passed. Even *she* realized how sincere I was in my apology.

When I arrived, Elias revved the engine with the gas pedal. It sounded smooth and powerful, just like my Elias. I walked past the hood and placed his lunch and my gift on the workbench he erected sometime this weekend. I didn't stay to talk, only to feed him and be humble in his presence. I peered at his face through my periphery and grimaced as I walked out quickly. This situation was icky and awkward, and I hated it.

I spent the rest of the afternoon at the public library researching the remaining volumes of my family's history. Stewing about if or when Elias would come into the house made me nauseous, so I packed a snack and hit the road—luckily I still had my rental car. Much of the information was similar to the last pieces I collected. Micah had the articles I requested ready for pick-up, and I added a few more before I sat and waited for them to be copied.

Today's most exciting information was about my great-great-grandfather winning government contracts to supply the army with lumber to build wagons, forts, and guns during the Mexican American War in 1846. As I said, I'm not sure how that affected me, though the article was entitled, "Farnsworth sinks fortune into Mystic Creek Valley." That tidbit would be an excellent question for the Mystic Tax Assessor when I visit next week. It's nice to know that my ancestors gave back to their community. Maybe that's why people looked at me in a funny way.

"Here you go, Abigail. I think your research is paying off. Keep it going." Micah smiled and handed me a thick stack of papers. Why did that sound like I was one step closer in a scavenger hunt I hadn't sign up for? *Hmm.*

I pushed on the exit bar and stepped outside, only to realize I wanted to invite her over.

"Hey, Micah. Do you still want to come over and see all the stuff I'm giving away? I could make some tea and cookies to sweeten the offer, literally?" I felt so needy, but she seemed excited to come.

Her eyes brightened, and she made tiny fingertip claps, keeping her voice down. "I'd love to!"

"Terrific. After you're done with work Thursday?" I offered, and she nodded. Learning from my past behaviors, I shoved my papers under my arm and immediately put our appointment on my calendar. *This thing was becoming part of my brain.*

When I returned to the house, I ran to the barn to check on Elias, but the door was shut. *That's weird.* I slid open the giant door and walked to my newly restored car, but Elias was nowhere to be found. There was, however, a note tucked under the windshield wiper.

I was able to restore the engine and fix the exhaust system. Your car is safe to drive. Please register it before you drive it. You should also transfer your insurance from the Corolla to the Buick. I'm going back home tonight. We'll talk later. Elias

I reread the note, hoping I missed the part about him forgiving me, but nothing was said. I'd lost him—maybe even forever. I glanced at the workbench to see if he'd eaten lunch. Neither the figure nor the note was anywhere around. I hoped he had read how sorry I was. I worked hard to express myself clearly, hoping he would understand and forgive me. How long will I have to wait for a reply? Not long, I hoped. I was anxious already.

Without waiting another minute, I bolted for the house to stop him, but his truck was gone. I didn't notice it was missing in my rush to reach him. I couldn't breathe, and it scared me. I tried to remember to do that breathing exercise, but I couldn't remember the sequence. I sat on the stoop, fanning my hands before my face, trying to settle myself down when Amy the Great emerged from the tall grass.

She bawked a steady rhythm, and I understood what she was trying to do. Minutes later, my head cleared, and my chest heaved less. Amy kept her steady pace, and, once my shoulders drooped, she walked over and sat between my knees. Of all the things the universe could bring me, it was a fucking therapy chicken. This one act of kindness exempted her from being roasted forever. She let me pet her back and rub her head with my thumb, purring like a sleeping cat. Finally, I felt better.

"Thank you, Amy. Are you sure you're a chicken and not some sorcerer in chicken's clothing?" Her purrs continued in a tick-tock sound until I stopped wallowing in pity. All I could do was keep moving forward since I'd done what I could to repair what I created.

There were no texts, emails, or emojis from Elias as I fell back into bed later that night, and my heart sank even further. I needed to unburden myself to someone. Unfortunately, the only person who might have listened was Seneca. *Would she still be pissed at me?* She was my only hope, and, as Elias said, I needed to get over myself. This was another relationship I had fucked up and was mine to repair. I rolled over and resolved to make things right.

The phone kept ringing and going to voicemail. I tried two more times, and the same thing happened. I wouldn't sleep until I got this off my chest, come hell or high water. Seneca would forgive me, so I sent her texts. Several, actually.

Hey, Seneca. It's me ringing your damn phone off the hook.

Please don't be pissed off at me anymore. I am sorry for not keeping you in the roller-coaster loop of my life.

YOU MATTER TO ME! Please call me back.

I'm finger-painting my apologies on the wall in my blood. PLEASE call me back.

That did it.

"What the fuck, Abby? I'm trying to sleep; what's your problem that you can't wait for a goddamn answer?" I could feel the gust of anger through the phone. I'm pissing her off on top of what already pissed her off. What *is* my problem?

"I'm sorry," I whispered.

She screamed at me, "For what this time?"

"For . . . everything. I have been a bad friend and a sucky communicator. For not calling more often or asking what was happening in your life—everything." I sighed, feeling lighter for having purged my heart.

Moments passed without a single word. "You do suck—and thank you."

"I miss you so much, Sen. Are you okay since we last talked? Did your dad close his business? Please come and visit me." I hoped she would.

Her exasperated tone settled into one of pain. "Things have been tough. I'm not going to sugarcoat it. Dad closed the store today, so I didn't want to answer the phone; I was wallowing in despair. We had a sale, so most of the merchandise is gone, and Dad said he's using the money to move to Cleveland. Don't ask why. Our lease is up Tuesday, so, yeah, I'll come and visit you. I have nowhere else to go anyhow."

I jumped up and danced on my bed. "I'm sure you have so much to process. I'll send you the address and take care of you this time: food, housing—everything. I owe you so much. Thank you so much for forgiving me, Sen. I badly needed your forgiveness today. I'll see you Thursday?"

She hummed. "Yeah, Thursday. And, Abs . . . I miss you, too."

Chapter 21
Reunited with Seneca

A BIGAIL

The highlight of this fine Monday morning was that the internet was on, and I could start shopping online. *Whoopee!*

Researching online was a big deal because, after checking the local sewing shop, I found that most of the fabric I'd like to use to restore my furniture was only offered at high-end textile outlets. So, shopping online it was. The woman at the store recommended a furniture restoration company a few towns over, though I'd have to schedule that visit much later. I wasn't prepared to hear the astronomical price they would quote me and the even more dejected feeling of not being able to afford it. Money was tight, and there were more pressing projects to complete first.

I had four bedrooms to clean from ceiling to floor before I could consider anyone viewing my home. I'd been weighing the pros and cons of having the carpets professionally cleaned, but Elias felt the house deserved to have all the floors refinished. *See? There he was again! Infiltrating my head, my heart, and my pocketbook.* I suppose I should get a quote for that, too. I didn't know about prices and what was involved with each project. All I saw was me moving chairs, couches, and everything out to the front lawn while the work was completed. I mean, I had a garage, but there were probably mice in there, and you know how I hate those. That was Elias' department. But what if he didn't come back? Then, I'd never get to use my garage, so the floors wouldn't get refinished, and I would never have anyone over.

It was time to revisit my original plan. Micah would help evaluate the stuff I would get rid of, but I needed a professional to help with the rest. I knew one person who wouldn't take advantage of a young woman, but he lived several states away.

"Hello, Mr. Brickner. It's Abigail. How are you today?" I've learned to be a professional on the phone to compensate for my high-pitched voice, which resembles that of a prepubescent boy.

"Why, hello, Abigail. To what do I owe the honor?" *I loved it when he spoke like that.*

"I want to get a list of all the antique furniture in my house and how much they are worth. I'm cleaning out a ton of clutter and would kick myself if I threw away something of value."

"That's a very wise decision, dear. I think you'll find a comprehensive list of everything of value in the house in that packet of information. There is no need to hire anyone since this valuation occurred less than three years ago."

"Oh." *Did I bother to look through that envelope?* "Great. I'll take a closer look at that packet today. Thanks, Mr. B. Also, do you think restoring all the hardwood floors is a better investment than cleaning the carpets?" *Why not get the most bang for my call and ask?*

I heard him breathing and making pondering sounds. I guess this was a big decision after all.

"Abigail. When choosing where to spend your money, always consider resale benefits. Would you get more money for a historic home with refurbished floors or old, unfashionable carpet? I think you know the answer to that one, right?"

I may be young and inexperienced, but I knew the answer he was pushing for. "Refurbished floors. I get you, Mr. B."

"You're a smart cookie, dear. I'm always here if you need me. Goodbye, Abigail." He didn't wait for me to say goodbye. He was a very busy man. He was the most grandfatherly person I'd had in my short life, and I was grateful for his guidance, however long it lasted.

Three-floor restoration calls later, I had appointments scheduled over the next two weeks. I aimed to list what I wanted to eliminate, take pictures, and post those items online. It was a big job, and the most important one, before I started any other projects upstairs. I used Amy's eggs to make breakfast for dinner, along with bacon and a new potato pancake recipe I was getting into trying new menu options for when I opened for business. My days were beginning to fill up, and I wanted to take some time to usher Seneca around the area. We both would benefit from knowing what this sleepy village offered. Guests would not only enjoy a comprehensive listing of what to do in the area; they would want firsthand experience with various restaurants, shops, and activities. I'd ensure I did them all, including wine and my best friend. She'd be here Thursday, and I wanted to love this place as much as possible in the time I had.

Tuesday was another busy day of cleaning and purging. As it turned out, there were twenty sets of sheets for this place for five beds. Even if every room had two sets, I'd still have ten extra. Math! *I could do math*. I was so proud of myself. I opened every one of those sets and pulled out the worst of them to make rags. I also washed the fabric shower curtains and hung new clear plastic liners. I tore down all the window coverings and wiped down all the mini blinds hanging behind them. Blinds would have to suffice until I decided how to restore these rooms.

That got me thinking. If I could restore three of the five rooms by the end of the summer, I could start renting them out for profit. I'd live in one room, and Seneca could live in another. Worst case, she could sleep in my room while we rented out hers for a busy weekend. This plan was indeed one of my best. I'd commit this one to paper.

By midday, Elias had still not answered, and that icky feeling washed over me again. Wasn't forty-eight hours the maximum time to respond to a note? This was starting to feel like I was being ghosted, and I couldn't allow that to happen. It was time to call him. I brushed my teeth and pulled my hair into a ponytail. I knew he couldn't see me, but I didn't want to look gross speaking to him on the phone.

"Hello?" he said sweetly. I fully expected him to let it go to voicemail, so I was thrilled to hear his sexy voice.

"Hi, Elias. I miss you." I coached myself to stay calm at all costs. Give him a reason to want to speak with you. *Cosmopolitan Rule #5.*

"I miss you too, princess." *Yesss! All was not lost.*

"I should have a pet name for you, too," I suggested coyly.

"Like what?" His voice went husky, and I loved that he put away the reason for my call to banter with me.

"I don't know . . . darling?"

"Yuck. I'm not a 1950s Hollywood husband."

"Definitely not. Quite the opposite. How about baby?"

"Too generic. We can do better." *We are still a "we!*

"Did you like it when I called you sugar? It's over the top, but what do you think?"

I bit my lip and walked in a circle again, think of the perfect name.

"Too much. Acceptable choices include Mr. Big, Hercules, Big Man, or my favorite, Daddy." *Oh, no, he didn't!*

"OMG, Elias. You're kinky!" I shouted.

"I told you, you don't know the half of it. I'd sure like to experiment with a few of them, but I've not had the right partner. Unfortunately, you and I have some things to work through first." His sexy, fun tone turned serious. "That is if you still want that."

I jumped on the chance to answer. "Yes! Definitely. That's what I want . . . Daddy." My pussy clenched just saying those words. I never had a dad, daddy, or even a pop. I didn't see it as disgusting or wrong. It was the idea of being protected like a father would. Just not *my* father. . .

"Christ, Abigail. Do not say that to me unless you are prepared to play out that scene," he growled.

"I would do that with you. I'm so very, very sorry for upsetting you like I did. I trust you to know what is in your best interest, and I'm working every day to put my past attitudes about myself out of my mind. You make me want to be a better woman for you."

Tears trickled down my face, and I was happy he couldn't see me crying.

"Do it for yourself and no one else. You deserve to feel good about yourself all the time, Abigail. Do you understand what I'm saying?"

I nodded. "I do."

"I do, who?" He goaded me.

"I do, Daddy." We both let out a groan. "When am I going to see you again?" I needed to feel his hands gliding down my body, his lips on mine, and his cock inside me.

He cleared his throat. I could envision him stroking his beard and thinking, I'm not sure what turns me on about that, but it does.

"You and I still need to have a few more conversations about how to improve our communication. I will not go through these feelings ever again with you. We have to do better."

"We will. I promise." I crossed my heart and fell onto the sofa, exhausted.

"Alright, then. Good night, Abigail."

"Elias? One more thing. Can we have phone sex, Daddy?"

ELIAS

Fucking, yes! Game on!

"Where are you, Abigail?"

"In the front parlor, on the sofa. Call me Abby," she whispered. It looked like my little girl was only too happy to role-play with me and a pass to a family-friendly pet name.

"Are you my little girl, Abby?" I needed to be sure that was how she wanted this to go down.

"Yes, Daddy. I want to touch you," she purred.

"Where do you want to touch me, sweet girl?" My voice melted with seduction.

"On your cock, Daddy. I want to feel how thick you feel in my small hands. Can I touch myself, Daddy?"

"Geezuz, Abby. You're very good at this game. I'm in my office, and Paul will be back from lunch any minute now."

This was so hot I couldn't control my breathing. I unclasped my belt buckle and shoved my pants down without even unzipping them. Gripping my red-hot cock and stroking it while she breathed into the phone sent jolts of electricity through my body, and my balls pulled higher.

"Touch yourself, Abby. Shove your hand down your pants and find that wet, hot clit and make those small circles you love when I touch you." She gasped, and I knew she was doing my bidding.

"Daddy, you feel so good. I want to come for you. Can I come for you, Daddy?" I loved when she begged for me.

I dreamt of having the right woman to play with like this. This was how I wanted to be with her the time we fucked.

"Yes, sweetheart. Come for Daddy. I'm going to come with you." Fuck, this was amazing. I hadn't come this fast since junior high.

"Come now, Abby. Daddy wants to hear how much you like his fingers on your pussy."

Screams of pleasure pierced through the phone, extracting my blessed release.

"Elias!!"

"Abby!!"

I yanked on my cock, milking every ounce of fluid left in my balls. I heard the garage door slam shut, and I sat upright instantly.

"Baby, I have to go. This was beyond amazing, but I have ten seconds to get my pants up. I'll call later."

Chapter 22
The Girls Are Back At It

ABIGAIL

Double booking is a common ADD characteristic, thus exemplified by me, Always Falling Behind Abby. Learning that I screwed up my calendar, brought on panic, which added another layer of loathing, forgetting Micah would arrive thirty minutes before Seneca was due to arrive. I prided myself on having placed both arrivals in my external frontal lobe, aka my phone's calendar. What I notoriously kept forgetting to do was to look at said calendar until the ten-minute reminder pinged me.

"Hey, Micah. I'm so happy you could make it. Come in." I pushed the door back, allowing her to enter the foyer unobstructed, and her mouth fell open.

"Look at that pastoral mural!" I think she may have swooned. "It's original, right? Wow. I could sit right here all day and look at it." She stepped in farther, and I shut the door.

I cleared my throat. "It is incredible, but let's go into the parlor for a snack." *Look at me being all hostessy.* "As promised, I baked some magic bars. I didn't know if you had any allergies, so I made lemon squares, too. Coffee or tea?"

I pointed to the coffee table adorned with beverage napkins I found while rifling through the drawers a few days ago. It appears I am the proud owner of several boxes of "You're Either Inn or Out of Mystic" beverage napkins—one thousand, to be exact—showing the play on words about staying at an inn. They will be great for spills or propping up a wobbly table.

She sat down, swiveling her head in all directions. "Uh, tea, please."

I hustled to the kitchen to microwave some water. There was no time for a kettle today. I had to get Micah started on one project so I could properly welcome Seneca when she pulled up. Minutes later, I zoomed back into the front of the house with a hot mug of water and three kinds of tea. I really am pretty accommodating when I apply myself. I'm going to be a great innkeeper. *Good talk.*

"So, Micah. I made a logistical error today and will have to cut our visit short, but I want to have you back soon to go through some things when we have more time. Another guest is arriving on short notice, and I can't reschedule with her. Do you mind?"

Her face fell, but she covered her disappointment well. "Of course. Things come up." She eyed my cookies or the old clock on the table. I wasn't sure.

"Why don't you make your tea? Then I'll give you the two-dollar tour. We'll finish back here so you can enjoy your cookies for as long as you'd like. Sound good?" You would have thought I pulled a rabbit out of a hat at her outburst.

"Oh, Abigail. I'd love that. Thank you for not canceling on me. I've dreamed for years about what it might look like. *"How could I deny her puppy-dog face?*

True to my word, I moved Micah through the main floor and up the main staircase before I received a text from Seneca that she exited the expressway and would arrive in fifteen minutes. Ushering her down the hall, I gave her three minutes for the bedrooms and an exciting trip down the servant's stairs, finishing outside at the gardens. The spring air was merciful today, with a light breeze and lots of sunshine allowing her a quick stroll through what soon will be a beautiful garden.

"My word, Abigail. The potential for these gardens is spectacular. I hope you have a good groundskeeper lined up." She trailed off as she pushed through the overrun slate walkway toward the pool. "Oooh!" She whipped around wide-eyed. "You have a pool! Boy, would I love to swim in that one. Would you invite me over for a swim? I won't be any trouble. Truly."

This woman was a kid in a candy shop. She shuffled around, stopping at several landscape features, including a broken birdbath, a spinning metal wind catcher, and several birdhouses. "I love birds," she whispered. *Great. Mary Poppins had arrived.*

"Micah, you are welcome to sit and watch the birds whenever you'd like. As a matter of fact, I'd be thrilled if you'd feed and keep those houses all tidied up. I don't know a thing about them." She clapped her hands like she won the lottery. Making people happy wasn't hard when you knew what motivated them. Clearly, this was Micah's jam.

Horn toots sounded as we exited the path to the driveway, and a piece of home slowed to a halt. I didn't know whether to cry or attack her as she approached me. Seneca took control of the situation, and I was relieved.

"What the fuck, Abs? You said a big house, not a mansion. Where's the footman to grab my stuff? Does the chef do made-to-order meals? Are you the house manager?" She looked to Micah for confirmation. To her credit, she raised her shoulders while her eyebrows slid up to her hairline.

Judging by the popping sound in my back, I realized her hugs were crushing me. Seneca was all bluster on the outside but sweet and loving on the inside. We were the same age, but she looked older than I did. It wasn't that she spent every moment she could in the sun it was her DNA. My bestie was one-eighth American Indian and another African American. Her dad was white and looked older than his years. People used to think she was my older sister or super young mom. Either way, we were as connected as two friends could be without sharing blood.

"Sorry to disappoint you, Sen. I had to fire the footman, and the chef only made mutton." I couldn't keep a straight face. I patted her shoulder in consolation, "You're looking at the sole employee of this here home. For you, though, I'll do made-to-order meals, but you're hauling your crap upstairs on your own." I pointed to her SUV, and we walked over to the hatchback.

"Oh, and this is my friend, Micah. She's never seen the house either. She's the librarian here in Mystic. Let's grab a few things and head back inside for some cookies."

We each grabbed a bag and dumped them in the kitchen, continuing to the parlor.

"Shit, Abby. It's like stepping back in time. What are you going to do with all this stuff?" She picked up knick-knacks along our route, then placed them down, only to keep doing that as we passed through the house. I let my friends chat while I pulled the iced coffee out of the fridge. Seneca was a coffee freak, and I wanted to impress her with my new coffee skills.

There were several topics I stayed clear of while Micah was visiting. It wasn't that I didn't trust her; it was that I didn't know her. Mystic was like middle school. Everyone knew everyone else's business, and I wasn't ready to share mine beyond moving in. *This reminded me that I needed to invite the neighbor ladies I met last week for a meet-and-greet when I was settled.* The good news for me, though, was I wasn't settled and wouldn't be for a long time.

Micah left after drinking her tea and scarfing down five cookies. She was a nice person, and I wouldn't mind hanging out with her even if she was at least a decade older than me. Elias was more than a decade older than me, too. Did that make me an old soul? *Things to ponder.*

After we walked Micah to her car, Seneca barely hit the front porch before starting in on me.

"Cut the shit, Abigail. There is no way you got this house up and running yourself. Who is he? Who helped you? The guy you spouted on about over the phone?" So much for subtle.

"Let's get your stuff inside, and I'll bring you up to speed over a bottle of wine." I didn't wait for a reply and headed out the door only to hear her snarky comment.

"Day drinking. Bring it on!"

"He said that?" Seneca was my fiercest protector.

I tried to look unaffected, but I missed this side of her the most. No matter what stupid, ridiculous thing I said or did, she would spin a logical reason to defend me without knowing all the details. Growing up, whether I was right or wrong didn't matter to her. She would chastise me after the fact in the privacy of her bedroom; never in my house. Girl talk was strictly prohibited at my house. Everything uttered in private or in the open came back to haunt me later. It was like Aunt Eleanor bugged the house as if I was a convicted felon on parole. I suppose to her I was. But you can't hold stealing a pack of Tic Tacs when you're six over a teenager a decade later. My philosophy was simple: adults drew the lines, and kids were obligated to cross them. Present company included.

During our senior year, Seneca and I devised a scheme to steal our teachers' coffee mugs and move them onto other teachers' desks. To be more devious, we superglued them to their desks once we moved them around. Why? No reason. Only an epic senior prank. Mr. Ruggers almost beat up Senor Nelson when he saw his "I'm History in the Making" mug on his desk. Priceless. The only other prank that still lives on to this day was that we printed fake money with our faces on the bills. We hid them in every locker, file cabinet, manila folder, backpack, and music folder we could access. Talk about a legacy! "It was the best of times. It was the worst of times," I would say on reflection. My English teacher, Mrs. Pearson, would be so proud that I remembered the opening line to *A Tale of Two Cities.*

My bestie seemed a bit flustered when she sensed someone else was moving in on her turf. I needed to admit to my selfishness and defend Elias.

"He did. Sen, when I tell you I almost broke that man, I did. I must be the blindest bitch in the world not to see how much that man likes me. Why else would he put up with all my bullshit? *You* barely put up with it!" I pointed to her face, and she rolled her eyes in agreement.

I topped off our glasses, which almost fell off the sofa. Thank goodness reaching for those cookies distracted me, or I'd be on my ass.

"Let me get this straight. He's everything you've ever wanted in a man. He treats you like a princess and fixes everything around here, but you decided you aren't worth it? What the fuck is wrong with you? He's right. You *are* a train wreck, even if you are adorable. Sweetheart, it's time to love yourself despite your past. Can you do that? For me—and him? For you?"

My coming to Jesus moment shouldn't begin with a pound of sugar and three glasses of wine. My head was cloudy, but my sight was clear. This was my line in the sand, and, if not now, when? I know I'm worth it, but how much am I worth? That was the blurry line I had trouble finding.

Chapter 23
Besties in the Village

ABIGAIL

Our heads were pounding the following day, but our butts were moving. Foraging for food was our first errand, and I wasn't about to cook anything in my state. Seneca drove my car out of the barn through the opposite door, and I hopped in my rental car as we set out onto my sleepy street for our "Mystic Experience." After dropping the rental off at the rental return, (another thing I forgot to do on Monday), our next biggest challenge was where to eat.

Best eggs or best French toast? Two diners on opposite sides of the street a half-mile downtown from each other both touted the best breakfast in the village. I didn't care which one we chose because we were returning tomorrow to try the other one.

We agreed last night that we'd act like tourists for the next forty-eight hours and afterwards, stop spending money we didn't have. Granted, I was sitting on almost seventeen thousand dollars after getting my house up and running and renting a car for two weeks. I'll never have this kind of money again, so I will enjoy some of it with my friends.

"Deese is da best eggs," I mumbled, stuffing another forkful into an already stuffed face.

"I know!" Seneca pointed her fork at me. "Great choice. Do you see that guy over there? Don't look."

I looked. "Where?"

"Sit still," she hissed. He's by the window, wearing a baseball cap, drinking coffee, and looking hot.

I swiveled in my chair again. "Him?" I pointed.

"Abigail! Stop pointing!" she hissed again, grabbing my hand.

It was too late. He stood up, grabbed his bill, and walked to the register, looking at us from the corner of his eye. One moment, he was paying, and the next, he was standing at our table.

"Hello, ladies. I couldn't help but notice you looking my way." *Gulp.*

Thank goodness Seneca was quick on her feet. "Yeah. Um, are you in the construction business? You look like you might do that." She pursed her lips and scanned his body head to toe and back up again. *Smooth.* I slunk into my seat.

He chuckled. "I am. Restoration work." Seneca and I shared a knowing glance.

"Really," she said, dragging out the word. "My friend here just moved into a historic home a few weeks ago and might be interested in your services."

Damn it! Why did she have to say it like that? I need my floors refurbished, not my pussy.

He shifted his feet and shoved his hands in his pockets. His dirty blond hair fell over one of his eyes, and his eyes beamed with potential services he could render.

"Floors!" I blurted out. "Just floors. Stripped, sanded, and stained." My God, that sounded like an exotic dancer's after-hour show.

Men like him shouldn't lick their lips unless they want a Seneca in their face.

"Maybe you should come by later today and check them out." She licked her lips as she pressed her big breasts tightly against her sheer T-shirt.

Fuck my life. She wrote my address on his hand, conveniently nestled beside her chest. "There you go. We'll be there in a few hours." It's a wonder her fake eyelashes didn't fall into her hash browns the way she batted them.

"Alright then." He cleared his throat again. "Have an enjoyable day, ladies." He appeared to change his gait as he walked toward the door. No doubt, after rubbing against Seneca's tits, his tighty-whities were choking his dick. The bells that rang as he opened the door alerted me to the fact that my dear friend invited a stranger into my home under the pretense of restoration when she was blatantly transparent that he would be restoring her sex life. I hoped she wasn't including me in that game.

I shook my head and shoved the rest of my potatoes into my mouth. "Hussy."

Prude."

"Bitch."

"Killjoy."

"Fine. Have fun, but count me out. I know everything about you but don't plan on me having a threesome. No way."

She mocked tears. "Just when I was having so much fun." She ground her fists into her eyes.

"Fuck off. We're out of here." I stood to pay the bill and walked out of the restaurant. I needed air. I forgot how much trouble she could get me into. Elias would have a cow—two cows—if he knew what Seneca was planning. Good thing I planned on another round of phone sex tonight. Best friend be damned.

The only stipulation on my spending was no knick-knacks; no matter how funny they were, I had more than any human should have. I'd take pictures instead. I needed a wardrobe fit for a proper proprietor if I wanted to be taken seriously. My closet resembled a discount store of holy T-shirts and ripped jeans. My finest dress was a faded sundress from the sales rack of a discount retailer purchased for my high school graduation. *I should add that to my rag bag.*

Seneca and I discussed her dad's decision to close the store and move to Cleveland. It seemed he had caught the love bug too, and felt his daughter was old enough to manage her own life.

"It wasn't my choice to live with my father; it was his. 'Save money. Keep me company,' he'd say. *Whatever.* I suppose the couple of grand I did sock away is handy," she said flippantly.

"You've done well for yourself, considering your line of work. At least you only had to work one job. I worked two and still had trouble making the rent." I strolled through the shop and picked up a very expensive dress, casually eyeing the price tag. "Will I ever be able to afford two hundred dollars for a dress with pineapples?" We both doubled over laughing.

We picked through hundreds of clothes in every shop along Main Street before turning the corner at an upscale resale shop. The door chime tinkled as we walked through to the retro-designed shop steeped with clothes labeled by decades. Normally, I didn't confine myself to a genre, but I was feeling the 1980s and perhaps some early 2000s.

With my arms loaded with possibilities, I yelled to Seneca.

"Fitting room, Sen!"

"Coming!"

With my best friend trailing behind me, we synced our fashion reveals by the giant mirror on the wall.

My first outfit was a gossamer-overlay silk blouse in white paired with fitted black leather pants that slung relatively low on my hips. Depending on how I accessorized, I could have been a pirate or a dominatrix in this outfit. *Watching those modeling shows was paying off.*

"Holy shit, Abs. That's hot as fuck. I bet you Elias would like it." She winked and twirled in her paisley mini dress and white go-go boots.

"You don't even know him—though this will get his attention." I turned, catching myself from all angles. Yes, this would do. "Your outfit is a must! We'll need to find a place to go dancing soon."

We must have made ten reveals before the sales lady came by. She looked put together, dressed in tailored tan pants and a cardigan sweater in blue. Chunky gold jewelry and a silk patterned scarf made her look like a Diane Keaton wannabe.

"My, my, ladies. I'm Sheila. You are tearing this place up. Have you narrowed down your choices? Let's take a look at what you picked."

She sat down, crossing her legs as she settled into the loveseat across from the mirror. Seneca and I shrugged our shoulders. I guess it couldn't hurt to have a third opinion.

For my first outfit, I chose a white blouse and black pants. In minutes, Sheila jumped up and ran through the store, grabbing this and that and returning with a pile of accessories she dropped on the loveseat.

"Here," she said, pulling me in front of the mirror. She clasped two necklaces, three bracelets, and a thin black patent leather belt on me.

"Now you look complete. Oh, wait one minute. What size shoe are you?" She disappeared again, bringing back three shoe boxes of my size. Holding up a strappy four-inch heel in patent leather, "These are for nighttime and dancing." She put those down and unboxed a chunky black heel with a silver buckle. "These are for work or standing for long periods of time." And, lastly, a cool pair of ankle boots with a kitten heel. "These are for when you're feeling sassy. Shoes make the woman as much as the man."

She wasn't wrong. I loved shoes, and shoes loved me. My dream of having a closet with hundreds of shoes in every style and color started today. I loved color, and, now that I had a few bucks, I'd brighten everything in my life.

I held the strappy heels, "Do these come in ruby red?" A giant smile appeared on the woman's face.

"Darling! You have fabulous taste. Give me a minute." While she dashed away again, I looked at Seneca as she clucked her tongue.

"She's got your number, girl. Did you see how she upsold you with another three hundred dollars of accessories? Be careful with that one, Abs." I felt panicky every time she laid another item on me.

"I feel you, but I can use all these extras with lots of other outfits, so maybe just a few to get me started?" I asked as if she was paying my bill.

"Your money, honey. You're living here now. You can come back anytime. I'm just saying you don't have to feel obligated because she ran all over this store for you."

Thank goodness Seneca was there to keep me from being impulsive. After picking out three outfits and accessorizing them, I politely informed the saleswoman I was done for the day. Seneca handled her shopping spree much better. She had a plan for specific things and stayed in her lane like a horse with blinders. Ultimately, she got the paisley dress, white boots, and two scarves.

"Scarves make your outfits pop. Young, old, it doesn't matter. A fuchsia scarf with all black says sassy every day of the week." She popped her hip and snapped her fingers above her head. Yeah. Seneca was all kinds of sassy. That's why we were best friends. I was the silent but deadly friend, and she was the firecracker. *And, no, I'm not a fart!*

We managed to get back to our car in time to grab some ice cream and get home. Little Miss Firecracker had made a date for us, and I didn't want to be rude.

The knock on the front door startled me, given that my pants were down at my ankles and I had changed into work clothes in the living room. *Don't ask.*

Seneca bolted for the front door before I could finish pulling myself together. Striking a seductive pose, she yanked open the door, brandishing her perfect smile all over her face.

"Hey. We've been expecting you," she purred. To me, it sounded more like the opening line of a thriller movie.

"Hey. I'm Derrick." He said in a deep, throaty tone, thrusting his well-formed chest in her face.

"Did you find the place okay?"

"No problem. I live a few miles from here, so . . ." He pulled his cap lower over his eyes, looking sheepish.

I stepped into the door frame alongside my brazen friend. "Hi. I'm Abigail. This is my house. Please come in." I extended my hand, and he shook it professionally, following me inside.

I could feel his eyes on my ass, and my ego loved the attention. However, my pussy self-corrected herself, making me trip on the floor mat. I belonged to Elias and not some hot, muscular carpenter guy.

"Please sit down. Can I get you something to drink?" I could at least be polite. Seneca perched herself on the opposite side of the sofa while I kept my distance in an armchair off to the side.

"I'm good. Thanks. So, what can I help you with?" He pulled a pencil from his ear and a notepad from his front pocket. If I could only get my head out of the gutter, I might be able to get my floors fixed.

I gave Seneca a keep-your-mouth-shut look and began explaining my plans to do this work in stages since my finances wouldn't allow me to do it all at once.

"This isn't uncommon in homes like these. We won't know what we're dealing with until the carpet is pulled back. Do you have an idea where you'd like to begin?"

I liked his demeanor—it was validating, assuring, realistic, and oozing with charm. *Knock it off, Abigail.*

Seneca took her moment to shine. "Upstairs—in my room." *Ugh. She's been here for two minutes and already owns a room.*

"Follow me." As we walked up the grand staircase, I could feel him staring at my ass again. I hope he didn't need reminding who was interested in him.

I pointed out the five bedrooms and the office that needed to be done. He pulled back the corner carpet of each room to get a quick look at the state of the hardwood beneath it, making various faces ranging from not too bad to cringe.

At the end of our tour, we sat down again in my bedroom to discuss his findings.

"Although I can't say for certain, covered floors usually clean up nicely, provided they aren't covering up a problem. Please note that I can't fully quote this job without seeing the wood firsthand. I want to take some measurements and then work up a quote for the carpet removal and the basic restoration of the floors. This will be a time-consuming, messy job, so everything in the room must be removed. I'll add that fee there as well. Once you've reviewed that quote, I can see where to fit you into my schedule. Plan on upturning your house for at least two weeks for the upstairs alone."

My face blanched. "Weeks? It could take me a month to move all the stuff out of one of those rooms." I twisted my fingers, feeling nauseous again.

Seneca gently hugged me from behind as panic set in. "Listen, babe—one step at a time. You don't have to make any decisions today. We'll make a plan. You always do great with a plan. Okay?" She kissed the side of my head and looked over to Derrick for backup.

"Seneca is correct. These are big decisions, and, like I said, I can't even schedule you for two weeks. You might consider a yard sale or purging those things you don't want to put back in these rooms. Let me break down this project into phases, and I'll have it to you in a few days. Sound good?"

He stood motioning for the door. I was paralyzed with another monumental task. Weren't there any easy things for me to do around here? Like picking a color for a wall or where to put a chair? I could do that in my sleep. Running a house, especially one of this size, was daunting.

Seneca motioned for him to take the side stairs out of the house. I'm sure she plied him with a dozen reasons he should come back and see her. And, if history proved me correctly, she'd offer to barter the price down in blow jobs. My girl loved to suck dick.

My phone rang, and the sun burned brighter, seeing Elias's name pop up on the screen. He'd know what to do.

I didn't wait for his greeting. "How do you know to call me when I need you most? Are you psychic or something?"

His deep, throaty voice made all my troubles evaporate.

"More like psychotic, princess. Is everything okay?" He picked up the strain in my voice.

I picked at my shirt hem, choosing my words carefully.

"Everything is fine. My friend, Seneca, came down to visit me for a while. We went shopping, and now I'm panicking about how much this house will cost me, and I'm unemployed."

He didn't respond immediately; instead, in his methodical manner, he contemplated my situation.

"I like that you're staying calm and sharing your thoughts. They are all valid reasons to feel overwhelmed. Are you remembering that all your awesome ideas aren't going to happen all at once?" His steady voice and reassuring tone helped me to find reason in his words.

"I'm trying. A floor restoration guy was here today to give me a quote on restoring the hardwood floors upstairs. It's not the cost so much, as it's the purging, moving, and a million decisions during the process that are making me insane." My voice hitched, but I had to keep my shit together. Elias shouldn't have to deal with a crybaby whenever something isn't easy. He was right. I did need to grow up and get over myself.

"Last I saw, you had already begun that project and made progress in the dining room armoires. Try shifting your focus to those bedrooms, and I'm sure—in a few days—you'll have plenty to throw away or sell. Can your friend help you post your stuff?"

He was brilliant! Of course. Seneca could help me with that. I bet that between Micah taking stuff and my selling the rest, I could move all this junk out in a month. By the time we were done, I could have Derrick start working as soon as his schedule opened up.

"Princess? Where did you go?" Oh my God. My mind kept wandering off.

"Sorry. My mind was chasing a squirrel, so to speak. Thank you for helping me through another house dilemma. I don't want to burden you with my troubles, so tell me what you're up to."

I heard him humming, and he was probably stroking his beard. "I've been working with Paul on a few plans for the shop. I told you about my friend, Reilly. He had me over for a beer and to play pool on Sunday. I've been doing some purging of my own around the house, but that's about all."

"Wow! You're always thinking and planning. I like that about you. You're the opposite of me. I guess we balance each other that way." I didn't want to pressure him about when I'd see him again, but tomorrow wasn't too soon either. "Do you hang out with any other friends?"

What if he didn't have any other friends like me? What if I alienated him? *Abigail, don't fuck this up!*

He chuckled. "I have a few friends from college I talk to every once in a while. I belong to the Masonic Temple in Pittston. Occasionally, I help with charity work or hunger relief events. It's a good way to meet people and help my community."

"Amazing! You never mentioned that. I don't know much about that group, but, if you're a member, it must be worthwhile." *I wonder if we have one in Mystic.* I sighed to myself. If Elias came to stay for good, he'd want to keep being a Mason.

"You do. I looked it up. You can stop wondering." *Damn! It's like he can read my mind.*

"I'm starting to think you are psychic," I giggled.

"Do you have a dress, Abigail?" His voice deepened, and the hair on my skin pricked up.

How convenient that I just bought one.

"As a matter of fact, I bought one this morning." I got up and walked to my closet, eyeing the deep purple, flouncy short dress hanging on my new hangers. The neckline was a deep V, and the skirt was made of three layers of silky material.

"Put it on, and show me." God, I loved how he ordered me around like he owned me. I dropped the phone on the small coffee table in my sitting area and peeled my clothes off at lightning speed. I all but ripped the dress off the hanger and slid it over my naked body, fluffing my loose hair around my face.

"I'm changing to video mode. There. What do you think?"

I bit my finger, watching him take me in. He had trimmed his beard shorter, and I could see how full and pillowy his lips really were. I remembered what that mouth did to me, and my pussy clenched under his scrutiny. It had only been a week, but it felt like a month. I needed him like a child needed their daddy.

His eyes hooded slightly, and he licked his lips slowly. He hissed the word, "Fuck," and my clit began to throb.

"I have shoes, too." I stepped back into my closet and pulled out a pair of sexy silver-glitter slingback heels decorated with a thin, long bow over each toe. I shouldn't have spent the money, but they were worth it seeing Elias's eyes glaze over.

I watched as he took a deep breath and covered his mouth with his hand. When he shook his head, I thought he might hang up on me. Didn't he like the look? Did I look ridiculous wearing this dress—I barely filled it out.

He pulled the phone closer to his face and spoke slowly, "You are fucking stunning. Do NOT make plans for tomorrow night. You're going on a date—with me. Now, you'll excuse me while I jack off to the picture I just took." His smile was devilish, and he blew me a kiss. "See you soon, sweetheart."

Uhhhh! I fell into the armchair, feeling tingly all over. Remembering his face filled with desire made my clit pulse. I wanted him to fuck me in these heels with my ass in the air. I wanted to be taken so desperately that I stripped off my dress and plunged two fingers into my wanton pussy as I worked myself so quickly it left me panting after I came. Fuck! This man was my soulmate—my everything! I wanted to please him in naughty ways as much as in proud ways. He deserved to have a classy lady at his side, but no one needed to know what happened behind closed doors. Tomorrow night would be epic; I'd make sure of it. Now, what to do about Seneca?

Chapter 24

First Dates and A Vision for Seneca

ABIGAIL

Today was an epic day in all aspects of the word.

First, I made an incredible stuffed French toast with fresh strawberries and crème fraîche. Seneca strained using the manual orange juice press, insisting that an automatic version be on my must-have list. If I were going to be an innkeeper, that gizmo would save me a ton of time.

After we satisfied our palettes, we cleaned up and headed to the detached garage to find some garden gear. Sunshine painted the sky blue, and the air smelled of dew. Anything life threw me seemed possible and my date with Elias was a dream come true. The beauty of the morning was soon destroyed as rancid smells poured out of the garage door, making my skin crawl and Seneca almost puke up her breakfast.

"Dis-gus-ting!" She screamed. "What the fuck died in here? Open the side door, and let's get some air flowing. I'm not staying in here for one more minute." She busted through the doorframe and kept walking toward the gardens. Like a puppy, I followed in tow. I'm not sure why I haven't been in this very obvious building since I moved in, except I hadn't needed to look there for anything. Elias didn't bring it to my attention, leaving me wondering if he had never wandered in. *Maybe I need to start thinking more for myself.*

The next epic moment clocked me upside the head when Seneca began identifying various flora.

"Those are annuals and will come up every year, so don't tear those out. These things that look like grass are, in fact, grass—ornamental grass. We can cut them down, split them, and let them be."

"Yes, ma'am. When did you learn about plants? You never mentioned this to me." How could I not know about my best friend's talent for gardening?

She walked further into the growth, stringing leaves and twigs through her fingers, stopping only to smell them.

"My mom insisted I knew where food came from when I was young. You may recall her being part American Indian. 'We come from Mother Earth. Everything we need, she provides.' I'll never forget that. She tore out some bushes that spring, and together we planted a small garden with cucumbers, green beans, tomatoes, and sunflowers." She paused, staring into space.

"We bought plants the first year, and after that, we harvested the seeds for the following year. She said this was the time of year we started our seedlings. Dad hated that we made a mess of his table, but he stayed out of our way." She sighed and continued walking.

"Sen, what happened with your mom? One day, she dropped you off at school, and the next, she was gone. You didn't stop crying for a week. Your dad said you could stay at my house for as long as you wanted, but I thought he went crazy. Even crazier—my aunt agreed to it."

Somewhere in the thick of these gardens, we found a wrought iron bench and sat down, pulling our knees to our chins. It's been ten years since her mom passed, and I hoped Seneca would finally unload her whole story.

She sat opposite me, deep in thought, fighting back tears.

"You're my best friend, Abs, so it hurts me that I never gave you the whole story. It's water under the bridge now we're adults, but you deserved to know." Another minute clicked by before she spoke again. "The truth was that my mother contracted pancreatic cancer, and my father refused to support her wishes to do nothing. Two days after she told us, she was gone, traveling the world as fast as she could before she died. I still don't understand how she could leave me—us—behind."

"Are you kidding me? Who does that? I don't know much about cancer, but you'd think spending every moment with your daughter would override any thoughts of seeing the world alone." I was shocked.

She sighed deeply. *Hmm.* "You'd think. All I have left are postcards from Italy, Greece, Egypt, France, and London. Each note was scribbled with, 'Wish you were here! Love you.' Do you have any idea how fucking hollow those notes were? She didn't want me there with her. She didn't love me," she screamed, reliving the trauma. "It took years of therapy for me to be able to understand those messages. 'Wish you were here'—so I could share these moments with you. 'Love you'—I couldn't put you and your father through the pain of watching me suffer."

"In the end, I chose to believe the therapist. Cancer does shit to people, and I decided to remember her with love and courage."

"As I recall, you were attending her graveside service less than three months later." I reached for Seneca's hand, offering what little support I could.

Huh! "The ironic part was that she was back five days before she passed, and we had to take care of her anyway. Thank goodness for morphine. We kept her sedated until her heart gave out."

My girl suffered for years after her mom's passing. I was content to know she found her peace. *It was time for something happy.*

I jumped up and took her hand. "Let's put those gardening skills to work. We'll remember your mom's best gifts."

For the rest of the afternoon, we worked together to hack down anything that wasn't a viable plant. For now, we made a compost pile at the side of the garage for convenience and emptied the worst of what was left there. Calling it a day, it was time to revisit the *Garage of Death* now aptly named.

"What do you want to do with all the dead animal carcasses?" *Seneca was kidding, right?*

"Make soup?" Even to me, the thought gave me the willies.

"Wrong! Don't ever say that to me again. There are only a few mice; seriously, Abigail, you're sick."

I had mouse traps all over the house, so why not also put a few out here?

I directed her to the cabinet under the kitchen sink to find more traps while I found a few things to start our seedling project. I noticed some bags of fertilizer and a few puddles on the concrete. This place needed waterproofing. I closed up the side door and walked to the lift-up door, making a note in my head to add these chores to Elias's To-Do List. I wondered if I could get Elias to build me a potting bench in his free time? *Ha. Free time. I'm his free time.*

SENECA

I'm not one to have visions, but I stopped short on the way to the house as I passed a budding rosebush. My mom's favorite flower was the rose. It wasn't lost on me that she was around in the wind. The sudden urge to build something magical here filled my heart and cleared my head. I would create something incredible, memorable, and meaningful in honor of her that I could look at forever. I could help Abby grow vegetables for her cooking and maybe even a garden where the community could work and reap the fruit of their labors. *Whoa.* That was quite a download of information.

Although I don't know what my friend would think, the idea was sound. She had her hands full already and didn't specify how long she wanted me to hang around. This idea needed careful delivery and timing. Since she mentioned Elias was coming to take her on a date tonight, I'd use that time to draw up a plan. Abby loved a good plan; I'd give her one in three phases.

ELIAS

I didn't plan a trip to Mystic this week. Honestly, I wasn't going to see Abigail for several weeks. I needed to flush this girl out of my system or die trying. I used every moment since I got home to scrutinize my life, what I wanted, and what needed to go. I started with old clothes. Not typically a dude thing, but, in the event I chose to pursue a relationship with Abi. . . someone . . . I wanted to look put together. Goodbye, ratty T-shirts, torn jeans, frayed button-downs, and those absurd silky shorts I used to play basketball in.

That took all of an hour, now onto the garage. Every project I started wasn't finished. It wasn't about money or time; it was more about inspiration. Several of these projects were inspired by Oria, the ex-girlfriend who treated me like dirt. Her name may have meant shiny or golden, but her heart was black as coal. While I appeared to look confident outwardly, she found every chink in my armor and lauded her superiority over me. She didn't mind my big dick, though. Oria found plenty of opportunities to "make it up to me," and I saw plenty of kinky ways to show her I wasn't a pussy but held back, afraid she'd use that information against me. After six months of learning about each other and talks of a future emerged, I noticed how little she gave to our relationship. Her hurtful ways and inability to be sincere took their toll on me, and, a few months later, I showed her the door. Patience should never be used as a weapon in a relationship. I gave her many opportunities to show me her commitment, and—each time—she let me down. I learned I was too patient in this regard.

I yanked apart those three projects I'd begun and made a scrap pile for future projects. The remaining piece was small in size but big in personality. I have an abundance of cutlery I've collected over the years for reasons I cannot disclose. Let's say that my college now has a new flatware pattern since they have been divested of the old style. This project inspired my childlike desire to build things from my mother's cutlery drawer. Spoons bent to look like legs and ears. A short fork for a tail and lots of wire wrapped to look like a body became my indestructible friend. It needed embellishments and polishing to make it look professional, yet it made me happy and calm. This was where I wanted to spend my time. Abigail's estate was the perfect place to realize that dream if we could work it out.

All the fight and anguish were out of me within forty-eight hours. Whatever ideas I had about waiting months to reconnect with her were out the window when she suggested phone sex and definitely when she put on that purple dress and sexy silver heels. My alter he-man ego took flight, and I blanked out when she agreed to call me daddy. I'm not a pervert; I'm a protector. It's a way for me and my trusted partner to build an even stronger connection than the norm. I wanted that so badly for me and Abigail. If she wanted a protector, she'd have it. If her biological father was too much of an asshole not to stay with his precious child, then fuck him. I'd shield her from the world.

Committed to making our relationship work, I pulled some clothes together and called Paul.

"Hey, buddy. We're slow now, so I'm heading down to see Abigail. Can you handle things for me? Call if you get a rush."

"Sure, boss. Have fun, but not too much fun if you—forget it. Talk to you soon. Don't forget to tell her what you've been thinking about. She needs to know."

I hung up mid-sentence. It's none of his business, except it is. If Abigail agrees to this plan, Paul will be more than an assistant manager to me.

Why was it that traffic was the slowest when you were in a hurry? My plans didn't include an overturned oil tanker and a ten-mile backup. It was time for a detour. The county road had already begun to fill up with like-minded travelers, so I rerouted through southern PA, over to Newark, and out the other side without adding more than twenty minutes to my drive. *Hallelujah!*

Beginning our dating life was nerve-wracking. I decided to start simple, like knocking on her front door.

"Wow! You are a giant. You weren't kidding, Abs!" the woman, whom I presumed was Seneca, hollered over her shoulder. "You must be Elias. Please come in." She waved her arm open for me to come in; her feigned sophistication was amusing.

"You must be Seneca, the long-lost best friend." I waggled my brows, shoving a hand in her direction.

"Precisely. Because I wasn't here when you two met, let me bring you up to speed. I know everything. I see everything and feel her pain, so tread carefully, my friend, because I'm watching you." She made a V out of her two fingers and pointed them at my face, then back at hers. I got the gist.

I ran a hand through my hair and fought hard not to laugh at her melodrama, "You are indeed the best friend. It never is, was, or will be my intention to hurt Abigail. You know her. She's unpredictable, impulsive, hilarious, and delightful. It's hard to be mad at her whether she deserves it or not."

"Damn, Elias! You know my girl." She lunged at me, throwing her arms around my waist. "I'm happy you took the time to figure her out. She's awesome, if not nuts."

My heart swelled, and I felt I had accomplished something in our short introduction. Gaining Seneca's approval was a big win for me.

A ruffle of purple arrived unannounced at the top of the stairs, and my sweet girl drifted down them one by one. Each step showcased a lithe, toned leg adorned with nothing but a shimmery shoe. I caught a glimpse of what she wore under that dress as she descended, and, if my eyes didn't deceive me, I'd swear she was bare. My dick jerked in my pants, and my chest felt tight.

She stared at me in my blue blazer and white, pressed shirt. I wanted to impress her and even pulled out a silver silk tie from my days as an engineer. Without overdoing my outfit, I pulled out my best dark blue jeans and polished brandy-colored lace-up boots. I know how to put myself together; I just don't like all the work involved. But, for Abigail? I'd put in the work.

When she reached the bottom step, I stepped forward and handed her the small bunch of flowers I had picked up in the village on my way in. Abigail was something out of a fairy tale, and I needed a minute to let this moment imprint on my brain.

"You look amazing, Elias." She touched my lapel, dragging her finger down its length. "You didn't have to bring me flowers . . . but I'm glad you did."

She smelled like vanilla and peaches, and made my mouth water. The dress was more spectacular in person, and I loved how it dipped into a low V below her pert breasts. My mind whirred like a finely-tuned engine when she leaned in for a kiss. It was soft and full of promise, and it took all my concentration not to pass out. It took a lot for a man my size to be knocked me down, yet this woman had only to look at me with those sultry, hazel eyes and pouty lips. *Fuck! I was in deep.*

"You smell like dessert. Can we skip dinner?" *Idiot! Keep to the plan. Woo her, dumbass.*

She grimaced. "No chance, Big Guy. I'm starving, and I need to show off my guy." *She was good.*

"You're on. I made a reservation down by the river. Let's get going."

As expected, when asked about her day, Abigail lit up like a firecracker, filling every moment of our drive with her garage escapades and grueling gardening endeavors. Tonight was about exploring her needs and wants. Before this night was over, I expected to clearly understand her life's trajectory and how I was to be a part of it. *Too many expectations? We'll see.*

Chapter 25

To Know Me is to Love Me

ELIAS

My pocket-sized woman allowed me to pick her up and set her into the cab of my truck. I should consider a better vehicle for nights out. I quickly made a left turn over the Mystic River Bridge and entered the posh parking lot of Enchanted Cuisine, an upscale seafood and steak restaurant. The reviews on this place were off the charts, and so were the prices. Today, I would spare no expense to woo my woman, pampering and assuring her she was deserving of such luxury.

The look on her face was priceless when we walked up the few wooden steps and through the artistically designed, plated glass doors. Her face flushed, and she turned to me, full of anxiety.

"Are we in the right place, Elias? This looks really expensive." Her eyes darted in every direction until she saw the flowing river on the other side of the dining room. "How about a few appetizers, and then we can go?" she winked.

While we waited for the hostess to return, I pulled her tightly to my chest and whispered into the shell of her ear.

"Tonight, you are my little girl, and I'm your daddy. When the server isn't present, you will address me as such. You'd be wise to accept that my little girl deserves the best, regardless of the cost. She is deserving of all things good and then some. You will behave with gratitude and appreciation for this evening without prompting. Do you understand me, Abigail?"

"Yes, Daddy," she whispered. I was elated to have her word. Every expression of her insecurity was minimized immediately for my benefit. She would learn over time that being uncomfortable was not a reason to run away.

I quickly snuggled into her neck and whispered, "Good girl. You're doing great."

The hostess witnessed my exploration of Abigail's neck and blushed. I was feeling proud getting two women to blush at the same time. The hostess cleared her throat and signaled me to come forward.

"Sorry for the wait. Please follow me." I ushered Abigail by her lower back around each table until we were seated in a remote corner near the water. I'll be sure to make another reservation soon because, once summer hits, this place will be jammed. Our menus were placed before us, and, once the hostess left, I took both of Abigail's hands and pressed them lightly in mine.

She was fascinated with the river and the raised Bascule cantilever drawbridge as we took our seats. Always the engineer, I explained what she was seeing and why it was so special.

"Sweetheart. When you open the menu, you cannot raise your voice. Do you understand? You can have whatever you want. Do not let the prices affect your decision. Alright?"

My tone was stern, and I hoped to instill calm in her mind and body. The first time I went to an upscale restaurant with a client, I thought I would throw up because of the outrageous prices. Embarrassed, I ordered an appetizer and said I wasn't that hungry.

As if she anticipated her cries, she pulled her hands from mine and covered her mouth.

"How bad are the prices?" She mumbled through her fingers.

"Bad," I reassured her, smiling from ear to ear.

"Oh my God. Okay, here I go." Daintily, she opened the cover with one finger and slapped her hand over the other, squealing. "Oh my God, oh my God, oh my God!"

"Breathe, princess. I told you to behave." I opened my menu and felt the bills in my wallet fly away. "We are both worth every penny of this menu. Now, let's find something fabulous to eat."

The waiter came to take our drink orders, and I ordered a shrimp cocktail for us to share. I ordered a bottle of her favorite white wine and studied her youthful face. Tiny, semi-noticeable freckles sprinkled her cheeks, giving her more color than her alabaster skin could produce. The sun looked good on her.

"I've never had real seafood. Those takeout places only serve battered fish, and it's gross." She made a nasty face, and my mind wished I had a still camera positioned next to the table to capture every delightful, sexy, fascinating expression she made. It would make for an exotic coffee table book.

Dinner arrived, and, ultimately, we shared my lobster and her filet. We stuffed our faces and played a short version of twenty questions, solidifying my initial observation that Abigail was highly intelligent. Sadly, it was her ADHD that camouflaged her accurate IQ. Her ability to absorb the big picture of most concepts we discussed attracted me. However, she got lost in the minutia, and that saddened me. I could only imagine how much more amazing she'd be if she went to college to spread her wings. My initial assessment still held that she would be incredibly successful in anything she did once she focused on a specific trajectory.

I heard knocking on the table, and my attention returned to her face. My mind wandered off again. It happened a lot, but somehow I managed to get stuff done.

"Tell me where your mind went?" she purred. I think she figured me out, too.

I stood and moved my chair beside hers to better view the river. *Or I just wanted my hands on her.*

"Always to you, princess. You're a marvel of a woman. You keep surprising me with how smart and tenacious you are." I slid my hand down her thigh and softly leaned in for a kiss.

"Daddy?" Hearing her say that name sent shivers up my spine, and my pants grew tighter again.

She continued. "Thank you for a lovely dinner. I've never been to a fancy restaurant like this. I'm glad you didn't tell me where we were going. I might have chickened out." She simpered. "I like surprises." She threaded her left-hand fingers over the one I had on her thigh and maneuvered them higher on her leg.

My breath hitched, and I wanted out of this place fast. I signaled the server and paid our bill quickly, leaving a fat tip. Within minutes, we were outside in the brisk spring air as sunset descended.

I didn't want to rush this evening like a horny teenager, so I directed her up the boutique-lined street, window shopping and learning each other's tastes. Cool April nights didn't attract many shoppers, so no one noticed when I pulled her into the little downtown gazebo. I pressed her against the opening pillar, keeping my growl low.

"Do you want to play, baby girl?" My voice was husky, and my breathing became labored.

Her hands pushed inside my coat, finding my nipples and pinching them. "I do, Daddy."

"Fuck, baby. It would be best if you learned to play fair. Did Daddy see correctly when you came downstairs that you were missing something under your pretty dress?' My dick pressed at her chest, giving her all the information she needed to know I meant business.

"Sort of," she bit her lip and averted her eyes to the buttons on my coat.

I slid two fingers under her chin and lifted her face to mine. "That's a yes or no question, Abigail. Are you, or are you not, wearing panties?"

Her plump lips were dry, and she licked them. "It's a thong, Daddy."

"That would be a yes, sweetheart, no matter how tiny. Do you need a punishment to remind you to be truthful with me? I already told you that I don't lie and that my honor is my most valued trait. Do you want me to see you that way, too?"

The truth hurt, and a single tear fell from her sexy eyes. She nodded and buried her head into my chest. She liked this game, and I was just beginning to play.

I pulled her back by her shoulders, forcing her to look at me. "You will not hide from me, Abigail. I'm not mad at you. I'm not even disappointed. We are establishing ground rules for our relationship, and, if we don't hold each other accountable for them, we won't have a strong foundation for when things get tough."

ABIGAIL

He literally had my back against a wall. There was nowhere to run, and he called me out on my shit so many times that it became pointless to try any longer, so I answered him as honestly as I could.

I played with the buttons on his coat, undeserving of looking him in the eye. "I understand, Daddy. I don't want to lie to you, ever. Truly."

He lifted my chin, not allowing me to hide from his stare. "Omitting details and necessary information are also called lies. I'd rather you tell me your thoughts than deliberately withhold information you think I might disapprove of." Both hands cupped my face, holding me still as he searched my eyes. The kiss that followed was hard and very convincing. He pulled away just as my legs began to wobble.

For him to take me seriously, I had to break the daddy/little girl scene; I wanted him to understand why I am the way I am. Our role-play was hot and sexy, but now was the time for honest, open dialogue.

"Elias, my whole life has been about survival. With that comes tons of white lies and skirting the truth, first with my aunt, then with homework, guys, and bosses. I would start to tell the truth and, after making stupid decisions, would get punished anyway. I felt trapped and worthless. I had to find a way to cover up or deflect my failures whenever possible. Over time, it became part of my nature. It is one that I'm not proud of, but now that I have my own life and money to live it with, I don't have to make excuses anymore. I tried to be honest with you before, but my emotions took over, and I fought back. I manipulated the situation to what I thought was my advantage, except it hurt you. Imagine what an eye-opener that was for me. You were the first person who spoke to me honestly without imposing your own agenda. I'm ashamed of how I treated you and want to make it up to you. Will you let me?"

I managed to unload my consciousness without crying, though now I'd like to run and hide from these huge emotions. They scared me, and I needed to purge them from my mind and body so I could settle down. I shook all over at the intensity of their wake, and yet I didn't want to leave his arms.

"We'll get there, sweetheart. Just keep talking with me, and I promise things will all work out. It took a lot of courage to see the error of your ways and communicate that to me. My little girl is growing into a beautiful woman right before my eyes."

Christ! Did you see how he pulled me back into our role-play? He's masterful.

"So, Daddy, when can I make things up to you?" I was done talking for the night. My head was pounding from the delicious wine, and now my clit purred as his hands slid around my ass. *Or was that me purring? Either way, my body was humming.*

"Now," he growled, pushing my dress up around my waist, not caring who might walk by. He pushed me onto the gazebo bench, unbuttoned his coat so it hung around my legs, and pushed my knees higher. When he looked down and saw the tiny swatch of material covering my bare pussy, he clucked his tongue.

"Sweetheart, your answer to the panty question should have been 'no.' I can see your slit through that lace, and there couldn't be enough fabric to cover my thumb." It wasn't a moment before he ripped aside that tiny shred of fabric and inserted one of his fingers deep inside me. I gasped at the intrusion and coldness of his digit. He kissed me deeply, moving his tongue the same way he moved his finger.

"My God, Daddy. That feels so good." I moaned when he turned that digit upward, grazing that perfect place. "Yes! Daddy, yes, there."

He laughed devilishly, pulling his finger out to suck my juices. "Not yet, little girl. You still owe me a punishment."

His fingers plunged into my soaking pussy again, and I moaned loudly. "Fuck, Daddy."

"No more outbursts like that, or we're done. Do you want an audience?" *Shit! I didn't think about that.*

"No, Daddy. I'll be quiet. Please don't stop." His face was as intense as my desire. If he didn't make me come this instant, I would scream.

Daddy growled again and shoved his fingers even higher, scissoring them until I smacked my hands over my mouth. "You will learn to control your outbursts, little one. Daddy will let you come when he's ready for you to come.

"Open your mouth," he commanded, and I lowered my hands to my sides. He pushed his thick, long fingers into my mouth, forcing me to taste myself.

"Do you like the way you taste, baby girl? So sweet. Like honey to my senses." I sucked his fingers, surprised by the taste of my essence. It smelled sweet, though the look on his face was sweeter. His eyes hooded over, and he moaned so low his chest shook. He was getting off on this, and I would capitalize on this moment as well.

I simpered again, "Again, Daddy."

"Fuck, baby girl." He repeated the deep thrust of his fingers, but, instead of two, he used three. The stretch was so intense that it took him a minute to work through my folds to get them inside me. He pumped them several times until I was breathless. "Take it, sweetheart."

His rawness excited me in ways I never thought possible. From sweet and kind to sounding like an animal, it blew me away. I felt empty when his fingers stopped their invasion. His low growl filled my ears, and his eyes turned dark and menacing.

"Suck," he commanded. My chest heaved, and my heart soared at his command. I took all three fingers, choking on them as he slowly pushed in and out. I'd become an animal just like him, lost in lust and pleasure, unable to hear the outside world. I didn't know myself at that moment, but I trusted Elias to protect me like the daddy he was.

I felt ravaged. He wouldn't let me come, and my juices trickled down my thighs as he pulled me to standing. I pulled my dress down, looking left and right to be sure we were still alone. Time stood still, and my head was woozy. I'm pretty sure we broke the law, but, on the flip side, I now have a greater appreciation for a gazebo. We literally left our mark on it. *Note to self. Bring a disinfecting wipe over tomorrow to clean up.*

Elias pulled me into his body and kissed the top of my head like a pleased father would an obedient child.

"You were a very good girl, Abigail. You listened and gave Daddy what he wanted. I'm very proud of you." I sighed audibly. *When had anyone told me they were proud of me?*

My body fractured at his praise, releasing deep-seated emotions I must have stuffed down my whole life. I sobbed giant tears and collapsed in his arms. I couldn't have known that hearing those five words would bring me to my knees. What was happening to me?

Elias stroked my hair as I mumbled several incoherent thoughts even to myself, and we began our walk back to the car. He didn't ask if I was alright or needed anything. He only stroked my hair and whispered sweet nothings to calm me down. His arms around my shoulders were warm, strong, and safe. It felt like new neuropathways were opening up in my mind, and I could see the world in a new way. Elias was changing my world in so many new ways that I could never reciprocate them, so I kept on crying. Besides a house and a barn, what could I offer to someone like him?

He hauled me into his chest like a baby and stood up. "Come on, princess. Let's get you home."

Chapter 26
A Three-Way Pact

ABIGAIL

Whoever said crying was for babies didn't know me very well.

By the time we returned to his truck, I had dried my tears, but Elias—Daddy—had more plans for me that couldn't wait.

"I believe dating is good for us, Abigail. Did you have fun tonight?" He nodded, suggesting I mirror his motions.

"Yes, Daddy. It's been lots of fun. Are we done playing?" I frowned, pouting.

"Only if you want to be, but be warned. Daddy can say goodnight, but Elias has a whole list of filthy things he wants to do to you."

Eeek!

"I want to play with Elias." I unbuckled my seatbelt and crawled across the console to plant a big, wet kiss on his sweet, pink lips. He pulled me into his lap, and we made out while he massaged my breasts through my dress.

"Enough!" He exclaimed. "Damn, woman, if I don't get you home soon, I'm going to blow my wad in my pants, and I'm not a goddamn teenager. Buckle up!" My peals of laughter filled the cab as he squealed the tires on the pavement.

What once was a ten-minute trip from Mystic Square to my home now became four. Every traffic light was a suggestion, and we coasted through every stop sign. We were breaking laws all over this town. Elias screeched his tires at every stop sign and almost threw me through the windshield when we pulled up the driveway, throwing the gear shift into Park before stopping completely. "Out!" he ordered.

I think he forgot Seneca was home because he had his shirt off by the time we entered the side door, his belt undone, his pants unbuttoned, and a delicious line aiming under his boxer briefs. Seneca pulled her head from the refrigerator doors, freezing him in place.

"Hey—ho! Hi there. I guess your date went well. I'm just…" She closed the doors and turned her head to look out the windows.

I pushed Elias up the back stairs while fluffing my hair. "Hey, Sen. Going upstairs now. Toss me the whipped cream, would ya?"

She gave me a big wink and threw me the can. "Safety first, Abs." I aimed a finger pistol in her direction and a "Roger that" wink back at her.

"Lock up, Sen. Nighty-night." I scampered up the stairs to find my man naked, sprawled out on the bed, and his hand warming up his dick for me.

"Don't you look delicious?" I licked my lips, drawn to the liquid pearl calling out to me. I reached for the zipper at my neck, letting my dress pool onto the floor. My strong, intense, sexy man spread his legs wider, jerking on his shaft to entice me. *Did he think seeing him naked wasn't enough to fall to my knees?* "Geezus, Elias. I've missed you."

My tiny hands wrapped tightly over his steel shaft, relieving himself of his hands. His crown was purple and leaking, and I licked that pearl like it was my favorite flavored lollipop. His throaty response turned me on even more. I squirted whipped cream on his crown and licked again. The sweet and salty combination complimented the tang I still had on my tongue from my own juices, melding them perfectly. It was erotic and dirty, and I loved it. Being naughty was a good thing for the first time in my life.

"Sweetheart, that tongue of yours is something else. Take all of me in that pretty mouth." *Damn straight, I would.* He stepped closer and pressed my lips apart with his thick head, and I grabbed his ass for leverage. I wasn't an experienced cocksucker, but I could be a good student when I wanted to be, and today I would be a star pupil.

"That's right, baby. Suck me hard." I remembered his previous instructions, relaxed my jaw, and breathed through my nose, allowing him to penetrate my throat. I gagged each time he pressed into my face, but I held to my decision to take more of him each time I had his big dick in my mouth.

"Fuck. Yes. Deeper, baby," he said after each gentle pump. I forced myself to take him back farther, but he was too big. When I pulled off to suck in more air, I whimpered.

"You're too big. I'll never get all of you in my mouth." I wiped my face of saliva and fallen tears.

"In time, you'll be able to take more. Trust that you can one day, but know that it doesn't make you a failure if you can't. I'm a big man, Abby. You'd have to be some freaky witch to take all of me." He wiped my tears with his thumb, giving me an encouraging smile. I thought he would help me up, but, instead, he pushed my head back onto his cock, staring at my face as his cock slid in and out each time. I must have been quite a sight, for—a few pumps later—he held my head and pressed himself deeply down my throat.

"Swallow, Abby. Every drop. Ye-es, yes. Good girl." He didn't command me but told me like it was good for me as his cum shot down my throat. High praise and encouragement were good for me. Elias not giving up on me gave me more confidence. I felt it even more when he pushed and supported me to go beyond what I thought I couldn't do.

I didn't think I had another tear to pour out of my body, yet a few more fell as I realized I'd leaped over another hurdle in my life.

"Thank you, Elias." I sat back on my heels and resolved to do better at everything.

"The pleasure was all mine." He winked, holding his hand out to help me up.

I chuckled. "I don't think so," as I walked back to the bed.

Elias spent the next hour licking, flicking, and sampling every part of my body without using his dick. If he was trying to break me, he succeeded. I hoped he planned on impaling me with that big dick of his, or I'd have to go for a sneak attack in the middle of the night. Luckily, he flipped me over, smacked my bottom, and fucked me hard. I came so far and hard that I blacked out, only to find myself on my stomach.

He straddled my ass and massaged my cheeks. "One day, little girl, Daddy will teach you how strong and courageous you truly are right here." A thick finger trailed its way from my pussy hole to my butt hole and penetrated that tight ring of muscle.

"Holy fuck! That smarts!" I screamed. *Why did people think this was pleasurable?*

He shushed me. "You're clenching. You have to relax. Breathe, sweetheart. I've got you." He pushed another finger into my wet pussy and painted my hole with my juices and reinserted his finger again. "Breathe out when I push in. There you go."

I'm a fucking porn star tonight. So what if I felt proud of my accomplishments? Some of the things we did tonight weren't for the faint of heart, and, once I got the hang of it, it felt amazing. Elias kept massaging his finger around my opening, then driving it in at various speeds, measuring my responses to each. After the first two pumps, I was soaking wet.

Elias reached his other hand around to my clit, making small, light circles as I whimpered at his ministrations. It didn't take long before he had me pressing my ass onto his fingers like a dog in heat. "Elias, please. I'm almost there. Please don't stop." I implored him to keep going, and my prayers were answered.

"Fuucck, Elias. Oh my God, yessss!" My ass locked down on his finger, and he puffed out a large sigh.

"My God, Abby. You looked so fucking hot, begging for my fingers. I can hardly wait to see my cock penetrate that tight asshole of yours. Fuck, you are perfect. Where have you been all my life, sweetheart?"

All his life? I wasn't even born when he hit puberty. He may not have had the love he deserved as a youngster, but I'd give him every hug, kiss, and word of praise for the rest of my life to make up for those years. Now that he was back with me, I wouldn't ever give him up—ever.

He rolled to his back, pulling me on top of him. "I've been here. Waiting for you to find me."

I was moving slowly this morning. My girl parts were sore from the three times Elias brought me to bliss, and only a shower and a cup of coffee could get me going.

Elias carried me to the shower and personally washed all my bits, insisting that only Daddy could do a thorough job. *Who was I to argue?*

"Thank you, Daddy. Can I wash you now?" I swiveled my shoulders demurely.

"You've wiped me out, sweet girl, but if you want, you can rub anything clean you want." He backed up to the wall of the shower and spread his arms and legs wide while I used my small hands over, in, and around all his crevices until he grabbed my hands and ordered me to kneel. "Clean out Daddy's cock, baby. You've earned it."

What started as a quick shower took longer than necessary, but Elias was happy, and so was I—right after he ate me out on the vanity. We were like two children who found the best toy in the world. Playing with Elias never got boring, and, soon, he said Daddy would teach me more fun ways to play. I couldn't wait.

As we both entered the kitchen, the smell of coffee was intoxicating. Seneca cooked bacon and eggs while soft rock music played in the background.

"Good morning, lovebirds. I'm surprised you can walk after the screams I heard all night." We all laughed as I looked at Elias, who was embarrassed.

I poked him in the chest. "I told you we'd need to add insulation in my bedroom. I can't have our guests hearing us fuck all night long." He had the decency to keep walking past me and pouring himself a cup of joe.

"What's on tap today, kiddos?" Seneca added cheese to our scrambled eggs and then stared at me with a weird smile on her face. What was she up to?

I looked at Elias, inquiring if he had anything specific he had planned. "Don't look at me. I came down for a date. I don't work here—yet." He blanched and hid behind an old newspaper.

I marched over to him and ripped the paper out of his hands. "What does that mean? Something on your mind, Big Guy?" *This pet name would come in handy.*

He looked to Seneca for help, and she shook her head. She turned off the stove and set up breakfast on the table. After she poured herself a cup of coffee, she motioned me to the coffee pot.

"You best get yourself some coffee. I have a few things I'd like to run by you this morning." She eyed Elias, and he picked up his fork, stuffing his face with eggs.

Through muffled words, he muttered, "Yeah, I have a few things on my mind, too." He eyed her back.

"I'm first," she jabbed a finger in his direction, and he sat back in concession. *Look at my two favorite people vying for my attention. I felt so special.*

I wasn't the most astute person, but I could tell something was up, and I sat down with my coffee and oat milk creamer poised for a presentation. I could handle almost anything as long as Elias didn't dump me.

"Shoot," I said, nodding to Seneca.

She cleared her throat and sipped her coffee once more. She pulled out two pieces of paper from under her plate and pressed them to her chest.

"Before you get crazy on me, please let me give you my whole pitch." *Me, crazy? Never. A pitch? Should I be concerned?*

"Here goes. I've been thinking about you and your new house and stuff and, well, about me. You have this amazing house and garden, and I can only imagine how daunting a task it would be to do all the things you told me about without some help." She looked up and gulped.

"Continue," I said encouragingly. I knew where she was going, but I promised not to interrupt.

She smiled and pressed her papers again. "It's a win-win; I could help rebuild the gardens and help you grow some vegetables. Maybe we could build a walking path meditation garden. Remember the one we walked at the botanical gardens a few years back? It was so cool."

Her excitement was contagious. I smacked the table as I remembered our outing. "Oh my God! That would be amazing. I'd love to design one of those." She wiggled in her seat at the prospect of building something magical. Elias thunked his mug down and hummed at the idea.

"Was there anything else you wanted to say, Sen?" It sounded as though Seneca would be staying with me for several months. Did I want that?

She put her papers back under her plate and looked at me straight. "This home is a new start for you, Abs. If you're okay with it, I'd like it to be a new start for me, too. I love to garden, and we wouldn't be in each other's space all day so you wouldn't get sick of me. I'm tired of working inside a store with shitty bosses. I have too much energy to stay seated all day. You know that. Also, I can help wash and change sheets after guests leave and be your right-hand girl. The only thing I'd ask for is room and board. I have some money stashed away to get me through for a while. What do you think?"

Seneca sat on the end of her chair, waiting to spring up and hug me. I wanted to say yes immediately, but I also had to consider what Elias wanted to say. He could throw a wrench into this whole plan, and then what would I do? Here was a perfect example of learning to be patient and think logically, so I took a deep breath and looked at Elias.

"Everything you said sounded great, Sen. It would only be fair for me to allow Elias to share his thoughts before making any final decisions. Is that cool with you?"

She deflated into her seat and sighed. "I suppose so." My friend and I are both learning not to be impulsive. It's a process. I opened my hand and motioned for Elias to speak as I ate my cold eggs.

"I have to say, Seneca would fill a huge gap in the renovations of your property. You should certainly consider her services and the additional expense." *Very practical, just like a daddy.* "I have a few ideas of my own, keeping in mind we are both committed to building our relationship. I could keep my service station in Pennsylvania going with the help of my Assistant Manager and chief mechanic. He'd get a bump in pay, and I could move down here more permanently. If you'd allow, I'd like to rent space in your barn, converting half of it into a mechanic shop servicing the Mystic area. It would bring more traffic to the area and to your B&B, which would be two more sources of income for you instead of finding another job."

I held my hand up to stop him. I needed to digest what he was offering. He had previously mentioned bits and pieces of his ideas, but I hadn't put them all together.

"If I'm hearing correctly, you want to move in with me? You want to help me make a living from this place? Are you sure, Elias? That's a huge move. What will your clients say? Your parents? Oh, what about your friend, Reilly? Don't you help him every week? What will he do?"

I could feel a panic attack ramping up. It was easy for Seneca to make the move. She didn't have any responsibilities; Elias had a ton, and the thought of him picking up and making me more important than any of those things was remarkable. My heart felt like the Grinch when his heart grew three times. *I told you I felt like a cartoon at times.*

He kept seated and gave me one of his stern Daddy looks. "I've already spoken to Reilly, and, although he's bummed about it, he knows how important you are to me. He even offered to come down and walk the whole property with us to see if any fencing needed fixing or any garden work you might require. No interference, Seneca." He winked at her—*such a charmer.*

"I was being straight with you when I said you should make the other half of the barn a studio. We could make a very cool ceramic area and cut in a big window for daylight, allowing you to paint any time of the day. With a few updates, you could practically live out there. Then there's all that acreage. You spoke of a corn maze or sculpture garden; the options are limitless." He stared out the window, deep in his visions.

"Geez-Louise, this is a lot to consider . . . I want it all!" I proclaimed, jumping up and down."

I have no fucking clue how much all these ideas will cost me, but I love them all, and I love you both so much for wanting to help me make a go of this place. It warms my heart."

Arms flew around me from low and high, enveloping me with love and support. It felt like I won a second lottery.

I know I've loved Seneca since we were kids, using the word love in a super awesome sense. But I love-love Elias, as in forever-I-do. Using that word flippantly with Elias would diminish what we had. Was our love the real thing? I'd never been in love before, so how would I know? On the other hand, I knew that true love came with sacrifice, and he made tremendous sacrifices for me to make our future together. I also knew love was kind, and no one was kinder than Elias. Everything he did or said oozed kindness, and all I had to do was not shit on him with my self-deprecating words or low self-esteem. That was the only thing he asked of me. I loved Elias and couldn't wait another moment to tell him.

I took his hand and looked up at his handsome, rugged face. His eyes sparkled, and I fought back tears at how lucky I was to have a man like him.

"Elias, would you walk with me?"

Skepticism flashed across his face, and I hurried him out the side door. I kept pulling him faster because I was impatient and wanted to jump onto his body, show him my revelation, and tell him at the same time.

"Slow down, Abigail. Where are you taking me?"

I took two steps to each of his until the path ended at the barn. There were open fields that went on seemingly forever, and trees lined up like soldiers on the right. Hills of greening grass covered the acreage to the left and open fields as far as the eye could see. This was all my land, and it made sense to stand in front of it and share my heart with him.

Elias stopped abruptly. "Whoa. Look at all of this land. I haven't been past the barn, but it goes on and on, doesn't it?" He looked down at me, placing his hands on my hips and lifting me into his arms. "You are the heiress to all this property, right?"

"Uh-huh." My brain went offline when he stared at my lips. The anticipation of his mouth on mine never ceased to diminish. "I need you to put me down. I need to tell you something."

He let me slip to the ground, not knowing what to expect. The crinkles at the corners of his eyes became more evident, and his brow creased, waiting for me.

"What I'm about to tell you is something I've never said to anyone. It's not a joke or something I take lightly, so here goes." I wiped my hands on my jeans and began walking in a circle.

"I think . . . I love you. Okay, not think—I do, but not in an amazing 'like' kind of way, but the real thing, I love you." My arms flexed out in front of me, alternating every time I said the word love. Was I trying to convince myself? I must have looked like an idiot to him. Who walked in circles and spoke to themselves when the person they should be speaking directly to was standing in front of them? *ME! That's who.*

He shook his head and threw me over his shoulder, swatting my ass. "What the fuck, Elias. What are you doing?"

Long legs walked me to the first bank of trees to our right and flipped me onto a low branch. Now, eye to eye, he said, "Start again, Abigail." He had a way of getting my attention, and this time was no different.

I pushed my loose hair back behind my ears, taking calming breaths. I looked up and peered into his light brown eyes filled with care—or was it desire? Either way, they took my breath away. "I love you, Elias."

He replied by kissing me deeply, ending with a sensual pull on my bottom lip. "I love you too, Abigail. It's about time you figured that out," he teased.

I stared at him intently, my hands cupping his face. "What do you mean about time? It took as long as it took." Then it struck me: when did he realize he loved me? "When did you figure it out?" I pulled on his now shorter beard, feigning annoyance.

He paused, answering matter-of-factly. "It could have been when you were having a breakdown in my parking lot. Or, when you were doing a little dance, as you freaked out over a mouse. But, definitely, when I overheard you talking to Amy the Great while pulling weeds. You're priceless, Abigail, and thoroughly entertaining. I want to watch your antics for a lifetime." He chuckled and stepped closer between my legs, kissing me like it was his mission in life.

When we came up for air, Elias returned me to the earth. Hand in hand we walked and talked—about Seneca and her plans for helping me—and he agreed that I could use the help. Having a friend to support me while I figure out my next move would be good. I stopped him when we reached the barn, needing clarification from one of his statements.

"You said 'lifetime' out there. Did you mean that?"

He kissed me again. "I can see that you still need convincing. I plan to love you until death do us part."

"Holy shit, Elias. Are you proposing to me right now?" Amy strutted out of a bush and clucked about in a circle. I jammed my hands onto my hips, watching Elias's head swivel in confusion. "See! Even Amy wants an answer."

He pursed his lips and jammed his hands on his hips, "I . . .This . . . We," he replied, shaking his head, presumably looking for his words. "No. Not today."

I was crestfallen. He still wasn't sure, and rightfully so. I was a wildcard. I could respect his need to see if this move would work out. Marriage was a big deal, and rushing into it was a bad idea.

He grabbed my shoulders. "Abigail! Get out of your head. I know what you're thinking and stop it—now!" "Give me some time to plan something special for you. Can you be patient, little girl?" *If he kept talking to me that way, then no!*

"Fine!" I yelled like a brat. "I can be patient!" I ranted every word like a five-year-old not getting their way.

"Good." He walked into the barn humming a merry tune, and I ran to the house to tell Seneca I was in love.

Chapter 27

Found Money and Philanthropy

A BIGAIL

So much for beautiful spring days. I'd secretly wished for a rainy one to go to the tax assessor's office and find answers about my great-great-grandparents. Per my previous conversation with Mr. Brickner, I spread out the contents of the yellow envelope he gave me over a month ago. I'm not proud that I didn't recognize the importance of those documents, but I'm older and wiser now, and I asked Elias to help me understand what I was looking at.

Clutching steamy cups of coffee, I picked up the document labeled *Land Survey.* "One hundred and sixty acres looks so small on this page." I chuckled at my wit.

Elias rolled his eyes. "Let me put this in perspective for you." He pointed to a bracket at the bottom of the page. "This is called a legend. It gives you a reference for everything on the map or survey in this situation."

I wasn't stupid. I'd seen a map and a legend before. Wrapping your head around one hundred and sixty acres was like envisioning a billion dollars. You can't do it if you've never seen it all piled up before you.

Wanting him to feel proud of me, I pointed to each symbol. "Blue lines for rivers, bumps for hills, peaked bumps for mountains, and the line segment says one inch per ten acres, and there are—let me see —sixteen of them. What's an acre?"

He palmed his beard several times, "Well done, princess. An acre is about the size of two football fields, shy of the end zones."

Doing the math, my head spun. "Who the hell is going to mow all that grass? Not me!"

Elias bent over hysterically. What was he laughing at? He grabbed his stomach, his eyes watered, and he stomped his foot.

"What's so funny?" I said indignantly. I would not be laughed at this way. I was serious about the grass.

"Princess, you are the funniest person I've ever met—mow the grass." Laughter bounded from him again, and my ire was up.

I shook a finger at him and shrieked, "Stop that!"

It took a minute, but he pulled himself together and wrapped his big arms around me in a bear hug. "Abigail, no one cuts the grass. They never have, and we probably won't either. Cows eat the grass. We farm the land. I'll mow around the house and the eventual sculpture garden, and we'll let nature do its thing. Sound good?"

Since he put it that way, that's fine, though I really should stop more often and think about what I'm saying before I say it.

"Now that you've had your laugh, walk me through the rest of these."

Elias took his time reading through each document, ensuring I understood them. The antique inventory I discussed with Mr.

Brickner was magically there, and I almost fell off my chair when I read the bottom line.

"One and a half million dollars! For furniture and knick-knacks? I'm an heiress all over again. Christ! I almost gave those ugly lamps to Micah for nothing. Do you think I should hire someone to go through all the junk I want to toss in case it's worth something?"

He rubbed his brow. "It's not a bad idea. I'm sure we could go through and get rid of the obvious junk, like those cactus beer mugs. Let's go through all of it tomorrow and separate the junk. Call Micah to see if she wants to join us. We'll have a party of it, okay?"

I climbed into his lap and kissed his delicious lips. "Thank you, Elias. You do make my life better."

He returned the kiss and pouted. "You just like that I do stuff for you."

I pouted back like a little girl, "You do the best stuff, Daddy."

I could feel his cock rise to the occasion, a sly grin forming on his lips, "Only the best for my little girl. Now get the fuck off my lap, or you can kiss this day goodbye." He pushed me gently to the floor and stood abruptly to march out of the room.

Guess who's laughing now?

Thankfully, the tax assessor's office was open on Friday. This was another historic building with elaborate moldings and beautiful staircases. They were everywhere, from the library to the school we passed on the way over, this building, and the bank we needed to stop at next. I'm not a history buff—though I've seen enough historic signs when our eighth-grade class went to Washington, D.C.—but living in Mystic was a step back in time.

The lobby sign directed me to the second floor, and I knocked on the appropriate door. A woman in her fifties, wearing an audacious pair of neon blue glasses, greeted me kindly. "Well, hello to you two. How can I help you today?" She studied me and Elias and made whatever assumptions she might, inviting us to have a seat.

I slid off my slicker and put my purse in my lap. Elias had the envelope of the articles I had Micah copy from the library, and, with any luck, I'll have another treasure trove of data to think about.

"I'm Abigail Farnsworth-Burton, and this is my friend, Elias. We're here to look through some historical documents regarding my family. Could you help us?"

I barely finished speaking as the woman's face turned ashen. *Why did people keep doing that when I introduced myself?*

She sipped her water bottle and cleared her throat. "I heard you'd moved to Mystic. What a lovely surprise to have a member of the Farnsworth family back with us."

I looked at Elias, then back to the woman. "How long has it been since a Farnsworth lived here?"

She didn't move her mouse, or look in a file; she knew exactly how long it had been. "Twenty-five years."

"I'm sorry we didn't catch your name." It wasn't a question, and, by the tone of his voice, Elias must have known she was holding back information.

She shook her head nervously, answering weakly, "Excuse me, I'm Mrs. Hutchinson. Ellen Hutchinson."

Elias sat back in his seat, telepathically giving me the go-ahead to continue.

I nodded my head once. "Mrs. Hutchinson, there seems to be a great deal of information about my family that I'll need your help discovering. Are you ready for a million questions?" My grimace was intended to be friendly, but I knew something was up, and I wouldn't stop until I knew everything about this place, my family, and the people who befriended them or hated them.

Mrs. Hutchinson stood, pressing her hands together. "Let's get started then. Follow me."

Elias and I silently followed Mrs. Hutchinson, holding hands as we walked down three flights of stairs into the archive room.

"Please don't be daunted by the sheer magnitude of the documents in these boxes," she pointed out, "This wall houses almost every document from Mystic's inception to the turn of the twentieth century."

Like the volumes of old books I'd already looked through, Ellen recited the protocol for interacting with them. Elias seemed impressed. "The office is open until four-thirty. Please let me know when you're finished, or I'll come to you just before closing. Do you have any questions?"

"Elias, would you pull out the last article in the envelope? I think it will help Mrs. Hutchinson understand the importance of my findings." He grinned, knowing exactly what card I wanted to play in this poker game. He handed her the article, and we waited for the expected outcome.

Her jaw dropped, and the paper slapped her thighs. "You know," was all she could utter.

I closed my eyes, relieved that my intuition guided me right where I needed to be. "I do. It seems great-great-granddaddy won big in the war against Mexico. If I'm not mistaken, his contracts with the government for timber and food brought this area quite a few perks—this building, for instance."

I could barely contain my glee when Elias touched my shoulder.

"Mrs. Hutchinson, we aren't here to stir up any controversy; we are only here to learn all the details of how the Farnsworth Estate came to be and who the last family members were to live in the house. Thank you for your assistance; we'd like to get started."

The assessor left the room, her brows creased and her voice mumbling under her breath. I wasn't sure why she was so conflicted. It wasn't her issue, only her problem to help us. There was more to this story, but today had already been a big win for me. Ezekiel and Agatha Farnsworth became more and more real every time I dug up their past. So far, I'd only learned good things about them; I hope today would be more of the same.

Our time was almost up, and we tabbed over a dozen pages we thought were important. Ezekiel was a crafty dude and very well respected. He sat on several village boards and appeared to have a way of doubling or tripling his efforts yearly. He wrote several doctrines on behalf of the Whig party, encouraging progress and using Mystic's resources to fund them. I suppose when he hit it big, he didn't wait for progress; he made it himself. The question was, did my family still own these "effects of progress." That was my goal, and I wouldn't stop until I found out.

"Did you have fun, princess?" He smacked my ass as I climbed into his truck. *Fun?* Interesting choice of words.

"More validated than fun, I'd say. Seeing the look on Mrs. Hutchinson's face—that was fun. Great fun, in fact. I thought she'd pee her pants when I showed her that article." I giggled, buckling my belt.

"She'll definitely have a skid mark in her undies today. You'd have thought I'd found the key to some national secret. I wonder what they're all hiding?"

That's the million-dollar question.

I looked over the notes we made, and a thought occurred to me. "Do you think that they think we're going to make a stink about taking these buildings back? What do I need with a park? I already have a one-hundred-and-sixty-acre park. I'm happy they have a great school, library, bank, and everything my family provided. If Seneca comes through as planned, the Farnsworth family will have a community garden. They should be happy I'm back—of course, they don't know that yet."

Elias rounded several curves on our way back home, lost in thought.

"All that would make sense, but something happened between your great-great-grandparents dying and the last Farnsworth leaving. Maybe you'll write the next Great American Mystery in your free time when you figure out why."

Too tired to respond, we hummed our agreement.

Dinner awaited when we arrived, and Elias went for a beer.

"Any luck, you two? Is the name Farnsworth worth anything around here?" Seneca flipped burgers in a pan and tossed caramelized onions and mushrooms in another. It smelled so good, and not having to cook felt luxurious.

I kissed her cheek, grabbed the buns off the counter, and placed them on the table. I gathered condiments from the fridge and answered her questions.

"Funny, you should ask. The Farnsworth name dates back to pre-1832, and the family owned half of this town. To answer your first question, hell, yeah, we found a goldmine of answers.

Seneca turned off the heat and pivoted toward me. "You're not fucking with me? You own this town, village, whatever?" Her expression of dismay was priceless.

I filled three water glasses and answered, "Not the whole place," and burst into laughter. "The downside to all this information was that the tax assessor, Mrs. Hutchinson, and probably others, think I'm up to something. Me? The one who can't put a solid plan together is trying to take over a tiny village in Connecticut? They're off their rockers if they think I could pull that off."

Elias sat silently, pondering my predicament. Of what exactly, neither of us knew. That was a great mystery, and I didn't have time to worry much about it. I had renovations to make, gardens to plant, and a business to establish. All this other bullshit would have to wait.

He took a long pull from his bottle and picked at the label. "The way I see it is these people will come forward out of fear and disclose their issues. You sit tight and wait for them to come to you. Maintain the upper hand. It's a good strategy." He pursed his lips and nodded, affirming his plan.

"Did you pick up this strategy from sports or *CSI* shows?" I was being a brat, and he took the bait as planned.

"I'll have you know, I'm not only pretty, I'm smart, and, yes, my wrestling coach beat that concept into my mind for years. It worked almost always, so why recreate the wheel?"

"Do you think there was espionage, murder, or, better yet, a Hatfield vs. McCoy family war? Ooh, that would be juicy." Seneca loved family wars, especially mafia ones. What if Big Man Farnsworth was a villain? You could have a target on your back, Abs."

Oh my God! I'm going to have a panic attack. "STOP," I yelled. "It's none of those things—I hope. Can we drop this for now? It's giving me anxiety, and I want to enjoy your burgers."

"Sorry, Abs. Let me get the sweet potato fries out of the oven, and we can eat." Seneca finished gathering our food, and Elias spun his bottle on its edge.

I gave him a look, "What's with you?"

"I don't know if I want to open a shop on Farnsworth property. Your reputation could kill my business," Elias deadpanned.

I smacked his arm hard. "Fuck off, Elias. My reputation is spectacular, and I haven't given you one reason not to stay here." *Okay, maybe I had, but we were past that.*

He rubbed his arm like a mosquito had bitten him. "Like I said earlier, you are entertaining if not nuts."

I gasped, feigning hurt. "But you *love* my nuts!"

He choked on his beer. "I think you have that backward, Abigail. It's *my* nuts, you love."

"O M G! Will I have to sit with you two, sexing up our dinner? Knock it off."

We were ashamed enough to blush, sending silent promises for a rematch later. Dinner was terrific, and Elias shooed us out of the kitchen while he cleaned up. I wouldn't fight him on it, so Seneca and I snuggled up on the parlor sofa with her garden plans.

"Before I begin, I've laid my concept out in stages, so don't freak out when you see what I did. First, I've divided the garden into genres: edible, fragrant, and meditation. We'll put the edible garden closest to the driveway so you don't have so far to collect them, and, if you decide you'd like it to be a community garden, it would be easier for people to access it. See, I left a huge gap between it and the next garden, so you have room to expand."

My friend was totally in her element, and, as she explained the rationale behind her plans, I saw her come alive. She hadn't been as passionate about anything since she got an A in biology and promised to become a biologist. It was exciting then, though seeing her morph into her true calling inspired me to support her efforts.

"I'm in shock, Sen. You have truly outdone yourself. You thought of everything for the present and the future. I can see it now: a dozen gardeners reaping the fruits of their labor and bringing our neighborhood a place to share its joy of the earth. Well done, friend."

I kissed her cheek and laid my head on her shoulder. Looking at the sketches, I pointed to a section by the barn. "What's this?"

"I love this next garden. It's all about fragrances. I have to research to find the best blend of smells, like roses with something else. Lavender is paired with another plant that blends well. Does this make sense?"

"I like vanilla with both of those plants. I also enjoy lemongrass with oranges or mint. You have a lot of research to do. I wouldn't even know what would grow well in this area."

Elias entered with a tea tray with some fudge cookies I had stashed at the back of the pantry. "I'm a fan of sandalwood and patchouli." He set the tray on the table and poured each of us a mug of hot water.

"Aren't you a man of many interests?" Seneca said haughtily, snagging a ginger-orange tea bag.

"He's a renaissance man," I injected proudly.

"He's something, alright," Seneca muttered. "Come to think of it, you arrived at the best part, the meditation garden. You're building that one," she looked down her nose and pointed in his direction. He was smart enough to keep his mouth shut.

"Abs, you'll help me with the design. I was thinking of having two designs. The first would be simple, like a heart or butterfly; it would be easy to navigate without being boring. The second would be more Zen, with signage of meditative thoughts from the masters, water features, and stone sculptures. I want the path to reflect ascension, you know, like when you've finished walking through it you reached your higher self."

"Geezus, Seneca. You have put real thought into this. I'm so proud of you. Would you print some pictures of paths you like? Elias, I'm sure, could build whatever you like, but I want it to be accessible to anyone. I wouldn't want to exclude someone because they had to hop from stone to stone." I had my mental challenges to deal with, and I wouldn't want to alienate a guest due to their disabilities.

Elias put his cup down, ready to jump into this conversation. "Not only can I build it, but we can get an ADA certification to promote your gardens as accessible for the handicapped. If we combed your property, we could find most of what we needed regarding structure. Seneca, would you create a detailed drawing, and can we add some numbers to the project? As you said, building this in phases would be best. This project sounds costly."

I patted my friend's hand and reassured her that her vision was appreciated and doable. "I want you to know how incredibly impressed I am with you. Your vision of three magnificent gardens will happen over time. I want to commit to your first garden immediately, with the provision that we'll make it as accessible as possible. I also want to have some signs showing your future project. We'll stake them in the areas you've recommended. It will signify to the community and us that we are committed to our visions."

Seneca shed the first tear, and I followed suit, dazed and amazed at what our brains conceived.

Elias shook his head at our blubbering. "You two have no fucking clue how easy those ideas are in comparison to the actual work necessary to get all these projects completed. Tell me again, Abigail, how much money do you have to work with?"

Another million-dollar question.

Chapter 28
Purging and Pretenses

E LIAS

I watched Abigail and Seneca snuggle, which warmed my heart. I was deeply moved by how they leaned on each other while building dreams together. I loved their witty comebacks and how they held each other accountable for what they promised one another. Reilly and I were the same way, which reminded me I owed him a call.

He picked up right away. "Hey, loser. Did you get the girl?"

I scoffed. "Of course I got the girl. Why would you doubt me?"

"Because you're pathetic with women when you're stressed, that's why."

"Fuck off, loner. Did your woman ever come back to you?" It was a dick move, and his answer confirmed it.

"As it happened, she didn't, and I told her not to bother calling again. Apparently, Pierre didn't live on a small town farm. He was sophisticated and dumped a bunch of money on her shallow ass."

My friend was hurting, and I could only help with a distraction. "Can you get someone to watch the farm for a few days and come over to Mystic? I have a shit-ton of work that needs more than two hands." Silence echoed through the phone.

"It's possible. Ed owes me a few favors. Will Abigail mind?"

Good question. "She's been wanting to meet you, so I'm sure she'll be okay with it." I wasn't mentioning Seneca. She'd distract him just fine.

"Let me work out the details, and I'll call you later. Send me the address."

"It's about time you listened to me. We'll have a great time. I'll teach Abigail how to make barbeque and set up a bonfire. See you soon, dork."

"Who were you talking to?" The long T-shirt she wore as she towel-dried her hair boiled my blood.

"Who? Oh, that was Reilly. His joke-of-a-girlfriend dumped him, and I invited him down for a few days. Are you cool with that?"

I made all sorts of assumptions, and, like Reilly, she needed a distraction before answering. I pulled her hips to my face and pressed a kiss at her belly button. She dropped the towel and chastised me.

"You're trying to distract me from the fact that you asked your friend to visit without asking me first. I know you, Elias McGinnis. You're going to have to get punished for that."

My eyes hooded hearing the word punishment. I was a bad boy, and she could do anything she wanted to exact her vengeance.

"Be a good boy and take off your clothes and get on the bed." I did as she said, not wasting a moment as she twisted her hair in a tight knot on her head and affixed it with a rubber band.

"You've been a naughty boy, and the mistress of this house will not stand for your insubordination. Do you understand, Elias?" Abigail, the dominatrix. I did not see that coming.

"Yes, ma'am." She giggled. *So much for the scary dominatrix.* "Spread your arms out for me. There." She turned and reached into a drawer, retrieving a pair of long socks.

"These will make you feel more comfortable while I teach you a lesson. You will listen to every word I say and do everything I ask, and, if you behave, I will reward you with the biggest orgasm of your life."

"Yes, please. I'll be a good boy." *Fuck!*

"Good." She tied my wrists to the bedposts, not well, I noted. My sweet girl needed her Eagle Scout to teach her about knots you can't escape. I played along with her because the scene she set had me on fire.

I lay there as she slowly lifted her shirt, revealing her almost-bare pussy and pert breasts. I noted they were fuller, and her tummy wasn't as hollow. My girl was fattening up, and I loved what it did for her confidence. She crawled up my body, dragging her breasts along my legs, stopping long enough to press her bosom around my fully erect cock. Her velvet skin and raspberry-red nipples delivered pre-cum to my purple-tipped cock, which she lapped up like a good kitten.

"This is the best punishment ever," I sighed heavily, realizing I made a terrible mistake.

Abigail stopped immediately and dried off my dick with her hand. "Well, then, perhaps I need to clarify my point."

She rolled off my body and the bed and pulled up a Victorian armchair, hanging one leg over the arm, exposing her wet pussy.

"Can you see clearly, baby? Do you need me to come closer?" She taunted me, and my dick ached to have her mouth back to where it started.

"Closer, please," I begged, but she didn't move an inch.

"You don't deserve consideration when you forget to give me mine. You'll see what you can and imagine what you can't. Either way, you will neither touch me nor fuck me." I swear that chair turned her speech into a queen.

She twisted her nipples between her fingers, licking her lips and letting her head loll backward. Fuck, was she gorgeous. My dick stood proud, jerking when she moaned, and I silently begged her to come back to the bed. Abigail ignored me as she slid one hand down to her glistening pussy, looking only peripherally to see my agony. She brought her other hand down to spread her pussy lips and tapped at her engorged clit, and that's when I lost it.

"I'm sorry! So sorry, Abigail. I didn't think you'd mind, and you were busy, and-and . . ." My pleading was pathetic and pained. She was right to punish me. I had to remember this was her home, and, until we were married, I didn't have a stake in this place.

She graced me with a response: "You should be. I would do anything for you, Elias. I only ask for your consideration when you make plans. I have plans, too, you know: floor restoration and furniture restoration. These things are hard enough to accomplish without having company."

Shit. She was right. I was going to tear out the carpet in the other bedrooms this weekend, but I needed Reilly for the furniture.

"I forgot, sweetheart. You are right to be upset. I'm very sorry." She tutted her pink tongue and tapped her finger to her head.

"What to do, what to do." She walked around the bed to the back staircase and went down buck naked. Too bad I could hear her whole conversation through the vent.

"Hey, babe. Whoa. Did you forget I lived here?" Seneca was at the kitchen table, trolling the web.

"Nope. Elias has been a bad boy, and I'm teaching him a lesson."

"You're a badass in the bedroom, girl. Do you want the thing?" Seneca said slyly.

"Both of them." Abigail returned the tone. *Shit. What was in store for me now?*

I heard the stairs creak and knew whatever Abigail had planned came from the kitchen, and my mind whirred at all the possibilities. Spatula? Yes! Whip cream? Hell, yes. Tongs? Holy shit, no!

She sidled up to the bed close enough that I could smell her essence. "Did you miss me, baby?"

My mouth was parched, and I wanted to wet my tongue with her juices. "So much, sweetheart."

"I brought you two gifts. Would you like them?" Her seductive words and swaying hips shut down my logical brain, and I could only answer, "Yes."

"Good boy. Close your eyes and don't open them, or we'll start all over again in the morning. *Gulp.*

I knew immediately by the sound of the whoosh that she was going to use duct tape on me. *Fuck!* She better not rip the hair off my chest with that shit, or I'm going to beat her ass red with a flogger. Luckily, she only put it over my mouth. I'd heard stories of athletes taping one of their buddy's ass cheeks together and ripping it off as a gag, more like hazing—and painfully embarrassing. So far, I was ahead.

Unfortunately, the next item she used was far more painful—a feather duster. For such a big guy, you'd think I had thick skin. Sadly, that was not the case. I'm not ticklish by regular standards, but when Abigail traced my tattoos or the insides of my thighs, my whole body seized up with tingles to the point of pain. Now, she was using it against me, and I had to give her props for her ingenuity.

I couldn't speak, but I screamed anyway. The tiny flicks she made over my nipples put me close to unconscious. She slowly used her weapon of destruction to obliterate my desire ever to cross her again. My dick leaked and jerked as my body convulsed from her dusting. My feet worked to capture her around her waist, but she was too quick. She spun her body to face my dick so her pussy was over my face, and that's when I ejaculated onto her.

"Geezuz, fuck, Elias! You got me up the nose." She sputtered, trying to catch her breath. "You're a bad boy coming before I said to. You have another punishment you need to work off now." She stood up and carefully removed the duct tape, and I took a big breath.

"Fuck, Abigail. I couldn't help it. You tortured me, and it was hot."

"I guess you'll have to put your mouth where the honey is." She messed up that saying, but I agreed with her intention.

She mounted my face and turned herself back down to my cock. She sucked hard and popped off just the way I liked it. The humming sounds brought her sucks a whole new dimension of pleasure, and I forgot I was being punished. I pushed my tongue deep into her pussy, angling my nose to bump her clit. She squirmed each time, allowing me to gather every ounce of her honey. I could tell she was close when she ground her pelvis onto my chin, and I worked vigorously to bring my girl to release.

"Holy shit, that was good." She dismounted my face and rubbed her tits as I looked over at her wanting more. "I think I'll take a shower now."

"You can't!"

No sooner did the words leave my mouth than she smacked my dick. "No more coming for you tonight, mister. I'll be back soon. Don't wait up."

Again, why didn't I keep my mouth shut? "Nooo! Goddamn it, Abigail. Finish what you started. I learned my goddamn lesson, now suck me off."

By the time she went into the bathroom and shut the door, I was free from her binds and stalking her way.

I knew I scared the shit out of Abigail with my beet red face to my fucking purple cock—anger written all over me. When I flung open the door, she ran for the shower, hoping to find refuge. Let me be clear; starting now, there will be no refuge tonight. I lifted her weightless body and wedged her against the shower wall face-to-face. I kissed her hard, taking what was mine. She'd know that I was sorry and that torturing me would only poke the bear.

"I'm going to fuck you right now, so you'd better tell me to stop if you don't want me to." I bent to suck the hollow of her neck and waited only a moment before I impaled her with my angry cock.

"Oh! God, Elias," was all she said as I pummelled her pussy without mercy. Her cries of pleasure and pain didn't keep me from easing up. She'd lit every nerve in my body tied to her bed, and every one of them needed extinguishing.

"Abby. Yes. My God, woman, you've undone me. I'm at your mercy. Please forgive me."

She pushed my hair from my brow and stared through slitted eyes. We breathed each other's air as we melted into each other's arms, letting our passion fuse into one.

"I forgive you," she whispered, spreading butterfly kisses all over my face. "Take me to bed, Daddy."

And that's why I loved this woman so much.

I woke this morning to my little girl waking me up with her lips tightly wrapped around my cock and wishing me good morning when I unloaded down the back of her throat. She was a greedy little thing, but I would never complain.

Her phone pinged with an incoming email, and I left the bed while she scrolled through her messages.

"Six thousand dollars for the upstairs! I think I'm going to puke." I knew why she was sticker-shocked. Floor restoration costs a small fortune, but I also had questions about that estimate. I slid on my boxer briefs and walked out of the bathroom.

"Let me guess, your floor restoration guy sent his quote?" Her pouty face confirmed my suspicions.

"Show it to me." I sat down beside her and saw several items that could save her money.

"Reilly and I will save you more than a grand by ripping up the carpets ourselves. Another is moving every stick of furniture out of those rooms. We'll need to clean the shed and store all your upstairs furniture there so he can get in and out quickly. Also, have you gotten any other quotes to compare his?"

She shook her head. "I didn't have time. We met this guy, and Seneca had him over before we could discuss it. He seems nice, but I don't know whether he's taking me for a ride."

I tucked her under my arm, "It seems a little high for one floor, but let's call him and ask what the price would be if we took care of the furniture and carpet. I'll see if anyone else around here can come by and give you another quote. Always get two or more. Some pretty charming salespeople can empty your bank account."

"Yeah," was all she said.

I slipped on my shirt and pants and made a suggestion. "Let's go through those bags of junk you found. You might get lucky and find six thousand dollars." I gave her a wink and headed down the back stairs.

I peered out the side door to see Amy the Great sitting on my shoe. That damn bird had her own nest. Quietly, I opened the door, trying not to startle her. I stared her down, but she only gurgled, unaffected.

"While I appreciate your contributions to our household, I do not appreciate your ass on my shoe." I pointed to the decorated basket next to my shoes. "That is your nest; get in there." If I wasn't a patient man, the bird would be in a pan by now, but—instead—I gently lifted her and put her in her designated space, holding a hand up so that she stayed. I will now add "chicken trainer" to my resume. She stood up, turned a few times, dropped an egg in the basket, and jumped off the porch. *Wasn't she a little stinker?*

I grabbed the warm orb and walked into the kitchen, "Breakfast is served," I proclaimed. Seneca already had pancakes stacked on the table. *So much for my harvesting an egg for breakfast.*

"Good morning. How is our bad boy doing today?" I should have known this was coming.

"Why don't you ask Miss Abigail? She's limping a little this morning." I couldn't hold my laughter.

She poured her coffee and clucked her tongue like Abby did last night. I may have gotten aroused. "Seems like you two are made for each other. A couple of kinky cats, I'd say."

"Blow jobs and pussy licking aren't kinky, Seneca. However, the duct tape and feather duster crossed a line." She coughed out her drink against the cupboard.

"Whew! I've gotta get me some soon. I can't take you having all the fun." She rinsed out the sponge from the sink and cleaned up her mess.

"Don't worry. Good things are coming your way. Be patient." Little did she know that Reilly would make her blind with satisfaction. That boy loved a challenge.

"Better eat a big breakfast because we have a lot of work today. We can't do anything until we clean out the garage and go through all the junk Abigail wants to get rid of."

"That's right." Abigail entered the room looking edible. "I called Micah to help us, and she'll be here by eleven. I want to start in the garage. Garbage day is Monday, and I want all that crap by the curb."

"You're going to need a dumpster. I'll make the call, but it could be a couple of days before it's delivered," Elias offered. "By the way, have you checked your mailbox since you arrived?"

Two young faces stared blankly at me and then at each other. "Oops." Where would these two be without me?

ABIGAIL

Working together, we cleaned out the garage before Micah arrived. The plan was to move anything left in the garage to the barn. I mentioned to Elias that there was a possibility the garage had leaked, and he started a list for our next trip to the hardware store.

"We'll tarp the roof for now, then update it when the upstairs rooms are finished."

He was the boss of that stuff. I knew I needed to meet with a banker on Monday to see my available funds would cover the floors and the garage roof. With any luck, everything we wanted to eliminate will at least cover the floors. My list of projects was growing, and I began worrying that my eyes were bigger than my pocketbook. I'm not shocked, though the scale had grown dramatically.

Micah arrived wearing a sweatshirt and jeans, very out of character from the two other times we'd met—so much so that I hardly recognized her. She was wearing glasses now, and her hair was in a ponytail. She was cute in a fun-mom kind of way, and she made me feel comfortable and valued.

"Thanks for coming again, Micah. I know we didn't have time to go through much, but I've worked through the lower level, and this stuff isn't going to fit with my plans. If you see anything you might like, please put it aside. There may be some things of value

I've overlooked, and I could use your help pointing those out. I will have a yard sale soon and need to know the value of some of these things." I chuckled over my naïveté.

"I will do my best."

Between trips to the curb and repacking saleable items into boxes, we had lunch and chatted about the house and its decor.

"Now, here are pieces that might be worth something." She held up a severely tarnished old silver mirror and a brush with matted-down bristles.

"It's disgusting. I'd never use it, would you?" I asked quizzically.

"Never!" She shook her head in disgust. "Except it's made of silver. If you have an appraiser coming over, get a price on this. You could melt it down and use the silver for something else." *Hmm. I didn't think of that.*

"Great idea, Micah. Thanks." To her credit, she found several other objects worthy of an appraisal and a box filled with different small trinkets that she said weren't of value, but she'd enjoy the antique nature of those things. I walked Micah to the door and invited her to come back this summer when I had things more in order.

"I can't thank you enough, Abigail. This was lovely, and I appreciate your gifts. I'll treasure them. Let me know about that brush. Together with the mirror, you're sure to fetch a good price."

I giggled. She said "fetch." That's so old-fashioned, and she wasn't that old. She was almost out the door when she turned back. "I forgot to mention my niece, Lindsay. She's about your age and can help you with your website if you don't already have a person. She's very clever and has a good head for business."

I wrote her number down and flopped onto the sofa, exhausted. Another day zipped by, and I always seemed to get behind no matter how far ahead I got. I was supposed to contact Derrick and forgot. I was also supposed to review those articles Micah had copied for me. There was grocery shopping and bedrooms to sift through—it never ended. *Breathe, woman.* One day at a time.

Elias wheeled all the stuff we would sell into the garage and stacked the boxes tightly so we could bring down small furniture items tomorrow.

"Are you doing okay, princess?" He handed me some iced tea with a twirly straw. He knows me.

"My brain hurts. So many decisions in one day should be outlawed. Thanks for the drink." He kissed my forehead and sat beside me.

"You did well, sweetheart. You found some money in that stuff, and I found another floor restoration guy who can come out tomorrow."

"It's Sunday. Doesn't he have a family or church to go to?" I gulped down the whole glass, finishing with a belch.

"Classy, dear. He has both but said he didn't mind swinging by since his church is a mile away. He's bringing his family, so hop to it and show these people some Farnsworth hospitality." I gave him my stink-eye.

"I like your lemon squares. If not for them, make them for me." He waggled his brows like that would make a difference. *It did.*

I climbed onto his lap. "Anything for you." I pecked his cheek, laid my head on his shoulder, and fell asleep.

Chapter 29
Out With the Old

ABIGAIL

I don't remember going upstairs last night; I only woke up to pee and was starving. I slipped downstairs for a granola bar and glass of water before stumbling back up the stairs for another six hours of slumber. If I wanted a good night's sleep, all I had to do was make decisions—all day. I'll file this away for the next time I can't sleep.

Today was Sunday-Funday, and we needed a break. After calling the second restoration contractor to reschedule our meeting, I made some sandwiches, packed up a cooler I found in the basement, and informed everyone we were going to the park—my village park.

"Why the park? I want to see the Mystic Aquarium," Seneca whined.

"Quiet. If you're a good girl, I'll take you for dessert at that fancy-schmancy dessert place that guy from the cooking show opened a few months ago. Besides costing a fortune for dessert, I heard they were little works of art. I'm feeling inspired."

"I like dessert," Elias muttered.

"You behave, too. This girl needs to sit still and not move. There will definitely be no thinking today. My brain still hurts from yesterday." The ground was wet, so I set up under the gazebo—yup, *that* gazebo. I floated a blanket I found in one of the linen closets onto the floor, put my cooler on the wrap-around bench seat, and, without further ado, starfished a pose on the floor.

Elias snapped several pictures, and I posed for him like a pinup girl.

"This is not resting or appropriate for a park." Seneca insisted.

"Shut up. You're next." I challenged her. She stepped up like I knew she would and unbuttoned the top four buttons of her top and pushed her tits up tall in her bra. "Have a seat, Elias. I'll take these."

Seneca delivered some naughty poses and a few sweet ones to send to her dad. "Missing you, Pops."

Elias and I collapsed, and Seneca excused herself to find a bathroom. I closed my eyes, snuggling into Elias's chest as he drew circles up and down my arm. I listened to his heartbeat and counted the number against the second hand on my watch. He was so at ease with himself, and I was so bouncy. I would voice that thought, but I'd have to put a quarter in the "Don't Talk About Myself That Way" jar. I was old enough to recognize our differences in age and personalities. He wasn't immature, not in the least, so why would he want a girl almost fourteen years younger? Our Daddy/Little Kink was only a way to play, not a way of life for us. I wouldn't want it that way; it would become too uncomfortable for us in public. He said I was entertaining, except didn't the same act get boring? I wasn't sure how to bring up the topic, so I let it go for now. Instead, I counted his heartbeats and dozed in the morning sun.

"Hey, you guys. Guess who I ran into at the coffee shop? Derrick!"

I guess it didn't matter we were asleep. Seneca brought us company, and now we were awake.

"Hi, Derrick. Howse it going?" I said drowsily. "What's up, man?" Elias echoed.

"Sorry. I didn't realize you were sleeping, or I would have hushed her."

"What's that? No one hushes me." Seneca threw in his face. "Never mind. We're going to go to lunch and then hang out on the river. I'll catch you cats later." Her reference to yesterday's comment stuck.

"Safety first, Sen. Respond when I text you later." We waved her off, knowing she'd be alright with this guy—we hoped, anyway.

Elias's phone pinged. "Speaking of texts, it's Reilly. He can come down tomorrow if that's still okay with you."

"Sure. Tell him to bring some work gloves and a pillow. We're going to be busy moving furniture." I grabbed my phone and opened the list I was making of house stuff I'd need to add or replace—pillows and handcuffs.

ELIAS

Abigail and I finished packing the contents of the first bedroom's bookcases, drawers, and closet before continuing to the following two rooms. The plan was to have the first three rooms cleared and the carpet removed before moving the rest of us out of our rooms. By Wednesday, we'd all be living in the living room.

Between rooms, I've had to settle Abigail's mind that she was doing the right thing by moving forward with the floors. Knowing the base was completed, everything else in those rooms could be added later. We'd gone to the bank last week to open an account, of which her money was transferred from the care of Mr. Brickner to Mystic Federal Bank & Trust. They assured her she had enough money for the project but to be frugal about the rest. The manager helped obtain a safety deposit box large enough for Abigail's paperwork and supposed trinkets, though I felt there would be more to deposit before long. In addition to the box, he suggested opening a short-term CD until she could decipher the complete value of her inheritance. *We needed to discuss insurance soon.*

We sipped iced tea at the kitchen table later in the afternoon when Reilly arrived.

"Hey, brother. Nice place." We hugged it out on the front porch, turning to enjoy the generous front yard. "It's not a horse ranch, but it'll do."

I clapped him on the back as we entered the house. "Horses are for the backyard. It goes on and on and on."

"Shiiiit. Can I sell my place and move here, too?"

"No fucking way. I may have a parting gift for you, though." I winked at him and walked through to the kitchen.

"Ladies, let me introduce you to my best friend, Reilly. Reilly, this is Seneca, Abigail's best friend, and this is my girl. Hands off." Reilly made a show of hugging the girls and lifting them off the floor. He's such a dork.

I took special care to watch how Seneca received him. Her feisty nature and his charm were sure to create sparks.

"Welcome, Reilly. I'm so happy you were able to make it over. Elias goes on and on about missing you, although I think he misses the hard labor you subject him to the most." Abigail loved to bust my chops.

"Hey! I resemble that remark. This body is getting flabby, sleeping all day. If it weren't for the horizontal athletic program Abigail has so generously provided, I'd have a beer belly by now." *I suppose I earned the smack she landed on my arm.*

Seneca sat quietly, an unheard-of occurrence. She stepped around Reilly, bumping into his shoulder on her way to get him a glass of tea. "Sorry," she said demurely. Yep, I called it.

"I'll grab your things from your truck and meet you upstairs. You'll get the grand tour tomorrow, but we have work to do before sunset." I fake-punched him in the arm and left him and the girls to chat.

SENECA

"So, Abigail tells me you have a farm in Pennsylvania. How did you come by that?" I was curious. How many people in a lifetime say they own a farm? Two?

He stood across the island from me, checking out my chest. I'll admit I wasn't dressed well, but my bra held my girls upright and proud. I wanted to point to his eyes with my finger and raise them until he looked at my face, but I'd just met the man, and he was fine. He was lean but not skinny, with dark, straight hair that he tucked behind his ear. His piercing blue eyes captured my attention, and it was hard to turn away.

"I'll let you know I won it in a poker match. I have a keen eye for telling signs." He gave me a wicked wink. Who did he think he was coming on to? I wasn't a prude, far from it. Derrick and I played all touchy-feely for over an hour before I asked him to bring me home. I liked to have fun, but I didn't feel obligated to put out on a first date, even for this player.

"Poker, huh? It must have been quite a game. Are you sure you don't work a desk job? You can be straight with me." He wanted to play poker—OK, but I was calling his bluff.

He walked in front of me, crowding me into the center island.

"I'm not a player, Seneca, at a poker table or in real life. I like you and your spunk. We'll get along just fine." He put his glass in the sink and walked out of the kitchen.

What the hell just happened? That man was aggravating, and, no, we will not get along "just fine," as he put it. I'll make my judgment calls, but this fool didn't deserve me.

I found Abby upstairs, sitting on a bed in the first room. *We need to name these rooms.*

"I'd like to take pictures of each room," Abigail said, "so I remember where everything belongs. Then you guys can bring the big furniture down first, and Seneca and I can work on the smaller items. Okay?"

We nodded, letting her have control of the situation. Any of us could have taken the lead, but we needed to respect the woman whose house this was. While Abby worked, I pretended to look busy while checking out Elias's thick thighs and tight ass and that magnificent mechanical tattoo adorned with clocks and pistons. There had to be a story behind that kind of artwork. And—not to be outdone—was Reilly and his cut abs and long, muscular body that oozed sensuality. He could be eating turnips, and I'd drool watching him. *Note to self: cook for Reilly.*

Daylight made a final appearance at about seven, and no one was interested in cooking or going out. Pizza and salad were a phone call away, and Elias left money by the front door as we filed up the stairs to shower. The den didn't have an attached bathroom, so he used mine. I wasn't complaining, but he was so damn long that when it was finally my turn, the water was freezing.

"Come on! You assholes used up all the hot water." I screamed my displeasure for the whole floor to hear.

"Give it twenty minutes, and it will get better," Elias yelled.

"Pizza is here, get the door," Abigail yelled.

"I need five more minutes," Reilly yelled.

They could all fuck off. I stomped down the hall to answer the bell, gave the kid his money, and told him to keep the change. *No change for you, Elias.* Abby and Elias were probably fucking anyway, and screw Reilly. I didn't wait for them to come down and popped open the steamy box of cheesy goodness. Ironically, Reilly was the first to appear just as I took a rather sizeable cheesy bite of an oversized slice.

"You look hungry," he commented, smirking, looking superior to me.

I wouldn't dignify his comment and continued swallowing the burning hot cheese like a pelican swallowing a fish. Ultimately, I had to pull part of it out so I wouldn't choke. You'd think that asshole would ask if I was okay, seeing as how I was struggling.

"Bit off more than you could chew? I've got something else you can choke on if you're interested." He shifted, cupping his dick.

I shook my head, running his disgusting words through my mind. *Unbelievable! I just met this guy and this was how he spoke to me?* No fucking way was I going to inflate his ego by responding to that comment. If watching a girl choke was a turn-on, then he made Elias look like the mother fucking Eagle Scout he claimed to be.

I collected my plate, another piece of pizza, and a water bottle and stormed out of the kitchen and up to my room. That fucker better stay the hell away from me or he'd leave here without his dick attached.

ABIGAIL

Seneca was gone when Elias and I made it down to the kitchen. Reilly was eating alone, looking at his phone, and I felt like a heal screwing around upstairs with his friend forgetting he had given up his week to help me.

"Sorry, Reilly. I'm glad you didn't wait for us. Did you see Seneca?" I scooped up two slices and a can of soda and set them on the table. The salad was already there, and I filled a glass with ice while Elias took his food.

He shook his head and pocketed his phone. "She was miffed the last time I saw her. I think she's in her room—probably about the cold water."

Maybe, but that didn't track with Seneca. She flows better than that. I'd leave it be for now.

"Want to watch a movie after dinner? We finally have internet, so we're ready to roll." Elias always knew how to lighten up a situation. I couldn't have been the only one feeling the tension.

"Sure. I'm not sure if I'll make it through, though. It's been a long day, and I'm exhausted," he stood and excused himself to get his room ready.

"Use our bathroom," Elias called behind him, and he waved, hearing the offer.

"What's up with him?" I asked Elias.

"I wish I knew. He was fine before the showers, then he wasn't. Do you think Seneca's disappearance had anything to do with it?" Elias stuffed half a piece of pizza in his face, looking at me as if something was wrong.

"Let me text her. Hang on."

Are you in your room? Are you okay?

Yeah, I'm fine. I'm not feeling sociable. I'm going to shower and then sleep. Have a good night.

So long as you're okay. Did Reilly say something to you?

Nothing I couldn't handle. Night, Abs.

I put my phone down and looked closely at Elias. "I thought you said your friend was cool?"

He looked indignant. "Because he is. What are you implying?"

"Sen said that he said something, and she didn't feel like dealing with it, so she went to her room. Seneca rarely backs down, so it must have been a doozy."

Elias scrubbed his face. "I was afraid of this. I think Reilly likes Seneca more than I thought he would. He only acts like an ass when he's crushing on someone."

"Hmm, my ass. You better find out what he said and tell him to make it right with Seneca. I'm not having hard feelings in my house. Understand?"

"Yes, ma'am."

Chapter 30
Shared Spaces

ABIGAIL

Once the bedrooms were clear and the hallway carpet was hauled to the curb, the house felt lighter and cleaner even. The best news was that the floorboards were in good shape. The bad news was that Reilly would have to leave earlier than planned, so we canceled our plans today and packed up our rooms—Seneca's and mine—while Elias and Reilly packed up the den and moved all those bookcases out to the garage.

"Dude, why are you leaving so soon? I can't move all this shit without you," Elias begged.

Reilly shoved his hand through his hair, gave me a side look, and then turned his back to speak with Elias privately.

"Isn't it obvious? Seneca hates me, which means Abigail hates me, and I don't want to drive a wedge between you two." Reilly checked his phone like he was receiving some critical information, but I knew it was bullshit. I asked Elias to confront him on what he said, and he was being a pussy and not giving a straight answer. I'd pushed Seneca this morning, and she would only tell me he made a lewd pass at her and that he was a dick. There had to be more because Seneca got off on besting assholes, so I pressed her again.

"Honey, you eat dicks like this for breakfast." *Okay, maybe that came out wrong.*

She adjusted her bra, lifting each bosom in its cup to ensure they were up and even. "I don't know, Abs. Something about him unsettles me, and I can't put my finger on it."

I pondered. "Does he creep you out?" I said cocking my head to the side.

She pressed her lips as she looked upward. "No, more like his intensity. How he looked at me was intense, as if he knew something about me, and it freaked me out. How could he know I loved sucking dick?" She smacked her hand over her mouth.

"He said that to you?" I was aghast.

She pressed her hands onto the countertop and leaned in. "He suggested that, when he saw me with my mouth stuffed with pizza and the grease dripping down my chin, I'd like what he had to offer."

I smacked the counter. "No fucking way!" I leaned onto my forearms and enjoyed this story more than I should have. "I bet you looked hot."

"Abigail! I did not." I understood that she felt indignant, but hey, he's a guy, so . . .

I traced a finger over the marble countertop around the island until I stood before her.

"You like him, don't you?"

Her eyes blew wide, and her chest heaved. She shook her head vigorously.

"You do, and it scares you, doesn't it?" She shook her head again.

I pulled her into a hug. These big feelings are scary. If I've learned nothing these past weeks, it is that sharing them with someone helps to ease the anxiety of dealing with them alone.

"Don't be afraid, Sen. He's leaving later today. You don't have to act on them now; just let them flow, okay?"

She pushed me back and cupped my face, and said, "Why are you all of a sudden so freaking calm? That's my job."

I kissed her lips quickly, "Because you taught me well," and kissed her again. "Now get your ass upstairs; we have two hours to pack our rooms. Leave anything that looks like junk in the middle of the room, and I'll bag it up later to review.

ELIAS

"You're seriously going to run away from a little tension? You caused it, now be a man and apologize. As for your farm needing your immediate assistance, that's bullshit, too. Say you're sorry, and let's move on."

Were we back in junior high? I felt like a goddamned principal mediating my students.

"Fine. Later. Let's move the big stuff to the garage in case I need to make a quick escape."

I'd never seen him like this. Reilly doesn't "escape." He's more of a run-to kind of guy. I'd leave it alone for now, but I'd corner him soon enough and find the real reason he wanted to leave.

Abigail and Seneca walked down the barren hallway—the sound echoing off the walls. Abigail braided her hair into a loose crown like her great-great-grandmother wore, and Seneca piled her hair in a messy knot on her head. The two looked like sisters from another mother yet bound tight with history.

"What's the plan, fellas?" Seneca barked, still with an attitude. I didn't have time for drama, so I let it roll off my back.

I stood tall, stretching my arms and back, noticing Abigail's eyes laser into my muscles. "The plan is to get everything out of your rooms so Reilly and I can tear out the carpet after lunch. Rain is on the way, which works well for us since we need to arrange the living room furniture, allowing us to live there."

Everyone nodded and got to work. Abigail and Seneca pulled all their belongings together and moved them down by the bay window, and Reilly and I lugged their mattresses into the downstairs hallway. Before long, every closet and every room were bare except the carpet. I locked up the garage, and Reilly and I tacked down the tarps I bought a few days ago. I'm happy Abigail didn't forget to mention the leak, or she could have potentially lost a million-plus dollars in one storm. Her setbacks were my setbacks, and I would move heaven and earth to keep those from happening.

Organizing the living room and parlor was akin to children claiming the best bedroom.

Seneca staked her claim first. "I love you guys, but I'm not sleeping next to you while you rut against each other in the middle of the night. My bed will be by the giant mirror on the complete opposite side of these rooms."

Reilly was next. "Well, I sure as hell am not sleeping next to them either." He pushed the long couch against the fireplace and tugged his mattress five feet from Seneca's, who blew her lid.

"No way! You're leaving today, so you don't get a spot." I knew we were in trouble when she pointed a finger at him.

He smirked as he informed her otherwise. "News flash, sweetheart. I'm staying the rest of the week. My crisis has been averted. I'm sleeping here."

Have you heard the expression, "Don't have a cow?" Congratulations—we now have a tension-calf.

"Abigail! Kitchen! Now!" Seneca shouted. Abigail's face blanched, and she looked to me for support.

When they left the room, I jammed a finger into Reilly's chest.

"What the fuck, Big Guy? You were supposed to apologize, not throw fuel on the fire. Calling her "sweetheart" when she was that mad was an act of war, and, buddy, this war is yours to fight."

I left him there as he rubbed his forehead and cautiously entered the kitchen. Abigail was rubbing her friend's shoulders and speaking calmly. It felt ironic to have Abigail be the calm, collected one, but she rose to the occasion and helped her friend as best she could through the crisis.

"Three nights, Sen. That's all I'm asking for. You have my permission to kick him in the balls if he starts up with you again." Seneca chuckled and took a deep breath. She turned around and hugged Abigail tightly.

"I'll do it, you know," she whined. "Consider this a housewarming present. My sacrifice is your gain."

I stepped over and hugged them both. "Thank you, Seneca. I've never seen Reilly act this way before. He's usually chill and complimentary, but I told him to get his head out of his ass and apologize."

"Thank you, Big Guy," Abigail crooned.

"He better apologize," Seneca demanded.

"Can I join the group hug?" Reilly asked, approaching our huddle and waiting for a response.

"I'm sorry, Seneca. I don't know what came over me, but I'm sorry for being an ass. What I said was lewd and completely inappropriate. It will never happen again." *Of course, she took her sweet time answering.*

"I accept your apology," she choked out. I was proud of her for taking the olive branch. You can't move forward if you're holding onto the past. Reilly prudently put his arms around mine and Abigail's backs, averting any contact with Seneca.

When our huddle broke, we all returned to the living room and strategically placed the furniture for privacy. Abigail and I pushed the sofa to the bay window and moved the coffee table across the room by a side window, giving us enough room to place her king-sized mattress. We pulled the secretary over in front of it, cutting off a direct line of sight to the others. I didn't mind sharing the space in the short term, but I wasn't sleeping in my clothes, and neither was my girl. As we moved the furniture this last bit, the cover fell down, revealing several cubbies filled with envelopes of varying sizes. A lap drawer opened, and a letter addressed to Angela Farnsworth spilled out.

What the hell? "Uh, Abigail. I think you should see this."

She flipped the envelope several times, feeling the contours of its contents. When she found the courage to open it she began to tremble. "Help me, Elias," she cried. I hugged her from behind while she read the letter.

March 10th, 2004

Dear Angela,

You may not remember me, but I am a distant cousin and have only just learned of my mother's inheritance. Sadly, she passed away last month, and I found the contents of this letter among her things. I hope it brings you joy knowing you are a very wealthy woman. Please get in touch with the number below for more details.

Best Always,

Reginald Armstrong (Lillian Farnsworth's son. She took her family name back when my parents divorced.)

Contact person: Mr. Anthony Brickner, Esq. 247-553-2200

"Did your attorney ever mention this to you?" I was annoyed. She should be annoyed, too.

"No! But I'm calling him right now." Abigail ripped the paper from my hand and went outside on the side porch to make her call. She returned quickly, deflated.

"He didn't answer," Abigail said emphatically. "I left a rather angry message that he call me the minute he got my message. How could he not have told me about this letter? He couldn't deny he knew because his fucking number was written on it, and it was dated twenty years ago. Did my mom ever see this?"

I reread the date and realized she couldn't have received it. She was already dead. Did Reginald write this letter and not send it? There was no postage on the envelope. I'm so confused. I folded the paper, tucked the letter back in its envelope, and left it on my pillow.

Seneca ran to hug her, and she stood confused. Reilly was clueless, and Abigail didn't care at that moment. This was a mystery for the history books. She emptied the remaining documents from the secretary and put them in a paper bag to review later. This inheritance was getting trickier by the day.

Our new living arrangements were almost complete when the doorbell rang. We stopped moving around as if we were hiding something, and our eyes shifted left and right. Abigail threw her hands in the air, still annoyed from earlier.

"We're not hiding anything, geez." She opened the door, and, to our dismay, it was the police. *Fuckty-fuck!*

"Hello, Officer. Can I help you?" She pasted on a pleasant smile for the man.

"Are you Abigail Farnsworth?" She nodded. "I'm Officer Hutchinson, Ellen's husband." *What the actual fuck?*

"Wow, yeah, hello. Is everything okay? Am I in trouble?" Abigail threaded her fingers together, wringing them white.

"No, ma'am, although you can't leave that carpet lying on the curb like that. I know you just moved in, and garbage day is tomorrow, but you should get a dumpster if you plan on leaving piles like that by the street."

"Oh! Goodness, no. I knew that—I'm doing that—it won't happen again."

My girl was stressed out, and I couldn't let her feel that way alone, so I crossed the room and stood behind her in the foyer, extending my hand.

"Hi. I'm Elias McGinnis, Abigail's boyfriend. Is everything okay?" I could feel Abby lean into my chest for support or to keep from falling down.

"Everything is fine. This is more of a social call. Ellen, my wife, said you're quite the legacy around these parts, and I wanted to assure you that if you need any assistance, please get in touch with my office. We do regular nightly surveillance drives in this neighborhood, and the area Social Committee has us over to talk about self-defense and home protection now and again. I would encourage you to come by the Chamber of Commerce and learn all you can about Mystic and what it has to offer. Here's my card. Call anytime."

Stepping off the porch, he turned to wave, as Abigail quietly shut the door, eyes bugged out.

"Holy hand grenades! I didn't see that coming. Ellen's husband? That must have been a lively dinner conversation Friday night. Do they think I have nothing better to do than sit around drinking tea and eating crumpets?"

I'd learned to let it run its course when Abigail was in a theatrical mood. Once she was done burning off steam, she'd be ready to be rational, so I bit my tongue and noted the upside of not getting involved today.

Another exhausting day came to an end, and my plans for a bonfire literally fizzled out due to rain. Instead, I offered to run out to pick up barbeque for dinner and the necessary ingredients for s'mores. Hell, we'd do well to have some tequila handy, too. That was until Abigail's phone rang.

All eyes shifted to her ashen face, and I walked to my pillow to pick up the letter. She gave me a weak smile and waited to hear what this letter meant to Abigail.

ABIGAIL

"Hello, Mr. Brickner. I'm sorry for the harsh tone of my message, but it seems you left out a huge chunk of information regarding my inheritance."

"While it appears that I did, it was intentional. I was charged with keeping this trust intact and protected for the lifetime I cared for it. The enormity of this estate would have been too much for such a young woman, or anyone for that matter, to handle at once. You said it yourself that you weren't sure you were up to the task. My phone call last week sounded promising, and, although you don't know it yet, I was planning a visit next month to see for myself if you were ready for the final installment of your inheritance."

I began feeling claustrophobic and needed to walk. I pulled on my coat and hit the gravel driveway again like it was my personal treadmill. "Please continue."

"I have been the executor of this estate since 1962, long before you were born. My father was the executor for more than a half-century before that. Remarkably, his father held the estate from its inception in 1878. Since then, we have protected every Farnsworth interest, and you are no exception. These past two decades were the hardest in that we didn't want the house to stand unused, so we leased it to caring, respectful people so that when you were old enough, you could gain control."

My head was spinning, and I felt nauseous. My life was an episode of the Twilight Zone, and I had only begun to open my eyes to what was happening around me.

"That's a lot to take in, but please tell me, why didn't you contact me when I turned eighteen or twenty-one? I'm twenty-four now, so why the wait?"

He didn't respond quickly, and I knew another punch was coming.

"Abigail, dear. I waited until you cut ties with your Aunt Eleanor or were more settled in your life."

"Why? I left her house right after graduation. Wasn't that enough?"

"It could have been, but I was at your high school graduation, though you didn't know it, and I witnessed her coldness and disdain for having to be there. 'Pretenses,' I believe she said, was why she attended. I couldn't protect the estate if I thought she would abuse you in the process. The money and the property weren't going anywhere, and I'm sure you'd agree you weren't ready to accept such a large gift."

Tears ran down my face, registering how completely accurate his accounting was. He was at my graduation. He'd been hiding in the shadows since the day my mother died. That reminded me.

"Mr. Brickner, why didn't my mother get this letter? Did she know about the inheritance? Why was it in the secretary drawer?"

He chuckled at my rapid-fire questions. "She never received the letter because she didn't know about Lillian's passing. Her son, Reginald, must have left it in the secretary you mentioned. Your Aunt Eleanor was never notified because she was estranged from your mother for many years. They didn't reconcile until you were born, and your mom needed family support. Again, Abigail, your family is protected not only by the inheritance but also by my family. When I said you reminded me of my granddaughter, I was referring to you, though not by blood."

I sat down in the middle of the driveway, unable to hold myself up any longer. Mr. Brickner's family had shielded me for my whole life? Blood seemed to drain from my body and my brain sizzled with this new information.

"Abigail, are you still there?" His concern was touching. I liked the idea of him being my grandfather.

"Yeah, I'm here."

"I hope you're sitting down because the next piece of information I have for you will knock you on your bottom."

Dear God, please let it be good. I can't take much more.

"I'm sitting," I whispered.

"I'm proud to tell you that if my visit next month is successful, you'll inherit twenty million dollars."

I don't remember what happened next. Elias said he ran out of the house when he saw me lying in the driveway. He said he heard Mr. Brickner calling for me and told him I'd call back when I regained consciousness. Now that I had, I could hardly speak. Elias told Seneca and Reilly to get lost for a while, and I could hear them shuffle out of the room.

"Sweetheart, are you alright? Can you breathe? What did he say that made you pass out? He wouldn't tell me."

My darling Elias looked pale with concern. He swaddled me in a blanket and held me like a baby until I looked him in the eyes.

"Elias," was the only thing I said.

"Baby, listen to me. Whatever he said, we'll handle it together. I love you so much; please don't let this thing consume you."

Hmm. He loved me no matter what. That's nice. I pulled my feet out of his tight hold and sat up.

I mouthed, "Twenty million dollars," but the sound stuck in my throat.

"I don't understand, Abby. What did you say?" I tried again. He made the mouth motions with me, and suddenly he screamed, "Twenty million dollars? You have twenty million dollars? Fuck, Abigail, your luck keeps getting better and better."

Chapter 31
A Not So Subtle Night

A BIGAIL

I called Mr. Brickner back, and we scheduled his visit. The whole conversation was batshit crazy. All that money wasn't real until it was in my name, so I stuffed down the anxiety and hysteria and went on with my life.

For the rest of the week, Elias and Reilly fixed the tractor and used the land survey I had to mark the perimeter of my property. They assured me they would report anything of importance since I was tied up with Seneca and the garden. Elias noted that an official survey would cost several thousand dollars, and it wasn't important unless I was planning on flattening the whole thing, which I was not.

My garden was taking shape and I loved how organized Seneca was in her preparations. She staked out where she wanted things to go and kept a notebook full of ideas, lists of items to be priced, and equipment that would make her life "so much easier." Allan, the owner of the local hardware store, was kind enough to open an account for me, and Seneca was given strict instructions to keep to the budget. I may be a gazillionaire, but I didn't have the money in my account, and therefore, it didn't exist.

I hadn't spent time alone with Reilly and we had a few things to get straight before I tied myself to Elias for the rest of our lives. I entered the barn where Elias was tinkering with the tractor, and Reilly was building a wall from the far side of the room to the halfway point. Watching these hot men work was a hobby I'd gladly take up. I was alone in my thoughts when Reilly caught me licking my lips.

"Feeling happy, Abigail?" Reilly grinned, displaying his perfectly white teeth.

I walked over, my hands in my back pockets, and felt coy. "I am. And do you know why?" I intentionally tempted him. I wanted to know if my boyfriend's best friend would go to places he shouldn't with me.

"Because you like watching me work? I can take my shirt off if that would make you happier." He broke into a solid laugh and looked at his friend.

Elias looked at him like he would take him out back and shoot him. "Keep your fucking clothes on. She's happy because she got laid this morning." *Hell, no, he didn't just say that.*

I turned all shades of red. These two were trouble, and my man was in line to feel my wrath. I walked right up behind him and clutched his balls, causing his wrench to fall.

I hissed into his ear, delivering a clear message. "If you ever share our love life like that again, you won't have one any longer. Understand?"

The mewl he emitted was good enough for me. I rubbed his nuts, restoring blood flow, and walked back to a timid Reilly.

"Come on, Reilly. Let's go for a walk."

Elias laughed.

I hadn't made time to walk around my neighborhood but now seemed like a good time. There were six houses along my street and several more once you made the loop away from my house. Several were historic homes like mine, though none as big and stately. Gorgeous gardens started to bloom, and giant maple trees spread their branches like an umbrella over their lawns. One home had sculptured, twisted pine trees lining the walkway from the street to the front doors, while others used hedges to create a manicured look. It was fascinating and stuffy, all at the same time. Iron furniture seemed to be a staple on every porch or patio, as well as giant door knockers. *It must have been all the rage back in olden times.*

Reilly and I walked silently for a time before I began my inquisition.

"Elias tells me you've been friends since junior high. You must have some great stories you could share." I started with a softball. I watched crime stories, and this was how to relax the perp before you drilled the incriminating evidence down their throat.

He looked around as if help was on the way. *It wasn't.* "Yeah, we got into some scrapes here and there, but Elias was always a straight arrow. A solid guy, salt of the earth."

It was fun watching him squirm, but I had more important questions. "Cut the crap, Reilly. Elias is not an angel. He told me about his youth, strict parents, and dog. More importantly, he told me about his ex-girlfriend and what a bitch she was. I know Elias. What I don't know is why you're giving my girlfriend a fucking hard time. Care to explain?"

You would have thought I gave him a choice to be flogged or bathe in a pool of piranha. Instead, he blurted, "She's a bitch. She can't take a joke and is way too serious. I was flirting with her, and she took everything wrong."

Hmm. "That's not quite what she said," I commented, allowing him to defend himself.

He shoved both hands through his silky hair. "Then what exactly *did* she say?"

I stopped walking, and he turned in my direction. "She said you made a lewd comment, insinuating she'd be up for choking down your dick."

His face fell, and his eyes closed. "I didn't mean that."

"Fuck off, Reilly. You met her, like, five minutes ago, and you're throwing out suggestive comments. What's wrong with you? Is this your game? Do girls drop to their knees for you when you say shit like that?"

I saw a mom with a buggy walking down the street and decided to keep moving before we made a scene. The vibe I got from him felt like remorse. I'm not excellent with body language, but his face looked upset. We walked another block before he took my wrist.

"Listen, Abigail. I didn't come down here to be a pain in your ass. I didn't even know Seneca would be here. I just came off of a bad break-up, and she riled me up with her sassy attitude and big boobs. I'll keep my distance and keep myself in control until I leave if you'll let me finish what I came here to do."

I didn't respond, and we kept walking. We returned to my driveway, and I stopped again. His sadness muddied his piercing blue eyes, and I didn't want him to beat himself up. Unfortunately, Seneca was melodramatic at times, and although earned, she made Reilly her target.

"She accepted your apology, and so did I. You seem like a good guy, Reilly. We're going to be friends for a very long time, Seneca included, and I want us to feel comfortable communicating with each other even when we're pissed off. Yes?"

He wrapped his strong arms around me, and I smelled his woodsy skin. It was nothing like Elias's, but, hugging him back, he felt good.

"We're good." His smile was full and genuine, with no trace of insincerity. This was the true Reilly, and I liked having him around.

Elias met Reilly on the drive, and they took off for a few hours. They talked about tractor parts and topsoil.

I was alone again in my house with my thoughts and Agatha's journal. It had been a week since I last opened it, and I felt guilty not ordering those beautiful fabrics she meticulously chose to restore her—my—furniture. Projects like that were costly and would need to be done one by one, but, now that I'm a bazillionaire, I would do them all!

I made hot tea and curled up on the bay window seat to read more.

Ezekiel has the most unusual sixth sense about being in the right place at the right time. After a dinner meeting last night, he learned the government was handing out contracts for various goods and services. Wasting no time, he submitted several documents and was granted all of them. He would supply lumber for guns and forts and feed our soldiers during the war on Mexico. My husband was a patriot, and I am proud to be his wife.

There it was! These were the exact words described in that article about how Ezekiel became wealthy. I read on.

These years of toiling have finally paid off. We're millionaires! Gracious, I don't even know what that number is, except we're one of them. Our lively discussion of using this vast sum of money was exciting yet a hardship. So many people didn't fare well during these war years, and I felt our obligation was to help our community prosper and support those who remained. Ezekiel wanted a bank. I wanted an orphanage. It is times like these that feminine wiles work their very best, and, as such, we will purchase land tomorrow and build an orphanage come harvest season.

Holy shit! I set the journal in my lap and stared out the window. My family saved children, and it continues to this day. Agatha embraced her femininity to help her husband see the importance of saving lives before frivolous things like a bank. What a clever woman. I wanted to be like her and build a place that inspired and lifted my community, even if I didn't know how to do it. And, like Agatha's Ezekiel, I wanted a man like Elias to be by my side when I did them.

I heard a vehicle on the front drive, and the front door slammed shut.

"I'm back! Is anyone home?" Seneca belted to no one in particular.

"Over here," I called.

"What are you doing there?" She dropped several bags on the ground and kicked off her shoes.

I held up the journal and took a sip of my tea.

"Ooh. Did you find anything juicy?" Seneca climbed over the sofa to join me.

"Nothing that we didn't already know; however, I did get more insight into how Agatha thought. Take a look."

I pointed out the passages and waited patiently.

"Atta girl, Agatha. I guess it is true that behind every good man is a great woman."

We chuckled together. We heard the side door open and close, and another call rang out.

Both men were smiling, making us suspicious. "What are you two up to?"

They looked at each other, confused. "Nothing. We thought you might like to go out to eat tonight. Let's have some fun. What do you say?"

You didn't have to ask me twice, "I'm in," and Seneca clapped her hands. Reilly and Seneca better keep it together because I finally had an opportunity to wear my new white blouse and leather pants, and neither would ruin my night.

I overheard Elias reserving us a table at the new upscale Mexican restaurant we discussed on one of our rides to the village center. Seneca wore her new studded flair-bottomed jeans, stiletto heels, and a not-so-family-friendly halter top, topped with a matching blue denim jean jacket.

From my vantage point above, Reilly almost fainted watching Seneca strut down those stairs, and Elias worked not to stare at her voluptuous chest. The roles reversed when I came down next. Great-looking clothes allowed me to feel confident and sexy.

Elias looked at Reilly sharply, "What have we gotten ourselves into?"

We drove together in my newly restored Buick, and thank goodness our friends didn't poke at each other. The temperature heated up once the margaritas started flowing, and all bets were off.

I shared with Reilly Seneca's visions of her garden plans, and Reilly slammed his drink on the table, perturbed.

"Did you account for drainage and rainfall in this area? How about pesticides and fertilizers?

Elias dropped his head, knowing Reilly stepped into a minefield.

A rush of red spread across Seneca's neck and face as if he had smacked her. That man better run.

"Do you think I'm stupid? Just because I didn't go to a fancy college doesn't mean I don't know how to do my research. I have three, count them three, highly specialized master gardeners advising me on my plans, so I don't need your judgment."

She flipped her long, wavy locks and looked out the window in disgust. I gave her credit for not bolting, though we did have her locked in with our seats.

Elias reached under the table and gripped my knee, letting me know he had this under control.

"Reilly, Seneca has been researching these projects nonstop. When she's not weeding and cutting down plant matter, she's on the phone or the internet with gardeners around the globe. Trust me when I say she's got this under control."

I rubbed Elias's hand in thanks but cleared my throat when he moved it up to my thigh.

"I'd like to make an announcement. Given Seneca's reconnection to gardening, I'd like to pay for some classes to validate her commitment to my home and future career. Thank you, my dear friend, for investing in me. You never let me down."

We all raised a glass, averting tonight's first crisis—though it didn't take long for the second to emerge.

Dinner was over, and I bounced in my seat, waiting for Elias to tell me where we were going.

"I'm not telling you. It's only eleven minutes away, so control yourself." He gave me his stern Daddy look, and I immediately took control of myself. In hindsight, I could see my self-control improving, noting it was easier when Elias was nearby. I felt more confident about my ability to handle stress, like with the officer who came by yesterday. I was nervous and wary, but I didn't run or shy away from his questions. It felt good and empowering.

We crossed the Mystic River and turned into the marina. Music blared from a second-floor restaurant, and I pointed excitedly.

"Is that it? Are we partying at the marina? So cool, Elias. Thank you!" I cried.

We all jumped out of the car, but Elias grabbed my wrist before I could leave. "Have a good time tonight, little girl, but behave yourself."

Whoa. My stomach flipped, and butterflies swam through my body. Daddy wanted to play here—and *fuck* if I wouldn't stop him. This was going to be the best night ever!

Elias took my hand, and we caught up to the others, feeling excited until we heard, "Why are you all up in my face? I told you

I don't need your help. I know how to walk." Even in the glow of the parking lot lights, we could see Reilly roll his eyes.

"I know you know how to walk. Do you see the gravel under your feet? It's got to be tricky in heels."

I understood his desire to keep her safe, though he needed to work on his delivery. I found it ironic that he and Elias had trouble speaking to women. *Wait a second. Elias was tongue-tied with me, not every woman. Did Reilly like Seneca? Shit! Why didn't I pick that up earlier?*

As if he conjured a face plant himself, Seneca began to fall.

"Aaahh," she shrieked. Reilly caught her by the hips and pulled her hard into his chest. He wrapped his arms around her midriff and whispered in her ear.

Whatever he said, she softened, and he unwound his arms, brushing his hands down her backside. This did not go unnoticed by Elias or me.

Elias commented, "So close. He almost got ahead."

And I replied, "Yeah, those two are going to kill each other."

Reilly paid our cover charges, and the host led us to a secluded table far away from the dance floor. Sunday nights usually aren't a big party night, but the host said there was a bridal party, and they didn't care if others joined in, only that they paid for their own drinks. The DJ played all the best tunes from the seventies to current top-chart singles, and I had a groove I wanted to bust.

"Come on, Sen, let's boogie!"

ELIAS

My girl looked like sex on a stick, and I couldn't wait to grind up against her. Instead, I watched her bump asses with her buddy and slide all over the dance floor, interjecting herself into the bridal party.

I hoped she took notes from this party. Simple, sophisticated, electric, and fun. I hadn't thought about my wedding day at all until I met Oria. The idea of tying the knot with one person seemed overwhelming, but Oria ticked so many of the boxes I thought I wanted in a woman until months later. She embarrassed me in front of her friends and then belittled me to her parents. That night, I revoked any thoughts of marrying her. The package on the outside didn't match her inside, and I'd given up hope years later of ever finding the right woman—until fate stepped in.

Reilly walked to the bar and got himself a drink, and I forgot about him and Seneca as I spun Abigail into my arms.

She purred when I pulled her close, and my dick tented my pants. "Hi, Daddy." *Fuck, yeah.*

"Hi, baby girl. Do you want to dance with Daddy?" She was four inches taller in those stilted shoes, making it easier for me to grab her tight ass.

"Uh-huh," she mewled. "I was wondering when you were going to come out and play. It's been almost a week, and I missed you." Abigail pinched my nipples through my shirt, and I hissed.

"You are being a naughty girl tempting Daddy that way." I danced her to the edge of the floor. "I have a special surprise for you, but you have to be a good girl for me."

Her eyes lit up, and her exquisite smile spread from ear to ear. "I love surprises. What is it?" she squealed, tearing at my lapels.

I laughed at her exuberance, "It's not time yet."

We danced several more songs together, me imprinting my dick on her belly each time we pressed together and her grazing the back of her hand on my crotch every chance she got. We line-danced with the wedding party until I stole her away to suck her tits in a dark hallway. I wanted to fuck her against that wall, but when they called for the bouquet toss, the bride specifically called her name when she didn't see her on the dance floor.

"Oh, Daddy, please! Can I go and catch the bouquet?" She pulled on my shirt like a child, trying to get her Daddy's attention.

"You'd rather catch some flowers than fool around with Daddy?" I put her in an impossible position and felt like an ass for doing it.

She pouted, torn between her choices. "Go. Have fun." She clapped her hands, then fixed her blouse and ran down the hall. Abigail knew Lady Luck personally and, of course, caught the damn thing. Her luck was my luck because she was mine.

"Oh my God!" Abigail cried. "Throw them again; I can't keep these; it's for someone from your wedding party."

My girl had both class and humility to know how to handle herself in this situation. It made me proud.

"No, no," said the bride. You're part of our wedding, too. Please keep them and remember what a great night this was." She looked Abigail up and down, smiling. "Besides, who knows when it will be your turn to be a bride?" Abigail hugged her, and she walked over to show me her prize.

"Can you believe it? She was so nice." She wrapped her arms around my waist, and I knew the time had come.

"Stay here, sweetheart. I want to thank them." I approached the bride and groom and explained my situation. Moments later, I returned to my girl, grinning ear to ear.

The DJ ended the song and directed a spotlight to the edge of the dance floor where we stood.

I took my girl's hands and absorbed the glow from her delicate face. She couldn't know what was coming and looked around as the crowd drew their attention to us.

"Abigail Farnsworth-Burton, you are the prize in our story. You came into my life when I was emotionally lost and demanded I drive you to your future. What I didn't realize at the time was that you were driving me to mine. We may not have known each other very long, but it feels like we've been connected since—forever. I like who I am when I'm with you. I've become a better man when you challenge me. I can't imagine my life without you."

I knelt on one knee and retrieved the velvet box from my suit coat pocket, displaying the contents before her. "My darling, Abigail, will you marry me?"

I was told the room erupted when she said yes, but all I heard was her breathing as she kissed me. I placed the ring on her finger, and she swooned at the size of the stone. My brain went into hyperdrive, and I felt my body whoosh as if traveling through time, connections being fused together to complete a circuit. Electrons and neurons scrambled and rearranged themselves into a new and improved Elias, one that included Abigail, and I was dizzy from the effect. I was forever changed and cried tears of joy.

"Baby, Elias, don't cry. I said 'Yes,'" Abigail kissed me tenderly, assuming I hadn't heard her.

"I know. I can't believe my good fortune." I picked her up and spun her around to another blast of cheers. The DJ kicked the music up a notch, and I finally put her down, filled with bliss.

She laughed. "It looks like we both found our fortunes. Finding you was only a matter of time, and you were well worth the wait."

I kissed her hard and promised her this night would last forever.

THE END

EPILOGUE
The Grand Illusion

A BIGAIL

Our friend circle was small, and our families smaller, allowing us to choose a wedding venue on a fancy boat for a sunset cruise on the Mystic River. Seneca, her dad, Reilly, Micah, her husband, and, of course, Mr. Brickner and his lovely wife. Elias's parents sent their bland regrets via a message on a department store gift card. *Sorry we can't make it. Congratulations, and best always.* My heart broke for him; he deserved so much more. He shrugged it off, annoyed.

"Hey, princess. Let's go for a ride," he said, and we hopped on the golf cart Reilly had gifted us for our wedding. He waggled his brows and pushed me against the refrigerator.

I put down the lemonade pitcher before spilling it on the finger sandwiches I prepared. "Are we going to be long? The 'Ladies Who Lunch' want to see the gardens Seneca finished last week."

He nuzzled my neck, growling, "That depends on you, sweetheart."

Uh! That man.

He spun me around, and that meant he was feeling very horny. He wrapped a blindfold around my eyes and pushed me toward the door. *I may have read that wrong, and he was feeling kinky.* Either way, he escorted me to my chariot and buckled me in.

I could smell flowers blooming in the late June sun, wet dirt, and Elias's clean linen shirt. My insides twisted absorbing his scent. We weren't on the cart long before he stopped and took my hand.

"Princess, stand here and don't turn around." He carefully positioned me and removed the blindfold, and I saw the biggest smile since he proposed.

"My darling Abigail, you are my sun, moon, and sky. These meadows are made for your sweet, thoughtful soul. If you say yes, I'd like to give you this gift as a wedding present to celebrate our lives together on your family's land."

For a guy who gets tongue-tied, he sure waxed poetic when given the chance.

I stood on my toes and gave him a sweet kiss that turned x-rated. I giggled and rocked to my heels, nodding my head. "Yes. Gimme, gimme, gimme my gift!"

He spun me around, and my hands went to my mouth. I squealed into my hands so loud I almost broke my eardrum.

I spun back to him, tears leaking from my eyes. "It's a gazebo!" He nodded.

"You built that—for me?" I looked so proud and happy when he showed me the gift he made from his hands.

"For you, princess. For us to get married before our reception on the river. What do you think?"

The gazebo was whitewashed with elegant spindles, which he said came from a reclaimed Victorian house somewhere along his travels. The roof was pitched low, and a rooster weathervane proudly sat on top. *Amy would love that.* How did he hide this from me? Probably because I handled a million things near the main house, and he built it in a meadow two football fields away near a stream that runs through our property. *Yes, our property. That fight was a doozy, my fault. For posterity, it was a Farnsworth property.*

"Think? I can't think of anything more thoughtful or beautiful in my life! Thank you so much, Elias. You exceeded every expectation I ever had of you. I can't wait to marry you." *I may have knocked him over when I jumped into his arms, but he handled it well.*

He ran his hands over my back and threatened to lay me down in the tall grass and fuck the shit out of me. *His words, not mine.* "Don't forget all the good times we've had in a gazebo, little girl. Daddy loves playing with you out in the open." *Geezus, this man has game.*

If you were wondering what happened to our friends after our proposal, I didn't ask, nor did I care. The only thing that mattered was getting home and fucking the life out of Elias.

We burst through the front door half undressed, and Elias began making demands. "Get us water, and get the hell up to our bedroom." I didn't question his thought process, and, if rolling around on the disgusting floors that weren't finished was the only way to get in that man's pants, I was on board.

Like Hercules, Elias pulled my mattress up the stairs from the living room and down the hall himself. He ran back down for the bedding, and I was naked when he returned.

"Fuck, woman, you read my mind." We each grabbed two corners, snapped the fitted sheet into place, and ignored the rest of the linen. Elias locked our door and switched off the lights. The moon would be the only one watching us tonight, creating a romantic ambiance as it glowed through the paned windows.

He all but threw me onto my back as I bounced up the mattress. His growl turned my insides liquid when he unleashed his dirty talk, and I became unraveled.

"You made Daddy wait a long time for your pussy, little girl. You wanted those flowers more than you wanted my cock, and, now, you're going to wish you'd let me have my way with you at the party."

Oh, Daddy!" I called his name. "For God's sake, they would have looked for me and found us doing unspeakable things in the hallway."

He tapped his dick on my mound and corrected my way of thinking. "I don't give a shit who is calling you. When Daddy says it's time to fuck, you'll fuck me." *Good Lord, the things that man says.*

His cock was purple and ready to burst when he slid it in without preparing me. It was a blessing his dirty talk had me wet and ready. "Ah, Daddy, yes! That feels so good." He filled me to the hilt and pumped until I told him I was ready to come.

"You don't get to come until I tell you. Remember what happened last time?" *For the record, it was me who said that, but I wouldn't correct him. We were having too much fun.*

"Yes, Daddy." He pulled out as fast as he entered me and held his dick in his hand, stroking it slowly.

"You danced a lot tonight. Worked up quite an appetite, didn't you, little girl? You must be hungry." I moaned, knowing what would come next. He knew I loved to suck him, and tonight wasn't any different.

He climbed my body, trapping my arms, and hovered over my tits, tempting me with his swollen shaft. My clit pulsed, and my heart raced. My life had never been so good.

"Stick out your tongue and take me back, sweetheart. Way back." He adjusted himself so I didn't have to reach for the liquid pearl resting on his tip. He tasted salty and divine. Elias made the idea of deepthroating his cock a decadent, filthy treat I'd never considered before. His appreciation for my efforts was always rewarded.

"That's my girl. Your mouth is so hot and wet and feels so good. Yes! Keep going." His moans of pleasure transferred to my pussy, and the pain of not being able to touch myself was driving me mad. He knew exactly what he was doing and reached his arms back to rest on my thighs, pushing his cock deeper than I could take him on my own.

"Fuck! Yes. Christ, Abby, you're incredible." My gagging encouraged him to continue his gentle pumping. Elias didn't forget about my pleasure and slid one hand down my leg to my pussy. I tried to scream, but my mouth was too full. He rubbed my clit, applying the perfect pressure, and I tried to scream again, only to have his cock slide deeper down my throat.

Saliva dripped from the corners of my mouth, and breathing through my nose wasn't enough. I took the biggest breath I could and gorged myself on his thick cock, and he came hard down my throat. He sat forward, pulling his cock from my mouth and allowing me to swallow. He moved himself down my body, releasing my arms, and folded forward, holding me tight.

"I can't fucking believe how good you are to me. My soul left my body when I came, and I almost forgot you couldn't breathe. I'm so sorry." He stroked my sticky face and kissed me deeply. I cried, staring into his beautiful eyes, having pleased him so profoundly.

"It's okay. I'm alive—truly alive, but know that I could have pinched you if I thought I would pass out." *If I remember, that is.*

"You are so beautiful, smart, and brave. I can't wait until we're married." His declaration filled my heart with joy, and I echoed his words.

He rolled off my body and jutted his chin toward the bathroom. A shower sounded terrific, especially if Elias washed my hair.

We didn't emerge until noon the next day, and Reilly was nowhere to be found. Seneca strolled out into the kitchen like the cat who ate the canary.

"What?" she spat.

Elias got in her face and made an accusation. "Where or what did you do with my friend?" She looked unaffected.

She made a face, turning her palms upward. "How would I know? His mattress was empty when I woke up."

Why did I feel there was more to this story?

I pressed on. "Did you come home together last night?"

"No."

I tried again. "Did you see him before you went to sleep?"

"Yes."

It was like pulling teeth. "Then, what happened that he left without saying goodbye?"

Color rose from her chest, and she looked away bashfully. "We—may have kissed."

Elias jumped in, raging, "You aren't sure? How can you not be sure? I thought you hated him." He stomped around the kitchen island, waving his hands in the air. "The two of you act like children. Did you fuck?"

"Elias! Please don't talk to my friend that way . . . Did you fuck him?" I spun around, turning my question into an accusation.

I think her teeth chattered. "We were drunk," she wailed.

Dear Lord, please let her tell me they used a condom.

I hugged my friend and whispered in her ear, "Please tell me you wore a condom." She cried into my shoulder, "I don't remember."

Shit! Shit! Shit!

I pushed her hair back and reached for a tissue. "You better hope your pH was off, or this little slip-up could last you a lifetime."

Life was so much more relaxed after those damn floors were finished. Like any household project, it took two extra weeks to finish, but Reilly had left, and Seneca only spent half her time at my house and the other at Derrick's. He was so sweet. When he offered to pull up the carpet on the grand staircase and restore the wood for free, I told him he had lifetime pool privileges once I got it open. He was more than satisfied with that arrangement.

It seemed Seneca experienced a few days to freak out about her colossal condom crisis. I'm not sure Reilly and Seneca could be in the same room after that, let alone a lifetime with a baby. *They had better find a way to coexist at our wedding.*

"Sen, I promised to pay for some gardening classes for you, but they cost a lot." That was the laugh of the century. Do you have any idea what the monthly interest income is from twenty million dollars? I don't do math, so let's say it's stupid money.

"Really? Money is the problem? If you don't want me to help you, say so." Seneca was always defensive and always combative.

I sat her down at the kitchen table to explain.

"Pick a state: Utah, Indiana, Texas, Pennsylvania, or Michigan." Her face contorted.

"Fine. Pennsylvania," she said belligerently, cracking open a soda.

I held her hands and looked into her dark brown eyes, "Congratulations, you're going to Delaware Valley University for horticulture school starting this August." I smiled and squeezed her hands. "Take a look at the program, and—if you hate it—pick another one, but you're starting this August. By winter months, you'll study, and by summer months, you'll be my slave. Sound good?"

She jumped up and down with joy. "Are you fucking kidding? You'd do that?"

I stood up and hugged her tightly, "I'd do anything for you. You'll do your abroad studies in Japan and learn about Zen gardens. The moment you've graduated, we'll break ground on the third phase of your masterpiece."

There was nothing left to say but leave her to her research schools while I drank a glass of wine, pouring through the papers Elias dumped into that brown bag a couple of weeks ago. The floors were done, and the rooms were restored with their respective furnishings with the added brawn Derrick provided. I'd finished reading Agatha's journal and found several more volumes while putting all those books back on their shelves.

I was halfway through the bag when another similar letter appeared.

September 5th, 1958

Dear Mr. Bertram Langley:

Pursuant to your request, I have reread your petition for claiming lands originating under the Farnsworth Estate. Your situation of being married to a Farnsworth heir does not entitle you to any lands, structures, jewelry, etc., including any financial claim you feel you are owed under your marital rights. The law supersedes any discussion you and your spouse may have had, as well as decrees your deceased wife may or may not have made on her deathbed. They are considered hearsay unless she conveyed those intentions to me in writing.

Her bequest has been most generous, allowing you to keep your current home without forfeiture at any time now or in the future. The estimated cost of the house has been appraised at $87,500. The additional $20,000 cash to pay for any outstanding bills accrued while she was alive should more than cover your losses. The Estate will cover burial costs, as noted in my previous letter. Please submit those bills immediately so that you may be reimbursed promptly.

Regarding your children, they will have full access to your income and savings, including their childhood home, and you have control of how those proceeds will be divided before or after your passing.

I hope this letter answers your questions satisfactorily. Our business will be complete after we receive Amelia's funeral receipts.

Best to you and your children.

Regards,

Anthony Brickner, Esq. 247-553-2200

Holy Moly! This story gets better and better. I grabbed my tablet and did some quick research, finding exactly what I was looking for.

"ELIAS!" I screamed.

He ran down the stairs, sounding like a herd of elephants.

"Damn it, Abigail. I thought you were done screaming like a banshee." I liked how his nostrils flared like a bull when he was angry. I imagined steam rising from his ears like a cartoon, and it was hard to be afraid of him.

"Read this," I shoved the paper into his sweaty hand, admiring his shoulders and that fucking sexy tattoo. I smiled the whole time while I waited for him to finish.

His eyes became sinister. "Who is Langley?" he demanded.

"Do you remember Ellen Hutchinson's reaction when we went to the tax assessor's office? *She* is the daughter of that guy. That makes her a Langley, and God knows what he told his children about the Farnsworth Estate cheating him out of millions."

He busted out laughing, "Well, that explains a few people with an axe to grind."

"That's not all. Susan 'Someone' from the deed's office is a Langley daughter, and Henry from the realtor's office is the brother of Bertram Langley, who wrote this letter. It's quite a family affair."

He slapped his forehead, mind blown. "I can't get my head around all of this. All your answers were here this whole time, right under our noses."

I slid my arms around my man's sweaty waist, "I guess it pays to clean out your old shit and appreciate what's right in front of you."

THE END ~ AGAIN!

Don't go! More books in the *Dazed and Confused* series are in the making.

Start another fantastic Beth Gelman series today, beginning with *The Perfect Voice*, available on Amazon and other terrific retailers.

Thanks for being a Beth Gelman Insatiable Reader!

Beth Gelman books are now available on Barnes and Noble Press!

https://www.barnesandnoble.com/s/beth%20gelman

Visit my website and see all the good stuff. Oh! Enjoy my FREE Newsletter while you're there.

www.BethGelman.com

Don't forget to join my Facebook Page: Beth Gelman's Author Page

https://www.facebook.com/profile.php?id=61566436377146

Follow me on Instagram

https://www.instagram.com/bethgelmanwrites/

Follow me on TikTok too!!
https://www.tiktok.com/@beth.gelman.author

About the Author

The sassy and sensational Beth Gelman is a professional pianist and vocalist and has authored her fourth steamy romance. Authentic, resilient, loyal, and spiritual, she's not afraid to learn, fail, speak her mind, or try new things. She loves writing romances, especially romances that make her readers grow and appreciate their strengths and weaknesses. She loves her lattes, yoga, and every dog on the planet, along with her devoted husband. You can find out more about her at: www.BethGelman.com.

I would love to hear what you thought about *Always Falling Behind.* Please leave a review on your favorite bookseller's site, including:
Amazon, Goodreads, BookBub, Kobo, Apple, Google Play or Barnes and Noble Press

Follow me at:

Facebook: **Beth Gelman's Author's Page**

Instagram: **BethGelmanWrites**

TikTok: **Beth.Gelman.Author**

Visit my website and Join my Newsletter:

www.BethGelman.com

<u>CATALOG</u>
The Perfect Series:
The Perfect Voice
The Perfect Lessons
Making Perfect Sense
Novellas:

Socially Satisfied

Dazed and Confused Steamy Romances

Always Falling Behind

Acknowledgements

While we all come in various shapes and sizes, many of us struggle with invisible maladies that can diminish our quality of life. Whether our circumstances are mild or severe, we must acknowledge, prepare, and make a plan to succeed. Failure is not an option!

Abigail struggles with ADHD, Attention Deficit/Hyperactivity Disorder. It doesn't matter whether we agree or disagree with the dysfunctional nature of this malady; we only need to understand that the person suffering from it needs time, compassion, and love to help them find a way to live that makes them whole. For that matter, isn't that what we want for ourselves, too?

I am surrounded by wonderful, passionate, brilliant people who are affected by ADHD, anxiety, obsessive-compulsive disorder (OCD), and a plethora of other learning challenges. ALL deserve the kind of love Elias gives to Abigail. Seneca has her own bag of tricks coming in my next novel, but the way she unconditionally loves her best friend is a miracle for both of them.

For those of you caring for or suffering from any of the above mental illnesses listed, please consider gifting yourself with organizations designed to make your life plan an easier, more pleasant road. (See the next section for guidance.)

To Sam—You never cease to amaze me. Your maturation bubbles are popping all over the place, and seeing you bloom into the stunning woman you've become is a mother's greatest gift.

To Evan—It's not easy being a scientist living in only black and white. Life is filled with many shades of gray and too many variables to confuse the brightest of minds. Watching you balance the finite with the infinite is spectacular. I'm so happy when you take the time to sort it all out and make a plan to succeed. I wish I could say you only have to do it once, but I'd be a liar if I did. Keep believing in you because I'll never stop.

To All the Abigail's in the World—Keep making those plans! And keep starting them as well. It's okay to ask for help. It's part of the plan. It's okay to fail so long as you reflect on how to improve next time. *Always have a next time.* Find your people, plant yourself firmly in those relationships, and grow.

To All the Elias' in the World—You don't have to have yourself together to be a lifeline to someone else. Words matter, and so does delivering them with kindness. Kindness costs nothing and giving it freely to the sexiest thing you can give a woman/person. Be true to yourself first. Like the airlines say, "Put your air mask on yourself first, before helping others." Those are good words to live by.

To the Real Amy the Great—You have the best legs money can buy! Titanium!! Like Abigail's story, you can be trusted and leaned on for solid advice. Thank you for always having my back and saying the right thing when I need you most. #saltysistersforlife

To the Real Paul—I love our conversations! You are an inspiration and reminder that we all have our duties to perform, but our choice with whom we do them is our gift to those we love. You are one of my gifts. #KernPress

To Alecia—My badass writing buddy. The universe brought us together, and thank goodness we listened. You have become not only a loyal reader and writing buddy but also my soul sister, who gets me. I love that no matter what, we make the time to be present with one another. You, too, are one of my gifts. #MomsofADHD-children

To Jane—My devoted BETA. Thank you for making my book a priority in your busy life. Your opinions, and perspectives are very appreciated #InsatiableReaderForLife

To Nora—My angel who saw me through to the end of the story. Rest in peace, my angel girl.

To Daryl—the love of my life, who has been my Elias for almost twenty-eight years, you complete me.

Mental Health Organizations

The Road to Better Living

TAKE CARE OF YOU!

Your good mental health means the world to me. Whether caused by menopause, chemical deficiency, or DNA, you deserve the best care and comfort possible.

If you are suffering in any way, please reach out to one of these organizations for assistance. (These are only a few of hundreds to choose from.) Beth Gelman doesn't endorse any specific mental health organization. Please choose an agency that you and your health providers agree is in your best interest.

Anxiety & Depressions Association of America https://adaa.org/about-adaa

The ADAA is focused on prevention, treatment, and cure of anxiety, depression, and related conditions through education, practice, and research. The organization has a community of over

1,500 mental health professionals, many of whom contribute actively to research, education, and training.

The Trevor Project:

Crisis counselors are trained to answer calls, chats, or texts from LGBTQ young people who reach out on our free, confidential and secure 24/7 service when they are struggling with issues such as coming out, LGBTQ identity, depression, and suicide.

https://www.thetrevorproject.org/resources/article/resources-for-mental-health-support/

National Alliance of Mental Illness: https://www.nami.org/Home

What started as a small group of families gathered around a kitchen table in 1979 has blossomed into the nation's leading voice on mental health. Today, we are an alliance of more than 600 local affiliates who work in your community to raise awareness and provide support and education that was not previously available to those in need.

National Federation of Families: https://www.ffcmh.org/about

The National Federation of Families is a national family-run organization linking more than 120 affiliates and partners focused on the issues of families whose children – of any age – experience mental health and/or substance use challenges during their lifetime. It was conceived in Arlington, Virginia in February, 1989 by a group of 18 people determined to make a difference in the way the system works.

The JED Foundation: https://jedfoundation.org/our-impact/ JED believes that we can promote mental health and prevent suicide among teens and young adults by equipping them as individuals, strengthening their campuses, and mobilizing the communities and influences in their lives.

A Peek at The Perfect Voice

The first book in the Perfect Series

CHAPTER 1

RUBY

"Oh My God, Trudie, I just can't do it anymore! I'm so tired of being disrespected and being taken advantage of by asshole bosses."

My poor friend sat by while I mourned yet another epic work failure. Trudie passed me a third glass of wine. "Come on," she said, "don't give up yet."

I was trying to figure out where my life went sideways. I couldn't believe I was back living in my parents' suburbia home in the Midwest after another dismal attempt at "adulting." This most recent marketing position was a step outside my comfort zone, but once again, I was let go for some contrived reason.

I racked my brain trying to find a thread that connected the last two positions I've held and lost. All I knew was my ideas and contributions were recognized and praised by my immediate supervisor and that both misogynistic bosses thanked me for my ideas, took credit for the projects' success, and then "unfortunately" let me go.

As per usual, security marched me over to Human Resources to sign some papers and hear a "good-bye/good-luck" scripted speech. "We don't want to get into the 'weeds,'" the HR rep stuttered out. *Weeds? What the hell is that? Does that mean my boss was threatened by me? That's crap!*

Disgusted with corporate bullshit and my lack of control in the world, I stormed out of the HR office carrying my one box of pictures, a "*No Hablo El Stupido*" coffee mug, my Groot bobblehead, and the sock monkey plush that Trudie gave me when I landed the job.

Nearing the front reception desk, I heard mumblings of why I was let go from Dumb and Dumber, the two bimbos that sat there every day, filing their nails and batting their eyes at every Y chromosome they encountered, instead of doing their fucking jobs.

"I heard she slept with her boss," Dumb said to Dumber.

"OMG! I overheard she was leaking company secrets to our competitors," Dumber said to Dumb.

Whipping around to face the reception counter, I screamed "FUCK YOU! I've heard you're both raving bitches, but I'm not talking behind your backs!" at the two receptionists who loved to see one of their own fail. "Or…maybe…again, my jackass boss stole my work and passed it off as his own! I'm through with this bullshit! Perhaps you two lackeys should stop sucking your bosses' dicks to get ahead."

I was out of control and these girls were in the line of my wrath. *Too fucking bad! Two years down the tubes, AGAIN! Christ, why can't women have great ideas and get recognized for their contributions instead of their male bosses stealing their work? UGH!*

Placing my wineglass on my whitewashed nightstand covered with want ads and candy wrappers, I rolled onto my back in defeat. My fluffy white duvet with Madonna's *Vogue* album cover emblazoned on it flattened under my weight.

"Why does this keep happening to me?" I moaned as I hung my head off the side of my childhood bed.

I had been lucky as a kid. When I turned thirteen, my mom fought hard with my dad to get me a full-sized bed. "My baby Girl is growing up and needs a Big Girl Bed." Big Girl, indeed! Now look at me, crying like a baby and pity-drinking wine and scarfing down Oreos, trying to pick up the crumbled cookies of my life (and the crumbs in my ample cleavage and bedsheets.)

I had become a successful independent event planner even though I kind of fell into after helping a friend out at her wedding. I had a different degree out of college, but not a vision of where I wanted to go and what I wanted to do with my life, so I pulled my resources together and became the Go To Girl Assistant, LLC." I was the master of my domain. From there, I spun off into work as an executive assistant. I helped one long-term client for three years before I decided to work for another organization. My talents were praised and respected by my clients, and if I could have made enough money to move out of my parents' home, I would have kept that career. Hence, the recent decision to stay put in the safety of my parent's home while I got settled into a long-term career.

Doing her best to offer support, Trudie, my best friend from college, had come over to shore me up. Lying alongside me, she propped herself up on her elbows with her cleavage pressed into Madonna's nose, closed her eyes, and sighed. She knew I needed to keep venting this out.

"Listen, Trudie. You know my parents are the best. They have always supported everything I've tried. They were the ones who shook the cowbell at my marching band shows, brought flowers to my recitals, and called the local newspaper to do an article about the beautiful weddings I did down on the Detroit River. But even my wonderful parents only have so much patience with me. I'm twenty-eight years old and if I have to hear, 'we know you're doing your best, Ruby, but...,' one more time, I'm going to scream!"

When my dad's eyes drooped after hearing that my best-laid plans had gone south, a piece of my heart died. My mom even started to leave magazine and newspapers clippings for job opportunities around. Subtle, and a little passive-aggressive, I'd say, but I knew she did it out of love.

I saw some pictures and notes she made about turning my bedroom into her dream crafting space while looking for some sheet music a few days ago. Soft blue curtains with tiny little cherries, white IKEA storage cubes, and with a high-end sewing area were not going to happen until I moved out for good, which made my heart hurt. *Again, sorry to disappoint you, Mom.*

At breakfast this morning, my dad sat down at our worn maple kitchen table with his favorite hazelnut coffee in the "World's Best

Dad" mug I gave him in third grade and a copy of the *Detroit Free Press*. As he took his first sip, he looked up at me and let out a breath. *Yeah, I knew what was coming.*

"Ya know, Ruby, your brother could use a little help at his accounting firm. Why don't you give him a call?" My Dad turned slowly in his seat, and reaching for me, pulled me into his barrel chest, covered with his softest flannel shirt. I gazed over his broad shoulder and fought back the tears of yet another failure. His words sounded like, "See how well your brother is doing? Why can't you be more like him?" Stepping away with leaky eyes and an attempt at a smile, I fled upstairs to my room. I wasn't sure how much lower my ego could go. Didn't Dad know that I'm a creative person and Doug was more traditional and linear? I can't fit my square-peg self in a round hole any more than he can feel nuance. Why can't my parents see that?

Trudie sat up, arranged her legs crisscross style, and grabbed her wine off the nightstand. Do you know that look that a mama bear gives to a predator when her baby is in jeopardy? It has nothing on Trudie.

"All of those other careers have made you what you are today, Ruby," she soothed. "You loved being an event planner. You got to use all your creative juices, and it forced you to be organized. Your attention to detail is off the charts." She toasted into the air, spilling some wine on my comforter. Thank goodness it was a pinot grigio.

Trudie continued animatedly, "You were a President's Club saleswoman for two years, proving you are amazing at negotiating and persuading clients to buy whatever you were selling." She cocked her head to the side, giving me puppy dog eyes and then looked at the empty bottle. "Maybe we should switch to the hard stuff instead of opening another bottle of wine?" She just wanted to get me wasted so I could forget my troubles. *Not a bad idea.*

I looked around my room and took in the awards and ribbons of my previously happy life. Trophies dusted with time, pictures of me and my bestie making glorious music, me on piano, her singing. I saw playbills from a high school performance of *The Music Man,* and thanks to my mom, my acceptance letter to attend a distinguished music school in Michigan. In retrospect, I should have known that my above-average abilities would only take me so far.

Maybe I had needed to take an extra "beat" when I chose to be a piano performance major? That probably would have been a better financial decision. But my high school senior recital and college auditions were amazing. I played an intricate Haydn Piano Sonata in F Major and a deeply moving Chopin Mazurka in A Minor, and I felt so accomplished and proud of the final product. I fantasized that I was destined to become another Horowitz or Cliburn.

These pieces were game-changers for me. I hadn't played them in over two years, but when I heard the music, I was still deeply moved. Perhaps poetry in motion wasn't the best way to describe how I felt; maybe "the most erotic love-making you can think of" would fit the bill. *Which reminds me, I really need to get laid!*

"I remember your audition, Ruby. You were so jubilant, confident, and proud of all the hard work you put in. I can't remember you feeling that way about anything since then. What happened to that girl?" Trudie asked, as she licked her fingers to swipe the last Oreo crumbs out of the package.

Good question. Where did that girl go? I failed as a music major. I changed to business management, but couldn't get through statistics and finance. What was I supposed to do after failing two majors by my senior year, leaving me without a chance in hell of graduating in four years? Oh, and guess who was still paying for these "life lessons?" ME! I was drowning.

I sounded like a whiny bitch, but I was twenty-one years old and had no future to look forward to. I felt like a loser in my parents' eyes, although they'd never say that out loud, and I felt like a loser in mine because I kept changing my mind about a career. The only thing I had going for me was my resilience.

"Come on, Ruby! Pick yourself up, dust yourself off, and go find another degree to get the hell out of school," was my daily mantra.

So, I did what I should have done after my freshman year—I went to a guidance counselor. It was like seeing an accountant. You pushed all your receipts (credits) in front of them and they would tell you what your net worth was. Well, good news! Not only did I have enough credits for a piano and voice minor, but I also had enough credits for a management minor, too. *Yay me!* Except you can't graduate with three minors.

Suffice it to say, I found an area of study where I excelled and graduated with a bachelor of fine and applied arts with an emphasis in communications—on the five-year plan. Finally, I had a degree, (and only $17,000 in debt). More importantly, I could move on to the next chapter of my life! Or home, as the case may be.

Crap! By the way, how does one monetize communications?